Orphans of the Living

Orphans of the Living

A NOVEL

KATHY WATSON

SHE WRITES PRESS

Published in 2025 by
She Writes Press, an imprint of The Stable Book Group

32 Court Street, Suite 2109
Brooklyn, NY 11201
https://shewritespress.com

Library of Congress Control Number: 2025907740
ISBN: 978-1-64742-978-2
eISBN: 978-1-64742-979-9

For information, address:
She Writes Press
1569 Solano Ave #546
Berkeley, CA 94707

Interior designer: Katherine Lloyd, The DESK

Printed in the United States

For Stu, Aaron, Annie, Max, Hannah,
Levi, and Shiloh.
My why.

"When you work the ground, it will no longer yield its crops for you. You will be a restless wanderer on the earth." Gen. 4:12 (NIV)

Author's Note

This book is a work of fiction. It's also true. The picture it reveals of my mother and her family is the work of the original artist—my mother—and me, the art restorer who received it, torn and forgotten, and brought it back to life.

Throughout my childhood into middle age, I watched my mother burnish, then mar, and finally, cloak, the picture of her life. After her death in 2006, I left that painting to languish in a dark hall, unwilling to apply the deft, time-consuming chore of restoration. I simply didn't know how to see past the dirt, the frayed edges, the dimmed colors. The distortion.

Then one afternoon in 2016, I opened Michael Chabon's *Moonglow* and saw a way forward. Chabon took the heft and truth of his grandfather's life, made himself witness to events before his own birth, and wrote himself into the story. I followed his lead.

My mother's story took place in a precarious time in American history—on the failed promise of Reconstruction, the birth and horror of the Jim Crow south, the environmental disaster of the Dust Bowl, and the financial destruction of the Great Depression. In every curve of America's roads, racism and the sanction of those who were different was inescapable.

To restore her story as close to the truth as I possibly could, I chose to face these horrors honestly, and not to shy away from the difficult pieces of her life. Characters in this novel speak as history suggests they would have. At times, that language is vile and hard to read. The words and racial slurs my characters use are ones I have never used in my life. But to remove them would be to soft-peddle my mother's world, to take away the truth of it. I hope this note can serve as a warning for those who find any language difficult to read. I am well aware of my position as a white novelist writing racial slurs, and I made this choice for historical accuracy only.

This novel also includes depictions of events that will undoubtedly be triggering for some readers, including abortion, rape, and violent death. I would like to say these were rare occurrences in American life, or that they continue to be, but I fear the opposite is true.

The most remarkable aspects of restoring this painting of my mother's life were the many times I encountered documents, manifests, newspaper stories, football game programs, and other historical records that confirmed the scattered bits of light and shadow my mother left me. From them, I've revealed a textured, honest painting of her life. I think she would recognize it, in a certain light, and know it as her own.

LULA

Stone County, Mississippi, Jenkins Plantation, 1925

Lula knew it was nearly dawn by the sound of the cicadas in the oak trees. Two cicadas rippled the tiny drums at their throats, and a million others replied. Their calls rolled down from the trees like rain on flat rocks, into the thick June dark.

First light wouldn't be for an hour yet. The insects' rattles dulled the sound of thunder somewhere off in the distance. It might rain, soften the ground a bit so she and the children would not have to work quite as hard chopping the cotton.

She shifted on the moss-stuffed mattress and knew without reaching out her hand that Barney was gone. She'd watched him smoking his pipe last night and seen his opaque gaze drift away from the porch. In the lantern light, the yellow circles around his blue irises were as dissipated as empty pecan shells. Yearning for something far away, absent her and the children? Then he banged the pipe against the porch rail as if he'd come to a decision.

"Walkin'," he said, not looking back at her, his straight back disappearing into the twilight. A few hours after she and the kids had gone to bed, he stomped up the steps into the shack, not bothering to unlatch the door quietly, supreme over their sleep and shelter. He didn't reach out to touch her when he came to bed, just sent his heat radiating toward her under the thin quilt, and with it, the smell of red dirt, fertilizer, wood smoke, and whiskey. He must have walked home through the cotton fields, she thought. And now, he was gone again.

Lula listened to the pulsing wave of cicadas, more thunderous than the previous three summers she'd lived here. Barney told her these were a different kind of cicada, that they shed their brittle insect shells thirteen years ago and crawled under tree roots, heaving their naked bodies into crevices to wait out a divine signal. Now they winged up into the trees in the millions, filling the early cool hours, the hot midday hours, and the dwindling light of the evening hours, with torment. Lula felt as if her ear drums were filled with thin blades of grass rustling and vibrating, never ceasing, until night fell full-on, and the horde and their wretched tymbals rested for a few precious hours.

She wished she could shed her body, too, crawl naked somewhere dark and cool and wait out the years. But for what? The future spooled out as a long, unending row of cotton, and next to it, a hoe.

She was thirty-seven years old, already a mother eight times over, on the day seven months earlier when she realized Barney's late-night incursion to her side of the thin mattress had implanted a root—a weed among the cotton—who could not be chopped away.

Unless. She thought on it for days, and finally came around to it. She heard of other poor women doing it in Montana. It was the only way out.

"Maudie Marie, take the young ones with you and bring back some squirrels," she said, handing Maudie the old musket and a small leather pouch of wad and shot. When she couldn't hear the kids' bare feet anymore in the leaves and bramble, she knelt on the dirt floor, her skirt around her in a halo, holding a piece of fencing wire like a Samurai sword. She slid the wire through the dirt and under the hem of her skirt, searching for the opening to her vagina, pushing the sharp, rusty end at herself. Missing, missing, biting her lip against the pain, until finally the wire found the fissure between the outside world of dust and anguish and the inside ocean of blood and viscera. She gave it a shove, falling forward on her elbows in a cry.

She rolled onto her side and pulled the bloody wire from her womb, panting hard, warm blood and fluid dribbling down her legs into her twisted skirt and onto the red dirt floor. She pulled herself onto her knees, struggling to clean herself up before the children returned, heaving her bloody skirt into the wash tub, and kicking dirt over the small telltale lifeless pool.

She crawled back to bed and lay panting on her back under the quilt, sweat and tears flowing together into her ears. Her blond hair, beginning to gray at the margins, twisted loose from the knot at the base of her neck and lay in a damp, tangled pile, indistinguishable from the yellowed pillowcase. It was all gone now: Her delicate round face, transparent as a petal. Her softly curved breasts and hips. She had looked exotic against the dry, scrubby Oklahoma landscape of her youth. Boys rode by her father's ranch just hoping for a glimpse of her. Who would even look twice now?

She heard the children returning and Maudie's quick short steps. Vernon stepped heavy, long strides, Albert on his back. Leonard and Ernie ran in circles around Maudie and Vernon, singing bits of song Barney had taught them.

"Who's the greatest lover that this country ever knew? And who's the man that Valentino takes his hat off to? Why, it's Barney Google, with the goo-goo-goo-ga-ly eyes," they bayed.

She heard Maudie command, "Put that snake down, Ernie! Throw it over the fence into the pig pen."

Leonard flung back the shack door, and a rush of hot wind, dust, and spent black powder coursed into the room with the children. Maudie held a brace of four dead squirrels over her head in triumph.

They stopped at the threshold when they saw their mother in the corner, lying down at midday on a Sunday, a quilt high up on her chin. Maudie lowered the squirrels and laid them on the sideboard. The boys were silent until Albert, from his perch on Vernon's shoulder, began crying.

"Go on, back outside, all of you," Lula whispered. "'Cept you, Maudie."

She walked cautiously toward her parents' bed in the corner.

"I'm gonna go find Pa," she said, taking in her mother, diminished and worn down in the short hour they'd been gone.

"No! I'll be fine. Listen, girl, my skirt, it's in the wash tub. You need to take that tub out to the cistern, rinse out the skirt, and hang it on the line before your Pa gets back."

"Where's he gone? I ain't seen him since Sunday School."

"Never mind that. Just do as I tell you."

She grabbed the tub and lifted the worn calico skirt into the shack's dusty light. The skirt unfurled like a lost battle flag, the red stain glistening. Something else rattled at the bottom of the tub. She picked up the bloody piece of wire.

"What *is* this, Mama?"

Lula moaned, the great yellow ball of her hair a shroud, her bare shoulders quivering with pain. Where *was* Barney? She would tell him, mournfully, that she'd miscarried. Maybe he'd stay in for the night, a rough hand on her belly, a reassuring sigh in her ear. But she knew there was no such tenderness anywhere on the plantation.

By supper time, Barney had not returned. Lula lay on her side, rolled toward the wall. Vernon built a fire in the wood stove. Maudie and Vernon gutted and skinned the squirrels and cut them in quarters. Maudie melted a hunk of salt pork in the cast iron skillet, dredged the meat in cornmeal, and dropped the pieces into the hot fat. She chopped a big pile of collard greens, shoved them into a pot of boiling water, and sprinkled a handful of salt over the meat and the boiling greens. There was still corn pone left from breakfast. When the squirrel was cooked through, she'd fry the pone in the drippings. She worked diligently, as if the meal could draw her father home, cure her mother, and bring Albert out from under her parents' bed where he'd gone to be close to his mother.

Maudie heard a whoop from Ernie and Leonard and knew they must have spotted Barney coming up the hill. In a moment, he stood in the doorway, the last of the light catching his sweat rising in a thin mist around his shoulders. He stared at Lula.

"Lu, you sick?"

Albert whimpered from under the bed.

"Get out from under there, Albert." Barney crossed the floor and pulled on one of Albert's bare feet.

"Maudie, get this baby and go outside." His eyes were still on his wife.

"Lula?"

"There was going to be a baby. I lost it," she said, her voice stretched thin as bird song in a far-off hollow.

Barney took off his hat and crushed it in his hands.

"I should get the midwife, then."

"No! I'm gonna be fine. Don't want no darkie woman poking at me."

Barney glanced at the food hissing and bubbling on the stove.

"Maudie!" he called. "Come on back in here and finish making supper."

But Lula was not fine. The errant wire drove a fever completely through her.

By the third night, her thrashing and feverish mumbling

drove the children out to the porch. In the midnight hour, Barney pulled on his overalls and took the stairs out of the shack at a dead run. When the kids woke up in the morning and walked bleary with sleep back into the shack, they halted in shock at the doorway.

Their parents' mattress had been pulled off the metal bed springs, and with its stuffing of dry moss, lay on the dirt floor dangerously close to the stove, which spit red hot light around the cast iron fittings. Lula looked like a primitive voodoo doll tossed on the mattress, her legs helter-skelter. And next to her on her knees, a Black woman, her head wrapped in purple cloth, leaned over their mother holding a cup to her lips.

"You gotta drink this, Missus Stovall. Come on, open your mouth. That's it, yes, just a bit more."

Lula was barely conscious; Barney was nowhere to be seen.

"You children help me. You mother needs a clean dress; this one is soaked." She looked from face to face. No one moved. "Now. Help."

Maudie pried her feet from the cold dirt at the threshold and found an old cotton dress on a hook.

"You boys, out," the woman said. "You, help me," she said, pointing to Maudie.

"Mama ain't gonna want no Black woman see her naked."

"Would she rather die?"

She reluctantly knelt on the floor and helped the woman peel her mother's damp, sour-smelling dress over her head and then slide the other one on. She looked away, avoiding her mother's naked, translucent skin.

"What's your name?"

"Maudie Marie."

"Mine's Violet Byrd." They struggled together to pull Lula's arms into the sleeves. "How old are you?"

"I'm ten."

"You are old enough, then."

"For what?"

"Old enough to know your mother might die. There ain't much I can do, and your daddy doesn't have money to go for the white doctor. Not that he could do anything, anyhow. Your mama's got some poison in her blood, and the only way we can kill it is to keep pouring water down her and keep her hot. Fever is God's way of killing that demon poison, but your mama is so tired now, she can't fight no more, so we're going to keep her by this stove, keep the stove stoked, give her a fever when she can't make one for herself. You understand?"

She nodded, not understanding at all.

"Heat up some water. We've got to make her drink."

Maudie spent the day at Violet's command, adding wood to the fire and heating water, which Violet mixed with sorghum and salt. She would crouch on the mattress, holding her mother steady as Violet poured the mixture down Lula's throat, over and over.

"Pee," Lula mumbled late in the afternoon.

Violet scooped her up like an empty flour sack and carried her out of the shack into a screen of pecan trees. Violet leaned her against a tree and pulled her skirt up to her waist. "Help me hold her up, Maudie."

Her mother moaned, and let loose a weak stream of urine down the tree trunk. Violet hoisted her back into her arms and returned her to the mattress in the unbearably hot cabin.

By nightfall, Barney and the boys had not come back. Violet lit a lantern, pulled a pipe from her skirt pocket, and lit it with a fiery twig. Lula seemed little changed, just growing quieter and smaller, as if she were preparing to descend into a hole in the dirt floor. When it was fully dark, the door opened and a small girl brought in a plate covered with a towel.

"This is my daughter, Dora. Dora, this is Maudie Marie." The two girls nodded to each other. Dora left the plate and slipped out of the cabin. From under the towel, Violet pulled out a piece of corn bread filled with fried salt pork and green onions, handed it to Maudie, then ate one herself.

"You go on back out to the porch and get some sleep. I'll stay with her."

She hesitated. Violet took a long draw on the pipe.

"What do you think I'd do to her that ain't already been done?"

Maudie stood at the door a long time.

"Girl," Violet said, smoking the pipe in the dim light. "You done good today."

Her mother's dull white face and Violet's shiny black face were both illuminated in the red light of the wood stove. Her mother looked insubstantial, as if she might disappear before morning. But Violet Byrd was filled with fire.

At dawn, Maudie crept back into the cabin, sure she would find her mother's body lying stiff and cold on the mattress. Instead, Violet was on her knees, wiping her mother's face with a wet cloth. Her mother was awake, meekly submitting to Violet's ablutions, her hands crossed over her breasts like a corpse, her eyes red, her hair wild. Violet had let the fire in the stove burn out.

"Go find your daddy, Maudie," Violet said. "It looks like your mama is gonna stay right here with the living."

With all the ease the unwanted bud had planted itself in her womb, it came as a surprise to Lula how impossible it had been to end its occupation. It became evident that the wire had conjured the fever, but left the baby to float untouched in its watery world.

A month after the fever, Barney finally noticed her belly.

"I thought you lost that baby," he said.

"Guess not," Lula said, cradling Albert, rocking him to sleep. "Guess not."

Lula placed her hands on a small white sheet of writing paper where it lay on the kitchen table, hoping she might press her regret into it. She had written her two oldest boys in Montana countless times. She left them with her Uncle Fred three years earlier, never imagining she would still be separated from them, or that replies to her letters would never come.

How had she ever let Barney convince her to take the other five children, join him in Mississippi, and leave Ray and Glen behind? She could tell herself an embroidered story about how they were better off there, how they would grow into fine young men working on Fred's ranch. How she'd had no choice, with their Montana land played out, the well dry, Barney gone, and no money to buy two additional tickets, anyway.

"Don't you be bringing your boys, Lula," he'd written when he sent the six train tickets. "They're old enough to be on their own. You bring our children, and Nettie. But not them damn boys."

There was no way to stitch over the ugly, ripped seam. She had traded them for the security of the younger children and Nettie, the ones Barney wanted. And traded them, too, for her own sanity. She could not bear another day of the Montana farm, with its crushing debt and failure.

Her eyes roamed the shack, out the one window onto row upon row of infant cotton in the red dirt of early March, still mostly bare of weeds. Could anything be worse than this wretched existence? The Montana years seemed innocent and sweet by comparison. Barney planted this year's corn and cotton, but it looked to be no better than any of the previous ones. They were scratching hard just to keep body and soul together. Barney, of course, saw it his way, each year slightly better than the one before, as if death could be measured in degrees: Less dead *this* year than last. No, it was all truly and wholly dead, from one end of this shack to the outer edge of these blighted ten acres, their sharecropper's allotment on the Jenkins plantation.

She sat down to write the letter. Maybe this one would finally elicit a reply, if only a postcard. The others, carefully written in her straight penmanship, duly affixed with a two-cent stamp? Chaff in the wind.

"Nettie has left us and gone to work for Gladys Jenkins, the wife of the plantation owner," she wrote. "She lives in a little lean-to out back of their house, which I'm sure was built in slavery times. There's a handsome young man from town, Burnis Davis, who is courting her. He has a good job in the pickle factory in Wiggins. His mother told me proudly that Burnis is the great-grandson of Jefferson Davis, the president of the Confederacy. After living here with these darky people, I wish Davis and his soldiers in gray had won that war. Of course, your stepfather don't agree with me. These African people are a peculiar folk, always at rock bottom. I do not know why they carry on so. I can hear them over at their church this afternoon, just hollering and singing for hours. Except for one woman, Mrs. Violet Byrd, they have none of them ever said a kind word to me! You can imagine the Davis family don't think too highly of their son courting the daughter of sharecroppers, but Burnis keeps coming around."

She wrote to them of their half-brothers—Leonard, Ernie, Vernon, and Albert, the baby they'd never met—and of their half-sister Maudie.

And then she told them the news that sanded her down worse than the blistering winds of the Montana plain. "It seems I'm going to have another baby at my old age, sometime this June. I would trade this baby a hundred times over just to see the both of you again. I have no idea how we will feed and clothe another, and I can hardly bear the thought."

Would it matter if she reminded them again how their own father, Smith, had loved them? How life had been back in Oklahoma before he died of pneumonia, before Barney rode into their lives, promising security and abundance? No. Old wounds, old stories—they're best forgotten. She signed the letter, "Your Mama," her hope of a reply fading even as she sealed the envelope.

Now, in early June, she had resigned herself to the child. Both she and the baby were tormented by this turn of events, the baby thrashing away in the womb much as Lula had in the grip of her fever. As the four o'clock hour melted away, and the cicadas began their assault on her ears, she thought to impose as much pain as possible on the unborn child. She balled up a fist and dug her knuckles into her side, a warning. She would drag herself out to the cotton field this very morning, rain or no rain, and chop cotton as hard as she could. A stillborn baby was a better omen than raising another living child in this shack. The cicadas, drumming harder now, beat a cadence of shame down on Lula, but she was not moved by their condemnation. She was beyond forgiveness, either receiving it, or meting it out.

Early that evening, after Barney's nightly disappearance, Lula's water broke.

"Vernon, go fetch your sister at the big house," she said between pains. Maudie gathered the other kids on the porch. When Vernon returned with Nettie, Lula had already covered the wood kitchen table with a quilt. She was pacing, silent, her arms crossed, as if she still might judge whether the baby lived or died.

Nettie took her mother's elbow and they walked slowly back and forth across the dirt floor. An hour later, on the wood table, Nettie at her knees, Lula had a baby girl.

The baby cried, lying next to her mother, who would not

reach out a hand to comfort her. Maudie came in from the porch and carried her into her small bed behind a quilt wall. The crying slowed, then stopped. In its place rose a legion of cicadas, drumming, drumming, drumming into the midnight hour.

BARNEY

Stone County, Mississippi, Jenkins Plantation, 1925; Hanford, California, 1912

Barney stepped off the porch and shoved his pipe back into his pants pocket. Wouldn't do any good for the Black croppers to see him smoking when they had so little of the leaf themselves. How was he going to convince them to go along with his plan? That afternoon, under the big Live Oak, he saw how far apart they were.

"Now Barney, you say if we work together, we can make some money? I don't see how that can be when we still got the same acres to till, plant and chop, no matter whether we do it alone, or together," Joe Lee said.

"Well, we can help each other. I can bring my big mule, while you, Percy, you've just got that little donkey," Barney said, making eye contact around the circle of fifteen men sitting in the shade. A crock of tepid water and a ladle sat on a stone in the middle, each man taking a turn at the tin ladle.

"And you, Walter, you've got those big lazy boys"—the men chuckled—"while my fellows are just young 'uns yet. So see, I bring the big mule, you bring the big boys." Looks of unease passed around the circle.

"But really, men, there's another thing. You don't have to go to Mr. Jenkins, or his bastard Batson for all your furnish, or all your bacon and cornmeal. We can buy that together, share it." A murmur went up.

"Why would we do that, Mr. Barney?" Otis asked, incredulous. "You know if we do that, Billy Ray Batson will come down on us with that bullwhip of his. And you know nobody else is gonna sell us anything anyhow, on account of we are Mr. Jenkins's niggers. You know that!"

"I don't know that at all," Barney said, squinting at the sun as it moved west into the afternoon. They'd have to finish this talk soon. Batson was sure to check on them before long.

"Maybe y'all can't buy from the general store in town. But I can. I can buy a fifty-pound bag of cornmeal, and you all can buy what you need from me, *same price as I pay for it.* And same as with Jenkins, you can pay me after you sell your crop. I ain't interested in making money off you men. I'm interested in us all getting ahead, getting out from under Jenkins's thumb!" Puzzled looks passed between the croppers.

"What good would that do?" asked a man who had just arrived that winter from a plantation near Jackson. "Soon as I was getting along better over at the Hyde place, well, the boss, he beat me down something fierce just because I had a good horse and he wanted it. My only way out was to just hit the grit and find another place. But no matter what we do or where we go, we are always gonna be under someone's thumb."

Barney shook his head slightly, trying to hide his annoyance.

"They can't hurt you if you own your land, men! If we can make more money, we can buy our own land! Land is what *makes* us men! It's what sets us free from these bastards!"

All around him, silence fell. The men no longer stole glances at each other. They stared at the ground.

Isaiah stood in the middle of the circle, holding the tin ladle. "Mr. Barney, when was you born?"

"In 1873. I'm fifty-two years old," he said, straightening his back with pride. He looked much the same as he had in his thirties, as if a sculptor had kept at him year after year, rescuing his face and trim body from age and hard work; his full lips still lush; his long, narrow nose straight as a sapling; his hair, onyx-hued and thick; his blue eyes glittering large in the afternoon sun filtering through the oak leaves.

"And where was you born?"

"Pana, Illinois, but I don't know what—"

"You was born a free man in a free state, eight years after It surrendered. But it don't matter, because your people was *always* free. I was born in 1877, twelve years after It surrendered, same year as Jim Crow was born. I ain't never been free. Land ain't gonna make me free. And no fifty-pound bag of cornmeal is gonna make me free either." He dropped the ladle into the water crock and strode out of the circle.

Hours later, in the dark, the inky air damp on his bare arms, Barney walked toward Isaiah's place. He knew the other men met there late at night for corn whiskey. Maybe the whiskey would soften them up. He saw a circle of light up ahead and stepped into it. The quiet conversation around a low fire of pecan and oak whispered to a halt.

"Do you fellas mind if I join you?" he asked. Heads shook silently back and forth but the conversation did not resume. Barney cleared his throat.

"I've got some real fine Georgia tobacco, bought off a gentleman passing through on the train last week. Anybody got any whiskey I can trade it for?"

Grins broke out around the circle. Barney wouldn't squeal to the overseer about them drinking bootleg, and he was even willing to pay for a slug of it himself! A slim brown flask slipped out of Isaiah's back pocket, and when he handed it across the fire to Barney, Barney passed back some tobacco wrapped in flour sacking. They were even.

Barney took a slug of the hooch and steadied himself, hoping not to show how painful the needles of corn liquor were going down.

"Listen fellas," he said, his vocal cords tangling with the whiskey fumes in this throat, "I'm sorry if I showed any disrespect this afternoon. I know y'all have had it hard, harder than me and mine by a dern site. But I . . . well, can I tell you a story?"

They nodded. Stories kept at bay the dread of dawn and a day of fruitless labor, the fear of lynching, the constrictions of a life lived without a horizon.

"Well, I ain't got nothing now, you know that, no more than you do. Well, I got a good mule, and a few pigs and chickens, and I know Mr. Jenkins, he gives me more leeway, since he knows I've been farming a good long number of years," he explained.

"That, and you ain't a nigger," said the new man. The others laughed.

"Yep, that is true," Barney said. "But I wasn't always this poor. I have land, for all the good it's done me. Came here from Montana to grow strawberries three years ago, and bought ten acres over in Madison. But after I bought the land, didn't have a red cent left to buy equipment, or even put up a cabin for the family. The bank wouldn't loan a Yankee nothing. When I heard Jenkins was looking for more croppers, I had no choice. Keep thinking I'll get ahead, but it ain't never enough. Those strawberry fields, they're just weeds and stones."

Barney took his corncob pipe out, now that he'd shared more than a generous amount in trade for the rot gut. He took his time packing the pipe, lighting the leaf, letting the anticipation for his story build.

"Back in the aughts, I was in Nevada, mining for silver up in Tonopah." Barney puffed slowly on the pipe, thinking on how to tell his story, what parts to hold back.

He couldn't tell them how he hurtled toward destitution, driven by his rapacious lust for land, and more land, as if all land were the equal of Eden, with no regard for its variability or fecundity. Land—dirt with his name on it—was his solace, worth dragging his ragtag family, babies born here and there, around the West like bumpkins on a cheap nickel carnival ride.

It wouldn't do him any good to tell them that soon after he'd taken that fool's gander to mine for silver, he owned nine acres of farmland in California, and, why, he'd grown seven tons of alfalfa and ten tons of oat hay on that San Joaquin valley farm, and made $567 after he paid for all the seed and fertilizer. Or how he gathered up that $567—his brother's money, really, just loaned to him—and gone off to Mexico to buy a banana plantation. Or that he came back from Mexico with money in his pocket, and bought a farm in the brand-new town of Chandler, Arizona in 1913 with the slim remainder of his Mexico money, after he paid his brother back and then some.

It wouldn't help his cause any if he told them that in 1915, he cashiered himself out of the Chandler land and threw that money behind farming 480 acres in Montana—480 acres of worthless, barren, arid, rock-bound land—courtesy, in part, of the 1862 Homestead Act, signed by Mr. Abraham Lincoln himself, his hero. Or that the final sum of all his aspirations had been to trade away the money salvaged from that disaster to grow strawberries in Mississippi. Until there was nothing now to trade, and land an empty promise.

It wouldn't do him any good to tell them he had four rich brothers. Better to just be a poor man among the poor. All that familial wealth made no difference in Barney's life anyhow, because his brothers were not going to bail him out this time. No sir. They were going to sit on their millions and let him rot in the Mississippi mud.

Now, he would tell them about the bananas in Mexico. He'd tell them what he learned about working together with the banana farmers and how they spurned the men that tried to keep them under their thumbs. But even then, he wouldn't tell them everything about Mexico. He wouldn't tell them about Luzelba.

"Well, see . . . you ever hear of the United Fruit Company? No? Right around 1900, they started hauling bananas from the southern world—Jamaica, Guatemala, Mexico—and they were buying 'em cheap and selling them high all over the US. I thought maybe I outta be in the banana business, and so, in 1912, that's what I did."

But first, he went to see his brother George.

Barney cleaned up, put on his one suit, pushed his prized stickpin with the gold nugget into the right lapel, hitched up his buckboard, left the farm, and went to see his younger brother George at his Southern Pacific office in Hanford, California, nine miles away. He walked in carrying a banana and put it on George's desk.

"George, how many of these do you eat a year?"

"Bananas? Now listen, Barney, I sense a scheme somehow, involving bananas." George stood up from his desk. "And I don't have time for that today. I've got all the managers coming in at two o'clock."

"Well, George, I'll answer my own question. Every man, woman, and child in the US of A eats sixty bananas a year. Sixty!"

George raised an eyebrow and set his pen down next to his desk blotter, clean of inconvenient doodles or paperwork.

"That's near $15 million in bananas, George! United Fruit Company, you ever hear of them?"

George rolled his eyes and sat down. Railroads had been good to him. They'd fattened his wallet and cushioned his backside. It irritated him that his no-account brother, older by four years— still stick-thin, black hair with not a hint of silver, those piercing blue eyes—was tutoring him on business in his own corner of the world.

"Barney, that is one of the biggest corporations in the world. Of course I've heard of them."

"The way it works out, they can grow those bananas for about one cent apiece and sell them for two cents apiece. They own the market, and a damn lot of farmland in Guatemala, Jamaica, and Colombia, but they don't have a toe-hold in Mexico. Too small for them. Why last year, little farms there grew just 750,000 bunches of bananas worth about $2.5 million, and sold them right at home in Mexico. United Fruit is paying no attention."

"You've been to the library again, haven't you?" George sighed. For a man of only thirty-five, he wore an older man's resignation, his hair receding without a by-your-leave, his jowls heavy with scotch.

"You are not telling me you want to take on the United Fruit Company, are you?" asked George. "Because if you are, I think you are a bigger idiot than I thought you were when you went off to mine your fortune in Nevada. You need to just go back down the road to the farm. You did real well the last three years. Find yourself a wife, have a few children. They're great farm hands." George let a small, mocking smile escape. "Next year, I bet you can even afford a new Model T Ford, that is, as soon as you pay me back the $500 you owe me."

Barney sat rigidly in the leather arm chair in front of George's desk. His brother had a way of making him feel small, as if George were a grand, strutting rooster and Barney nothing but a little bantam hen.

"I don't want to take on United Fruit, George. I want to skirt about as far around those fellas as I would a bucking bronco. That's why I'm telling you about Mexico. You know where bananas grow down there?"

"No, but I bet you're going to tell me."

"They grow only in the wettest, hottest spot in Mexico, on the Isthmus of Tehuantepec. Remember how you were telling me about that new railroad from Salina Cruz on the west coast, 124 miles to the Gulf Coast? Those small farmers, they can get their bananas to the coast now, East or West, instead of just growing them and selling them in Mexico."

George fidgeted in his chair and straightened his vest, checking the time on his vest pocket watch.

"Look, I know it won't be long before United Fruit swoops in there and takes it over. I just want to go take a look, see if I can buy some land and bananas, and make a business of it before they do."

"Well." George ran a hand around the collar of his starched white shirt. "Well, that's not a half-bad idea, Barney. God forgive me for offering you an ounce of encouragement. I do have some contacts on the Tehuantepec Route. Maybe they could help you. I'll give you a few names. Good luck to you."

Barney stood up and planted his feet in front of George's desk.

"Oh bother. Why did I think I would get off that easy?" said George, looking up at the ceiling. "What exactly is it that you want, Barney? Because money is out of the question."

"I want you to be my partner."

"In *what*? You haven't got anything to partner *in*. And that would require money, as you know, which I am not going to consider."

Barney worked hard to suppress a scowl. He swallowed. He glanced around the room, the rich teak-paneled walls, the thick carpets on the floor. His hand fluttered up briefly to the stickpin in his lapel.

"George, I've got $500 in the bank from the farm proceeds this year. All the bills are paid. Yes, I know I owe it to you, but let me put it to better use. You don't need it, do you?" he said, waving his arm around his brother's luxurious office. "What is $500 to a man of your position? I want to just go down there, look around. If I find some good land, and I can find a way to grow bananas and get them to market, all I ask is that you'll postpone calling in that loan. And that you'll help me with transportation, maybe just pitch in another hundred if I really need it. And if you do, why, I'll give you a 60 percent stake in our enterprise. You know I'm a good farmer, and I'm good for it. I am."

George's secretary called him on the intercom.

"Mr. Stovall, the men are in the conference room."

George sighed. He'd been worked over plenty by Barney since they were kids on the farm in Pana. Their father, another dreamer like Barney, had ripped them from their placid, safe farm in Indiana and subjected them to homestead life, an experience he said would toughen them up, make men of them. All George could remember was howling wind and rancid pork. But Barney? He reveled in it. He learned to ride and shoot, and herded George, Luther, and JB into afternoons rambling across the landscape. Only their older brother Emile had cuffed Barney good, put him in his place.

Hell, Barney even managed to get George to call him Barney, when everyone knew his name was Hiram. What was wrong with Hiram, for pity's sake? It was a right respectable name. Barney sounded like the name of an old goat, a carnival barker, a day laborer—certainly not a name fitting the son of Barzilla and Elizabeth Stovall. No, the old man would roll over in his grave if he knew his favorite son was wandering the earth as Barney Stovall.

George watched Barney across his desk, his hand caressing that stickpin with the ugly gold nugget stuck to the end, like a turd on a toothpick. "Tell me again, Hiram, why the hell I am calling you Barney?"

"I like the sound of it. Besides, Hiram means 'exalted brother'

. . . did you know that? You should be happy to have me off the throne. And Barney means 'strong as a bear.' That's what I aspire to, George. Not living life as your exalted brother, but a bear, roaming the West, wild and strong."

Damn that Hiram and his useless trips to the library.

"Besides, I got tired of people calling me 'kike' every time they heard Hiram."

The secretary whispered again over the intercom. "Mr. Stovall?"

"Tell them I'll be there in two minutes," George said, standing again.

"All right, Barney. You've got two years to return the $500, with my share of the profits, but I'm not in for another penny. Not one more, and I mean it."

"Just the hundred-dollar cushion," said Barney.

George shoved his pen into his vest pocket. "Don't push me," he growled.

BARNEY

Aboard the SS *San Juan* in Route to the Isthmus of Tehuantepec, Mexico, 1912

In early January after Barney laid in his third cutting of alfalfa, he walked his cow, his horse, and his mule down the road to Milton Hall's place. Milton hitched up his buckboard and carried Barney and his trunk to Hanford, where Barney caught the train to San Francisco.

He peered in the dingy ticket window at the Hyde St. Pier.

"Need a ticket on the SS *San Juan*, steerage, to Salina Cruz."

The agent licked his thumb and snared a ticket in the drawer.

"That'll be sixty dollars. Arrives in Salina Cruz in thirteen days."

Barney stuffed the money under the ticket window.

"Food'll be tolerable," the agent told him. "You got blankets there in your trunk? Steerage is cold this time of year." Barney nodded.

The agent scratched at a red line of dry, flaking skin above his dingy white shirt collar, his mouth and mustache a waning moon.

"Hope you like chinks and Mexicans. White folk generally don't travel steerage." He gave Barney a reproving look head to toe: brown trousers drooping with age around the knees, scuffed farm boots still thick with winter mud, a collarless shirt, and a worn plaid wool mackinaw.

Barney pulled the ticket from the agent's hand. Turning loose the sixty dollars burned at his fingertips. It was a bigger chunk of the $500 than he cared to part with, but he had no choice. No way he was spending $140 for the luxury of a cabin, and besides, then he'd have to tolerate a lot of swelled heads, folks like George or Luther. Fat heads, Barney chuckled to himself as he wheeled his old trunk toward the San Juan's gang plank.

By late afternoon, Barney's gut had already adjusted to the roll and pitch of the old steamer on the rough January sea. He poured a sour-tasting cup of coffee from a large urn and found a seat at a table in the steerage galley. He carried a pen, a ledger, and a book, *Growing Bananas in the Tropics*, and bent his head over the work. Land, labor, a place to live, a couple of donkeys. Bribes. Would he need bribes? The books said so. A Mexican sat across from him, sipping his coffee.

"Where are you going, señor?" asked the man, a gentle smile on his clean-shaven face.

Barney looked up at him, a slender fellow, not very tall, maybe a decade younger, a thick accent, thicker charcoal hair. His deep-set eyes held a certain benign curiosity, as if the answer to his question would give him something pleasant to think about in the hour before sunset. Barney tapped the book in front of him.

"Tehuantepec. Seeing if I can buy some land, grow some bananas. And you?"

"My home is north of there, in Oaxaca City. I just finished dental school at the university in San Francisco. I'm going home to start my practice. My name is Luis Bolon." He stuck out his hand to Barney.

Barney shook it slowly. "Barney. Barney Stovall."

Barney knew nothing about dentistry, nothing about Mexico,

save what he read in his agriculture books, and nearly nothing about Mexicans. That Mexicans had teeth and needed dentists had never occurred to him, or that Mexicans themselves might be doctors or dentists or anything, really, but thin, one-dimensional characters . . . labor . . . a flimsy backdrop in Barney's limited worldview. Now Luis's curious eyes made a lie of that. This man had far more education than he did, knew two languages, dressed in better clothes—a fine linen shirt, a vest and suit of charcoal wool—than Barney.

A bell chimed on the upper deck.

"Ah, that is my call to dinner," Luis said as he stood. And a cabin. He had a cabin, not a steerage compartment.

"Say, after dinner, perhaps you could tell me more about your country, maybe what you know about Tehuantepec?" Barney asked.

"That would be very enjoyable, Mr. Stovall. Please come up, and I will buy you a cigar in the lounge."

Barney thought about Luis all through his supper of fish stew and rye bread. How had this young Mexican lived such a deliberate life in so short a time? He had an education and a plan for the future. Did the solid surface of Luis's life bore Barney, or did he envy him for it? He watched his fellow steerage companions, mostly Chinese men and a few Mexican families. The Chinese men were likely heading south to build a railroad. What was passing between the Mexican families, the mothers and fathers and stoic children? A glance, a light touch on a shoulder, a hand sweeping dark bangs off a small forehead. Barney felt alien, alone, an uncommon feeling for a man of thirty-eight who had successfully avoided the entanglements of marriage and society. The whispered vowels and clicking tongues of Spanish and Cantonese spun together over the hum of the steam engines. Barney listened a while, hypnotized, surprised at a sudden unexpected desire for companions, a cabin to retreat to later, and someone's warm, soft sighs in his ear. He struggled to his feet as the ship made a sudden hard roll to starboard and found his way to Luis.

The men stood on the forward deck, the night clearing and full of stars. Luis lit a cigar and passed it to Barney. They smoked together for some time in silence, their smoke disappearing behind them.

"So, Luis, you got a sweetheart waiting for you?"

Luis gave him that soft, contented smile again.

"Yes, señor, I do. Isidora. We will be married next month." Another accomplishment that had alluded Barney.

They talked long into the night, finally retreating inside against the cold. Luis described the Yucatán and its southern terminus in the Isthmus of Tehuantepec, his own home state of Oaxaca, his Mayan people, the countryside's steep rolling hills of coffee beans, the sound of geckos at night, his passion for a bowl of posole and red chili, his adoration for the Virgin Guadalupe.

Barney told Luis about his boyhood in Pana, his rich brothers, his peripatetic search for success as a farmer, a miner, a land speculator.

"Just never seem to be in the right place at the right time. But I got a feeling that this time, I'm gonna hit the mother lode," he said. "On my own, without my brothers and their stodgy ways, wearing blinders like plow horses. Don't need 'em, don't want 'em."

Luis smoked in silence.

"You remind me of Saint Paul, kicking against the goads. The more you kick, the more the harness will eat into your flesh."

Barney grunted. "I don't hold much truck with scripture. I only kick at things that deserve to be kicked. Just trying to find my own way in this world, and seems like there is always someone throwing up a gate I can't pass through."

Luis nodded, recognition in his dark eyes.

"Can I ask you a question, Luis? Why were you down there

in the steerage galley this afternoon? You've got much finer digs up here on deck."

"Ah, my friend, you are not the only man without a home on this ship. Your fellow American passengers on my deck do not think kindly of a Mexican man in the cabin next to them, or sitting at their dining table. I, too, have gates that will not open for me. And so I came below, to where my people are, and instead, I find you, with your book and a mind for conversation."

In the morning, after Barney's cup of metallic coffee, white bread, and prune jam, he wandered up to the deck, hoping to find Luis. The sun's rays, still low on the horizon at not quite eight in the morning, slipped across the ship, illuminated the wet deck and turned the three masts into slender golden spars of light. Barney looked east into the sun, tipping back his head and shading his eyes, when something on the foremast caught his attention. A man was slowly inching his way along the uppermost yard arm, pulling forward with his hands, pushing backward with his feet. At first, Barney thought he must be a sailor, but that wasn't possible, dressed like he was. The man was wearing trousers and a morning coat, the tails of the coat flapping like loose sails. The boat was under steam power in the quiet, windless swells, and the sails were not set. Why was he there? When the man reached the end of the yard arm, he reached into his coat pocket and pulled out something small and dark and pressed the object to his forehead: a gun.

"Hey, hey you up there!" Barney yelled. The man, startled, nearly lost his grip and spun around on the yard arm, now hanging beneath it, still pressing the gun to his head. *Bang!* A spray of red exited the back of the man's head, and he fell into the sea.

"Man overboard! Man overboard!" Barney heard from behind him on the bridge.

"All hands to starboard!" Barney recognized the captain's voice. "Bear away!"

Barney ran to the starboard side and looked for the man's body on the waves, saw it sinking fast, but it wasn't alone. Shark fins appeared, plowing under the man, their sleek gray backs rising out of the blue water, stopping the man's descent into the deep. He appeared almost alive, animated, as the sharks pulled at his dead limbs, the water now swirling red, a tangle of morning coat and stripped trousers slapping the water. Barney gasped, as did Luis, who was suddenly beside him, along with the captain.

"You, sir, I heard you yelling at him. What happened?" the captain asked Barney.

"I was just looking up into the sun, and I saw him crawling along the yard arm, and then I saw the gun. He must have wanted to make sure he fell into the ocean when he pulled the trigger. Are you going to try to . . . pull him in?"

The three men looked over the side again.

Only a pool of red and a flash of brown wool remained on the surface; the sharks had already abandoned the pile of rags. The ship steamed away from the vanishing red swirl. The captain was off, looking for who among his passengers might have chosen this clear, golden morning to take his life.

"My God," whispered Barney quietly. "I've seen men die before, but not like that."

For the next twelve days Barney and Luis, driven by their natural affection for conversation and the shared horror of the passenger's suicide, met each other on deck after the midday meal and walked the circumference of the ship. After each lap, Luis would set a centavo coin on the deck.

"It measures our accomplishment for the day," he said with a rakish grin, as if the seven-hundred-foot circumference of the steamer was the summit of Mount Everest. Barney thought the tiny idyll a playful gesture. To Barney, life was hard work, devoid of humor, and camaraderie. He didn't know who was on his side (if he had a side) and who was his enemy. He thought frequently of the man hanging from the yard arm, angling his body toward the sea. Would he finally be alone like that, no hope, a feast for sharks?

"So, your people in Mexico, they get along?" Barney asked one day.

"Get along? You mean, do we live in harmony?"

"Yeah, I suppose I mean that. In America, everywhere I go, seems like there are Brown people and Black people, red, yellow, and white people, and they find plenty of reasons to be at each other's throats. Times I think it would be better if we were all just one color."

"White, of course, Barney?" Luis asked with a chuckle.

The question stopped him is his tracks on the varnished deck.

"I don't know. I never thought about it."

"Have you ever heard of the NAACP? National Association for the Advancement of Colored People?"

Barney sighed. "Yep, I heard of them. Read all about those New Yorkers in the *Tonopah Bonanza*—Black and white folk together—who got their backs up about riots that happened right in my old stomping ground in Illinois. That's what got the NAACP started. Did you know that?"

Luis shook his head. "No, I didn't. But sometimes I came across their newspaper, *The Crisis*, when I was in school. I admire them, Barney. I think perhaps they might not want the whole world homogenized, as you suggest, though. What if, instead of everyone born the same color, we simply just took each other as we are, every color equal, like wildflowers in a field, each as beautiful as the next?"

Barney fell silent for a full turn around the deck.

"I met this man, a Negro," Barney said, "named Charles York. 'Bout thirteen years ago. When the coal miners there in Pana had been on strike for nearly a year, the mine owners, with the help of two of my darn fool brothers, they went down to Alabama, and they brought back three hundred poor devils to cross the picket lines. You know, they told them they were bringing them up for jobs in new mines, never told them nothing about being strike breakers. Anyhow, Charles, he was one of those, and he brought his wife and two babies with him.

"I wish I'd never met Charles that day. Fact, I wouldn't even have been in Pana if old Barzilla hadn't gotten so sick, my mother with a couple of young ones, Jesse and Edna, still at home. I'd been gone since I was twenty-two, made my way to Los Angeles—big city compared to Pana—but I just wanted to get a long way away from the farm. Don't remember why now, or even how I picked LA, must have jumped a freight and got off there. Just itching to be on my own, I guess. And damned if I didn't hire on to a farm in Los Angeles, a dairy, milking Ayreshires. I liked it there. Went down and registered to vote first thing. Like my daddy would say, 'That's what Abe Lincoln would do.'

"My mother sent a letter asking me to come home, help out when Daddy just folded up. Came back and took over the farm. My peckerwood brothers were right there, but they'd already gone to work on the railroads and the coal mines. Salaries and a 'Mr.' in front of their names, britches too clean to stoop to dirt farming.

"Anyhow, I'd gone in to town one day for supplies, and I see Charles and his wife and kids standing on a corner, looking lost. I'd heard rumors about these strike breakers coming to town, how my brothers had gone down there to fetch them. I knew they didn't do it to help out the Negro man, no.

"So I stopped the buckboard and asked the man if he was lost. He told me how they had come up from Alabama, promised a job, but the mine owners had nowhere to put a family, just the single men. Put those single fellas up inside one of the mines, or in an old warehouse they called the Alabama Hotel. Drinking and whoring and gambling, no place for a family. He had not a red cent, his wife looked scared, the babies were cold. Knew our bunk house was empty, but I also had an inkling my brothers would not take kindly to Negro strikebreakers living at our place. Likely to mar their reputations, you see, regardless of the fact that they had trucked them into town themselves.

"That's not how I was raised, though. My daddy would give hospitality to anybody, any time, unlike my skinflint brothers. He'd say, 'That's what Abe Lincoln would do.' And he should know, because my great-grandfather and my grandfather, Hezekiah Owen Stovall, came west from Kentucky with the Lincolns, first to Indiana and then to Illinois. They parted company in Decatur, and my grandfather and his parents came down thirty-five miles and bought the farmland in Pana. My grandfather Hezekiah was just a boy, the great Abe was just a boy, and they crossed together out of Kentucky on the Rolling Fork of the South River.

"I thought, well, Abe Lincoln wouldn't leave them standing there on the corner. So I took 'em home. And there was hell to pay, Luis, I tell you. Hell to pay. My dad, he was a strange old bird. Liked to sit on the porch roof in a rocking chair, he did indeed. He'd sit up there, and when he saw my brothers coming up the road, he'd fire his pistol into the air, and I'd come running in from the field, stand at the bunkhouse with a shotgun. Finally, Luther and George, they just gave up, let us be.

"So then I'd ride Charles in every day to work in the mines, and he told me all about Alabama and the Jim Crow laws. You ever hear about that? What in tarnation makes people so hellish?"

Luis just shook his head, kept his hands clasped behind his back, and matched Barney's much longer stride, listening intently.

"I told Charles, him and those miners, they had to stick together! And sure enough, they did. Formed their own union of sorts. Not that it did them any good, I'm sorry to say. Those white miners stirred up such hatred against those three hundred men. A massacre, they called it. Funny, though, whites and Blacks both died, and the white ones? They were killed by white lawmen. So you could pick your side, and in the end, with all that hatred, it didn't matter. You could die being right, or die being wrong."

Barney grew quiet and slowed his pace. The afternoon breeze was picking up, and both men's boots and shoulders were wet with wind-blown spray, the air full of salt and seabird calls.

"You said you wished you'd never met Charles?"

Barney stopped at the rail, Luis' stack of fifteen centavos at his feet.

"Charles was hurt in those riots, not too bad really, shot in the arm, just a flesh wound, and I paid for the doctor to sew him up. It was enough, though. There was no way his wife was staying in Pana, and Charles was not going back to Alabama.

"'There's nothing for me there but more misery,' he told me. And so you know what I said? I said, 'Move to Springfield! That's Lincoln's town. I know you can find a job there, better then working in a coal mine.' He trusted me, Luis. I rode up there and saw him once. He was working in a barber shop, cutting white men's hair. He said he could never touch a white man in Alabama. Progress, he called it.

"I stayed on at my folks' until my dad . . . He passed in 1901. My brother Emile was down in California, and he said he'd take on Mother and my young brother and sister, so we sold the farm, put 'em on the train. And me? I heard there was gold and silver to be found in Nevada, so I headed west to Tonopah, staked out a claim—nothing but me, a shovel, and a donkey. I never heard what happened until later." Barney pulled his damp old mackinaw tight across his shoulders.

"Heard about what?"

"Riots, in Springfield, in the Land of Lincoln, not the old South. Imagine that. That's what rattled those folks into starting the NAACP. Negros lynched. Negros run out of town naked.

Negro babies starved to death because no town would take them after Springfield turned them out. And Charles and his wife and kids? Those same white men who sat in his barber chair, they nailed boards over the doors and windows of his little house and lit it on fire. With them *inside*."

The two men stood at the rail and watched the sea heave, as if Barney's story had made it nauseous. The seagulls that followed the ship hung suspended in tall stacks of wind, their wings rising and falling in a funeral cadence.

"Barney, my friend, I am very sorry. But you can't believe that was your fault."

"Can't I? Just meddling in things I can't understand. My mother said I never could keep my nose out of anything. If I hadn't sent him there, if he'd just gone back to Alabama where he belonged—"

"Belonged? You would wish him to return to that—what did you call it?—'hellish' existence?"

"At least he'd be alive."

"Is that the answer, Barney? Alive, but still a slave?"

"I'll be damned if I know."

After Barney's supper of boiled beef and potatoes, he met Luis on the deck.

"I never answered your question this afternoon," Luis offered.

"What question was that?"

"You asked if we get along, we Mexicans. Harmony, yes?"

Barney nodded.

"No, I am sad to say. We may all have the same brown skin, but over the centuries, we found other ways to divide ourselves, kill each other, eat each other: our tribes, our gods, our land, our superstitions." Luis lit a cigar and pitched a spent match over the rail. "There is no one righteous, not even one."

BARNEY

Isthmus of Tehuantepec, Mexico, 1912

In the early hours of February 2, 1912, a Tehuano wind gathered itself into fluttering wings of airstream somewhere 124 miles to the east, on the Gulf of Mexico. Drawn by the Pacific Ocean, a moth to flame, the Tehuano bucked and rolled west across the shallow Isthmus of Tehuantepec until it amassed the strength to climb the Sierra Madre de Oaxaca, hurtle through Chivela Pass, and onto the shore of Salina Cruz. There, at full power, the SS *San Juan* steamed to meet it, an ancient wind and an iron ship tangling on the rough sea.

Barney and Luis stood on the bow, hats gripped in their hands against the wind and pitching waves, watching the arid coast of Oaxaca come into view. The *San Juan*, supplying every ounce of power to its sole engine, steamed through the two breakwaters of the recently erected artificial harbor. "Thanks to President José de la Cruz Porfirio Díaz Mori, proving even an evil man can do the right thing on occasion," Luis said.

The ship passed a dry dock, more than six hundred feet long, Barney estimated, where one freighter, hoisted high as if it would fly away across the world, was branded United Fruit Company. The sight of the ship in Barney's first glimpse of Mexico seemed ominous, a warning: *Beware All Ye Who Enter Here.* He shivered in the wind, even though it was already eighty degrees and climbing at nine in the morning.

The two men, having shed their sweaters and coats, rolled their steamer trunks down the gangway. Luis was headed to the railway station on the other side of the harbor, where he would take the first of three trains, hopscotching north, to Oaxaca City. Barney looked into the heart of Salina Cruz. All the contours of the journey ahead—a bewildering country, a mysterious language, attempting to farm a fruit he only knew from eating them while walking behind a plow and mule on the California farm. The whole idea suddenly seemed ridiculous.

They stood in the hot wind, their shirts and pants snapping like sails, and shook hands.

"I have not known many friends in my life, Luis. And now that I've found one, it is one sorry sodbuster who must tell you goodbye."

"Ah, patron, my country awaits you. I hope you will find the riches you dream of. Someday you must come to Oaxaca City. Isidora and I would welcome you any time."

"And I would say likewise. But I don't seem to have a home at the moment. Wonder if I ever will."

Salina Cruz reminded Barney of San Francisco after the 1906 earthquake, when every man, woman, and child frantically wailed on the collapsed and bent city until it rose again. Along the dirt streets of Salina Cruz, a throng of men in short sleeves and Panama hats dug foundations, pushed wheelbarrows of wet concrete, and hauled wagons of wood posts. A fine limestone dust blew through the windy streets. No adobe for this new Western outpost; it was erupting in concrete, speedy and sure. The newly christened railroad had given Salina Cruz gravitas: gateway status to the Gulf of Mexico. Rumblings about the Panama Canal, set to open in two years, imbued the city with a sense of urgency. Mexico had to rake in its fortunes before the canal made the Tehuantepec Route yesterday's news. Barney felt that urgency himself, a thrumming panic.

He wandered aimlessly, tugging his trunk behind him, looking for . . . what? Something familiar, something that might ground him in this strange place. Inscrutable syllables of Spanish flew past him in the wind, along with the aroma of pork fat and corn. It occurred to him he needed a place to stay, something to eat. If only Luis were with him, interpreting the sights, sounds, and smells.

He turned a corner onto a broad avenue lined with Brasil and palm trees, their trunks rising from the rocky soil, surrounded by bursts of purslane. Houses crowded right up to the avenue's edge, their occupants and home life sealed from view by heavy wooden doors and iron fittings. The avenue led him to a central square, like the ones he'd seen on his rambles to small California towns east of Los Angeles. Small cafes with tables and chairs arranged in the pale, sandy dirt; a butcher shop with chickens hanging by their feet, fly-covered strips of beef on hooks; an old man strumming a guitar outside the open doors of a cantina.

It was midafternoon, the wind was dying, and Barney realized he had walked for hours. The wheels on his trunk had begun to squeak, or maybe it was the soles of his old boots? He couldn't tell. The sight of one man brought him to a halt. Not a Mexican, not a white man, but a Black man, sitting at a cantina table, staring at him like a preacher inviting him to the altar to repent. The man stood and reached out his hand.

"Ezra Sykes."

Barney grasped his hand.

"Barney Stovall. You speak English!"

Ezra grinned, lips cracked from the wind and heat, a few teeth missing here and there. A deep gash ran over his left eye, healing now, like a tom cat who has spent too many nights under the porch. He rubbed his hand over his short salt-and-pepper beard and waved Barney to a seat.

"Come down to these parts from Louisiana 'bout ten years ago, worked on the railroad in Guatemala. And you?"

"California, just off the SS *San Juan* this morning. Here to . . ." Barney stumbled over his words, his mouth dry, his pitiful plan, as he saw it now, stuck in his throat. "Grow some bananas." Barney peered closely at Ezra, measured him to be at least his height, but muscled and thickset around the chest like that prize fighter Jack Johnson; maybe his age, thirty-nine, or a little younger. He watched for Ezra's reaction to the banana plan and saw a flicker of disbelief, his copper eyes examining Barney's blue ones with pity.

"You're a long ways from Guatemala. And Louisiana," Barney observed.

"Thought I was leaving the South when I came down here, but I found out ole Jim Crow, he got here before me, on the coat-tails of the United Fruit Company. Made me take my hat off to the white man—no offense to you, mister—couldn't marry an Indian woman, couldn't live or eat where I wanted, was paid dirt wages. Didn't leave Louisiana just to live like that again, so I got out of that boiling jungle and come up here."

Barney eyed the food in front of Ezra: a half-eaten pile of yellow rice, a jagged quarter of a giant tortilla slathered in mashed beans and wild greens.

"You hungry, mister? I've had all I want," he said, pushing the plates toward Barney.

Barney wiped his dusty hands on his pants and lifted the tortilla to his mouth without hesitation. Ezra waived to a young Mexican girl leaning against the cantina door frame.

"Una cerveza, Lola, por favore."

Barney eyed Ezra around the edges of the tortilla. *He speaks Spanish too? Damn.*

"Mr. Sykes, you know anything about growing bananas?"

Ezra tilted his head back. The setting sun rolled across the plaza into his open mouth like a wave. He howled, the laugh echoing under the cantina's palapa roof.

"Bananas? Why yes, mister, I've been on both ends of a boatload of bananas, from the end that is growing, to the end that is shipping. And I hate those goddamned bananas. 'Nother reason I left Guatemala."

The beer arrived, and Ezra pushed it across to Barney.

"If you're thinking of growing bananas, mister, you need this beer more than I do."

Barney took a long pull on the tepid beer; the tortilla, barely chewed, clawed its way down his throat.

"Well, now, I have reason to believe that I can get some land, somewhere east of here, maybe Acayucan—some land that's already planted in bananas—and when I harvest 'em, I can take 'em over the Tehuantepec railroad to Medias Aguas, and from there, onto the connecting line to the port at Veracruz, onto a steamer and up to Galveston. I've already lined up a buyer there."

Ezra whistled.

"Well that takes money, mister. A lot of it."

"I got money."

Ezra reached over and pulled the beer back in his meaty hand.

"Well, why'm I feeding and watering you then?"

Ezra and Barney drank some more beers, Barney buying this time, fifteen cents a bottle, and as the sun went down and the cantina filled with weary construction workers, Barney hired Ezra. Ezra shook his head back and forth as he pumped Barney's hand up and down. He would be Barney's guide and interpreter for an enterprise in which he had no interest, and zero confidence. But moving anywhere was better than sitting still in Salina Cruz where he was drawn to bar fights. No one here on the western edge of the isthmus seemed to want a Negro on a construction crew, even one whose strong back made him the perfect hod carrier.

Ezra grumbled "I'm just this mister's burro" while pulling Barney's trunk, Barney trailing behind, down a narrow side street, out of town to a small cabana on a rocky outcropping above a sandy wash. There was a dog tied up outside, and a woman's things hanging on hooks inside. The night was moonless, the stars raining needles of light on the sand. Barney pulled a blanket from his trunk, rolled himself into it on the Saltillo floor, and listened to coyotes yip off in the distance. Soon, Ezra was snoring from his spot on a sisal bed. Barney didn't give in to sleep for a long time, clutching his money belt and its remaining $438.50 against his aching chest like a poultice.

In the morning, Ezra made his goodbyes to the dog and a pretty Mexican woman who had come to make them tortillas and eggs. Barney watched them from the road, unsettled by the spiraling of black and brown limbs as they kissed at the cabana door. At the train station, Barney gave up another dollar to buy them tickets. The train labored over the mountains and down into a dense rain forest so lush, Barney wondered if the train and tracks might liquefy in its rich fecundity.

By late afternoon, they reached Acayucan. Ezra found them a room to share in a hotel.

"No ole Jim Crow here," he told Barney happily, the slash above his eye winking. The door to their room opened on an interior courtyard where chickens scratched and three young children ran in circles chasing a baby burro. A teenage girl stirred laundry in a cauldron set over a fire and hung wet sheets from a rope strung across the yard. An old woman sat under the shade of a jacaranda tree, pressing tortillas.

"Lordy," Barney said as the carnival of laundry and whirling children surrounded them.

"Let's go find us some bananas," Ezra said.

Barney spent the evening in a state of confusion. The thick, perfumed air weighed on him, sweat soaking through his shirt in circles as big as pumpkins. Ezra propelled him into three successive cantinas, where all conversation immediately ceased: a Black man with a gash over his forehead, a white man sweating profusely. What a pair, Barney thought. Ezra stuck out his hand.

"Money, Barney. I got to buy these fellas beers."

Barney swiveled to follow the conversation, looking from Ezra to the farmers. There were nods yes, nods no, laughter, mostly after what Barney took to be Ezra's jokes. Occasionally Ezra would roll his eyes in Barney's direction, and he got the sense that Ezra was mocking him. He caught a few words he understood: plantano, hectar, meses, ano, Frutas Unidos, and one word he heard over and over. Luzelba. What was a luzelba?

By the end of the night, Barney had shelled out for two dozen beers. On the way back to the hotel, he peppered Ezra with questions.

"What have we got, Ezra? Acreage? Workers?"

Ezra kept chuckling to himself.

"Well, I found us someone who just might partner with you. But I'm not sure you're gonna like it."

"Just tell me!"

"You know that passel of kids running around the courtyard this afternoon, chasing the burro? The kids' mother owns the hotel. Husband ran off to join the revolution, and she's got five hectares— that's 'bout twelve acres—of plantanos—bananas—and no one to manage or harvest them. That's your new partner, if you play it right."

"A woman?"

"Not just any woman. Luzelba Tamay. They say she's a beautiful, young thing, fierce, a *Tehuana*."

"Tehuana? Like the wind?"

"More like whirlwind, what they say. Women round here are the merchants, set the rules, 'cept for those set by the government, which ain't too kind to women. And the farmers? They say United Fruit is already sniffing around."

"What do they want?"

"They want bananas, you damn fool. And the land under them. They come in and offer sky-high prices for the bananas, and that scares off all the other buyers. Then after everyone else goes away, next season, they won't pay shit for the bananas, and all the farmers lose their serapes, end up selling their land cheap to United, just to keep from going under. Seen it happen all over Guatemala."

"Well, I heard about that. But I didn't think United Fruit was paying any attention to Mexico . . . too small. But with the railroad . . . Damn. So what's gonna make this Tamay woman partner with us?"

"Well, that's what you gotta figure out. You the brains of this outfit. I'm just the burro."

Barney was up at first light, the timid new sky and fresh air unspoiled by heat and humidity. It suited his farmer métier to leave his room early while Ezra slept. He made his way through the courtyard, quiet now, a few chickens roosting here and there in the dirt. Out behind the small hotel, the rain forest had been peeled back to make room for acres of bananas, now leafy, fruit setting, stretching high up the slopes into the mist.

Barney walked up the hill through tall grass. Up ahead, through the trees, the grass swished. A woman with a thick braid down her back was swinging a machete against all comers threatening to swallow up the bananas. She floated through the Sargasso

Sea of grass, the machete swinging one way, her braid the other, her breath in the sunny grove rising like smoke above her dark hair.

Barney counted the task before her—clear these twelve acres—nearly impossible for one woman alone, not to mention one with three kids and a hotel to run. On his left, a handcart held a pottery pitcher, a sharpening stone, and a second machete. He rolled up his sleeves and hefted the machete, feeling its weight and balance, and strode into the grass, setting himself six feet from the woman's threshing right arm, and met her stroke: right, left, step forward, right, left, step forward. For the first time since he departed San Francisco on the *San Juan*, he was at home in his surroundings, his hand married to the machete.

The woman glanced briefly at Barney, nearly losing the measured rhythm of her swing. But she kept sawing the grass, saying nothing, and Barney kept meeting her stroke for stroke, until they reached the top of the orchard. They stopped, both of them breathing like plow horses.

"Thank you, I do appreciate your help," she said, crossing the newly swathed path toward him. "But you've just wasted a half hour of your time. I've already told your compadres I'm not selling to United Fruit."

Barney stared at Luzelba Tamay and dropped the machete.

"I hear the angels singing," he said.

"How is that, señor?"

"You are Luzelba Tamay, you speak English, and you don't want to sell to United Fruit!"

"All true. And since you have been making use of my machete, perhaps you could tell me your name and how you come to be in my bananas."

Barney needed a drink of water. If sweating up the hillside wasn't enough, Tamay's nearness made him dizzy, as if she had beaned him with the flat side of her machete. Every heaving breath she exhaled was like warm acacia honey. She barely came up to the middle of his chest and couldn't weigh more than 110 pounds, but she seemed larger somehow, a July harvest moon, low on the horizon, taking up all the space between them. Barney didn't know what to do with his hands, found it hard to speak his own name. What did he know of women, save for a fleeting crush on Fanny, his neighbor Milton's wife. His own brief interludes with wan American women who tittered behind handkerchiefs were no preparation for this fiery woman. Her bronze skin and dark eyebrows, drawn now into a disapproving scowl, were rare earth to him, nothing like the pasty blond acquiescence of young school girls in Pana, Illinois, or the grasping women along Hollywood Boulevard in Los Angeles. How had he gone so long thinking those were the things women were made of? Luzelba Tamay was a different species.

"I'm Barney Stovall, and I've come from California to buy some land . . . or some bananas . . . ship them to the US, where every man, woman, and child eats sixty bananas a year and—"

"I'm not selling, I told you."

"I'm not United Fruit! I'm the farthest thing from United Fruit you can even imagine. I'm the opposite of United Fruit."

"Really? You're an American. How do I know you're not representing United Fruit?"

"All the money in the world I got, it's right here," he said, slapping the money belt slung across his chest. "This is it! There's no United Fruit behind me. I'm agin' everything they've done in your part of the world, and what they're gonna do, if we let them."

"We, señor Stovall?"

"We, if you please, Mrs. Tamay."

"I prefer Luz. Let's work our way down the hill to the water pitcher."

By work, she meant pick up the machetes again and make another pass through the banana plants down to the hand cart. Barney stayed one step behind her, all the way down. Luzelba Tamay was the most perfect thing he had ever seen.

BARNEY

Acayucan, Mexico, 1912

Luzelba and Barney sat in the shade, passing the water back and forth. Barney wasn't a religious man, but the water tasted holy. His fingers stung where they grazed her hand on the pitcher. Luz and Luis, these two curious people, were changing the way his heart beat, how the valves opened and closed. He hiccupped and held his breath, letting it out slowly.

"Ma'am, may I ask how you come to speak English?"

"When I was sixteen, my father sent me to nanny for the American attaché in Veracruz. I was there three years. He knew he'd leave the hotel to me one day—I was his only child— and he saw English as essential.

"And now for my questions. Why do you want my bananas? Why should I sell them to you?"

Barney rolled out his plan, the same one he'd told to George, to Luis, to Ezra. But for the first time, each word held promise, as if Luz had blown on his dice and he'd rolled doubles. He believed it now, saw it all: bins of bananas loaded off the dock in Galveston, the buyer clapping him on the back, closing the deal. The money . . . his future, his stake. His proof to George and the rest of his brothers that he had chops, was not just a dreamer floating from one tangent to another.

"And so, Mrs. Tamay—"

"Luz."

"Luz," he said tentatively. "My associate, Ezra Sykes, he's down at the hotel. He'll help me hire workers to finish clearing the fields, and I'll arrange the harvest and transportation, and pay you well for the land and the bananas—"

"No."

Barney faltered. "No?"

"Mr. Stovall, do you know anything about women in my country? We are not allowed to own anything. This land, this hotel, they are not even mine, even though my father left them to me. They are my husband's to dispose of as he chooses. At the moment, he has chosen to follow Zapata into revolution." Luz threw pebbles at the cart as if it was a target.

"Do you know, when he left, he wanted me to come along, bring the children. Be his soldadera. Come for the fighting, stay to cook his meals and wash his clothes, all of my children on my back! The irony is, if the revolution succeeds, which I do not for a moment believe will happen, the women fighters, the soldaderas, they will have some sway. Perhaps they will fight for reforms. But it is more likely that my husband will die a foolish death along with the revolution, and I will be left to pick things up again, with no protection from the courts or the police.

"So will I sell you *my* land? It is not my land to sell, and yet, it is all I have: mine, and not mine. It is a shadow of a real thing, but it is all I have."

They sat silent for a while, Barney uncertain what to say next.

"But Mr. Stovall, I will sell you my bananas. *If* you agree to one thing."

"Name it," he said, surprised.

"You must convince my neighbors not to sell their bananas or their land to United Fruit. Because if they do, in one year, my land—the shadow of my land—will be worth nothing."

"Well, Luz, that is a tall order. How can I possibly convince them of that?"

"We will buy their bananas together, you and I. Partners. I may not have land, but I have money. We can pay better than they would get selling just to Mexicans. They must never know it came from me, for they would never sell to me.

"And then you will take their bananas, and my bananas, to Texas, and send me the money. For one more year, United Fruit will get nothing from Acayucan."

"That's a mighty big risk. Say I do talk them into it, what makes you so sure I'll send you your money after I sell the bananas?"

She smiled at him for the first time. "Because you asked that question. And because you can swing a machete."

For the next two months Barney, with Ezra at his side, talked one banana farmer after another into selling to him, even though United Fruit sent two slick operators in linen suits carrying cases of tequila and cigars to compete with them. Barney was able to convince them in his plain farmer manner that they could always sell to United Fruit in the years ahead if they wanted to, but this was the time to profit and hold onto their land, see what would become of the banana market. Sixty bananas for every man, woman, and child in America! Why, they were sitting on a gold mine! Ezra told his own stories of how United Fruit raped the farmers in Guatemala and the Caribbean.

Late at night, Ezra, Barney and a handful of farmers sat drinking and swearing and laughing together in the cantina. Sometimes, they were smoking cigars and drinking tequila courtesy of United Fruit. The youngest of the bunch, Fabio Chuc, told Barney, "We can drink their liquor tonight, and I can tell them no tomorrow."

Barney convinced them to work together to clear the fields of grass to keep pests down and make harvest easier, pulling out his copy of *Growing Bananas in the Tropics* to show them pictures. He sweated hard next to them every day, Luz's spare machete in his hand. Luz held his money belt for him now in her apartment. Trust went both ways.

By April, Barney had lined up transportation for thirty hectares of bananas. Bunches of bananas—about nineteen thousand of them, if he'd calculated right—loaded on mules and wagons would go to the train station, be transferred to cargo bins, and travel by train to the port of Veracruz where, on June 11, Barney and the bananas would set sail on the SS *Mexicano*, bound for Galveston.

Ezra, for the most part, had come around.

"Stopped calling me 'mister,' now calls me Barney," he told Luz on one of his frequent evening visits to her apartment. Visits conjured from this or that or the other thing, just to stand on her doorstep and tell her about his day. Sometimes she would come out with him, if her children were sleeping, and they would walk in the dusk through the bananas, heavy now with fruit.

"He's sent for his girl *and* his dog in Salina Cruz. Says he likes it here. He ain't sure why, but he says they seem to hold no grudge against a Negro. Says some of the farmers even asked him to stay on, help manage their bananas. Says even *you* asked him."

"I did. He works hard. The other farmers like him. I think maybe next season, we can form a cooperative, manage these bananas together, just as you have shown us."

Barney felt walloped. Acayucan would go on without him. He could hardly blame Luz. There really wasn't a place for him here in the banana business. He owned no land, wasn't likely to get any, and in his meticulous planning, he had laid it all out for them, all they needed to know to export their next crop. All that was left was to introduce them to his buyer in Galveston.

What surprised him was that he didn't care so much about the money anymore. What mattered were his compadres in the cantina late at night, Ezra telling him to hitch up his britches, the ferocious Tehuano wind. Luz.

She must have read his mind.

"Barney, you can't come back."

"Well why not, Luz? A man can go wherever he wants in this world, and I—"

"But a woman cannot. I am here forever. I have the children, and the land that is mine and not mine. I have a husband."

They walked in silence for a while.

"I received a letter from him today. He says he is coming back in July, if he lives that long."

"So, he will just pick up where he left off, is that it? Is that what you want?"

"What I want does not matter. I cannot even divorce him. I cannot leave my land, or my children. My only choice is to carry on, to save money against the day . . ." Luz caught her breath. "The day my children and I can make of life what we want. And who knows when that will be."

Barney wanted to pluck an answer for her out of the velvet blue sky, the light suspended like comb in a honey jar, a perfect abeyance of time and consequences. He caught her by the arm, and then he froze. What if she came into his arms? His romantic repertoire was limited to five furtive minutes with a prostitute in Nevada City.

"No, Barney," she said gently to him.

It was enough of a reproach; he dropped her arm, embarrassed, and started back down the hill. He made it three steps. Luz put her arms around him from behind, and with as much effort as it takes to blow the duff from a dandelion, they fell together onto a pile of dried grass. She quickly unbuttoned his shirt, then the front of his trousers.

She knew, from his surprised eyes, that Barney knew less about love making than he did bananas. She led him, gently, to her own buttons, then drew his hands to the tender, soft places he never considered would be his. They were quiet in the rustle of the grass, kissing, caressing, Luz pressing her nose into his sweaty shoulder, still ripe from the day's labor. They rocked silently in the evening breeze.

When they were still, limbs slung around each other, breathing in unison, Barney closed his eyes, holding the image of them together for as long as he could. Luz pulled her skirt from the grass to drape over them both.

"Do you always say no before you say yes?" he asked.

"Only with you."

"Luz, why can't we go on forever? You can come with me, to America. There's land there, far as your eye can see or your heart can imagine. You can start over. We can. You can own land in your name, I'll make sure of that."

"Don't spoil this moment, Barney. Tomorrow, you will carry my machete into the bananas, and I will tend my babies. And then you will go. This is where I belong, and over there"—she gestured north over his bare shoulder—"is where you belong."

Over the next few weeks, it was almost as if their lovemaking had never happened. Barney rushed to arrange the harvest, timed so that the bananas were vibrant yellow when they arrived at the dock in Texas. Luz let Ezra use a small piece of land behind the hotel to build a house for himself and his Cecilia. Barney helped him build the forms, mix straw and mud, and pour the adobe bricks.

He only knocked on Luz's door when he needed money to pay a farmer for his bananas, and looked mostly at her cheek bones, not her eyes. He was afraid to ask her to walk with him again, afraid she would say no, afraid she would say yes and then rebuff his advances. He wanted her again and again and again without end, but the futility of that made him reluctant to take anything less, even a few more nights in the warm grass.

On a humid night in late May, he stood at Luz's door, leaning from one side of her sisal mat to the other like an anxious race horse.

"We're nearly all in now, Luz, it's almost all harvested. I need $100 to pay one more fella, and then tomorrow, I can go over it all with you, how many bunches we'll be shipping, and what I think we can get for them."

Luz left him on the stoop and went to get the money. When she came back, he was looking up the hill into the bananas, finding it hard to face her.

"Barney, will you walk with me tomorrow night, once more? A time to say goodbye?"

He took the money from her and nodded, a man sealing his fate. He headed toward the cantina to hand off his final payment. He should feel elated, on the precipice of success, but the thought of saying goodbye to Luz and Acayucan pinned him in on himself, unable to see beyond this one miserable goodbye. The night was dark, no moon, most of the stars hidden away. A light, warm rain began to fall, and later, Barney figured it must have muffled his hearing. Or maybe he was just remembering Luz in the grass, a vision that rendered him senseless. Whatever it was, he didn't hear the two men slide close.

An arm around his neck and a sharp kick to the back of his knees propelled him to the ground, where the pointed toe of a cowboy boot began to work on his ribs. He tried to get up, but a pair of arms pounded his head back into the wet street, while the disembodied cowboy boots kicked him repeatedly in the kidneys. No one said a word, just grunting at their own exertion as they reduced Barney to a pile of hurt. In his barely sentient state, he heard an American voice whisper in his ringing ear.

"You won this year, Stovall, you son of a bitch, but you ever come near Acayucan's bananas again, and Tamay will get what you're getting, maybe worse." The United Fruit men went through his pockets and took the $100.

"That's for the cigars and the tequila," said the disembodied cowboy boots as they kicked him in the ribs one final time. Barney lay in the rain a long time, chasing consciousness, until Ezra found him, cold, wet, and bloody.

"Aw, Barney, you're supposed to be the brains of this outfit," Ezra said, scraping him off the street and onto his shoulder.

"And you're the burro," Barney whispered.

When Barney opened his eyes, he was in his room at the hotel, Luz leaning over him.

"United Fruit," he said. The sound of his own voice made his ears throb.

"I know," she said.

"How?"

"They have sent a few notes . . . Threats."

"You didn't tell me," he said, and Luz shrugged. "They took the money for Fabio."

"Don't worry, we've taken care of it. I gave another $100 to Ezra for him."

Barney noticed for the first time that he was shirtless, and that his chest was bandaged tightly.

"The doctor came. He says if you don't piss any blood, you will probably live."

"That's good to know," he said, trying vainly to sit up. Luz lightly pushed him back onto the pillows.

"Luz, we've got ten days to get those bananas to Veracruz. Help me up."

"You are not going anywhere, señor. Ezra and I, we will finish the harvest, get the bananas to the train. And if you promise me you will stay right here until then, I might even let you come with us." She smiled at him, a warden's intimidating smile. Barney wasn't going anywhere.

Ten agonizing days later, the three boarded the Tehuantepec train. He braced himself against the concussion of wheels on track, still aching and bruised. Luz sat next to him, her stiff upright posture concealing all her curves.

"I keep thinking United Fruit might make another visit," she said.

Ezra sat slumped in a seat across the aisle, his Panama hat pulled down over his eyes, exhausted from the last days humping the bananas from the fields to the train.

In Medias Aguas, they and their bananas changed trains, and made north for the port at Veracruz.

Finally, Luz relaxed. They sat on the shady east side of the car, and while Barney braced himself against the train's insistent torture, the motion lulled Luz to sleep, her head falling to his shoulder. It wasn't a walk in the tall grass, but it was all he would have.

The SS *Mexicano* was waiting for them. Barney arranged the final transport of the bananas to the ship, Ezra translating. In an hour, the ship would leave for Galveston. The three friends, like tinted layers of sedimentary rock—shale, sandstone, and limestone—turned heads as they walked through Veracruz, arm in arm.

At the gangplank, they parted. Barney touched Luz's shoulder and shook Ezra's hand. Nothing to be done about it, he thought.

"I will write," he said to Luz, and she nodded, knowing he wouldn't.

"Luz, I . . . " she let him stutter. Ezra moved away down the dock. "I wish you would come with me. Ezra could bring the children later."

"You wish the impossible. But it is a lovely wish all the same."

Barney stood on deck and watched Ezra and Luz grow smaller, mirages in the blue haze.

On June 17, 1912, the SS *Mexicano* steamed into Galveston. Barney's buyer met the ship, and took possession of 19,800 bunches of bananas—each bunch 140 golden bananas—and paid him $1.50 a bunch, $29,700 total. In the afternoon, Barney wired $19,800 to Luz. He wired George, as he promised, sixty percent of the profits: $4,740. He put $3,160 in his pocket—more money than he would have again for twenty years.

He picked up a copy of the *Galveston Daily News*, and there on page twelve read, CHANDLER, ARIZONA: NEW TOWN WITH PROMISE. He sent a wire to Milton giving him his cow, horse, and mule. He sent a second wire to George asking him to sell his farm. He bought a train ticket to Arizona. If he wanted to forget Luz and Acayucan, Chandler seemed as good a place as any.

Barney stared into the shadowed, deep eyes of the sharecroppers around the fire, his story complete. Had he convinced them that working together would be better?

"That Ezra sounds like a mighty fine fella," Joe Lee said, raising his corn liquor in a salute. The others nodded. Barney slapped his palms against the knees of dungarees, and smiled.

MAUDIE MARIE

Stone County, Mississippi, Jenkins Plantation, 1925

The boys stood around the wash tub on the kitchen table, eyeing its contents. Vernon stuck a finger toward the bundle in the middle and poked hard, three times. The bundle mewed.

"Does it have a name yet?" Ernie asked his brothers.

"No, Mama says it don't need a name. We're just supposed to call it Baby," said Leonard.

"Yes, she's going to get a name," Maudie said, coming in from the yard with eggs in the front of her apron.

"Get on outta here," she barked at them. "Pa said you was supposed to head down to the field. Everybody's got to work a little harder till Ma's feeling better. Take Albert with you."

Lula lay on the bed in the corner, still asleep. The morning was creeping toward seven, and still she hadn't gotten up for the day. Maudie picked up the baby, whose whimpering had bloomed into a full-throated cry, and swung her softly, singing "shh, shh, shh" as quietly as she could. Her mother stirred.

"Ma, you got to feed this baby."

"Bring her here, then."

She lay the baby next to her mother, who reluctantly opened the front of her nightgown and pushed a nipple toward the baby's mouth, now open in an anguished cry. Lula's breast filled her mouth, but the crying did not subside. Lula pushed on the side of her breast, holding back the unresponsive flesh from the child's tiny mouth. Lula grimaced.

"It's no use." She pushed the baby aside, as she had the last two mornings.

"Ma, what do I do? She's so hungry!"

"I don't care. Truly I do not." Lula rolled back toward the wall, and Maudie caught the baby as she rolled toward the floor.

She wrapped the baby in a blanket, carried her down the hill toward the cotton fields, and saw her father and a clutch of Black croppers and some of their wives and children hoeing her family's cotton field. *What in the world are those people doing here?* In the very middle of the field, just two rows over from where her father hoed, she made out the distinctive purple head wrap of Violet Byrd. She waded through the knee-high cotton. Barney watched her carry the baby toward Violet and kept chopping.

"Missus Byrd, my Ma doesn't have any milk for this baby," she said over the baby's piercing cries. "I don't know what to do. She's gonna die if I don't find her some milk."

Violet laid her hoe in the cotton and stood, rubbing her back with the palms of her hands.

"All right, child." She reached out her dirty hands for the baby. Maudie Marie clutched the yowling baby tighter.

"What you gonna do with her?"

"Why, I'm gonna fry her up for breakfast. What do you *think* I'm gonna do? There are some other women with new babies, and I'm going to find one who has some milk to spare. You can either come with me, or give me the baby. But unless one of us moves, you are right, that baby is going to die, sure as this cotton is bound for Atlanta."

Barney was moving down the cotton row toward them.

"Pa, Missus Byrd wants to take the baby on over to *her* side of the plantation, to some women over there."

"You go on and go with her, Maudie. It'll be just fine. And then you'll know where your sister is."

"But Ma—"

"Your Ma is not gonna care whether this baby is drinking darky milk or white milk. She is just not gonna care," he said, returning to his place on the chopping line.

She followed Violet out of the field and down the road that separated their cabin and field from the Black sharecroppers. Violet took long quick steps, and Maudie trotted to keep up with her. Was the baby soothed by the gentle rhythm, or was she simply slipping away? She peered at her under the jostling blanket, and the baby seemed to be looking up into nothing. She picked up her pace. The road rose, then fell, and she saw a small village of sorts, thirty cabins set in irregular rows among pine, oak, and pecan trees. In the three years they'd lived on the plantation, she had never ventured down this road, and it had taken on a mysterious, dark aura—a place where the residents spoke some hidden language, ate strange foods, and would cast spells on her if she came too close or spied their secretive ways. To her surprise, the shacks looked little different from hers. Small children chased each other and a few chickens through the dust and pine needles. Women sat on their porches darning clothes or shelling peas. And one held a baby at her breast.

"Morning, Clemmie Mae," Violet said. "This here baby was born two days ago, and her mother's milk hasn't come in. Not sure if it ever will. She's the one had the bad fever. When you finish feeding little Dewey there, do you think you could suckle this one?"

"Let me see her."

Maudie held the baby toward Clemmie Mae in outstretched arms—an offering, a prayer, the baby growing more quiet and limp in her arms as the minutes passed.

"She's a pretty little thing, for a white child," Clemmie said. She pulled Dewey's fat cheek from her breast, handed the sleeping baby to Violet, and reached out to Maudie Marie, who stepped hastily onto the porch and released the baby into Clemmie's arms.

Clemmie gathered her in. With two fingers in a V clasped around her breast, she guided the nipple to the baby's cheek and brushed it lightly against the pale skin. The baby didn't move. She brushed the nipple against the baby's cheek again and again. Finally, her small mouth formed an O. She turned her head, ever so slightly, toward Clemmie's ox-blood-shaded nipple. Maudie Marie watched, fascinated, as Clemmie slowly brought the baby's tiny bone-china mouth to her earthenware breast until the baby took hold, and sucked.

"She's gonna be all right now, child," Violet said, clasping Maudie's shoulder.

"Violet, you know, I can't do this for long, I just ain't got enough milk to feed two babies."

Maudie looked back and forth from Clemmie Mae to Violet, her fear returning.

"Don't worry . . . ma'am. I will bring you some eggs. And some pork! We got some good salt pork and corn pone. I can make that for you each morning, with some bacon fat. I can—"

"Hold on, Maudie! You'll fatten her up so much, she'll never get off the porch!"

Both women laughed, and for the first time in three days, Maudie drew a peaceful breath.

"You're gonna have to leave your sister here with me, girl. But you can come back and see her, and yes, please bring me some eggs. We ate our last chicken yesterday. And some diapers, and a blanket. A nightdress too."

Maudie walked alongside Violet on the road back to the Stovall's cotton field, the pace slack now. It was getting on to nine, and the June sun made the clotted air rise like smoke from the weeds and stubble along the road.

"Missus Byrd—"

"Call me Violet, child."

"Yes, ma'am. Violet, why are all you people in my family's cotton field? Don't you have your own to chop?"

"Well, your daddy," Violet chuckled, "he's convinced all the men to help each other. Says we might actually make some money after the furnish is paid back. I think he's a damn fool. Biting off more trouble than he can even imagine. But we shall see."

At the Stovall's cotton, Violet strode back into the rows, making straight for Barney. Maudie Marie watched from the road, how her daddy took off his straw hat and offered Violet a reverential nod. Violet stretched her chin to the sky, and then to Maudie's surprise, raised her finger and shook it in his face. Barney smiled. The look on his face—affection? admiration?—confused her. She hurried on to the shack to gather up the eggs, the diaper rags, and whatever else she could think of and then headed back toward Clemmie Mae's. When she passed the field this time, Barney and Violet were on opposite ends, chopping cotton, separated by six men and Maudie Marie's towheaded brothers. Their backs were to each other, their hoes rhythmically hewing the red clay soil. Maybe she had just imagined her father's deference to the powerful woman in the purple head wrap. The thought that she was mistaken made her sad.

She spent the afternoon in the shade of Clemmie Mae's porch, juggling first Dewey and then her nameless sister. The baby already seemed stronger, less fretful. When she fell asleep, Maudie laid her on a folded blanket on the porch, heated a kettle of water on the wood stove and washed diapers for both babies, and hung them on a line stretched from the shack to a pine tree. Neighbor women gathered in clutches nearby. She felt sure they were talking about the white girl doing chores at a Black woman's house. As the sun edged behind the oaks and pines, she fried up four eggs, crumbled some corn pone into them, and placed the plate on Clemmie's lap.

"Ma'am, I suppose I should go home. I still have to cook supper. Should I take the baby home, or leave her here? I don't want to be no trouble, but surely she will be hungry again before morning."

"She's fine, girl. I'll manage. You come back tomorrow, you hear? And bring more eggs."

Maudie picked two mirliton squash from the vine by the front door, chopped them up along with some salt pork, and added them to the pot of black-eyed peas she had started soaking that morning. Her mother still lay on her back staring up at the rough ceiling, looking to Maudie much like the baby had in her blanket that morning, as empty as a January cotton sack.

"Where's the baby?" she asked, her voice a monotone whisper. Maudie didn't answer. She heard Barney and the boys coming up the road.

"You should ask Pa." The peas started to boil, and Maudie busied herself with washing the breakfast dishes. Barney washed at the pump outside, pushing the boys' dirty heads under the spigot to loud cries of dismay.

When he came into the shack, Lula asked again. "Where's the baby?"

Barney and Maudie exchanged looks.

"Violet Byrd took her to a wet nurse. She'll come home when your milk comes in, and if it doesn't, well, she won't for a while."

Lula clenched her fists and beat them against her thighs.

"I won't have it, Barney. I just won't!"

"Shut your mouth!" Barney's face, drawn with anger and exhaustion, folded into itself. He leaned against the wall by the bed and watched Lula a while as tears rolled down her cheeks. He rubbed his face, rearranging his anger.

"Lula, I don't think we have a choice," he said softly. "That baby would not have lived another twelve hours, and you know that. I know you don't want her, I know you feel poorly, but we have to provide for her somehow. And she needs a name, Lula, if only to put on her tombstone." Barney paced the foot of the bed, thinking. "Remember that girl who was born to your great uncle J.C. Rowland, name was Nora? JC, he was in the Thirty-Third Missouri Regiment, a private in the Union army. Died in St. Louis in 1862. She's in your family bible. Then your grandfather George raised her."

"What is it you like, Barney?" Lula asked. "The name, or the Thirty-Third Missouri Regiment? That war is over and gone, and the wrong side won. Why don't you just leave them all in their graves?"

"Well, you are wrong. Abraham Lincoln's side won. If Nora Rowland's father did right by Lincoln, joining up and dying, then that is good enough reason to name a baby after her."

"You would argue with a fence post, so what good is it if I disagree? Name her what you will."

"I like the name, Lula. And she needs a middle name."

"Mae!" Maudie Marie called from the stove.

"Where did you come up with that?" Lula asked. Barney and Maudie exchanged the same conspiratorial look again.

"Mae it is. Nora Mae Stovall, June 7, 1925," Barney declared.

Maudie spooned up the peas and yelled for the boys. Even her mother ate dinner that night. The sky grew dark, the cicadas yearned in earnest for mates, and Barney disappeared from the porch.

Chapter 7

LULA

Stone County, Mississippi, Jenkins Plantation, 1925; Oklahoma, 1893–1911; Arizona, 1911–1914

Lula lay on her back and rested her fingers in the hollows of her cheeks. Her skin felt like every acre of farmland she had ever known, from Oklahoma to Arizona to Montana: dry, dry, a sucking dry that left the top soil and the outer layer of epidermis a blasted shell, a dusty covering for what surely was nothing good beneath. She was the daughter of an arid West, a landscape grasped at by people seeking a toehold that would not wither and blow away.

Mississippi, now, that was a different story. What it lacked in common comforts and human decency, it made up for in humidity. Still, Lula's skin was indifferent to it, refusing, much like Lula herself, to drink in the atmosphere.

"I wonder who has that baby now," she whispered into the shack's tepid, dusty air. Barney and Maudie had named her Nora Mae, but to Lula she was still nameless, a week after her birth. *Best not name your demons.* A part of her—not the maternal part, the part that had loved her first eight babies, but the poor part that had no sovereignty over few possessions—could not stand the thought of a Black woman holding and feeding her baby. It made her so angry she almost got up and did something about it.

As the afternoon heat, wet and crushing, pushed her back against the damp sheet, she thought instead of other times, other babies. And another husband.

OKLAHOMA TERRITORY, 1893–1911

Her earliest memory was a small slice of a day in a sparkling blueberry pie sky. She wandered barefoot around the flat, dusty mesa sucking on a rag soaked in sugar water. A sugar teat, Pappy called it.

"Lula, come on and climb on Pappy's back," he said, squatting down to boost her onto his shoulders. He and his cowboys had cattle to move, but there was just something about this little yellow-haired girl.

"This is your last summer before you go off to the school house, baby girl."

"Don't make me go, Pappy!" she said, flailing her arms and the spit-soaked sugar teat around his cowboy hat. "I wanna pony and my own cow and some boots!"

Lula could see over his hat toward the ranch house. Her mother was tying on a bonnet against the August heat, coming toward them, waving and smiling as she picked her way through the sagebrush and broken rock. Her indulgent father; her sweet-tempered mother.

"Ah now, Janette, can you just leave her with me today? We're riding up to bring in that big herd near the dry wash. Easy day. She can just ride in my lap, keep me company. Can't you, girl?"

Janette laughed and reached for Lula. "John, you know I got three babies that need tending, and this little stinker and her sugar teat have got to pick the green beans and help with the babies so I can get a fire lit under that laundry. Come on, you little cowpoke." Just a slice of a day, like so many.

One morning in her twelfth year, her mother was braiding

her hair when Lula declared, "Mama, that Smith Wilkerson is a fine-looking man!"

"Well, Lula Rowland, my goodness, he's almost old enough to be your father! Why, he must be—"

"He's twenty-nine, Mama, and he sure can sit a horse."

Janette pulled a little harder on Lula's braids.

"Well, I never!" she laughed.

Lula laced her fingers together and grinned. "Well, I ain't never either, but I'm done with school this year, and I saw him smiling at me at the church picnic."

"Young lady, you are *not* done with school. Your pappy and I have decided. We are sending you in to Norman to high school. You can board there, and come home now and again."

"Mama, no!"

"Lula, yes."

Five years later, done with school and books forever, Lula married James Smith Wilkerson in the church yard under the big pine tree. He plunked her down in a newly nailed together four-room farmhouse, not even a mile from Janette and John. His father-in-law offered him a sure enough future: Work for him for five years, and he'd sell him five hundred acres at a very reasonable price, and grant him his grazing rights on another thousand acres.

Smith bought Lula a bolt of gingham and a sewing machine, and she stitched together a life. They rode out in the early morning on two dappled mustangs, teasing and dreaming. They built a herd and a brood. In 1907, Pernetti was born, followed by Ray in 1908 and Glen in 1909.

The land was dry as an old corn cob, but the farmhouse was a lush oasis, awash in laughter, babies bawling, Smith singing cowboy songs and reciting poetry:

"I never saw a purple cow
I never hope to see one;

But I can tell you, anyhow,
I'd rather see than be one!"

He hauled his babies around with him, even tying the newest young one against his chest in a blanket as Lula's uncle, Powhattan, showed him. Lula scratched out a summer garden, sending Nettie and Ray out to gather cow pies to till into the sallow soil and haul buckets of water from the well.

The winter Glen turned one; Smith rode in from feeding cows one bitter, cold afternoon; and asked Lula for a shot of whiskey.

"Just coughed all day, Lula, and my chest aches."

Smith fell stiffly into bed and begged all three kids to pile in with him.

By morning, he was burning with fever.

"Nettie, you run down the road to Pappy and Grammy's. Tell 'em we need the doctor," Lula said.

Lula slipped behind Smith in the bed, adjusting his tall, thin frame against her chest so that he could breathe better. She stroked his damp hair, laying her lips against his ear, rocking him gently, whispering like she might to one of the babies. "Shhh, shhh, shhh."

Far off, she heard the clattering of wagon wheels striking the frozen road. She and Smith each gathered in a breath, and let it go. Only Lula breathed in again.

For the Rowlands and Wilkersons, Smith's unexpected death drove a stake through two families and their happy and virtuous plans.

"Just ain't got the heart for this place anymore, Janette," John said in the spring after Smith's death. "We got more than Lula and the babies to worry about. This ole land is more played out as the years go by. I can't run as many cattle anymore. What will we do when we all have to depend on this ranch, with no one quite like Smith to carry it on?"

CHANDLER, ARIZONA, 1911–1915

At summer's end, John sold the ranch to a neighbor. John, Janette, their young children, and Lula and her three children drove two wagons piled high toward Chandler, a new town rising out of the Arizona desert with the promise of plentiful irrigation water and a pleasant climate. They bought ten acres three miles from town, enough for a few cows and a small dairy, and lived in two canvas tents while John and some hired hands built a two-story Sear's-catalog house, complete with electricity and indoor plumbing.

All the luxury could not diminish Smith's loss. For Lula who wanted nothing more than to be Mrs. James Smith Wilkerson, life felt like a keeping on, not a living. Janette and John gave her and her three children the upstairs room and then worried that she might never leave them and rejoin the world. She carried baby Glen with her everywhere, as if he might turn to stone if she let his feet touch the ground. Nettie, try as she might, could barely remember her daddy. And Ray? He was just plain a terror, throwing rocks at the neighbors' shiny new windows and refusing gestures of consolation from Pappy and Grammy.

John found Lula sitting alone in the kitchen at two o'clock in the morning, staring out the window at the moon glow on new hay fields.

"Baby, you got to move on. Those children, they need a daddy, and you need a husband. Why honey, you're a good-looking woman, and only twenty-three years old! You got a lot of years that need living."

"Pappy, why on earth would I want them? Nothing is going to be good again. Nettie, Ray, and Glen . . . They'd be better off without me."

"Lula! Please, honey, listen to your Pappy."

Lula stood, patted him on the shoulder, and made her way resolutely to the stairway. For the next three years, she dutifully groomed and dressed and fed her children as if they were cattle bound for auction.

In July of 1913, a tall man road a roan horse up to their front door, tied up at the fence, and rang the bell. Lula answered. He took off his new cowboy hat, still buff-colored and stiff. His sable eyebrows rode in toward the bridge of his nose in a thick, questioning line. The hat, however long he had been wearing it, had done him no good. His narrow, smooth face was sunburned, his lips cracked, his blue eyes shiny with fatigue. He was unmistakably dressed in new clothes. His snap-front shirt even had creases down the sides. His boots showed no wear. A carpetbag valise was tied to the back of his saddle.

Whatever the man had been expecting, it wasn't Lula. He spun his hat through his fingers as if it might speak for him. Lula waited, unsmiling, a perfect Mona Lisa, without the secret, the mirth, or the mystery.

"Ma'am. Good afternoon. My name is Barney Stovall, and I stopped to inquire about the land across the street. The fella at the land office said there's one hundred acres for sale in this section. Is your husband to-home, perhaps, who I could speak to?

"That would be my father you'd be wanting, Mr. Stovall. He's out in the milking barn around back."

"Thank you kindly, Mrs. . . ."

"Wilkerson. Goodbye now," she said, closing the door on the man's piercing blue eyes, his hat still dangling from his fingers.

At the barn, Barney introduced himself.

"Mr. Wilkerson, I'm Barney Stovall—"

"'Fraid you got my name wrong. I'm John Rowland. You must have met my daughter, Lula. She's the Wilkerson. Widow."

Barney rolled up the sleeves of his new shirt and joined Lula's father on the milking line. It seemed the most neighborly way to find out about that one hundred acres, and well, about the dairyman's widowed daughter too.

Ten buckets of milk later, Barney thought maybe he'd stay a while.

"'Barney Stovall is feeling mighty tickled these days and all because he met with fine success while boring for water on his ranch in Section 15, 3½ miles out of town,'" Pappy read to Lula from the *Arizona Republican*. "'Mr. Stovall struck a good flow of water at 335 feet. The well furnishes some of the clearest and finest water in the district.' Lula, listen to that! Barney is famous! You could do a lot worse than a man with one hundred acres and good irrigation to boot. Water and land—why that's the stuff a family is made of."

"Are you forgetting something?"

"Well, he'll build you a house too, with plenty of room for more babies."

"Love, Pappy. What's a family without that?"

"Do you not feel a shred of love for the man? Why, he's handsome, keen, a man of means, and he's surely got his mind fixed on you."

"Not a shred, Pappy. Not yet. And then there's the children. Nettie seems to like him fine, but the boys, he just rubs them the wrong way."

"Well of course, child. Those boys have had their beautiful mother all to themselves for three years. They just aren't ready to hand the reins to a new cowboy, Lula, surely you can see that. Give 'em time!"

But letting time unspool was not Barney's way.

"Marry me, Lula. What are you waiting for? Neither of us is getting any younger. I've got dreams, you know. But I need you, I need children . . . and land. This hun'red acres, it's a good start, but the West is wide open, boundless, far as the eye can see."

Barney was walking Lula around the plot where he hoped to build a house.

"A house just for you, Lula, with room for the three kids, and as many more as you like."

Lula was stepping hesitantly, grasping her skirts with one hand and shielding her eyes against the setting sun with the other.

"You look troubled, Lula."

"Are you saying you want to move on from here? Because I really don't want to leave Pappy and Ma. We're just starting to feel settled here."

"Well, now, I'm not planning to head off at a dead run, but sure, someday, Lula. A man's gotta find his way in this world, one step in front of the other. I went to Mexico, and that gave me part of the money for this hundred acres, but you know, already, we're surrounded by other land owners, and we can't grow any bigger. We may just have to move on at some point. Land, Lula. That's what puts money in the bank. And you want the best for the children, don't you? Your parents won't live forever. I'm sorry to say that, sweetheart, but it's true."

"Barney? Do you love me?"

Barney kicked a dirt clod, stooped, picked it up and aimed it at the trunk of a tree.

"See that? That ole red dirt, crumbling against that juniper, that's me. I have just been steadfastly looking for treasure my whole forty-one years, just sailing through the air, nothing stopping me. But you, you pretty thing, you are that juniper. You've knocked me to the ground. I tremble whenever you walk into the room. I can't imagine life without you. Is that love?"

Lula thought maybe that was love. It reminded her of how she felt the first time she saw Smith, and every time after that too, even when he lay stiff in a juniper box. But she didn't feel it now.

Maybe it would be enough if only one of them trembled.

On January 22, 1914, at the courthouse in Phoenix in front of Superior Judge John C. Phillips and two clerks, she took Barney's hand and promised, in spite of that, to love him till death did them part.

If marriage to Smith had seemed like a fusing of spirits to Lula, the quick vows and paperwork at the courthouse made Lula feel like a piece of property, a successful financial transaction. Barney lost his ardor later that evening, initiating a fumbling interlude in their Phoenix hotel room. She noticed that he kept his eyes closed through much of the lackluster proceedings in their marriage bed. So she closed hers too, and instantly, Smith appeared, raised on his elbow next to her, stroking her bare belly, smiling. She wondered who Barney imagined behind his closed eyes.

Still, on the train ride home to Chandler, Barney was kind, pulling her close. Perhaps he was just having first-time jitters, having never married before after so many years of bachelorhood. In some ways, it made her feel more inclined toward him, a man innocent of lovers' ways, a creature who needed her and the womanhood she had hastily packed away when Smith died.

That night, back in Chandler in their newly constructed farm house, Lula went about seducing Barney, a tact she had never needed with her eager first husband. It seemed to light a spark in Barney, and now, eyes open, he uncoiled Lula's yellow hair, ran his fingers through it, and buried himself in her. It gave her hope.

Chapter 8

LULA

Chandler Arizona, 1913–1914;
Chouteau County, Montana, 1914–1918

Lula peered around the kitchen door and warily eyed her Uncle Fred. He sat with Barney and her pappy in her parents' parlor, smoking a cigar, waving it authoritatively as if he held their fortunes in its curling plume.

"I'm telling you, Barney. Montana. Why now, *that's* the finest open space in America. And the government, well, they'll even stake you."

He pulled a brochure from inside his jacket and laid it on the table between them. On the cover, the Milwaukee Railroad tempted in big letters, Uncle Sam Sends You an Invitation.

"The Homestead Act, it grants a quarter section—160 acres!—to any man like you who claims it. As long as you prove it up in five years, just keep it under cultivation, you get full title to the land. And there are dozens of quarter sections right next to each other in Chouteau County. See on the inside of this here brochure, the president of the railroad himself says it's like the government is opening the vaults of the treasury and bidding each man help himself!"

Lula snorted quietly. Fred owned fifteen thousand acres of prime ranching land and a big brick house loaded with finery.

Why was he promoting this railroad brochure? It was a scam, Lula was sure, having watched her Uncle Fred maneuver his way into wealth. Where her pappy simply worked hard, Fred schemed his way to that acreage, one piece of chicanery, one back-slapping bank visit after another. Why was the man here, anyway, in her parents' modest catalog house in Chandler?

Lula took a glass of milk and sat at the kitchen table. She'd been married eight months now, was three months pregnant, and had a sour feeling at the bottom of her stomach where the new baby lay. Barney and his blind land lust, wheeler-dealer that he was, was no match for Uncle Fred.

Barney was a stranger to her still, and Ray and Glen showed no signs of warming up to him. Did her boys sense her own reticence, or was it something cold and rigid of Barney's own making? Sweet little Nettie, doted on by her younger brothers, and increasingly by Barney, was often a deterrent to all-out war between them. Barney expected complete and total obedience, and no matter how many times Lula said, "Barney, you have got to just let boys be boys," he would not stand for the slightest bending of his rules.

"They've got to respect me, Lula. Plain and simple. They are wild animals, those two. I don't know how you let them grow to be such downright jackasses."

Lula slipped out the back kitchen door and crossed the road to her own house. Her three children were asleep. She paced in her kitchen, stoking the wood stove, waiting for Barney to come home. At midnight, she gave up, and went to bed alone.

Fred's courting of Barney Stovall started with a letter John Rowland had written to his brother two months before.

"My new son-in-law snuck a whole boatload of bananas into Galveston right under the nose of United Fruit and turned a pretty profit. You should see what he's done already with his new farm. I'm mighty impressed."

That was enough to bring Fred on a brief visit to Arizona. He was Chouteau County's bull-roaring champion, a member of the local bank board, an enthusiastic waver of the Montana flag. He and his cigar-chomping fellow ranchers and railroad owners were looking for farmers to occupy Montana, buy feeder calves and bulls and fencing and wheat seed and tar paper and children's shoes, fill the church pews, school benches, and tax rolls. Small, nearly insignificant figurines on their painted canvas of wealth and security, but necessary ones after all.

The next morning, Lula found Barney pouring over Hardy W. Campbell's *Soil Culture Manual*, a promise of dryland farming triumph—a gift from Uncle Fred—that would someday lay face down and abandoned in a wagon rut. But this morning, it held Barney in thrall.

"Just listen to this, Lula. Mr. Campbell says, 'The semiarid region is destined to be in a few years the richest portion of the United States.' He teaches you right here in this book how to do it: the science of capillary attraction. You can make the earth just suck up and hold onto the rain until you need it. Why, it's a downright miracle."

Uncle Fred had made a lot of promises the night before: offers of farm equipment, operating capital ("Interest rate? Now don't you worry about that. We'll talk about it later. It'll be low—so low we'll just have a good laugh about it."), and inside information on the best quarter sections available through the Homestead Act. All Barney would have to do was sell his Arizona land and come to Montana. Fred would introduce him to all the right people—investors even. Easy money.

"Why you'll have a ranch the envy of just about everyone I know."

She examined each hook and sinker as Barney ran through Fred's glorious depictions of wealth and status.

"What's the catch, Barney?"

"The catch? There ain't no catch. He's being straight with me. Dammit, Lula, he's your uncle! He wouldn't con me."

The train from Phoenix to Geraldine, Montana, would take three days and two nights. Lula stood on the platform, her children clinging to her skirts. Her belly, now six months full of Barney's child, was an unwieldy obstacle in a day already filled with plenty of them: trunks, boxes roped tight, everything they owned pitched toward an uncertain future. Lula smiled at her parents the way a doctor might at a dying patient.

"Don't you worry now. Barney says he's got it all arranged. Fred will meet us and put us up at his place until we can build something of our own." If there was any grace in that moment, any hope, maybe even a shred of happy anticipation, it was buried by John and Janette's most fervent fear that they might not see Lula or the children again. When the train pulled out, John threw his hat on the ground and stomped it with his boot.

The Montana episode did not come apart all at once. Like a single loose thread in a heavy coat, it unraveled slowly, barely noticeable, over six years. At the train station, Fred sent a hired hand with a wagon instead of coming himself. When they arrived at his ranch, he wasn't there to meet them. The hired hand pulled the wagon up to a swaybacked bunk house and started unloading their trunks and boxes.

"But Uncle Fred said we were staying with him," Lula said, pointing to the house across the field.

"The missus says there ain't no room. Says you'd be happier here anyway, in your own digs." It was December, just days before Christmas, and Lula had never felt such cold. The dry wind crept under her skirts and assaulted her thin Arizona skin. She was stunned, too, at the inhospitable welcome. Her aunt, whom she'd never met, didn't even send down a warm dinner to the weary family.

"Now, don't you worry. I'll have us a better place soon. Looky there, Fred's got a whole cord of wood for us, all cut and stacked. I'll have us warm in no time," Barney said, a tinge of forced bravado in his voice.

The winter froze hard that year in Chouteau County, a 1915 New Year's Day welcome of seventy below zero. There was no way Barney could dig any sort of foundation for a house under those conditions, and he hadn't secured any land yet, so they endured the bunk house, which seemed to slip off its moorings, day by day, much like the Stovalls themselves. The boys spent their days in pitched battles with each other. Nettie sat in a cold corner crooning to a baby doll. Lula lugged her belly around the two-room bunk house, trying to cook and do laundry while navigating the children and unopened trunks, their whole world those two rooms and the empty, flat, snow-white landscape outside two narrow windows. It was too cold to do more than run quickly to the well with a bucket.

Barney was gone most days, looking at land and quarter sections. Some days he'd dress to ride one of Fred's horses, old canvas pants over long underwear; and some days, he'd put on the only suit he owned, carefully tucking his prized gold stickpin in the lapel. The suit from his California days was little protection from the fierce cold, but Barney, proud to the last shoestring in his old brogues, would just throw a cowhide around his shoulders in the buckboard.

"Where might you be going today?" she'd ask.

"Now, don't you worry, little mama. Just talking with some fellers your uncle put me on to, some who might invest in our enterprise."

March brought a thaw and a baby. Maudie Marie Stovall was born in the bunk house, delivered without incident by Uncle

Fred's doctor. Lula clung to her, a warm morsel in a cold and dreary predicament. Barney seemed pleased, and a bit awed, touching Maudie's fingers and toes with the reverence he might give a gold nugget or a survey marker. Glen and Ray ceased their warring long enough to welcome their new sister, badgering Lula for chances to hold her. The fire roared in the wood stove. Icicles dripped in rivulets off the roof. Barney took the day off from his scheming and blustered his way through cooking corn cakes, salt pork, and eggs. It felt to Lula, from a certain angle—memory held in abeyance—like a family.

In April, Barney finally got what he came for: land.

"See here, I've got us a quarter section, 160 acres, through the Homestead Act, in Section 20 for just a twenty dollar filing fee. But that's just the beginning. Can't run many cows on that size spread. So look at this map. See these two other sections . . . 17 and 19 . . . these are quarter sections that link up with ours, and they're for sale, and we're gonna buy them."

Lula peered at the plat map, tendrils of mountain ridges, streams here and there, stretching through Sections 17, 19, and 20. To her uneducated eye they looked more like spiders' webs, snares for the uninitiated.

"Why are they for sale? I thought this was prime land."

Barney rubbed his temples and stared at the ceiling of the bunkhouse. "Lula, some folks just haven't got the gumption to make it out here. And they don't have investors. We do."

"We do?"

"Fred has introduced me to some fine people. Why, there's the owner of the Marshalltown Buggy Company of Iowa—they're starting to make automobiles!—and he's just opened a store in town selling buggies. And autos someday, he says. He's cosigning with us to buy this south half of the northeast quarter of Section 19."

Lula's head swirled. It was like trying to follow a shooting star, these half and quarter sections speeding through Barney's mouth like meteors.

"And Russel Henry. He's cosigned with us here to buy another quarter section in 17. He's a fine man, owns the dry good store over in Fort Benton."

"Why doesn't he just farm on his own?"

"Some men just want to be shopkeepers, but the lure of ranch land . . . All they need is to find a good farmer like me, and they open their cash registers! Fred has talked me up pretty high to these fellas."

With a flourish, Barney laid two mortgage promissory notes on the kitchen table. The kids were asleep, even the baby. The bunkhouse groaned against a dry spring wind that brought no rain. Lula stared at the line where her name was required. The mortgage buying Emma Bullet's place was $1,237. The mortgage buying George Butler's place was $1,960. She had never associated her name with so much debt.

"Barney, I . . ."

"Sign Lula. I can't build us a house until we secure this land. We'll have 480 acres, and that's just a start!"

Lula sighed. Whether it was an omen or not, Maudie Marie cried out, taking both parents' eyes away from the spray of white pages on the table. They watched the baby's quilts rise and fall in the washtub until she fell back to sleep. They turned back to the papers, which seemed to shift under the lantern light. He nodded at the pen, and Lula did as she was told.

By May, Barney and Lula chose a home site in the middle of their quarter section in Section 20—a high, flat plateau surrounded by rock outcroppings, just set back from the dirt road, a stream flowing down just behind what would be their back door. Barney hired some local boys to help him dig a foundation and a well.

There'd be no tar paper shack for his family, he said. A proper house with windows and bedrooms, made in the adobe fashion he learned in Mexico, but from Montana sod. People drove up in their buggies to watch him at work since no one had seen such a variation on a simple cut sod house. Barney built a big trough and filled it with straw, dirt, limestone, and water, and shoveled the concoction into frames. He worried that the bricks wouldn't set if it rained, but no rain came, which seemed a blessing at the time.

In June, they moved in, the prairie flowering, the creek full of spring optimism, the stars at night beacons out across the land that Barney loved already.

"It's ours, Lula," he said the first night as they lay in their own room after months of communal sleeping in the bunkhouse.

She clutched his hand under the blankets.

"Lula, are you happy?"

She wrapped her other hand around his rough one. "I'm afraid, is what I am, of the cold, the dark. And lonely. It's so empty out here. But I'm not *unhappy*, Barney."

Barney pulled her on top of him and slipped her flannel gown up over her hips.

"Well don't take on any worry, you pretty thing, my Rebecca of Sunnybrook Farm. Some day you will love this land as much as I do, you know that? You know, you are the prettiest woman in all of Chouteau County."

"I wouldn't know that at all! I haven't seen a one of them," she sighed, but Barney had already moved past the question of her happiness and was wrapping his legs around her thighs.

Finally, the weather was fine enough for Lula to wrap up the baby and bundle up the three kids and ride with Barney to town in the buckboard. While Barney had not scrimped on housing materials, fencing, or livestock—they now had two horses, six pigs, two dozen chickens, and one hundred head of cattle—Lula had not spent five minutes in town since they arrived in December. She wandered down the wood planked sidewalks of Geraldine in a trance, buying fabric, coffee beans, canned peas, sugar, and even, at Barney's insistence, some face cream for her chapped skin. Barney gave Glen, Ray, and Nettie three pennies each for a bag of candy, and stood proudly in the mercantile as the boys were measured for their first cowboy boots.

"You boys are ready to ride the range with me now," he declared, but both boys—Ray, seven, and Glen, five—were only interested in kicking their new boots and sucking on their candy. Lula watched them from the fabric bolts and saw Barney's face drop. *Oh Barney, quit trying so hard,* she thought. Her sympathy surprised her, since Barney's bravado usually made her cringe. But the months in the bunkhouse when they could not escape each other had shown her his tenacity, his doggone will to make it, even if he did treat her and the children as assets—or in the case of Ray and Glen, liabilities—on a balance sheet.

So she embraced the only role she could out there on the prairie: a producer of assets. Vernon Leslie was born in 1917 on the day the US declared war on Germany, followed in short order by Leonard Burnett in 1918 as the Spanish flu swept the country, hitting Montana especially hard.

And all the while, Barney toiled at turning the prairie around them into productive farmland, dragging a huge Campbell Soil Compactor behind his two horses, grazing his cattle from parcel to parcel across his 480 acres. It all seemed to work. He managed to sell a few tons of wheat and put by some hay for the cows in the winter. He'd driven thirty pretty fat two-year-olds to the auction yard. They were not getting rich, nor were they falling behind, if you didn't count Barney's small but frequent cash withdrawals from the Mexico and Arizona proceeds. But then, the rains were regular in those years.

Barney and Lula had reached a kind of détente. He would buy

up every quarter acre that presented itself, though none had since his original purchases, and she would scrimp on every penny, the enterprise's bean counter.

They sat on the front porch one evening in June 1917, Leonard wrapped tight in Barney's arms, Maudie Marie and Nettie playing at their feet, Glen and Ray chasing each other across the yard with carved wood guns Barney had made them in the evenings.

"They say in the papers we're all going to have to help with this war," Barney said.

"What can we do?"

"Well, we could plant a victory garden," he said with a grin, pointing to an early bed of carrots, cabbage, and onions in the side yard. "And then they say we should have wheatless Wednesdays"—Lula began to laugh—"And meatless Tuesdays, fuel-less Mondays, and gasless Sundays."

By now she was laughing so hard she startled the baby who began crying from his perch on Barney's shoulder.

"How about if we simply don't eat except on Thursday?" she asked, breathless. "Because, by golly, Barney, we have already cut our rations to the bone."

"I think that's all for the city folk. But I do have to go into Fort Benton next week and register for the draft."

"You? You're forty-four years old! What do they want with an old man like you?"

Barney sat up straighter in the rocker and moved Leonard to his other shoulder. "Just the law, honey, and nothing will come of it. But see this little bundle here? Not bad for an old man."

LULA

Chouteau County, Montana, 1918–1922

For a few years it seemed that the old, frayed coat of the Stovalls' existence had stopped its unraveling. The war brought higher beef prices. The rains came as regular as a farmer could hope for in a land determined to remain barren. The 1918 flu passed them by, even as it took five thousand of their fellow Montanans, including a family of five just east of them who starved to death.

Lula was carved by these things, hardened by the Montana cold and the prairie wind, her youthful vitality depleted by each subsequent baby, until she barely recognized herself in her one mirror. No longer the tempting yellow-haired girl, she was a graying frontier wife, a mother of six. Barney's own youthfulness—his ramrod-straight stature, sleek black hair, and unwavering blue eyes— made her feel, in comparison, as if she was hitched to the wrong wagon. But there was nothing to be done about it. When she thought of her dear Smith, he was a thin cowboy silhouette against an Oklahoma sky. She'd even forgotten his face. She was resigned to a meager existence, even if Barney still dreamed the impossible Montana dream that a vast, productive ranch might emerge from the scabby prairie and make him rich.

But then the rains stopped. Over two and a half years, from the spring of 1919 until the fall of 1921, a mere fifteen inches of rain fell across Barney's land. By the time Earnest Newton Stovall was born in 1920, the well water was often muddy. Barney could no longer pretend that the dry spell was just a passing thing. He sold off cattle and ran through all but a pittance of his Mexico and Arizona funds. Now he dressed in his California suit once again and rode into town, leaving Lula to worry and to chores alone, even though Glen and Ray could have handled all that was left of the Stovall operation by themselves.

Glen was a big boy even at ten years old, reaching to Barney's chin. And Ray, at twelve, though slight and wiry, made up for it with a kind of cunning meant to keep Barney off-kilter. The boys' hurts grew as deep bone bruises during the Montana years, as they counted Barney's moments of affection for his own children as ample evidence that he cared nothing for them. They adopted a kind of slothful response to any orders Barney gave around the ranch, leaving Lula to cajole them into helping. They disappeared for hours, often days, frightening Lula and relieving Barney, who hoped they might never come back.

"Why can't you treat them with just a little kindness?" she asked one night as they lay in bed. That afternoon Barney had captured each of them and whipped them with a harness line for failing to do their chores.

"Why can't they treat me with respect? And you just make it worse, fawning all over them! You never back me up, giving them just more excuses for not doing what I tell them. We should have left them with your pappy in Arizona!"

"Oh Barney, how can you say such a thing?"

But he had already turned away, pulling the blankets and all talk of reconciliation to his side of the bed.

Things grew dire around the Stovall place. Barney sent the boys out to hunt deer and grouse to keep meat on the table, and Lula rationed her canned fruits and vegetables through the cold fall and winter of 1921–22. Barney came home from town one day laden with books from the library on potato growing.

"That Emma Ingalls is coming to town next week."

"Who is that?"

"I told you about her. She's the first woman ever to serve in the Montana legislature, made sure you women got the vote. And now she's proposing that Montana ratify the Woman's Suffrage Amendment to the US Constitution! Lincoln would have admired her. She's going to give a talk next week at the Grange in Geraldine. I think we should go."

Lula set down the last jar of canned chokecherries.

"Barney, you cannot be serious," she said, her voice rising. "What do I care about the vote? You want me to vote? I vote for a satisfying meal. I vote for warm clothes for the children. And while I'm at it, I vote for a decent dress for myself. I wouldn't have anything to *wear* to your lecture. And I vote for water that doesn't taste like dirt!"

Glen and Ray smirked from their school books across the room. The baby let out a yelp. The little girls stopped chopping onions and venison for hash. Vernon and Leonard looked up from their game of marbles. The room rolled to a stop, like a buggy on the crest of a hill.

For a moment, Barney stood still and rigid, as if he were resisting something, perhaps the urge to slap Lula. Instead, he picked up the library books and a lantern, and slammed the door behind him. Lula watched him from the kitchen window for a while, the lantern illuminating him reading in the nearly empty and freezing cold pole barn. She thought about calling him in for dinner, and then she thought better of it. He could eat cold hash if he wanted.

A month later, Barney reinvented the ranch.

"Potatoes, Lula. That is the future. We're going to plant potatoes this spring." Barney had come in on the buckboard that afternoon with the first supplies she'd seen in months: flour, beans, coffee, cornmeal.

"Where did you get the money for all this?" she asked.

"Don't you worry, Mrs. Stovall. I still have supporters here in these parts." He laid two notes on the table. "Mr. Schmidt, he loaned me $225, and Mr. Bergeson advanced me $331.35 for seed potatoes and equipment."

Lula's face turned white. "How will we ever—"

"Trust me! Potatoes are the answer to this godforsaken dry land." Barney planned to head into town the next day for a wagonful, while the weather was good and the roads clear.

"We'll keep 'em in the root cellar. In March or April, just as soon as it thaws, we'll have them in the ground. You'll see."

"Won't they need water too?"

"We'll drill another well. Everyone's doing it."

On the blue, cold dawn, Barney rousted Ray and Glen, and the three set out in the wagon for town.

"We'll be back before dark," he told Lula. She looked skeptical.

"Why don't you ever believe me, woman?"

She watched the wagon for a long time as it crossed the flat prairie, until it was an insignificant speck on the horizon. She chastised herself for her lack of faith, but try as she might, no wellspring of optimism made an appearance.

By three o'clock, the blue sky vanished into a wall of dirty gray cotton clouds, and a wind dropped down across the plains.

"That's a snow sky if I've ever seen one," she told Maudie, watching the storm move toward them.

By five o'clock, a driving snow blotted out the landscape and the road. She set a lantern in the window and paced, juggling Ernie on her hip.

At seven o'clock, the door flew open, and Ray fell across the threshold, covered in white.

"Dear God! Where are Barney and Glen?" Lula cried as she and Nettie pulled him into the house.

"'Bout a mile back. The buckboard—Barney ran it off the road, lost the whole load. Wanted me and Glen to stay and help him haul up all those taters, but the horse ran off as soon as we unharnessed her. I told him to go to hell."

"Ray!"

"That stupid old man! Glen is dumb enough to stay with him, but I'm not freezing to death."

Lula grabbed Barney's old mackinaw and a hat, and pulled on her boots.

"Ma! Where are you going?"

"Ray Wilkerson, if your father could see you right now, you would disgust him."

She grabbed the lantern from the window sill and started off down the road. She had no idea how long she'd last in the blizzard, but she trudged, one iced boot in front of the other, calling, "Barney! Glen!" It took her fifteen minutes to find them, coming toward her into the circle of the lantern's glow—Glen with Barney's arm wrapped around his shoulders, Barney dragging a leg behind him.

"Lula! The potatoes, they'll be ruined, every one! They'll freeze by morning! We've got to go back for them."

"What is the use? We've no horse to pull the wagon, and you are close to freezing to death. It's time to give up, Barney."

By first light, Barney—muscles torn in the fall from the buckboard, ankle and leg wrapped tight in old rags—hobbled down the road to the potatoes and found them soon enough on the featureless prairie, looking like a burial mound in the snow, each frozen as hard as a stone.

For two weeks, he rarely left his bed, brooding, his leg a purple passion play against the raging white snow outside the window.

One afternoon, Lula brought him a bowl of barley soup, and he pulled a crumpled sheet of paper from under the blankets.

"I found this on the bulletin board at the feed store the day we bought the potatoes."

Lula flattened the paper against the quilt.

"Come to Madison County, Mississippi, strawberry capital of the world!" it read, followed by, "Go south and grow up with the country," in big strawberry-red letters.

The Madison Land Company, Dr. L.T. "Strawberry King of the South" McKay, and Episcopal Bishop Hugh Miller Thompson weighed in, promising riches growing strawberries on prime land that you could buy for as little as three dollars an acre.

"And see here? It says Mississippi has the lowest debt ratio in the whole US of A, at nineteen dollars per capita, and Mississippians are one-third healthier by official figures than us Northerners."

Lula had no idea what debt ratio was or how you would tell if a person was one-third healthier than another, but what she did get—her fingers trembling as they held the flier against Barney's hip—was that Barney was buying it. It was another way to get rich on land, land, land, like a glutton whose mouth is open wide for cultivated black earth.

"Barney, you aren't really . . . I mean, you don't know these men. This sounds, well, I don't know, but how could it be true? Three dollars an acre?"

"For heaven's sake woman, this McKay fellow is a doctor, and Thompson, he's a preacher, a man of God. Do you think they'd make this poster and send it all the way up here to Montana if they was liars?"

One month later in early May, still cold, the clouds bearing not rain, but ill-will, Lula pulled the buckboard up in front of Uncle Fred's manse, and sat still, the reins wrapped around her fingers like prison chains. Behind her in the wagon, Nettie held Ernie while Maudie Marie, Vernon, and Leonard huddled close to their big sister, rough boxes and trunks piled around them. Ray and Glen sat on the bench seat on either side of their mother, who had spoken barely a word to them since she returned from the Western Union office in Geraldine the afternoon before.

"Y'all wait here," she said.

Uncle Fred was startled to see the Stovalls and all their possessions in his front drive. "Where the hell is Barney?" he said from the open front door.

"Uncle Fred, could we go inside?" Lula asked.

In the front hall, all the further Fred invited Lula to tread, he repeated himself. "Where is your husband?"

Lula considered the question as if it was a riddle that stumped her. "He's gone to . . . grow strawberries in Mississippi."

"Well, I'll be a son of a bitch." His voice rose. "Do you know how much money he owes to people around here, people I introduced him to, vouched for him to? What am I supposed to tell them now? And me, why he owes me almost a thousand bucks, plus interest."

Lula crumpled into a chair and stuck her fists in her eyes. She wailed, "I don't know what to do!"

Fred paced back and forth across the travertine floor. "Well, if you're thinking you can stay here, Lula, that is simply not possible."

"No, no it's not that. I have tickets."

"Tickets for what?"

"The train. Tickets for us, to join him in Mississippi. He thinks he can make enough money there to repay you and these other folks. He asked me to tell you that. He's just done wrung everything out of this land that he can, but without water . . . I couldn't even bring up one bucket of water this morning to wash up!"

Fred stopped pacing and looked down at his dusty boots.

"Well, he tried, I will give him that. Lotsa folks ain't making it, but he's just giving up too soon! Why, in another year, the rains will return and then—"

"Those rains would be watering our graves. I fed the children the last of the dried venison for breakfast. I don't even know what we will eat on the train . . . " Her voice trailed off. "But Uncle Fred, that is not the worst of it."

He peered at her with dread. What could be worse than a wagon full of starving children and worn housewares and clothing more suited to a burn pile than a train trip to Mississippi?

"He sent me six tickets."

Fred looked at her quizzically, and then it dawned on him. "But there are eight of you."

"Barney says I can't bring Ray and Glen. Says he won't have them no more."

"My god, Lula."

"I don't know what to do! We can't stay here or the children and I will starve. But the boys . . ." Her fists were white against her cheeks.

"Uncle Fred, they are good boys, and if my pappy had not died last year, I know he'd send for them. But you are all I have now. They can work hard! Will you please let them stay with you? As soon as I can convince Barney, I'll send tickets for them, I promise you!"

Outside in the wagon, the wind whipped at the departing children like a jealous lover. Ten minutes went by. Fifteen. Twenty.

Finally the door opened. Fred called Ray and Glen over. "Boys, your mother has something to tell you."

Lula's face had long passed white and was now nearly transparent. Ray and Glen were ashamed for her, sorry that Uncle Fred—a man they disliked almost as much as they did Barney—was seeing her so distraught.

"Boys, you know that I love you with all my heart."

Glen began to back up, like a boxer dancing away from a blow. Ray did just the opposite, leaning in, as if he might strike them.

"You are going to have to stay here with Uncle Fred for a while."

Glen started to cry, but Ray's face hardened.

"It's only for a while, just until we get enough money together in Mississippi to send for you," Lula pleaded.

"Barney don't want us, does he," said Ray.

"No, no, it's not that," Fred explained. "It's just, why, he knows you boys are almost young men now, and the little children, and your mother, they can't stay here. You can bunk with the hired hands, work here on the ranch—"

"Not unless you pay us."

"Ray!" Lula exclaimed.

"Well, I ain't a slave to no one."

"I'll pay you, if you work like a man. But you are going to have to grow up and show some respect. After all, I'm—"

"Glen!" Lula cried.

The boy was running, vaulting the fence line, heading for the low hills on the edge of the ranch.

"Glen, come back! Glen!" But her voice was lost on the prairie.

Lula cried all the way to the train station. Nettie gave Ernie to Maudie Marie, climbed up onto the bench seat, and took the reins. When she had cried so that nothing was left, she reached behind her into a box and pulled out Hardy W. Campbell's *Soil Culture Manual.* She pitched it into a wagon rut behind them. It started to rain, but it was too late for all that now.

GLEN

Twin Bridges Orphanage, Twin Bridges, Montana, 1924–1926

In Cottage Four, Bed Seventeen, Glen tossed from one side to the other, the stories in his head chasing each other into deeper, darker corners. During the day, he was the matron's worst nightmare, even at fourteen years old, mushrooming over her where she stood at the door to the washroom. At nearly six feet, he was the biggest boy in the cottage, maybe the whole orphanage of 237 strays. He was no longer a boy, no longer a tiny stream barely dimpling the landscape. He was the headwaters of a mighty river rising up out of solid rock.

"Stovall! Get in there and do your business!" Mrs. Pike, the matron, said, pointing to the door again, stamping her foot.

"Name ain't Stovall. It's Wilkerson."

"Your name is Stovall because that is your name on this wall," she said, pointing to the list of the fifty boys who lived in Cottage Four. "And you will always be Stovall, you stupid lummox," she hissed.

In the night, his anger pooled into despair. In the October dark, with the smell of cattle and hay and pigsty climbing in the open window, the room awash with snoring and whimpering, he knew an epidemic of bed wetting was sweeping over the sleeping porch. Each morning at five, frantic boys caught up their wet sheets and heaved them at the radiator, hoping for the miracle of evaporation and absolution. By six o'clock, Mrs. Pike would inspect the beds, and those whose bladders had let loose the anxious urine of abandonment would most certainly feel her misplaced wrath. Just last night before lights out, she had tied shoes on the hands of poor Edward, the small elfin boy of nine who lay in the bed next to Glen.

"There! That'll teach you to do evil with your hands in the night!"

Glen clenched his thighs and rolled onto his side, staring at Edward, whose halting breath came and went as if it might change occupants before dawn.

I've got to get out of here, Glen thought. *Get out and go back north to Chouteau and kill Uncle Fred. Drive a pitch fork right through his head!* He seized on anger as his only reliable companion, not his fifteen-year-old brother Ray, over in Cottage Five, who seemed resigned to their fate.

"You wait, Glen! You wait until spring when he's got to move all those cattle with two less cowboys. He'll come back for us, I promise you! He just don't want to feed us through another winter," Ray said. Kept apart all week, Ray, Glen, and the other siblings were allowed to meet for an hour on Sunday on the front lawn of the Castle, the main house, its turrets a fancy gimcrack on an otherwise beatdown orphanage.

"What makes you think I'd go back with him? I'd kill him first!"

"You think that's what Ma would want? Her uncle, dead?"

The invocation of her name riled Glen, as it always did. "She left us! I'd kill them both if I could. And Barney too."

"Well, if it ain't Captain Blood, the pirate! You been reading too many comic books, Glen. You think murder's going to fix anything? Ma had no choice. I don't blame her. Now Barney, you may have a point there, that dirty bastard." Ray squeezed his carnivorous eyes together and sucked his teeth.

Glen jumped up from the lawn and paced in a circle like an ox in a threshing pit. The day was hot, and he'd taken off his undershirt, wearing just the telltale orphan overalls and the old hand-me-down lace-up boots that were already too small for him. The work at Uncle Fred's place—branding calves, bailing hay—and now on the orphanage farm had carved its furrow on him. He was made to cultivate muscle. Every potato, every slice of brown bread, every morsel of salted pork he ate lay thick on his shoulders and thighs. As he paced, his overalls moved like mountains on a fault line, rising and falling with hidden power.

"Naw, really, Glen. Simmer down! You look like you're going to light out for Mississippi on foot. You just bide your time. No use going to prison over the death of one stupid sod farmer. I hate him too, but I got a life to live." Ray was practical like that, keeping his powder dry. All Ray wanted was money and a girl, maybe a bottle of whiskey. He'd had a snort once and couldn't shake the memory. Fat chance in the middle of Prohibition. Besides, vengeance was a waste of time. Someday, Fred or Barney might be useful.

But Glen was pure in his malice. He hated the matron and the way she tormented the smaller, defenseless boys. He hated the superintendent, Harvey Stiles, for doing nothing about it. He hated his father for dying of pneumonia in Oklahoma when he was still a baby, leaving him with not one memory of Smith Wilkerson to cling to. He hated his stepfather Barney for marrying his widowed mother, for dragging them to Montana in the first place, then uprooting them again—well, most of them—to grow strawberries in Mississippi. He hated his mother for leaving him with her Uncle Fred. He hated Fred for dumping them in the orphanage.

But most of all, he hated Barney for sending only enough train tickets to Mississippi for his mother, his sister Nettie, and the younger kids. What did he have against them? He couldn't see how he must have looked to Barney, a growing wedge of a boy who stared him nearly straight in the eye, challenging his every order. And Ray? Conniving, manipulating Lula. That's what Barney saw. Things that a boy like Glen, who was smaller in his own imagination, was blind to.

Sunday afternoon mail call: Nothing for Glen or Ray. That their mother had no idea they were at Twin Bridges never occurred to Glen. That she might have written them letters Fred never passed on, well, that hadn't dawned on him either. So he sat alone on a bench under the cottonwood trees, and watched kids tear open their letters, watched them grip the edges as if they were life preservers, watched them cry or grimace. Watched one boy wad up his letter and stomp on it. Randall Smythe, who lived in Ray's cabin, walked the perimeter of the lawn and sat on the bench next to Glen.

"I thought you was one too," he said. "Because you never get any letters."

"One what?" asked Glen.

"A real orphan, like me. My folks, they died of the flu when I was just a baby. Been here ever since, me and about twenty of the others. But I heard you've got people. What they call the rest of you is orphans of the living," he said, his voice soft, sad. "You *got* folk, they just don't want you."

Glen knocked Randall backward off the bench into the cottonwood leaves and duff and broke his nose with his first rolling punch. It took less than a minute for the staff to pull him off the wailing boy and lodge Glen in the Cottage Four attic, where he would remain for five days, alone, with a bare mattress, a chamber pot, and a few sandwiches.

On Thursday, Superintendent Stiles opened the door and stooped to enter the attic. Glen lay on the mattress, staring at the rafters.

"Hello, son."

"Ain't your son."

"Now listen, Glen, there's no reason for such hostility. You are the one who bashed poor Smythe's nose in for no reason. I'm here to bring you back into the good graces of Twin Bridges."

Glen snorted.

"Well, young man, I can just leave you here, you know!"

"I had a reason."

"What possible reason could you have for hurting that boy?"

Glen's eyes never left the rafters. A minute passed.

"You know, you're right. Smythe just told the truth," Glen said.

"Well then, you see, Glen? You just come on down from here now, your punishment is complete, and we need you."

"For what?"

"Next Friday night, it's our boys against the boys over in Sheridan, first football game of the season. And you are the biggest boy we have, and the fastest too, I might add."

Glen stirred on the mattress for the first time. "I don't like being made fun of."

"Why, I'm not making fun of you, Glen. You run a football better than anyone I've ever seen."

"I'm not talking about you. I'm talking about those folks over in Sheridan. Come out to watch the orphans play in our stupid overalls, mooing at us like cows. I ain't doing that again." A week after he arrived at Twin Bridges, he played in the last game of the season. He'd been judged a good eighth man, and sent, a lamb to the slaughter, to play a game he didn't understand with players he didn't know, on a snowy cold January field.

Stiles, hunched over in the tight space, bobbed his head up and down and stepped from one foot to the other. Glen thought he looked like a quail darting through cheatgrass.

"Well then, Glen, have I got some good news for you. Carroll College, over in Helena, just donated their old football uniforms to us! And my Mrs. Stiles is already darning them, fitting them to you boys. There's a real nice one I'm saving for you, just your size. Number 16. Mr. Nells, the chair of the board, bought us a new football. And not just any ball. Why, this is a KN, made by the great Knute Rockne himself! You can pass it, throw it right through the air. Wouldn't you like to have a go at that, Glen? We've only got one week to get ready for the game. I've asked Mr. Brown to coach. He's been watching you horse around with the boys on Sundays. He thinks you're just fine."

Glen turned his head and took in Stiles for the first time, his Ichabod Crain stoop, his narrow-set cloudy eyes. He knew what Stiles was doing—using him. He glanced around the attic and gripped the grimy edge of the mattress. It had became a peaceful cocoon these few days, the clanking of the other orphans below of no concern. Mrs. Pike, no concern. Little Edward had saved some of his food and added it to the random sandwiches shoved under his door, along with his copy of *The Adventures of Huckleberry Finn*. It tickled him that a few of the boys he hated had been assigned to empty his slop bucket, especially Wilbur, a mean boy of fifteen who took smaller boys out into the wheat field and did something so brutal to them that the little ones always came back crying. All Stiles cared about, though, was that football game.

"Alright, I'll come down. On one condition. I'm team captain, get to pick the team."

"That's just fine, Glen. I was going to suggest that myself."

On Friday morning, in a mowed meadow wet with dew, Mr. Brown and Glen stood in front of all the boys deemed old enough and big enough to step into the old Carroll College uniforms. Glen knew who could buck a bale of hay, who fed the orphaned calves with a bottle, who offered him a seat in the dining hall. That's who he'd pick.

"You, you, and Ray," he said, pointing down the line. "You,

Tommy, you, Sam." He was getting close to his team of sixteen, all they'd need for eight-man football. Finally, he saw the tall, lean boy he was looking for, in the back row, with a piece of white tape across his nose.

"And you, Randall." Randall's head snapped up, and he eyed Glen with suspicion.

"Looks like you can take a beating better than most," Glen said with a grin.

Glen nodded to Brown, his job done.

"Well, now, that's it boys! The rest of you, you'll be cheering your mates on Saturday night. Squad, let's get to work."

Brown tossed the new football to Glen. Glen ran his fingers over the tightly seamed cowhide and let them linger on the soft laces. This new ball was tapered, slimmer, and fit in his big hand—a slice of ham in a biscuit. The boys fanned out on the meadow grass. Brown took them through blocking, running, receiving. Glen threw the ball in sweeping arcs across the field. By noon, Brown had worked out a defense and an offense, and put them head-to-head in their boots and overalls. As to who would control the ball and the plays, it was as clear as the sound of the meadow larks all around them: Glen Earnest Wilkerson.

On Saturday night, the Twin Bridges orphans, now officially the Saints thanks to the embroidery on their uniforms, blindsided the Sheridan High School Warriors with a passing game. The Warriors were geared up to defend against the flying wedge. But instead, the night's game ball, the KR, flew again and again from Glen's arm, and most often landed in Randall Smythe's outstretched hands.

The Saints beat the Warriors, 31–6.

Twin Bridges Orphanage lies at a farrago of the Beaverhead, Big Hole, and Ruby rivers, where they flow into the Jefferson. Children streamed in from all directions, but hardly made a ripple in their infrequent leave-taking. Hard to imagine who had it worse: The *real* orphans, as Randall called them, or the orphans of the living. Nobody wanted either sort. A child would arrive, and soon after, his or her natural childish optimism would be dispatched to a drawer in Mr. Stiles office, where he filed them alphabetically based on their capacity for menial work: chickens, cows, kitchen, pigs, plowing, sewing, shoe repair. Football.

Glen, having found his footing in the patched Saints uniform, spent the season bedeviling Mrs. Pike and protecting his little guys. He didn't swing any more punches. Didn't need to. He was Big Man on Campus, as Randall called him, the darling of the orphanage's board of directors. The team now made newspapers around the region with pictures of Glen, his big square head, his arm cocked high, the ball bursting from his hand. If the orphanage ever needed a recruiting poster, they would surely have plastered Glen's image on it.

So it was no surprise when Fred Rowland showed up one spring morning and cornered Mr. Stiles in his office.

"Well, Stiles, I'm come to take my boys back. Things are better now, on the farm, and I can surely take care of them, yes sir."

Stiles pursed his lips, his pale eyes quivering.

"You are aware, Mr. Rowland, that you have not paid the expected ten dollars per month for each of the boys—not one dollar—since you left them here eighteen months ago? That puts you behind $360." Stiles fluttered from side to side in his desk chair. All he could think about was losing his star football player, a testament to his stalwart belief in fresh air, backbreaking farm labor, and a little book learning on the side.

Rowland frowned at the superintendent. "That, I don't have, sir. Would you prefer I let them starve? Their mother left them with me against my wishes . . . uhum . . . But now, why, I've thought better of it, and it's time they came on back."

"You mean, now that they can work harder, Mr. Rowland?"

"And they ain't working here, Stiles? I seen those kids out there. I seen those newspaper articles. My Glen is your number one money-maker, in addition to having a good strong back. I just wonder what their mother, my niece, would say if she heard you were giving me any guff about collecting her boys!"

Stiles was puffing little bubbles from his lips and cranking himself up in his chair as if he might fly off. "Alright then, Mr. Rowland. If you'll just show me the document granting you guardianship and pay the state of Montana $360, I'll be happy to release Ray and Glen to you, that is, of course, if they want to go."

"You just try and keep them here, Stiles, and I will have the sheriff on you in a minute. Orphanages are supposed to send kids out, not lock them in!"

Rowland scraped his chair back and left at a trot. Stiles tried to follow him, but Rowland shoved him to the floor. By the time Stiles caught up with him, he was stomping up the steps of Cottage Five and calling out for Ray.

"Ray Stovall, you in there? I've come to take you home!"

Ray appeared in the doorway. "Well, it's about time, Uncle Fred! God Almighty! I'll get my things."

"Where's your brother?"

"He's over in Cottage Four, but I don't think you outta go after him."

"Nonsense! Meet me out at the buckboard."

Stiles was beside himself. He ran ahead to Cottage Four and found Glen in the school room.

"Glen, I need to speak with you."

Out in the hall, he launched, breathless, into Rowland's unexpected appearance when Uncle Fred burst in the door.

"Glen, get your things. You're coming home."

Glen stared from the frantic Mr. Stiles to his imposing uncle in boots and a Stetson hat. But he was taller than his uncle now, even with the hat, and sure about one thing.

"I ain't going nowhere, least not with you," he said, his voice low and steady.

"I said get your things! You'll do as I say, Glen Stovall!"

Glen leaned forward in the coiled crouch of a defensive back. He took two steps and wrapped his arms around Fred, twisted, and pitched him down the steps of the cottage. Rowland landed square on his hat.

"My name ain't Stovall," he said.

Through the school window, Stiles and Glen watched Ray and Fred, his hat tilted at an unnatural angle, drive away in the buckboard. Ray turned and raised his arm in Glen's direction, searching for his face in the school room windows.

The "little guys," as Glen called them, didn't need another reason to worship Number 16. Even so, the scene on the porch—a frightened Stiles, a squashed Fred Rowland, a triumphant Glen "My Name Ain't Stovall" Wilkerson—spread like range fire through the orphanage by dinner time.

Randall, now one of his best friends, slapped him on the shoulder and slid in next to him at the Cottage Four table.

"Well, I'll be. Guess we better start calling you Wilkerson, lest we wanna end up on our asses."

Glen grinned at him. "Yep. I clobbered you once already."

"So listen, Wilkie. They say we can go to the movies on Saturday, and I've even got a nickel for popcorn—"

"What'd you call me?"

"Just now? Wilkie? Saying 'Wilkerson' takes longer than hoeing a row of corn."

"Alright, if you say so."

"OK, Wilkie. Movies? Saturday?"

"Sure thing."

Wilkie, as everyone called him now, spent the spring and summer of his fifteenth year growing his last two inches, to six feet even. He ate like the plow horse he was. He rode the "little guys" around on his shoulders. He went to the movies with Randall. He tossed the worn KR around with his teammates, sending them long in the meadow, running hard over cow pies and mud puddles. He visited the attic now and again to read his hidden copy of *The Adventures of Huckleberry Finn.*

That's where he found Edward one night, rolled into a ball like a pill bug, crying on the old mattress.

"Eddie? Did Pike toss you in here?"

Edward uncurled toward the wall and wiped his red eyes. "I'm hiding out."

"From who? No, let me guess. Wilbur. Is he bullying you again? I warned him to stay away from you little guys."

Edward curled up again.

"Come on, Eddie. You can tell me."

"He grabbed me. Before breakfast this morning. I was in the milking barn—"

"What, he hit you?" Glen gently rolled Eddie over, looking for a bruise, a cut. The side of his face was scratched from his hair line to his chin, like he'd been dragged over gravel.

"What the hell!"

Edward burrowed deeper into the mattress, burying a thin, high sob in the blue ticking.

"Eddie!"

"He said if I told . . . "

"Tell me, little guy. I promise he won't hurt you again. I'll make sure this time."

"He, he . . . " Edward rolled onto his back. "He took his . . ." Edward pointed at his crotch. "He shoved it up my arse."

Glen's stomach lurched, supper exploding into his mouth.

"That son of a bitch." Glen jumped up and pushed open the attic door. "You go wash up, Eddie, I'll see you in a while. I'll be right next to you, all night. But I'm gonna go take care of some things first."

"Wilkie! Don't get into trouble!"

"Trouble? It ain't me who's gonna have trouble."

Glen found Wilbur in the milking barn, just where he knew he'd be, finishing up his evening chores. Glen watched him for a while from the door. Wilbur, at sixteen, had the stoop and pot belly of an old man, as if his young years had been wrung out of him. His face in the dim light reminded Glen of a puppet he'd seen in a traveling circus: wooden, hastily carved. His movements down the milking line were stiff and jerky, kicking cows when they got in his way.

"Well, hello there, Wilbur."

"What do you want, *Stovall*?"

The barn was quiet, cows stamping their feet against the silage, the creak of timbers here and there in the evening breeze, the last of the sun creeping through the walls to lay silver stripes on the hay loft above their heads.

"Seeing as how that ain't my name, I'm going to pretend I didn't hear you say that, as we have lots more important things to discuss."

"Oh? What would that be, your highness? Your skill with that stupid little ball?"

Glen moved quietly through the barn toward him, talking softly.

"I'd like to talk about the little guys, the ones I told you to stay away from."

"None of your business, Stovall. I'll do as I please. Tell it to Stiles."

"We both know that's a waste of time. So I think it's time we worked this out, just the two of us."

Wilbur laughed. His hands were on the last cow in the line, close to the stairs that led up to the hayloft.

"Ooh, sounds like you want a taste of what I gave that sweet little Edward this morning."

"How'd you know, Wilbur?" Glen slipped a knife, lifted from the kitchen, out of his overall pocket. He held it up so Wilbur could see, swishing it back and forth.

"Stupid me, I thought you were just bullying them. What a sick bastard you are. There's only one way I can imagine ending this, and that's to cut your dick off."

Wilbur looked around for a way to escape and bolted up the stairs to the hayloft. Glen followed slowly behind him.

"Get away from me!" he yelled, his wooden face splintering in fear.

"What's a matter with you? You can dish it out, but you can't take it? Time someone taught you a lesson."

Glen moved slowly closer to him. Wilbur backed up, skittering around a hay bale, his back to the hayloft door. A gust of wind jolted the barn, and the door, which had been closed but not latched, blew open.

"Watch out!" Glen yelled. Wilbur pitched over backward, across a bale, and disappeared out the loft door, making not a sound.

Glen and Edward lay side by side on their beds. Lights out. Edward heard it first.

"What's that?"

There was shouting coming from the barns, and soon, lights coming up the road to the orphanage. The boys, all but Glen and Edward, pressed up against the sleeping porch screens.

"There's a stretcher. A body's on it, under a blanket," Sam reported. "Geeze, they're putting it in the van. Wonder who that is?"

In the morning, the whole orphanage was called together on the front lawn of the Castle. Stiles, his hands behind his back, addressed them.

"Children of Twin Bridges, I'm sorry to tell you this morning that one of our own, Wilbur Taft, fell to his death last night from the hayloft. He must have gone up there to kick down some hay for the milkers and lost his footing. Someone didn't latch that door, boys and girls, and now we've lost a brother, may God rest his soul. We'll come together to mourn his passing on Sunday. That is all."

Glen found Edward. They walked out into the meadow, and when they were alone, Glen took him by the shoulders.

"Eddie, I didn't push him! I was threatening him, yeah, but he was just backing away, and suddenly, that damn door just blew open!"

Edward smiled, the scratched side of his face a welter of scabs. "You promised me he'd never hurt me again. Looks like you kept your promise."

Glen stared down at his hands, and when he thought of the knife, they trembled.

"If anybody ever finds out I was up there with him . . ."

"Who's going to pay any attention, Wilkie? I'm the only one what knows. And you know as well as I do, everybody hated Wilbur. Nobody cares. He was just an orphan. A little door to hell opened and swallowed him up. They'll plant him out there in that cemetery with the others, behind the barn. They'll forget about him in a week."

"Maybe," Wilkie said, with no conviction. "But I won't. And I bet you won't either."

"No. I ain't never going to forget."

Glen spent the night in the attic, reading *Huck Finn* by lantern light.

A rider along the road to the Twin Bridges Orphanage, one with a particularly sunny disposition, might view the eight-foot solid wood fence surrounding the acreage with a sense of community pride. Why, look at the lengths Montana is taking to protect those poor unfortunate children!

Truth is, the fence wasn't there to keep trouble out, but to keep orphans in.

A week after Wilbur had fallen from the hay loft, early in the morning, while the boys had gone down to breakfast, Glen pulled a canvas bag from under his bed and stuffed it with clothes he had snared from another football team's locker room, a comb, a harmonica, biscuits saved from a few breakfasts, and Edward's copy of *Huck Finn*. He walked out into the meadow by the road and pitched the bag over the high fence.

Late in the morning, Mr. Brown, Glen, and the rest of the Twin Bridges Saints were running up and down the meadow. Glen was heaving passes, closer, ever closer, to the fence. One particular pass arched high and long over all the boys' heads and sailed out over the fence. Mr. Brown gave an annoyed wave of his hand to Glen's "I'll get it!"

Just as he was shimmying over the top of the fence, he called down to Brown, "I'll come back in the gate. See you in a minute." And then the lunch bell clanged out over the field.

It wasn't until supper, five hours later, that anyone thought to wonder where Glen was.

Chapter 11

BARNEY

Stone County, Mississippi, Jenkins Plantation, 1925–1928

"Here's to your little Nora Mae!" The men around the big oak tipped their hats to the new father. They'd been working together in each other's fields for several weeks, and Barney felt a rush of pride that his little fiefdom was holding together, even if fear and dissent were lurking just below the surface.

"Now tomorrow, men, let's hit Virgil's fields in the morning, and Roland's after lunch. How's that?" There were murmurs and nods of approval around the circle. He had backed off his earlier grand scheme in which the men would all throw in together, skirting Jenkins and Batson, his overseer; buying their own supplies through Barney; and avoiding Jenkins' more costly furnish.

One thing at a time. This year, they'd just chop each other's cotton, harvest each other's fields. Next year, well, who knew how far they could go together? Barney reveled in the camaraderie, fragile though it was. It conjured up memories of Acayucan, and with it, memories of Luzelba. Her mysterious scent invaded him for just an instant, washing away the bitter taste of what he left behind in Montana—defeat, debt, and two boys he hoped never to see again. At least Lula had finally stopped agitating to send for them, even though he knew she was right about one thing: It would be a godsend to have two older boys to work the fields with him.

"Wishing won't make it so, Lula. You know those boys would just undermine me again, and we'd never get a lick of work out of them. They would just be two more mouths to feed. Best to let your Uncle Fred keep them."

The summer weather was kind to Barney and his dreams, sending enough rain to boost the sharecroppers' harvest of cotton and corn. The men around the fire late at night raised a glass of corn liquor to Barney. Even accounting for the rain, their harvests had been better than they expected. So maybe there was something to cooperative farming after all. But not everyone was convinced.

One fall afternoon, Barney hitched up the buckboard to go into town for supplies. He came upon Violet Byrd in her purple headdress on the road, walking to town.

"Mrs. Byrd, would you care for a ride?"

"Why yes, Mr. Stovall, I thank you," she said, walking to the back of the wagon.

"No ma'am, no need to ride back there. Please join me up front."

Violet eyed the bench seat.

"Mr. Stovall, they say you are a smart man, but carrying a Negro woman in the front of your wagon is likely to get you strung up."

"A neighbor can't offer a neighbor a ride?"

"We are neighbors like a shark and an anchovy. We both live in the same ocean, but the neighborliness ends there."

"Well, suit yourself," he said, jumping down to help her into the back of the wagon. "At least sit up toward the front so we can talk."

They rode along silently a while, Violet's purple-wrapped head leaning against the back of the bench seat.

"Mrs. Byrd, if you may—"

"Call me Violet."

"Only if you'll call me Barney."

"Then it's settled, God save us. Our Christian names it shall be."

"Well, Mrs. Violet, what do you hear from the men on your side of the plantation? About our work arrangement, helping each other."

"Are you prying into my community's affairs, Mr. Barney?"

"No, ma'am! I just want to know the men are happy working together, and sometimes, I just can't tell. Everyone . . ."

"Keeps you at arm's length? Why, yes, what did you expect? They hardly know you, and they been beat down by white men their whole lives. Do you know what a driver is?"

"A driver?"

"When our people was slaves, the plantation owners, they had a white overseer, and they had drivers, slaves in charge of keeping peace in the quarters, keeping the men working in the fields. That's what they call you. My men, they call you the White Driver, so I think it's safe to say, they ain't too sure about you yet."

Barney flicked the reins against the horse's back in frustration.

"Dammit, Violet, I'm only trying to help us all make some money . . . Any money! What have I ever done to make them think I'm—"

"You was born into that cotton white skin. You just have to give them time, prove to them that you are the man you say you are. You are that man, aren't you, Mr. Barney?"

"Well now, I'm the first to admit I ain't always the smartest fellow. I've made mistakes, here and there. But I ain't never taken anything that wasn't mine to take! And I have nothing against the Negro people. No, I'm a Lincoln man, born and bred. And he died for the union, for the people . . . all the people."

"So you ain't against us. But are you *for* us?"

"I am surely *for* you. Why, without you, my wife, and likely my daughter, would have died! And when it comes to farming, cotton don't know Black skin from white. There's nothing different about us out there under the sun. If the sun rises and sets on us both, then I am for us *all*."

"You talk like a man of conviction. You seem to think if you say it, you can make it so. You Northerners are all like that. But the South? The South is like molasses, stubborn and bitter-sweet, and it flows whenever it wants, wherever it will. And what it wills is this: no sharecropper, white or Black, can decide *anything* for themselves. It's the owners, the sheriff, the overseers. They hold all the power and all the law, and they ain't sharing it with a raggedy group of Black farmers and one White Driver."

This shut Barney up for a while. Was she right? Was he just kicking against the goads, like Luis said on the ship? Well, what if he was? The United Fruit men beat him near to death, and he survived. Uncle Fred was guilty of a massive dupery against him, and he made it out alive. Nothing had ever beat him down *entirely*. Maybe this was his time, a reckoning with the fates from which he would emerge victorious.

"How is Nora Mae?" Violet asked, extricating Barney from his argument with himself.

"Well, I don't rightly know. She is a fretful little thing, cries a lot. Here she is almost six months old, and Maudie Marie carries her everywhere with her, like a rag doll. Lula has not taken to her yet, says she won't as long as Clemmie is nursing her. But I think that's just an excuse. She didn't want that baby, but what am I gonna do about it?"

"Get a cow, Barney."

Barney came back from town near sunset with a scrawny cow tied to the back of the wagon. Barney named the cow Nora Mae just so there would be no question as to why he bought her.

His years working dairy cows in California and Arizona taught him how to fatten up that poor little cow in short order with oats and molasses and corn silage. In a week, Nora Mae was drinking Nora Mae's milk. Soon, Barney was sending a sloshing bucket of milk with Maudie Marie down to Clemmie's. In a month there was enough milk for most of the plantation's children, an item the other croppers took note of. Barney hoped they would.

Lula, for her part, seemed to show little interest in her baby daughter, even though Clemmie was no longer nursing her. She accepted her back into the shack like an infection, never holding her close or rocking her. That she left to Maudie. It was more than a year since the sepsis nearly killed her, but she still felt as if she had been poured out, as if death was lurking, ruffling the hem of her skirt as she stood at the kitchen sink or sat on the front porch in the evening. Barney tried teasing a smile out of her, something he had been successful at in Montana even in the dead of winter, but she seemed so far away, he gave up trying to reach her.

By the time Nora Mae was one, a birthday no one in the family took it upon themselves to celebrate, Barney and Lula had become shadows to each other, passing silently during the day and striving not to touch each other on their slender bed at night. Barney knew Lula did not want another child, and consoled himself with that. It didn't occur to him that his wife and children might need tending. What possessed him was a desire to win the affection of his fellow sharecroppers. Barney was barely a presence in his shack at night, surrounded by his six children and a sullen wife. All his thoughts were of his men.

They were all asleep one night in July, exhausted by a day of extreme heat and cotton, when a fist pounded loudly on the door.

"Barney! Barney! You gotta come quick."

It was Violet Byrd. Barney drew on his trousers and bolted down the steps, following her, barefoot and shirtless.

"What the hell's going on?" he said running as fast as he could behind her.

"It's Ira Williams. He's killed someone."

Barney followed Violet to the Williamses' shack on her side of the plantation. There, at the small shed behind the shack, Ira had crushed himself against the shed door, sobbing, a sow and her litter snuffling around his feet. In the dim light from Violet's lantern, Barney peered into the shed and saw two worn boots, legs, and a man's torso, drenched in blood. Ira's sobs grew to a wail.

"Barney, I don't even know that man! My coon hound started howling, and when I come out to check, I found this feller with a pig under each arm. I hollered at him to stop and he just kept comin' at me, and I shot him! Oh my god, I shot him!"

Barney put his hand on Ira's shoulder. "Quiet, Ira. Just calm down." Barney took Violet's lantern and waived it over the dead man. A dead white man. A dead pig thief was one thing. A dead white pig thief was another thing entirely.

"Ira, your ma and pa in there?" He nodded toward the shack.

"Yes sir. Pa come out and I told him, 'Get back in there.'"

Ira was the only son of Joshua and Belle Williams, sharecroppers who had wound down their years, their hands, their knees, in Jenkins' cotton. Now Ira, just twenty, worked their allotment and took care of his blind mother and wan father. It was left to Ira to keep them and their cotton in the land of the living.

"Violet, you take Ira inside. I'm going to get Batson."

Ira wailed louder.

"There's nothing to be done for it now, Ira. You ain't done nothing wrong, that I can see, not a thing but protect your own."

Violet hissed at Barney. "You know that ain't true. They gonna string this boy up."

"What do you want me to do, Violet. Dig a hole and bury him?"

"That ain't a bad idea."

The only thing that kept Ira from hanging was the dead man. Eustice Branch was the town drunk. Most were happy to be done with him. What he was doing in Ira's shed was of little consequence in the turbid eyes of the law in Mississippi in 1926. The charge was murder. The white jury, mustering up some semblance of compassion, perhaps induced by Barney's own heartfelt testimony about Ira and his family, found him guilty of manslaughter. The judge sentenced him to five years in Parchman, the state prison. Ira would likely live through it, but it was a death sentence for Joshua and Belle.

"What are you going to do now, Barney? You gave Ira up. I came and got you to do something to help that boy, and you just gave him up!" Violet's words sprang from her mouth like biting flies. They stood in the road, half way between Barney's shack and Violet's on the day after the sentencing.

"I got Jenkins to agree to leave the Williamses in their shack, no rent for the time being. That's something, Violet. Now, if we can just get everyone to pitch in a bit of food, why, we can at least feed them. My Maudie Marie says she'll cook for them."

Violet's face softened.

"We can take care of our own, but Maudie is a good girl, and I'll put her to work. I'll get the other women to help. The children can tend their garden, feed those pigs. But Barney, five years is a long time."

"Don't I know it. I don't know what else to do. But I'm thinking on it." They parted, each to walk back into their own worlds. Barney walked twenty paces and turned, following Violet's progress in the red dirt, her head held high, a long stride in her skirts, until the road dipped and she disappeared.

STONE COUNTY ENTERPRISE, MARCH 3, 1927

Petition for Pardon

His Excellency Hon. H.L. Whitfield, Governor of Mississippi: We the citizens of Stone County, the undersigned petitioners would respectfully show that at the spring term of Circuit Court of said county, 1926, Ira Williams, colored, was convicted on a charge of manslaughter and sentenced to serve five years imprisonment in the State Penitentiary. Your petitioners respectfully ask you to give this petition your careful attention and grant this negro a pardon for the following reason: We believe that with the punishment already inflicted, the ends of justice have been met, and that he is penitent for the crime committed. The said petitioners respectfully ask that you consider the fact that the said Ira Williams pled guilty to the charges preferred against him and accepted the sentence placed on him by the Court. Ira has a mother and father, both getting old and no other one to look for support to and are badly in need of his support. We believe that if this man is pardoned, he will obey all the laws of the state.

Respectfully submitted,

Nick Ladner, A.B. Davis, G.W. Murphy, W. E. Batson, Mrs. M. J. Batson, C. O. Batson, A.A. Lott, W. T. Parker, W.E.R. Davis, L.B. Lott, Thos. A. David, Barney Stovall, and many others

Barney stood on the bottom step of Violet and Reggie's shack and read them the legal notice from the Stone County Enterprise. He looked up to catch Violet's eyes as he read, and felt Reggie's anger.

"You have stirred up the hornet's nest now, Barney," she said. "How in the dickens did you get Batson's brother to sign that?"

"Just like I got everyone else to sign it. I just went around and knocked on their doors. Lotsa folks hired Belle to clean their houses and care for their babies, and plenty remember Joshua's touch with their horses and mules. And nobody thought he'd done anything wrong! Thought they woulda done the same thing if Branch had been pilfering their pigs. Mr. Lott, he even paid for the notice. We been caring for the Williamses now for going on a year, and I don't know how much longer we can do it *and* keep Jenkins from evicting them."

Reggie stomped past Barney and disappeared into the evening gloom.

"What's the matter with him? He told me he wants to go it alone this season."

"Barney, you have him scared. He's scared of Batson, and now this. You better not come 'round here no more, least not to my steps. Good evening to you." She disappeared into the shack and closed the door.

He stood for a while, waiting for Violet to rethink things, but the door remained closed. He turned and made for the Williamses' shack to read them the notice.

Already, the story of Barney's pitch to win Ira a pardon was well-known across the plantation.

Sheldon Jenkins was sitting on his veranda reading the very same notice in the paper when his overseer, Batson, road up on his big bay horse.

"Morning, Mr. Jenkins. I see you've got the *Enterprise*. You see that legal notice Stovall put in there?"

"Yes I have, but it appears to be more than Stovall. I see your brother's name, too, along with others. Hell, I might even have signed it if he'd asked me." Jenkins put the paper down and assessed Batson's mood. His overseer was rarely cheerful and never charitable, and that's what made him good at his job, in Jenkins' opinion.

"Right unhappy about it, I am, sir. That Stovall has stirred up the niggers, and I promise you now, if we don't put a stop to his endless meddling, all this business of them working together, it's gonna come to a bad end."

"Well, at the moment, I see no harm. And in fact, each of the last two years they've harvested more than the previous one, even with the damn boll weevil." Jenkins watched Batson's face turn inward and sour. Batson didn't for one minute like Stovall chipping away at his absolute power.

"You say that now, but you seen those croppers over in Georgia trying to start a workers' union. You want that here? Because that's my prediction. They're gonna get so full of themselves, they'll just show up here one day to this very porch making all kinds of demands, mark my words."

"Well, Batson, you may be right, but for the moment, we'll let them be, you hear?"

Batson stiffened in the saddle.

"Alright, but I'm not taking my eyes off Stovall. And about the Williamses. I got another cropper wants to work those ten acres out on the east end, and he needs a place. It's time we turned those folk out."

"No, we won't be doing that. Belle Williams was my nanny when I was a boy, did you know that? You want to foment an uprising, just try sending those folks down the road."

Batson turned the bay and spurred him hard.

On March 18, 1927, Governor Whitfield died, putting an end to Barney's long-shot last hope. Ira would serve out the rest of his sentence—three years yet—and there was nothing to be done about it. Barney trudged up the hill to the Williams place to give Joshua and Belle the news. He regretted even sticking his nose in; just like Violet predicted, it had done no good at all.

It was late in the day, the winter sun dropping beyond the horizon. He and the men had spent the day getting the ground ready for spring planting.

"Hardly seems worth it," Preston Bates told him that morning. "Whatever Mr. Shelden Jenkins don't take, why that is apportioned to the boll weevil. And what's left, with cotton prices gone to hell, won't buy a bucket of sand."

Barney had tried encouraging Preston and the rest of the men with mostly made-up stories of overcoming the drought and cold, jaundiced earth of Montana. "Men, even Jenkins was surprised at how well we did this year. You can't just give up! No, we just gotta keep on keepin' on. Where would you go that's any better?"

"You should ask Reggie Byrd that question. He took off last night. The women folk say he ain't coming back, either."

"What?" Barney put down his hoe. "They left?"

"No, not they. Just Reggie. Violet and the little girl, they're still here. Don't know what's gonna become of them."

Barney passed Violet's door and almost stopped to check on her, but hesitated. Maybe she blamed him for Reggie's departure. He'd cut a wide swath around her since she told him to keep off her porch.

In the early gloom, he came to the Williamses' yard and stopped short. Joshua sat in a rocking chair, and next to him, Maudie Marie and Dora were bent over a basket of laundry, darning a pair of overalls by the lantern light. Joshua was singing, *"Go down, Moses, way down in Egypt's land,"* to the tiny blond girl sitting on his lap. Barney's own Nora Mae.

The picture of domestic tranquility put a snare in Barney's throat. Nora Mae was nearly two years old, and he'd never held her, let alone sung to her. She glanced up from the circle of Joshua's deep, feathery voice, and gave Barney a quizzical glance, the kind you might offer a stranger.

"Hello, Daddy. What brings you over here?" Maudie asked. Barney looked from Maudie to Nora Mae to Joshua as if he'd never seen them before.

"Evening, Mr. Stovall. Your little Nora Mae, she likes my songs."

"Evening to you, Mr. Williams. I've come to bring you some bad news, I'm afraid."

"I suspect I already know what you're gonna say, sir. I hear the governor died yesterday."

Barney twisted his straw hat. He jabbed a booted foot onto the lowest porch step, just to steady himself. How could it be that his own daughters found comfort here, in this mysterious world, more foreign to him than the banana fields of Acayucan?

Chapter 12

NORA MAE

Stone County, Mississippi, Jenkins Plantation, 1928

Nora Mae caught a glimpse of Clemmie walking through the pecan trees, a baby on her hip. She pulled hard at Maudie's hand.

"Mama!" she cried. Clemmie turned to look and quickly moved into the twist of brown trunks until she disappeared from sight.

"Baby, she's not your mama no more. We got *our* mama. Come on, now."

Maudie Marie pulled her through the leaves up the hill to the shack where her other mother lived, the one who was a distant thunderstorm, a promise of rain and cool comfort that never materialized. This much she understood: The brown mama, the pale-yellow mama—neither wanted her. She bent down and bit Maudie's hand.

"Nora Mae!" she yelled in pain. "You got no call to do that!"

The baby bent down and kissed her sister's hand.

Once inside, Nora Mae watched her mother carefully, looking for signs, the way the hound who lived under the porch listened for his supper bowl. Her mother passed her once, not glancing at her, and then again, and again. Nothing. Nora Mae felt a pitch in her stomach, as if her belly might come undone.

"Mama!" she cried from the corner where Maudie Marie had deposited her. "Mama!"

"I don't have time for you now. Hush up," Lula said. When Lula was near again, Nora Mae jumped up and wrapped her arms around her mother's leg. Lula stopped, rolled her eyes, then bent and pried the girl's hands from her thigh. "I told you, no. I got laundry to do. You go play with your brothers."

Nora Mae stomped down the stairs into the dirt yard. She could hear her brothers playing down in the creek bottom and knew that if she went that direction, they'd throw dirt clods at her, or worse. She turned the opposite direction, toward the Black sharecroppers' encampment. She knew the back way, having crossed it many times, her hand in Maudie's. She wandered, a stick in one hand, a rock in the other. She beat on the pecan trunks with the stick.

"Bad girl!" she said. She kicked aside leaves searching for last summer's windfall pecans, and when she found one, she would smash it with the rock and run her fingers through the nutmeats and shells, casting aside the wormy, decayed nuts. This took a considerable amount of time. She put the nuts in her pocket.

She made her way to the Williamses' porch, where Joshua sat sleeping in his rocking chair. Nora Mae's quiet bare feet climbed the stairs. She stood looking down at him, her hand on his knee. He was as thin and faded as old wallpaper. In his sleep, his blue lips puffed out with each breath, his eyelids fluttered, some scene from a distant day at play in his dreams. She jiggled his leg.

"Well, hello little girl," he said, opening an eye. "You come to see Uncle Joshua? Where's your sister?"

Nora Mae shrugged. "Ta home."

"You come all this way yourself?"

Nora Mae nodded.

"Well, climb up here in Uncle Joshua's lap then. You want a song?"

She laid her head on his shrunken shoulder, her hand on his chest. He brushed his feet against the porch until the chair began to rock, the creaking of the oak against the porch planks setting up a rhythm.

"I got-a wings, you got-a wings,
All o' God's chillun got-a wings!
When I get to heaven I'm goin' to put on my wings,
I'm goin' to fly all over God's Heaven,
Heaven, heaven."

The beat and vibration filled her tiny body.

"You got wings, Uncle Joshua?"

"Why sure, child. We all do. You too! Someday, they gonna carry us up away from all the sad old earth. But you, honey, you got lots of livin' days, so don't you worry. You just wait, and someday, you stretch those wings and fly up into the sky."

Sitting up straight in his lap, she tested his promise, rolling her shoulders and flapping her arms. Nothing happened.

"But I wanna fly, Uncle Joshua, I wanna fly away now!" Tears beaded up on her lower lashes.

"Now, baby, it's not your time; them wings is too little. Why, I gotta go first, and when I fly up there, I will look down on you from the highest heaven, and I'll say, 'Hello, little missy! Me and Precious Jesus is up here awaiting for you!'"

She settled back into the shield of his chest and squirmed until she had her hand in her pocket. She was gonna save the pecans for her mama, but it was no use. She filled her fist with the sweet nutmeats, and with her other hand, twisted his palm up, and let the nuts fall in a trickle into his pale, knotted hand.

Joshua chuckled and then fed the nuts, one to her, one to himself, until his palm was empty. Then he fished for something in his shirt pocket and put a buffalo nickel into Nora Mae's hand.

She stared into his gauzy gray eyes. "I ain't never had no treasure."

He patted her head and rocked quietly for a while, the sun dropping into the oaks.

"Little baby, you better go home before the dark come."

The boys rushed into the Stovall cabin and begged for biscuits.

"You can have those cold ones by the window," Lula told them. "Where is your little sister?"

"We ain't seen her," Ernie said.

Lula sat at the table and put her head in her hands. "Where has that child got to now? Ernie, you take the shotgun and shoot some squirrels, and bring that girl back with you. Don't come back without her."

"Aw, Mama. She ain't nothing but trouble! You know she gonna cry and scream, and I'll have to drag her back here."

"Then drag her, Ernie. It's getting dark. Don't sass me. Just go."

Nora Mae made her way slowly home, making big, aimless loops, the nickel as deep in her pocket as she could stow it. Over the ridge, she heard the retort of a shot gun. The hollow ringing scared her and she struggled to pull herself up into an oak tree. She sat still, her bare feet rigid, not swinging like a carefree child's. She sat stoically in the branches, listening, hidden by the twilight.

Over the rise, she saw Ernie, two squirrels tied together and flung over his shoulder. He was not the worst of her brothers. He had blue eyes like their father, and sometimes those eyes softened when he looked her way. She tried to crawl into his lap now and again, but if the others were nearby, he would push her away.

Ernie aimed the shotgun up into the trees, where squirrels chittered and sped along. He fired again, and a squirrel fell to the leafy ground. Nora Mae clung to the branch, sure she did not want him to find her. Ernie moved closer, and as he did, a rustle, a slight movement caught his attention, and he fired. The shot blew past her, the lead missing her, and she fell from the branch with a screech.

Ernie pitched the rifle and squirrels to the ground and pulled her to her feet. Blood ran in rivulets down her face.

"What's the matter with you! Didn't you hear me? What were you doing up there? I coulda killed you!"

Nora Mae shoved her hand deep into her pocket. It was still there!

"I's just playing. I . . . didn't know it was you."

Ernie pulled off his shirt and wiped her face. "Damn it, now Daddy's gonna have my hide. You hurt? Does it hurt?"

"It hurts! It hurts," she wailed as the shock of her fall from the tree wore off. Her wail grew louder. "I's not a squirrel! I have wings! I'm an angel. I'm gonna fly away!"

"You stop that nonsense," Ernie said, shaking her. "You listen to me, stop it! We're gonna go down by the creek and wash your face." He traced a thin red scratch at her hair line. "And if you say anything to anybody about this, I swear I'll bring you back out here and shoot you for real and bury you. You ain't worth the lickin' I'd get."

She submitted to Ernie, let him wash her face in the turgid creek, the water the color of molasses in the late day. All that mattered was the treasure, hidden away. And the wings, though she could not summon them yet.

Five months later on a sweltering June day, she turned four. The tiniest, misbegotten Stovall was now old enough to know she was invisible. The nickel was especially heavy in her pocket that day. She brought it out, kissed it, and hid it away again.

Chapter 13

BARNEY

Stone County, Mississippi, Jenkins Plantation, 1929

Barney's responsibilities were growing like kudzu. The men depended on him to thwart Batson, the Williamses depended on him to keep body and soul together, and now Violet and her daughter Dora needed help to work their fields. Not that Violet asked. Barney felt responsible for her all the same and talked the other croppers into helping her plant her ten acres and chop her cotton. She worked right beside them, a column of color and beauty among the men, their tungsten skin and faded canvas overalls a mere duotone background.

What he didn't have time for was his own brood, an unsatisfying experience if there ever was one. He left the children to Lula, the gulf between them now wide and impassable. The boys showed no interest in Barney and joined him in the cotton only reluctantly. *How have I failed to win their affection,* he wondered. *Couldn't they see how important he was to the whole plantation, how this was just the start?* Before long, he'd have some money put by to plant his strawberry fields. Until then, his men, *they* needed him.

Barney just kept putting one worn-out boot in front of the other. No need to look back. He'd plant those strawberries one day, maybe even hire all these men away from Jenkins to help him. He was imagining that one night—the look on Jenkins's face, Batson's too—on his way home from the fire and the corn liquor with the men when he noticed lantern light framing the window at Violet's. He missed her, their conversations, her power, her irreverence, a thought that exploded around the liquor in his belly and stopped him short. He crept around the cabin and found the narrow step to the back door. He tapped lightly and stood back. The door opened a sliver.

"Barney, what you doing here? Are Joshua and Belle alright?"

"They're fine, Violet. Fine. I just . . ." Barney plumbed for a reason to be at her backdoor in the pitch black. "Well, I'm just stopping to check on you. How you getting by?"

"Not that it's your business, but we are surviving. Mrs. Jenkins, she give me a bit of work at the house, and thanks to you and the others," she said, letting the door creak open another inch, "we've got our cotton and corn in. I thank you for that."

"I never told you, but I'm sorry about Reggie."

"Well, I ain't!" she said, surprising him. "He was a damn cantankerous man. Lazy too. We are better off without him, even in our present circumstances."

Barney stood peering at her one eye and the side of her face through the narrow opening, her purple turban shed for the night, her hair wild and full, the lantern light from behind illuminating its dark halo. He smiled.

"Even just three inches of you, Violet, you are beautiful."

Violet slowly closed the door, snuffing out the lantern light. He limped home in the dark, his back tired, his mind confused.

In the fields the next day, they caught each other's eyes and looked away so many times that the staring and the turning away bore into the rhythm of their hoes striking the ground. In the afternoon, under the oak tree as they stopped for water in the shade, Clemmie Mae's husband Otis handed the ladle to Violet.

"Don't know if you can spare her, Violet, but perhaps your

Dora could come over and help with the new baby, maybe stay the night? Clemmie Mae is feeling poorly."

Violet nodded, and for a flash of a second, she saw Barney's blue eyes over the lip of the ladle.

In the dark, Violet's skin and the moonless night sky pressing on the window seemed one and the same. She had thrown wide the back door when he'd arrived after midnight and pulled him inside and into her arms as if their assignation had been planned by far more than the syncopation of their glances in the field that afternoon.

They hurriedly undressed each other, the still-hot July air rising off their bodies, their scents—hers of soap and candle wax and tomato vines, his of dirt and tobacco and corn silage—tumbling out of their clothes.

Barney was so hungry for her that his breath came in strangled bursts. No one had touched him for a long time. Her lips on his chest were mysterious as if they spoke another language.

Now they were quiet, their bodies touching from the shoulder, all the way down to their feet. Barney liked the long, smooth feel of her. The moonless, starless night made time impossible to track. For once, Barney was not thinking of the sunrise, the waiting cotton.

"Violet—"

"Shh," she whispered. *She doesn't want to think of what's next either,* he thought. It suited him fine. The minutes passed, or an hour.

"Barney, best if you go now."

"If you say so."

"And best if you don't come back."

"Why?"

"Do you need a million reasons or just one? Cause I can give you a million."

"Violet, no one will know, if that's what you're worried about. I'm not a bragging man."

"You think no one will know, but this plantation is thin as parchment paper. No one can hide anything or cover it up for long. No one will think a thing about you bedding a Black woman, but it will be the end of me. Dora and I will be turned out, and that there is your first reason in the million of them. And one is enough."

Barney dressed in the dark without saying a word. "One is not enough for me," he said at the door, pulling on his boots.

Barney called it luck, the kind you make for yourself by just wanting it so. Dora and Maudie were fast friends. They helped out at the Williamses' and at Clemmie Mae's, and sometimes got permission from their mothers to spend the nights together at the Williamses'. For Maudie, it was a night away from her sullen mother, her tormenting brothers, and her clinging baby sister. For Barney, it was a chance to test Violet's pronouncement that he should just stay away.

Three nights in that hot summer of 1929, he came to her backdoor at midnight. Three times, she let him in. They didn't speak of the million reasons anymore.

The cotton harvest was late, a conspiracy of boll weevils and a parched sky. Barney's men were nervous, worried that Batson's propensity to cheat them would be redoubled. None of the men knew enough math to add their own cotton weights, so for the last three years, Barney had kept a ledger of each man's deliveries to the cotton gin. When Batson claimed far lower weights at the end of the season, Barney trudged up the hill to Sheldon Jenkins' front porch to show him his meticulous entries, complete with receipts from the gin, on behalf of his fellow farmers. Jenkins was amused by the contest between Barney and Batson, and because harvests had been extraordinary, he'd order Batson to pay the men the difference.

"No need to be stingy, Billy Ray. Just give the men their due."

But this year, that sort of magnanimity seemed unlikely, what with the price of cotton dropping, and the harvest itself far from robust.

But one thing buoyed everyone's spirits. On the afternoon of September 25, a man carrying a small cloth satchel came over the hill from town, toward the men and Violet, who were harvesting the Grears' acres.

"Who do you expect that is?" Barney asked. They all stopped, their cotton bags near full at the end of the day.

"Why, it's Ira!" one of the men yelled. They all left their bags in the rows and ran up the hill to meet him.

"Ira Williams! We weren't expecting you for months yet!" Violet said, throwing her arms around the slender young man who looked, to an honest eye, diminished, faded, worn.

"They just come into my cell block this morning, called my name and said, 'Time to go!' I didn't argue with 'em!"

All twenty farmers gathered around him, jostling to hug him, holding him out at arm's length to declare he looked pretty good, considering.

"Let him go!" Barney said. "Ira, you go on up to your mama and daddy. We'll have a celebration tonight!" Barney said.

"No. No sir. I thought I hated cotton with all that was in me, but you have no idea how happy I am to see this cotton. And all of you. If it's all the same to y'all, I'll just stay here with you and pick to the end of the day."

That night, Ira joined the men around the fire, the liquor, the tobacco. They asked him for stories of Parchman, and he just stared off, the events of those years already the things of nightmares, not daydreams.

"I'm gonna be a good man the rest of my life. I've been to hell, and I ain't goin' back."

Barney patted him on the back.

"Ira, you couldn't have come home on a better day. We'll be harvesting your acres tomorrow. Or what there is to harvest. We've known better years while you was up there."

"I heard what you done, asking the governor for a pardon. And my daddy told me you've kept him and mama together, and alive. I never thought I'd see them again. It ain't no way enough, but I thank you."

"Not just me, Ira. Every one of these men, and their women, even their children, they all helped. You're . . . our brother." The chatter stopped. The pine spitting on the fire punctuated the dark. *Could* he have really said that? Even thought it? Of Black folk?

Barney tried it again. "*My* brother."

In the morning, they all gathered at the Williamses' acres. There had been fires down south in the pine forests due to the dry conditions, and the sunrise was pink with particulate. Barney never thought he'd miss the miserable, sweltering steam bath of a Mississippi morning, but today, dew was nowhere to be found on the cotton, and the air was electric, crackling, as if it might explode. He felt naked and uneasy under the ruby sky.

At ten o'clock, Tobias Grear returned from the gin and caught up with Barney on the picking line.

"That Batson, he's at it again. Here's my weight from this morning. He added it to the other days, and lordy, Barney, this don't seem right." Barney pulled his ledger from his pocket and looked at the numbers. Batson was shorting him.

"Damn it all to hell, Tobias. Now I'm going to have to go up and see Jenkins."

Barney was gone nearly an hour—an unsatisfactory hour at that—because, just as he feared, Jenkins was not as amused by Barney pleading the case for his fellow farmers as he had been in fat years. In the end, all he could get out of Jenkins was the suggestion that folks who rock the boat too many times might find themselves, and their whole family, hitting the grit. Jenkins ended the conversation by lifting the pages of the *Stone County Enterprise* in front of his face, no longer willing to entertain an audience with someone so inferior. Barney stomped all the way back to the Williamses' acres. What would he tell his men now? He'd have to admit he couldn't get them their fair share.

When he rounded the bend close to the field, he expected to see all the farmers and Violet stretched out in the rows, heads down, cotton sacks on their shoulders or at their feet. Instead, he saw everyone gathered in a rough circle, and in the middle, Billy Ray Batson on his big mare, and in his hand, a bull whip. Ira Williams was cowering on the ground. Barney started running.

"I told you, nigger, there ain't no place on this plantation for a criminal." Batson flicked the whip hard on Ira's shoulder.

Violet hollered, "Leave him alone!"

"Shut up, bitch, lest you want the same."

Barney ran harder, and when he passed the mule team reined to the cotton wagon at the edge of the field, he yanked off two of the leather wagon lines.

Batson lowered the whip on Ira three more times, the other farmers too terrified to stand between them.

When Barney was but a few feet from the bay, on Batson's blind side, he launched himself at Batson and pulled him from the saddle.

"You son of a bitch, leave that boy alone!"

Batson was surprised to find Barney pinning him to the ground, one end of the leather wagon lines wrapped tight around his right fist. Batson tried to heave the bull whip at Barney's face, but Barney was so filled with rage he grabbed the whip and tossed it into the circle of men. Violet realized Barney's peril.

"Let him go, Barney!"

Barney looked over at Ira, blood seeping through his shirt.

He raised his right arm and brought the leather lines down on Batson's face, again and again. Batson screamed, clawing at Barney, his face a bloody mess. Barney saw no way out. He would have to kill him. Grabbing the ends of the lines in each hand, he bent over and wrapped them around Batson's neck, and twisted, the lines tearing at Batson's skin. Batson, silent now, bucked his legs, flailed his arms.

"Barney!" Violet yelled. She rushed him, yelling at the others. "Stop him! Stop him!" Ira crawled up on his knees, threw his arms around Barney, and pulled him off Batson, who now showed little resistance. Violet pulled the wagon lines off his neck, and Batson drew a rattled breath.

"Stovall, you're a dead man," he said in a whisper.

Edith Jackson acquired her style in New Orleans, her schooling in Virginia, and her tenacity in the cotton fields of Mississippi. Inside her white columned Wiggins home, designed to look like a plantation house ("Why should the white folk get all the columns?"), she held court, the doyenne of Stone County Negroes, their only hope for cold, hard cash.

She sat regally in a high-backed wicker chair, receiving folks most days, and sometimes into the night. She was part of a secret network of Southern Black women bankers who held and loaned out the meager earnings of sharecroppers, woodsmen, housekeepers, Mississippi River boatmen, and a few bookies and con artists to boot. She seeded her bank with a considerable amount of her own cash, the sources of which were never discussed. And besides, every Sunday, Miss Jackson arrived in high style at the Baptist church, where her pious hats and upraised hands, not to mention her generous donations to the offering plate, induced a kind of holy amnesia in her fellow congregants.

Violet Byrd set on a small needlepoint chair in front of her, her purple turban in place, her best dress on, a broach at her throat.

"Miss Jackson, you heard all about Barney Stovall and Billy Ray Batson?"

"It has been told to me, yes. A dangerous situation, to be sure." Miss Jackson folded her hands and watched Violet closely. She was no stranger to violence, or drastic measures. But what of Mrs. Violet Byrd?

"Ma'am, me and the other croppers, we know Batson is out for blood. I washed up and come straight from the field. If we don't get the Stovalls out of here—tonight—Batson and his friends, they are going to lynch him, maybe his sons too."

"How many in the family?"

"There's Barney, his wife, and six children. Their oldest girl, Nettie, she's married to that Davis boy, and they're safe, I think, it being the Davis family and all."

"Mm-hmm." Edith shook her head. "What are you proposing, Violet?"

"We've got Barney's cotton wagon and his mule team. I think if we just pile all them Stovalls in there and cover them with cotton sacks, we can get them down to the train in Gulfport before Batson comes after them. He's hurt pretty bad. I don't suspect he'll be after them 'til tomorrow. Barney's got family in California, so we'll send 'em that a way."

"How much are the tickets?"

"Three hundred dollars."

Edith hummed and tapped her fingers on the arms of her throne. "That's a lot of money, Violet, to help a white man."

"I know, Miss Jackson. But he has been a man of his word to all of us. I'm sure you know about Ira Williams, and Joshua and Belle, but every cropper at Jenkins's place has made money, some for the first time ever."

Edith smiled. "Yes, child, I know, because I'm holding some of it. But I don't make loans on money I can never get back. That's just bad business. And if I fail, then everyone else fails too."

"Well, I didn't come empty handed," Violet said. "I brought this deed. It's to the land Barney bought seven years ago, to grow strawberries. Ain't been touched. Barney sent it along with me."

Edith looked it over. There was no way those acres were worth $300. She had half a mind to refuse, just give Batson his prey, let him hang a white man, and be done with it. No loss. She looked down at Violet, who sat stone still on her small chair, her face full of fear and anguish. There was also the chance that Jenkins would rein Batson in, that maybe this would all blow over. Or not. It might be to her advantage to help Stovall disappear. He may have made her some money, but he was a troublemaker, pure and simple, and rabble rousing was never good for business. She narrowed her eyes at Violet.

"Alright, Mrs. Byrd." She pulled a small leather wallet from the folds of her dress and counted out $300. "Don't waste any time. Sooner that family gets on the train, the better."

"Lu, we have to go."

"Why in tarnation did you beat him up? Have you lost all sense? Ernie said you almost killed him!"

"I don't have time to explain now. We've got to get what few things we can, a change of clothes maybe, and get out there in that wagon."

Barney and Lula stood in the middle of the shack, their six children wrapped in a circle around them. Maudie was crying. Nora Mae was wailing.

"I ain't going. I ain't leavin' Mr. Joshua," Nora Mae howled. Barney clamped a hand on her thin shoulder.

"For once, that child is right. I can't leave here without telling Nettie goodbye!" Lula said.

Violet arrived at the open door.

"Lula, there ain't no time. Batson's going to lynch him."

All the caterwauling came to a halt. No one said a word. Lula grasped her throat, warding off the hangman's rope.

"Boys," she said in a quiet low voice. "Get your britches and a shirt. Maudie, pack up some biscuits and put that ham in a towel."

In ten minutes, the Stovalls gathered what few things might fit with them in the cotton wagon. Out in the moonlit yard, Violet and four of the men packed the kids head to foot, covering them with half-empty cotton sacks.

Lula lingered in the doorway. She looked over the possessions she was leaving behind: faded quilts, a few pots, a stack of chipped crockery, a wash tub. Worthless. But those things had traveled with her from Oklahoma to Arizona, Montana to Mississippi, the only constants in a peripatetic existence.

"We always leave with less than we come with," she said, but no one heard.

The road rattled under Barney, rumbling through his chest. The flying departure made his heart pound, his head throb. He was terrified his men and Violet would pay the price for his recklessness. And now it was even worse. Violet insisted on driving the wagon.

"Why you, Violet?" Barney cried.

"Because I can lie better than all these boys," she said, sweeping her arm over the men. "And they are less likely to stop me on the road than some Negro man with a loaded wagon. They *know* he stole it."

Barney couldn't figure the money out. The deed to the land over in Madison wouldn't cover the cost of getting them to California, and he had no idea how Violet pulled it off. All the men took up a collection, and pressed another $30 into his hand. He'd never be able to repay them. Most of them will be scattered to the four winds in a year's time, he thought, especially once Batson metes out his punishment, whatever that may be. Better if fewer of them are known to be helping the Stovalls at all. Which brought Barney right back to Violet. In his fear, he could barely breathe under the weight of the cotton.

Brother. That's what he called Ira just yesterday. Brother! Now all of it was ripped apart, everything he wanted. Violet! Like a load of cotton at the gin, he weighed it all out: Batson, Jenkins, the white jury that sent Ira up for protecting his own, Lula's damned Uncle Fred, those United Fruit men, his contemptible brothers, all on one side of the scale. On the other side, Charles York from Pana, Luis Bolon, Ezra Sykes, Luzelba, the banana farmers, his plantation men. Ira. Violet. Who were his people, who his enemies? It was the same old conundrum he'd worked over on the *San Juan* seventeen years ago. And what of Lula and the children, even those boys in Montana? To whom did he owe his allegiance: The white world he was born into and lashed to, or the Black and Brown world that bewitched him, consumed him, filled him with passion?

He moaned, shifting in the narrow corner of the wagon, and felt Nora Mae's blond head by his knees. He'd barely touched the child in her mean little life. Never rocked her, never walked with her by the creek catching crawdads. He reached down and pulled her up to him, into the circle of his arms. She was tiny and fragile, and he could feel her heart thumping, faster than a small bird's. She must be terrified too. They all must be. He stroked her hair. Nora Mae searched in the cramped space between them until she found his hand. In his open palm, she carefully pressed an Indian nickel, folding his fingers over it.

Yesterday, Ira had been his brother and Nora Mae nothing more than a mouth to feed! A wail filled his throat, and he let it go, into the cotton and the pitiless night.

GLEN

Montana and Oregon, 1927–1929

The farmland running up to the orphanage fence offered Glen little cover. He crouched and ran, clinging to ditches and swaths of late summer's uncut hay, until he made it to a row of cottonwoods about three miles from Twin Bridges. He knew he should shed his telltale orphanage overalls in favor of the clothes he'd stolen. He opened the canvas bag, and there on top, the worn copy of *Huck Finn* gave him an idea.

He lay on his belly on a nearby stream bank, his hands hanging still in the cold water, until a trout swam by, nudging his cold white fingers. Glen had him in a second and slapped his head on a rock. With his stolen kitchen knife, the very same one with which he had threatened Wilbur, he slit the stunned fish up the belly, drenched his overalls with the blood, and cut a jagged swath right through the bloodied fabric. He didn't think anyone would believe a robber would throttle a hungry orphan without two cents to his name, but it might slow down the sheriff and the dogs, cast a doubt on his disappearance.

And besides, he felt a moment of solidarity with ole Huck when he bled the fish on his overalls, recalling Huck's similar deception in Pappy's shack. Glen was alone, more alone than he'd been as an abandoned boy, an orphan, a wielder of fists. Save for Huck. Huck was alive in his mind, barefoot and freckled. Glen could almost see him, almost smell the Mississippi. He threw the bloody overalls in the ditch so they would be easy to find and hitched up his new britches.

He was slipping through the line, away from those who would tackle him, haul him straight back to Twin Bridges. He knew better than to make for the railroad outside town. They'd be watching. That's how they found two Twin Bridges boys the year before. He walked, only at night, sleeping in barns or barrow ditches during the day, gnawing on his biscuits, picking a lone yellow apple from a tree. He walked north, toward the big rail hub in Butte, hoping to head west on a freight, see the ocean. He made it in three days, played out as a steelhead trout on a stout line. He walked down the Butte streets, crowded with pit miners, languages he did not know—Finnish, Italian—rippling the stippled air, thick with wood smoke and mining grit.

Safe now, he thought. He stopped at a bakery window, the rows of bread and rolls thinned out at the end of the day. Strays, like him. He fingered the empty pockets of his stolen jeans, wishing for a nickel. A man in white watched him from the counter inside and was suddenly at his side.

"Young fella, bakery closes at five o'clock. I leave the day-olds on the back stoop."

Glen perched on his haunches on a big rock overhang at the edge of the Butte rail yard, trains coming and going slowly on the parallel tracks, clanking as slack cars were caught up and pulled on west toward Idaho or east toward the Montana plains. Glen watched the play of cars rolling left to right like the quarterback he was, sizing up the speed, the distance, the leap he would have to make. The screech of steel on steel made him nervous, imagining his leg or arm snared between wheels and track. He watched intently, slowly tearing and eating pieces from a loaf of rye bread left outside the bakery's back door.

The last light of the evening receded west. In its afterglow, Glen saw shadowy figures slipping between the tracks, hopping silently over the linked cars. He stood, leaned forward, squinted. On the rail nearest him a boxcar sat, its open door a seduction. Men slipped in, disappeared. Glen shoved the bread back into his canvas bag and slung it over his shoulder, crouching again, ready to drop down onto the yard and make for the open door. But a whistle and a shout, men running toward him with dogs and lanterns and torches, kept him on the ledge. Right in front of him, the railroad guards jumped onto the open car and hauled out the tramps and hobos, tossing them on the tracks.

"Git on outta here! Git!" they yelled. The dogs whined and pleaded against their chains, but the guards held them back, laughing. The evicted escaped quickly into the night.

"That should do it for tonight, Stanley."

Stanley, the 'bo chaser, hopped up into the open doorway and wagged his lantern toward the engine, six cars up. The engine revved. Glen's hope for a ride dimmed.

The railroad guards sauntered back toward the station, lighting up smokes, laughing at the hapless hobos. Their voices faded. Glen was contemplating the open door of the freight car when he saw the strangest thing. From atop the car, a figure stood, leaned over, grabbed the open frame of the doorway, and vaulted inside. From up the tracks, Glen could see a lantern bobbing toward him. One of the engineers coming back to slide the door closed, he guessed. The engines revved again; the train quivered. Glen jumped from the rock and sprinted the last few feet to the car. He pitched himself over the threshold, his momentum rolling him into a corner. A second later, the engineer rounded the end of the car and rolled the thundering door closed.

Glen blinked, then blinked again. For a boy used to moonless Montana nights pricked by starlight—nights so vast and dark they could feel like the edge of the known world—this total eclipse was bottomless. The train heaved forward, knocking Glen back into the corner. In the deathly void, the chugging, rolling car seemed sinister, and a cold fear settled on him.

"Dark, ain't it?" said a voice from the corner directly across from him. He'd forgotten about his fellow traveler. He pulled his canvas bag to his chest.

"Yeah, a bit."

The man chuckled. "What's your name, boy?" the phantom asked.

"Wilkie."

"Where you headed?"

"Wherever this train goes."

"Well, then, when we arrive, you'll be there," the phantom said, and chuckled again.

The phantom's voice conveyed no malice. There was a laconic fullness to his vowels, and it reminded Glen of his mother's voice, that lazy Oklahoma twang. It had been seven years now since he'd heard it.

"You from the South, mister?" Glen asked.

"Born there, but moved north to Chicago when I was six."

"Do they talk like you in Chicago?"

The man chuckled again. "Only on my side of town, the South side. The Darkie side. Call it whatever you want. It's where my family went to get away from Jim Crow Mississippi. Fact is, my daddy, the damned old fool, he named me Jim Crow Davis. Said he never wanted me to forget the Man who was holding my chains. And it musta worked, because I can't forget."

"Your name Jim?"

"Sure thing. Why that surprise you? Never met no Negro man named Jim before?"

"Well, sir, I never met no Negro man period, Jim or no. But here in my bag, I got *The Adventures of Huckleberry Finn*, and there's a slave—"

"Ah, yes, Nigger Jim. That poor soul."

Glen thought on Huck and Jim and all that befell them. If this Jim was like *that* Jim, well . . .

"My mother, she left me in Montana, then her Uncle Fred put me in an orphanage. I ran away," Glen said. The pitch-dark car was a confessional; the phantom Jim, a priest. "And I made a boy fall through the hayloft door, and die."

The train picked up speed, the wheels and track rattling into each other, fusing into one long whine. Neither Jim nor Glen spoke for a while, waiting for their bodies to reach equilibrium with the train's velocity.

"What you want from me, boy?" Jim asked.

"Don't know. Just wanted someone to hear the truth."

"The boy that died. Did he deserve it, the shove you gave him?"

"I didn't shove him! Just threatened him. With a knife. Wilbur was . . . hurting the little guys, things I can't even say out loud. Wasn't right. Tom Sawyer said that there was right and wrong and you have to know the difference. And Wilbur was wrong. Up there in the hayloft, he backed away from me, wind blew open the door, and he fell. Bad timing, I guess."

"You could call it that, or you could call it fate. Your fate, his fate. Karl Marx said the happiest man is the man who has made the most people happy. 'Spect more people are happy with Wilbur dead, don't you think?"

"Yeah, I 'spect so. Everyone 'cept Wilbur. Who is this Karl Marx fellow?"

"Besides Abraham Lincoln, he was the greatest man what

ever lived. Lincoln, he emancipated *my* people. But we . . . you and me, and most everyone . . . We are all slaves of another kind, slaves to the Man, the people that own everything—our bodies, our labor, our coming and going. We don't even own our thoughts! But Marx, he had a way to emancipate us all, give us the power to come and go and work as we please."

"He did? What is it?" Glen and Jim were inching closer to each other.

"It's like a compact, an agreement. Everyone should work as much as they can, and everyone should get as much as they need. No more, no less. And your mind is free."

Now it was Glen who laughed.

"You mean, if you just work as hard as you want, you get, what? A house, food, pocket money, clothes . . . a car . . . no matter what? This man you're talking about, the Man who controls everything, like my Uncle Fred or Mr. Stiles at the orphanage, they ain't gonna give me nothing! I worked hard for them, and they treated me like a plow horse."

"Well, see, the problem is, that's because they *can*. You know what a revolution is, boy? The Man ain't gonna let go our reins unless we *overthrow* him. Tear him down. Institute a *new order* where everyone gets what they need, and no one gets bigger britches than anybody else. You know where Russia is? The people there, they had a revolution, and now the poor folks like us, they are in charge."

Glen thought about it for a while. "Is it working?"

"They say so."

"So is that why you're on this train? You going to a revolution?"

Jim's sigh was so loud and disconsolate, Glen heard it over the train's rattle and whine.

"No, Wilkie. Wish that I was! But one man can't make a revolution, and there's hardly enough of us Communists. At least not now. No, my older brother Parnell, he's working on a lumber operation in Oregon, little company town called Maxville, up in the corner near Washington. Southern fellas own it, and they brought up a bunch of Negro lumberjacks who know how to fell and haul pine trees. Parnell, he's the Negro boss; sent for me, said he had a job. That's where I'm going. At least I'll be outside, outta the city. I hate the city. The Man is everywhere."

"Do you think he might have a job for me?"

"Maybe, if we don't starve to death before we get there. I watched you from up top, eating a loaf of bread. You got any left? I got a jar of mincemeat here. We throw in together, and that be a meal. What do you say to that?"

"I say it's time we shook hands." Glen clutched his bag and crawled toward Jim's corner. In the dark, they laid out dinner on Jim's blanket and talked through the night and the dawn, though the rail car never gave agency to the morning light.

Glen clambered onto the boxcar a frightened, aimless orphan. The tenets of his worldview would scarcely fill a shotgun shell, namely that football was good, Barney was bad, nobody wanted him, and that he would have to bungle through alone somehow. By the time the train reached Maxville, Oregon, he was a Marxist, a boy with a mission, and Jim—his North Star.

The train rolled to a stop about nine in the morning.

"What now?" Glen asked Jim.

"Well, just you wait. When that door rolls open, we are either in Maxville, or a world of hurt."

Five minutes of silence passed, the sound of boots on gravel, muffled voices, and then the door rolled open.

"Jimmy Bird!" A tall, muscular Black man in cork boots and an old plaid wool coat jumped into the car and ran to Jim, pulling him into a tight embrace. "You made it! This is the third train through here since I thought you'd arrive. I was fearing you wouldn't make it!"

"Got confused in the Chicago yard. Took me a day to figure out which freight to hop. Then in Butte, had to change trains, and the 'bo chasers were mean bastards. Got thrown off one, finally caught this one. This here's Wilkie. He needs a job too. You got one for him?"

Parnell looked Wilkie over. "Looks stout enough. I'll ask the whitey crew boss if he needs another choker setter."

They jumped off the boxcar together, and now Glen saw Black men jumping from other freight cars down the line. Parnell waived to them, and they gathered in a circle.

"Fellas, this here is Maxville. Daylight's a wastin'. Let's go."

By eleven, Wilkie had a job on the white crew, and a bunk bed in the white quarters.

He caught up to Jim as the men headed to the chow hall, which, he soon learned, was also divided into Black and white.

"Why is it like this, Jim? Why can't I stay with you and Parnell?"

"Guess the Man is everywhere here too, Wilkie," Jim said, his voice low, disappointed. "Doncha worry. You come on over to our bunkhouse. After dark. For a visit. Don't want no trouble."

Glen's first job for the Bowman-Hicks Lumber Company was choker setter. He learned the job in less than an hour, dashing in to wrap the end of a steel cable around a felled and limbed tree, and then get out of the way. The donkey puncher, a man running a steam-powered capstan a ways down the line, winched the log to a horse-drawn cart that would haul the log to the nearby rail line.

He was starving from empty days on the road and his cold all-nighter on the train. Before he left for the woods, he wolfed down—too quickly—a pile of beans, fat back, and cornbread in the chow hall. The load on his stomach threatened to come up every time he bent over a log. The foreman, Carl Scruggs, had stiff, wiry gray hair like a terrier, and a mouth full of crooked tobacco-yellow teeth behind mean, thin lips. He bellowed at Glen constantly.

"Faster, then get the fuck out of the way!" The three other choker setters laughed at Glen's rabbity leaps through snaring piles of limbs and tree trunks, forgetting their own ineptitude only weeks before. By four in the afternoon, the whistle punk blew a final "All clear!" and a quarter mile away, Wilkie heard the powerful steam donkey sigh its last grind for the day.

On the two mile wagon ride back to Maxville, Glen looked up at the Wallowa mountains, sharp and tall and snow-tipped from last night's late September snowfall, the first of the season. As soon as the sun dropped into the Western valleys, the sweat chilled on his damp canvas pants and shirt. He had no idea how to navigate the camp or the four hundred workers. It was like the early days of the orphanage. He didn't know his place, or how to settle down to the plow lines.

A few days later, after dark, he made his way across the meadow to the Black bunk houses and knocked on a few doors until he found Parnell and Jim. He sat next to their potbellied stove.

"How you gettin' along, Wilkie?" Jim asked. "You eatin' OK? How're the men in your bunk house?"

"Well, chow's good. Lots of it. I was hungry enough to eat the north end of a horse going south first few days. But the fellas, I tried talking to them about the revolution, and they don't seem very interested."

Parnell and Jim burst out laughing and pounded Wilkie on the back.

"Of course they ain't! They think they are already kings of the hill. You notice how much better your bunk house is than ours?" Parnell explained. "That's how the Man does it. Makes whitey feel superior so there's no need for revolution. They always at the top of the heap."

"You be careful, Wilkie," Jim said soberly. "Sometimes work ain't the best place to talk about revolution. Makes the boss man nervous."

But Glen was a righteous boy, all of seventeen now. He cradled a white-hot loathing for Barney, and something not quite so absolute for his mother. She was bruised fruit, not rotten like his stepfather, and nothing was going to change his mind on that. So his boxcar conversion, from orphan to revolutionary, could simply not be washed away in the deep, bottomless blue of Wallowa Lake. For the next two years, Glen just plowed straight ahead, said his piece and made the boss man nervous, damn him all to hell.

That didn't stop him from excelling at every job on the crew, from whistle punk to tree faller. Or from earning the begrudging respect of the white crew, even as they grew weary of his preacher-thumping condemnation of the Man and the tragedy of class struggle.

Glen's brief education on the boxcar made him hungry for more, and when he found a worn copy of Marx's *Communist Manifesto* at the bottom of a book bin in the white school house (even education was segregated at Maxville) he added it to his equally worn copy of *The Adventures of Huckleberry Finn*. Sometimes when he wondered if he was doing right siding with Jim, Parnell and the forty Black lumberjacks, instead of his own 350 white ones, he would thumb to the back of *Huck Finn*. There, he'd read Huck's own tormented argument with himself. Was he going to turn in runaway slave Jim and secure a spot in both heaven and community, or save his friend Jim's hide? And then he'd revel in Huck's decision. "All right, then," said Huck. "I'll go to hell."

The Black crewmen, who worked alongside Glen, offered more enthusiastic appreciation for Glen's skill in the forests, where he showed an unflagging impartiality toward the Black workers as he moved up the line of authority. By nineteen, he was running a crew of both Black and white workers, though the Black workers were still expected, by Glen's boss Carl, to handle the shittiest, most dangerous jobs.

There wasn't a football in camp, but he joined the camp's white baseball team, and socked the ball out of the rough grassy field into the woods more than any other logger. But when the team had the chance to play in a local league, Glen refused to pick up the bat unless the best Black players were on the team too—a gambit he lost. So he simply took up playing with the Black team, where he felt more at home anyway. Hell if he knew why, but he suspected the answer was buried somewhere in *Huck Finn* or the *Communist Manifesto*, or both.

Chapter 15

GLEN

US Army, 1929–1930

"I play a little football, yes sir."

The army recruiting officer at the Ashland, Oregon, armory appraised Glen with a new eye. Maybe there was more to this mud-splattered lumberjack than he thought. So far, all he'd been able to get out of him was that yes, he could read and write and do his sums, knew how to plow a field, pick hops and set a choker, pretty much like every other boy in Oregon in 1929. But something about his powerful shoulders, his muscled thighs the chair could barely contain, made the recruiter ask about football.

"Is that right, son."

Glen dug into the chair legs with his boot heels. He hated it when anyone called him "son," but he held his tongue. He wanted a regular meal, a bed with a clean mattress, money. He was done with logging camps, the cold, the danger, life slipping away at the tree line. Worse than being a Stovall back in the orphanage, he had no name. He was not a Wilkerson, nor a Wilkie, he was "Hey, boy!" . . . No one at all.

At least not at first. And at the end, he was just a "goddamnniggerlover!" That was what Carl had yelled at his back six months ago when he just walked away. Glen didn't kill Carl, but only for the love of his friend Jim. Jimmy Bird would have said,

"Don't throw decent money after bad, Wilkie. The Man ain't worth the trouble."

"Because, son"—there it was again from across the recruiter's desk—"it takes a special fellow to get into this man's army. It's a peacetime army. Lots of young men mustered out and sent home after the Great War. Not that many of us, now. Maybe 125,000 regular army, and nobody in Washington clamoring to add any more." Glen squirmed in his chair and glanced out the window at the ragtag March snow shrouding the Douglas firs.

"But there are a few generals who would like to see army football turn around here on the West Coast. You know our Jarheads lost to those navy midshipmen down in San Diego a couple a years ago, 123–0!"

Glen whistled.

"Tell me about your football playing, son. Did you play in high school?"

"Uh, yes sir, in a way." Glen sat up straight and conjured an earnest but sad smile on his handsome, square head and told the story he'd recited to himself that morning, walking in from the woods. "The flu took Mom and Pop in Montana, 1918. I was eight, only child. Ended up in an orphanage. They had a team. I was the captain, quarterback."

"Hmm. Who'd you play?"

"Local high schools. Beat 'em all too."

"You orphans beat the local boys?"

"Yes sir. Trounced 'em."

"Well now, son, that could be your ticket. Yes, it surely could. Give me a few minutes to make a call."

Two weeks later, after an audition in front of an army assistant coach sent all the way up from San Francisco, Glen was issued a single-breasted brown jacket with four brass buttons, a russet-colored belt, khaki shirt, black necktie, service cap, leggings, and a pair of boots. It was the first time in his life he'd put on an entirely new set of clothes. Soon, he was on a train, bound for Fort Lewis outside Tacoma, Washington. There was a base football team, he was told, and they'd see what he could do. Just as soon as he finished basic training, that is.

Glen was quite used to regimentation. The orphanage, the lumber camps. Take a number, stand in line, someone always shouting at him. But it was his choice now.

"Two hots and a cot," they said. Well that was just fine. Lights out at nine o'clock, the April Washington sky still hanging on to the sun. The glow didn't bother him. He was asleep, on the first clean bed he could remember, and when he dreamed, he was in a rail car, black and empty, save for one man: Jim Crow Davis. *Jimmy Bird.*

In Glen's waking moments, Jim was his invisible platoon buddy, his southern drawl whispering cautions about the Man, who at this moment was Glen's drill sergeant, barking marching and rifle cleaning orders. Or there was Jim's wry chuckle over the meticulous attention to tent pitching, or the futility of bayonet exercises.

"Me, now, Wilkie, I would just shoot the son of a bitch. Ain't that why you got a rifle? And really, you're a football player, not a soldier. Who cares if the football team is good at close-order drill? Only the Man, that's who."

One morning in class the squad leader pulled a manual from his utilities: SIGNALS.

"Whistles and arm signals, men," he said, tapping the booklet. "This is how we keep each other safe."

Jimmy Bird fell silent in Glen's head. Glen was filled with dread, the memory of Jim's last day creeping in.

The squad leader droned on, chirping out whistles and flapping his arms like a flightless bird.

"Danger. That's three short whistles, men, like this . . ."

But Glen was no longer in a classroom at Camp Lewis. He was in the Wallowas, in a dense copse of pine trees, high on a ridge. Down slope, two choker setters were slinging cables that hung from a highline around a bucked log. Further down slope, almost beyond the sound of Glen's voice, Jimmy Bird and two other Black loggers were limbing two massive pines. Glen hated this new highline, an aerial cable that swung bucked trees above the fray of brush and tree trunks down toward the donkey puncher.

"What the fuck's the matter with you, Wilkerson?" Carl barked the day they hoisted the highline in place for the first time. "Can't you see how much faster this'll be? No more logs hung up on trunks and slash!"

But Glen was terrified of the flying trees, swaying menacingly in the wind, as if they planned to exact revenge on the loggers who felled them.

"Only a matter of time, Carl, and you'll be burying someone 'cause of this thing," he said, pointing up at the cable shimmering thirty feet above them in the sunshine. Carl spit tobacco, just missing Glen's boot. "Only the damn fools will die, the idiots too stupid to get the hell out of the way."

Glen's job that morning was to send all the trees cut the day before, lying haphazardly on the steep slope, down to a waiting wagon. The rail yard was holding up a shipment for this final load. Carl was demanding that the job be finished by lunchtime. Glen was pushing his crew to limb the trees, hook them up, and maneuver them downslope as quickly as possible. He was rummy, tired from a late night lying out under the stars talking to Jimmy Bird, who seemed intent on escaping the human race.

"Wilkie, don't make no difference what I do. The scriptures, they say no matter where I go . . . If I make my bed in Sheol, God is there. But what good is that? Because the Man, he's there too. Heaven or hell, like my old man predicted, he ain't gonna let me go."

"What about revolution? Are you giving up on that?"

Jim chuckled. "I think revolution is for you whiteys. If it comes, it's gonna pass me by too. Ain't no place in this world for a Negro man to stand on his own."

"Listen, Jim, I've been thinking. Let's blow outta here. Remember when Bobby Billings left and came back in that army uniform? Why can't we do that, join the army? Got to be better than this. We could see the world, maybe. I ain't never even seen the ocean."

"Ah, Wilkie, the story is gonna be the same. White man in charge, Black man under his boot."

Glen paced the barren rock at the top of the slope, watching his crew. When the two men just below him set their chokers, stepped back, and gave him thumbs up, he signaled to the whistle punk halfway down the slope. "Give the all clear!" he yelled. The whistle punk, the newest member of the crew, gave two quick and one long pull on the jerk line, letting loose three bursts from the steam whistle: short, short, long. That was the donkey puncher's cue way down below to begin cranking the highline toward him, and everyone else's signal to move out of the way. Logs coming down.

Except on this particular morning, Jim did not move. He stayed bent over the tree he was limbing, while up above him, three elevated pine trees bore down on him. The other loggers jumped away, yelling at him, but Jimmy Bird ignored them.

Glen scrambled down from the ledge, yelling, "Jim! Get out! Get out!"

Jimmy raised his head and looked at him just long enough for Glen to know he wasn't planning on moving. Glen yelled at the whistle punk, "All stop! All stop!" But the punk just looked blankly at him, his hand idle on the jerk line. Glen dove toward the jerk line, but he knew, even as he crashed into the whistle punk that he was too late. A scream from Clem, one of the other Black loggers, told him all he needed to know. He pulled himself up and crashed down the hill, leaping over downed trees and slash. When he reached the massive pines, Jim was lying between them, flat on his back, his eyes open, his arms spread, as if to welcome an embrace. Glen knelt by him, ran his hand over his crushed forehead and then his chest, where a bright red pool was seeping through his blue plaid shirt like a vernal pond.

"Wilkie, he just, he just . . . " Clem sobbed. "He just stood up, let the log take him."

The next morning, Wilkie packed his two books and a few clothes into the same canvas bag he had arrived with two years earlier. He stood outside Parnell and Jim's bunkhouse, waiting. Fifteen minutes lapsed before the door slowly opened and Parnell stood in the wan light.

"Ain't your fault, Wilkie."

"Don't say that."

"Why? You think you coulda saved him? That boy, he didn't have no more reason to stay than to go, and yesterday, going just won out."

"That's what I mean! I coulda saved him, talked him outta it . . . I shoulda seen it coming."

"You think you're magic? Got all us Black folk figured out?"

"No! I just . . . loved him. I was his friend. I shoulda . . ." Glen was clouding up, rubbing his eyes on his sleeve.

"Where you headed?"

"I can't stay here. Every day, I'm gonna see him. And Carl, I might kill him. If he hadn't pushed us so hard yesterday—"

"Stop blaming yourself, or Carl. You think I ain't got the guilt too? What am I gonna tell my mother? She trusted me to keep him safe, bring him home. Except . . . home . . . Jimmy Bird, he was never home. Now, maybe he is, God rest his soul."

Glen and Parnell led a procession of Maxville loggers, Black and white, to the cemetery. They watched the preacher say a prayer and then he helped lower Jimmy Bird's pine box into the ground.

Glen pitched the canvas bag over his shoulder, turned, and didn't look back. A week later, he'd made it by foot and rail to southeastern Oregon and set to work for a small outfit logging lodgepole pine. He saved his money, walked into Ashland six months later, and found the army.

Glen's twelve weeks of basic training were a welcome distraction. No thoughts of the orphanage, the Montana years, even Barney and Lula. He kept *The Adventures of Huckleberry Finn* and *The Communist Manifesto* at the bottom of his wood footlocker the way a growing boy might discard childish things. Revolution was a fairy tale.

On his twentieth birthday, a good omen he thought, they handed him a regulation army football, and he joined the base team for summer practice. He was bigger than most of them, faster, cannier. Not that the other players were soft; they simply hadn't been thrashed as thoroughly by life, an experience that gave Glen an almost supernatural wiliness.

The team's fall schedule included games against Tacoma and Seattle colleges, where Glen in his Number 16 jersey played either quarterback or end, throwing or receiving a covey of touchdown passes. Newspapers starting taking note of Glen's game-altering presence. WILKIE DOES IT AGAIN! raved the *Tacoma News Tribune*. Glen embraced the team of poor farm boys, fishermen, and lumberjacks and before long, he was team captain once again, winning game after game.

On October 29 of that year, as the stock market crashed and reverberations were felt around the world, Glen was wrapped in a double bubble: army, and football. Reports of suicides and mass hysteria didn't invade the gridiron. Glen noticed the fans were as full-throated as ever, as if the ball was a talisman, and he its shaman. He burrowed more deeply into the game, until sweat and glory and aching muscles drowned out everything else.

By the next spring, the coach of West Coast Army football, Captain Leo McCormick, was sitting in the stands at Fort Lewis watching Glen sneak through the practice team's line like a snake in tall grass.

McCormick waited for Glen in the base commander's office after practice. It took Glen all of half a minute to determine the coach was on the level. He had the broad shoulders and narrow waist of the football player he'd been, warm inviting lines around his eyes, a neat triangular mustache. No mean yellow teeth like Carl, no hat-busting ego like Uncle Fred, no weaselly eyes like Mr. Harvey Stiles. And no penchant for betrayal like Barney.

"Son, your commanding officer and I agree. There's a uniform for you on the West Coast Army football team. What do you think of that?" he asked, holding out his hand.

Glen grabbed it enthusiastically with both of his, and pumped it up and down. For once being called "son" did not gall him.

In the morning, Glen sat next to McCormick in a premium, reclining seat on the train to San Francisco. The trip took the better part of two days. Glen was keenly aware that McCormick could have purchased a cheaper ticket for him. That he could have sent Glen to the snack bar for sandwiches and coffee at dinner time. Instead, he invited Glen to the dining car with him and asked Glen about his life. In return for McCormick's hospitality, Glen offered up his Spanish flu trope. No family, no home. It wasn't far from the truth, but those lines around McCormick's eyes made him want to return kindness with honesty. Yet the secret held. To tell the truth would expose his mother's abandonment, his anger, his longing. He wanted the coach to think better of him—that he was not the kind to be left behind.

The train's cocoon—Glen held and comforted by McCormick's sonorous voice and reassuring demeanor—made the arrival at the Presidio particularly disorienting. Glen was the newest, and last, member of the squad expected that year. Unlike the farm boys in Washington, his new teammates were savvy, urban—from Philly and Chicago and Los Angeles. They'd heard about his star turn at Camp Lewis, and they weren't having any of it, especially since Glen was replacing a much-loved player who had simply washed out of the army. No one would say what happened, and no one was ready to accept his orphan replacement. The jeering started almost immediately.

They thought they'd easily cow the new Number 16.

"What's that smell? Wilkerson, you bathing in sheep shit?" But Glen just smiled.

When the jokes didn't faze him, they took it to him on the field, plowing him into the rain-soaked Presidio playing field, again and again. From the sidelines, McCormick watched with interest, letting the hazing unfold, wondering what his new recruit might do.

What he did was play. A kind of lazy, insouciant play, as if he was just idling away the afternoon, with no particular interest in the beatdown he was receiving. Glen glanced occasionally at McCormick, saw him smile a few times. McCormick whistled Glen into the quarterback slot and watched as Glen's own offensive line rolled aside and let the defense sack him. Glen popped easily to his feet, tipped his leather-helmeted head toward McCormick, and called the same play, taking the sacking once again.

McCormick whistled a time out and called Glen to the sidelines.

"You OK out there, son? I can call a stop to this right now."

"I'm fine, sir," Glen said, wiping mud out of his eyes with a towel. "You ever break a horse, sir? The horse ain't got no use for you at all, not at first. And you just have to keep him on the lead, going in circles, slow and easy, until he tires himself out. Never let him think you're in any hurry. Then he's ready to pay attention. I 'spect we're about there."

While Glen and McCormick talked, the other players and a few men from the sidelines huddled up. Glen heard raised voices and, over the coach's shoulder, saw one player from the bench shove one of Glen's tormentors.

"Yep, right about now, sir." He winked at McCormick and headed back into the scrimmage. He called the same play again, and this time, his offensive line held. Glen dropped back and delivered the ball deep into the arms of a receiver. And just like that, it was over. A shout went up, his linemen clapped him on the shoulder, and Glen moved the ball down the field, unfettered. By the end of practice, his stock had gone up considerably. Only two players hung back, refusing to welcome him into the fold. Glen figured, *Can't win 'em all.* From a nearly forgotten corner of his mind, Jimmy Bird sighed. "The Man is everywhere, Wilkie, my friend. And sometimes, he wears a football uniform."

Chapter 16

BARNEY, LULA, and NORA MAE

Riverbank, California, 1929–1930

As if to underscore Lula's pronouncement on the steps of the sharecropper shack, that they always left with less than they came with, Barney, Lula, and their six children pitched a surplus WWI tent on five scrubby acres in Riverbank, California.

The land was 130 miles north of the farm Barney had owned before Mexico, before Arizona and Montana and Mississippi, before Luzelba and Lula and Violet and all these hungry children. Much to Barney's chagrin, he had reluctantly accepted the acreage from his brother George, who held random parcels throughout the San Joaquin Valley, because, well—and this was a notion the brothers shared, perhaps the only thing they had in common—land was power. Money could disappear, as the whole world had seen in the stock market crash that occurred a month to the day after Barney and his brood fled Mississippi.

Winter, mild though it was in the valley, was coming on, and they had little to eat, no garden to rely on, not even the pecan trees and their resident squirrels that had sustained them in Mississippi. No trees at all! Barney walked the barren five acres. An irrigation ditch with a dribble of pale green water hugged one fence line. Rocks jutted regularly through the jaundiced soil and scrub grass. But it was his now . . . Well, nearly. He was still on the hook for it to George. A gentleman's agreement, as George had called it, though Barney had a suspicion he bought the land with the very money Barney sent from their short-lived joint venture in Mexico all those years ago. And perhaps because it was only ten miles from Modesto, where George and his brood lived in a grand estate, giving George a better chance to keep an eye on him. But never mind, it was dirt, and he would make something of it, if for no other reason than to drown out the heartbreaking memory of Violet and Mississippi.

He took a day laborer's job at a farm a mile down the road from a farmer who did not know him, his diminished fortunes, or his wealthy brother. Barney's new employer chalked up his haunted eyes to the general condition of the destitute, having no idea of the midnight train ride or the wrack and ruin left behind.

"Mr. Stovall, I ain't got no money to pay you," the farmer told him. "But I've got eggs and milk, some apple trees, and the tail end of the truck garden. You can have all that you can glean."

The next morning, Barney's five oldest children trailed him down the dusty road, shoeless, hungry. They carried a rusted tin tub Barney had found by the side of the road and spent an hour picking shriveled cucumbers and tomatoes and digging onions and potatoes. It was easy work after chopping cotton, and the boys and Maudie sang a few songs as they took turns carrying the tub between them back to the tent, eating yellowed apples and pitching the cores into the barrow ditch.

Lula had kept Nora Mae with her. No use burdening the family's gatherers with a child most likely to refuse all instruction. Lula could not figure out why Barney had suddenly gone soft on the girl, but ever since the terrifying night in the wagon, he often took her with him, riding her up front on the saddle of the horse George had loaned him, carrying her on his shoulder as he walked the fence line. Just last night, he lay on an old quilt in front of the tent, the tiny girl curled into his side, his hand on her head. She choked down a wave of jealousy at the memory. She hadn't felt Barney's hand in a long while.

Lula watched Nora Mae tossing rocks into the irrigation ditch. The child was calmer, less likely to pitch a fit since Mississippi. In the afternoon, after the children returned with the wash tub, the girl sat by the road eating an apple and a cucumber, waiting for Barney's return. It was as if the two had formed a partnership, and Lula had lost whatever influence she had over either of them. Nora Mae induced in her a kind of duality. She was ashamed that she had tried to abort her, and sorry that she had failed. The easiest path was to offer only enough of herself to keep the child from death—drowning, starvation—but not enough of herself that the child might mistake it for love. For love was something she left in stages along the road from Oklahoma in the big, looping trajectory of their lives. Was there any love left? Lula as yet could not tell.

Barney and Lula slowly pieced together an existence. They lived in the tent most of the winter, which meant dodging leaks inside and mud outside, but Barney installed a wood stove and ran a stovepipe up through the canvas roof. Lula enrolled the kids in school, all except Nora Mae who was too young, and spent her days mending clothes donated by the nearby Baptist church to hardscrabble families like theirs. She shortened the worn legs of an old pair of men's overalls, making Maudie Marie a pair of garden pants. She turned long-sleeve shirts with threadbare cuffs into short-sleeve shirts for Ernie, Vernon, Leonard, and Albert. She patched the elbows and worn pockets on a flannel coat for Barney. She took in the side seams of a voluminous, faded, flowered housedress for herself and darned handfuls of mismatched socks for everyone. Nora Mae sat at her mother's feet, rolling an empty thread spool back and forth across an old rug that covered the dirt floor.

Lula chuckled to no one in particular.

"Why are you laughing, Mama?"

"Nothing that concerns you," Lula snapped. She stopped sewing and sighed.

"Well, child, I was just thinking how nice it would be if we could cut off the old, frayed edges of our lives and start over, like this shirt here. You understand?"

Nora Mae stood and leaned on her mother's leg.

"Do I get new clothes too?"

"Sorry to say that box of clothes did not contain dresses for little girls, so no, nothing for you, but you ain't going to school, so you will just have to make do."

"I don't want a dress. I want a shirt like my brothers. And pants," she pouted.

Lula shoved Nora Mae from her knee. "Go on, now. I'm busy. No time for your nonsense."

Electricity had come to the San Joaquin around the turn of the century, and now, nearly thirty years on, the old ice house on the road to Modesto was an anachronism. Barney heard they were tearing it down, hitched a borrowed buckboard to George's horse, and brought home a load of timber, salvaged nails, some weathered straw, and even an old door with wrought iron hinges.

"What are you doing now, Barney?" Lula asked, standing in spring mud outside the tent.

"Building us an adobe house, Mrs. Stovall, like the one in Montana."

Lula flinched at the memory but said nothing. Couldn't be worse than the tent, she thought. Might give the boys something to do.

In days of driving, April rain, Barney and the boys built frames for the adobe bricks from the ice house lumber, then toted wheelbarrows of clay and sand from around their five acres, mixed in straw and old newspaper, even pages of Sears and Roebucks catalogs Barney found out behind the post office, and poured the slurry into the wood frames.

"Nora Mae, baby, you tear apart all these here catalogs," Barney told her. And she did, ink and mud up to her elbows. Soon, neighbors intrigued with the adobe operation dropped by stacks of old newspapers, even wood chips and sawdust.

By May heat, the bricks began to cure, and by June, Barney had laid a foundation for a nine-room house: a kitchen, a mud room, a living room, a cold storage room with one wall up against a natural berm, and four bedrooms. All-in-all about twelve hundred square feet.

George came out in his new Model A Station Wagon one Sunday afternoon in July.

"Well, I'll be damned," he whispered to himself. He slapped his accounts book against his palm and wandered out to where Barney and the boys were mortaring adobe bricks onto the foundation.

"What brings you all the way out here, George?"

"Just checking in, Barney. Seeing how my loan is progressing."

"Well, as you can see, we ain't wasting time. Should be done here about August and then we can start on the pole barn, get the dairy going. Already got some alfalfa up," he said, waving his hand out across a green swath where there had been nothing but scrub grass. "And I see there's twenty acres across the road for lease, and I'm gonna need that, or hay costs will kill me."

"Whoa there, Barney," George said, waving the accounts book. "We said $500, at two percent, which is two-point-five percent below prime, I might remind you, due in full in three years. What's a Guernsey cost these days. Seventy-five dollars? You surely can't think you're starting a dairy on $500. Why, you've spent just about that much on your ranchero here."

"Well, now, no I have not. Got most of the materials from

salvage, traded some labor from me and the boys for windows and linoleum, and I've still got $400 in my pocket."

"That'll buy you a few cows, but a few cows does not a dairy make."

"My point exactly. The Riverbank Cooperative Creamery is going great guns. Why, they're producing Challenge Butter for all of San Francisco with that new cream separator! I've got a built-in market for milk. They've already got a contract waiting for me to sign. They can take as much milk as I can produce. I aim to have ten cows milking by winter, twenty by next year, and once again, George, you'll be doing better off me than you ever expected. But I need another $1,500, and not a loan this time. Partners, just like Mexico. You'll get your equity back in five years, and ten percent of my profits until I sell. How else you gonna make money in this godforsaken Depression? I see your rail cars just sitting on the sidings like birds with broken wings. *That's* gotta cut into your bonus."

Lula, Maudie, and Nora Mae watched the men from the front of the tent. Maudie held an umbrella over her mother's head in the heat. Lula wore the old house dress she'd taken in from the charity box and clutched at the worn lace collar. It was never good when George and Barney stood toe-to-toe and stared each other down. Barney thought George an irritation, a man with little appreciation for his vision; Lula saw him as their only hope. From the shade of the umbrella, she strained to hear the men's conversation, but they spoke through clenched teeth, their words teetering on the hot afternoon breeze, then evaporating.

As Barney's sunburned lips spit his last words, Lula saw George step back. They said nothing to each other for a full minute. George turned his gaze on Lula and the girls. She felt exposed, as if he was savvy to her utter disappointment in Barney and their ragtag existence.

George took his wallet out of his breast pocket and pulled out a five dollar bill. He threw it at Barney's feet.

"Buy Lula a decent dress. That one she's wearing was our maid's."

George stomped toward his car. He yelled over his shoulder at Barney, "Fifteen percent of the profits, Barney. Fifteen percent."

Barney smiled and returned to his bricklaying.

Nora Mae ran from room to room, shouting nonsense just to hear the empty house echo. In the weeks that followed, Barney hauled home old bed springs, a broken-down table and chairs, dented pots and pans, flotsam and jetsam discarded at a time when no one tossed out anything with the slightest hint of use left in it. The daily junk delivery kept Lula and the children busy with repair: shimming table legs, hand sewing covers for worn cotton tick mattresses, making curtains from discarded muslin sheets with cigarette burns and a hint of mildew.

With its whitewashed mud brick walls and eclectic reincarnated furnishings, the house had a bohemian vibe. It pleased Lula more than she expected. The house was solid, cool against the September heat, secure. She was surprised to realize that when Barney promised electric lights by the next year, she believed him.

It was the first time in nearly a decade that Barney and Lula shared a bedroom with a door that closed. On their first night in the house, they stood at the room's threshold with a lantern, hesitant, as if the room was haunted.

Lula blew out the lantern, and they undressed in the dark, then lay like a knife and a fork in the silverware drawer, divided. Sleep was far away from both of them; conversation farther still.

Barney cleared his throat. Lula clenched and unclenched her toes against the clean, rough, bedclothes.

"Lu, I'm sorry."

"Sorry for what?"

"You want a list, or can you just forgive me?"

"Don't know what I'm forgiving you for, so, yes, a list."

"Well, goddamn it, woman, just forget it then. If this ain't enough . . . I built you this house, there's cows in the barn, I signed the damned contract with the co-op today. I'm sorry."

Lula said nothing. The day's hard work descended on them, and they slept, never further apart than they were, side by side.

GLEN

The Presidio, San Francisco, California, 1930

It was only three-and-a-half miles from Glen's barracks at the Presidio to Kezar Stadium, but it might as well have been three-and-a-half light years.

Two weeks after Glen slipped through his field hazing, McCormick posted the team's playing schedule: St. Mary's College, Santa Clara, Stanford, Oregon State College, University of San Francisco. Most of the games would take place at Kezar, the new, sixty-thousand-seat field at the edge of Golden Gate Park. The most people Glen had ever seen in one place was the two hundred folk in Maxville who came to watch the Methodist preacher bury Jimmy Bird, and the four hundred or so who came to games at Fort Lewis.

So early the next day, he pulled on his regulation gray sweatpants and sweatshirt and ran straight down Arguello Boulevard to Kezar, igniting a long, successive string of barking dogs, their challenges muted by the thick morning fog. He sat alone in the stands until the sun came over the eastern bleachers, a molten yellow peach in the dissipating mist. He tried to imagine what twenty thousand people—the expected turnout for their games—might look and sound like, but his mind filled instead with fear. On the roster, he was as a starting back, on offense and defense.

He shivered in his damp gear. He had no one to talk to about it. No parents, no brother. Where was Ray, anyway? No buddies, as yet, on the team. He would have to occupy that uniform with the big, black 16 as if he really *was* the Wilkie who made headlines in Tacoma. Not the impostor, not the abandoned orphan, who sat alone in wet sweats on the Kezar bleachers.

By the time of the first game against St. Mary's, though, Glen had settled into the laces and the team. The army Jarheads beat them, and every team that came after. Except Stanford, coached by Pop Warner, who wielded his nearly unbeatable single wing formation known as the Warner Attack.

The Bay Area newspaper sports pages took notice, too, of Number 16, quickly adopting his nickname, praising Wilkie's fast feet and faster hands, even after the trouncing at Stanford, calling him the "one bright spot" in the faltering army line.

"Boys, don't be getting a swelled head about it, no sirree, bobtail dog, 'cause the Big One's coming," Coach McCormick reminded them after each win, wagging the sports pages at them.

The Big One was the annual West Coast Army-Navy game, played since 1925 on Armistice Day, November 11, at Berkeley's Memorial Stadium. So far, the army had won or tied every contest, but McCormick was taking no chances. He called his starters together one wet September morning, tucked his chin in as if to duck a blow and said, "Boys, we're going to learn the Warner Attack. We've got seven weeks until the Big One. Those navy boys will never know what hit 'em."

Glen looked around the circle at stunned faces, especially Walter Kingsley, the starting quarterback, a particularly solemn New Yorker whose father was an English lord of some sort, too far from the British Empire to actually make much of it, but still. Kingsley's reserve was part inheritance, part chagrin. Glen knew the look, the "how the hell did I end up here?" stare, and decided that if he was going to make a friend, he might as well start with someone as ill-suited to an army football uniform as he was.

And a good choice, too, because McCormick leaned on Glen and Walter to bend the offensive squad to the single-wing Warner playbook. Glen and Walter even borrowed the coach's car to go watch Stanford play a home game, and sat in the stands mesmerized as Warner tweaked his own formula, going from a single wing to a double wing before their eyes.

"That's what we oughta do. One better than the old Warner," Glen said on the way back to their barracks.

The next day, they sold McCormick on the idea and lined up the team. Now Walter pitched out right and left to Glen, the line sweeping easily to protect him. Then they tried short passes and long balls, Walter connecting with Glen again and again.

Jasper Thorne and Sidney Nash found themselves sitting out more plays than usual. The two had it in for Glen since his first afternoon on the Presidio field, where their taunting had come to naught. They'd been football stars at their Alabama high school. "Littermates," Kingsley called them privately to Glen in the lilting remnant of his English accent. They weren't good enough or smart enough for West Point or Annapolis, but their daddies, army officers in the Great War, made a few calls, and here they were. They weren't destined for greatness, but they could make Glen and his new pal Walter miserable, and that was just about as good.

By the time the Armistice Day game rolled around, Glen and Walter's gear had mysteriously disappeared, tacks had been driven into the soles of their field shoes, mud poured into their rifle barrels. It put both of them on edge, watchful. But neither of them was prepared for what the littermates did two nights before the game.

Glen was on guard duty, walking the Presidio perimeter, when he was ambushed from behind and held down by Thorne and Nash in black painted faces.

"Get off me, you assholes!" The men grunted as they rolled Glen onto his back and pulled him into a small grove of redwood trees, where one of the them brought a fallen redwood branch down hard on his right knee. By morning, his knee was the size of a grapefruit.

"Who did this, Wilkie?" McCormick asked.

"Don't know, sir. It was dark, didn't see a thing," he said from his bed in the infirmary. McCormick paced back and forth. Kingsley stood at the foot of the bed watching Glen, his lips pressed in a line as straight as the crease in his dress uniform pants.

"Well, you suit up, Glen, we'll want you on the field, but you can't play."

"Maybe not," Glen said, staring straight at Kingsley.

Two mornings later, Glen hobbled on crutches into Memorial Stadium, filled rim to rim with seventy thousand fans.

"Knee's better, sir. Put me in," he begged McCormick.

"Sit down, son."

Through two quarters, neither team scored. Glen grew agitated watching Kingsley throw perfect spirals that slithered out of receivers' hands, or run plays for puny yardage. The new Warner Attack withered without the Kingsley-Wilkerson connection. At halftime, Glen threw down the crutches and started trotting painfully back and forth behind the army team's benches, McCormick eyeing him with concern. By the end of the third quarter, with no points on the board for either team, the stadium growing restless with the tedium of it, Glen and Kingsley had their own huddle while the army defense was on the field.

"Walter, I gotta get out there. Tell Coach you need me. Look at me! I'm running. Hurts like hell, but if you can get us to the goal line and throw it to me, by God, I can catch it."

By the end of navy's fruitless possession, Walter had convinced the coach to pull Nash and put Glen in. Glen hobbled to the line, carried six times—five yards here, ten yards there—his knee screaming like all the sirens of San Francisco's finest roaring down Market Street at the same time. McCormick pulled him out, subbed Nash back in.

"You boys get us to five and goal, and I'll give you Wilkie back again," McCormick hollered in the huddle, the stadium roaring at the prospect of an army touchdown.

On third down, army was on the navy eight-yard line, and McCormick whistled Glen back in. Walter and the line swept left, Glen went right over the goal line and turned, just as Walter flung a tight spiral high over the navy defenders. Glen reached for it, pulled it in, rolled forward on his knees, and disappeared into a black hole of pain and unconsciousness. He never saw the stadium go wild or the army parade its donkey, or the National Anthem at Retreat parade. And he never saw the score board record the final score: army 6, navy 0.

Glen's bed in the infirmary was covered with newsprint. Stories in the San Francisco and Oakland papers, even the *L.A. Times*, told the story of Glen "Wilkie" Wilkerson, his shattered knee, his English quarterback, and their improbable victory in Berkeley. In and out of consciousness on Wednesday, the day after the game, Glen watched fractured faces come and go, including McCormick and the other players, minus Thorne and Nash, of course, which would have been a dead giveaway had anyone been paying attention. Whenever Kingsley was off duty, he sat in the chair next to Glen's bed, where some strange blood infection—the result, the doctor said, of the trauma and the swelling in his knee—kept Glen in a fever for nearly a week.

When Glen woke up, the first thing he saw was Kingsley, smiling.

"I have some thoughts on Thorne and Nash," he said.

"Do you, now?" Glen smiled back.

McCormick picked that moment to enter the ward. "Walter, I need to talk to Glen alone."

McCormick sat for a long time without saying a word.

"Wilkie, you told me once you didn't have any family."

"No sir," Glen said, an uneasy feeling swirling in his stomach. "None to speak of."

"Well, there's a fella in my office right now says he's your brother Ray."

Glen's head on the thin pillow felt like it weighed a hundred pounds. He flicked his eyes toward the ceiling.

"Uh . . . yes sir, I—"

"And before you go spinning another yarn, he's told me all about your mother, your stepfather . . . and the orphanage."

"Sir, that was a long time ago. I ain't got any idea where those people are now. Last saw my mother . . . eight, nine years ago. Heard she was in Mississippi. She could be dead for all I know."

McCormick resumed his quiet appraisal: Glen, plastered against white sheets, his hands gripping the thin blanket. Then he paced the room and came back to stand at the edge of Glen's narrow bed.

"She's not dead. She's here, in California, not more than a hundred miles east of here. But she thinks *you're* dead."

Glen's poison-spiked blood made an unnatural thrumming in his ears, fingertips, the soles of his feet.

"I don't understand. . . . What?"

"Seems the orphanage reported you missing to your uncle. Said they'd found your clothes, torn, soaked in blood. Figured you'd come to a bad end."

"Well, I'll be damned," Glen whispered low to himself.

"Sorry, son, I didn't catch that."

"No sir. It's just, I had no idea, all this time. How did Ray find me?"

McCormick swept his hand across the newspapers strewn on Glen's bed. "Hard to miss if you're reading the sports pages."

"Can my brother come up? I'd like to see him."

"I'd say that's just a start, son."

"Start of what?"

McCormick resumed his pacing. "Wilkerson, I don't know why you lied to me. Well, wait, I think I got an inkling. Maybe if my mother left me behind, I might want to rub her outta my life too, invent another reason for being in that orphanage. But that was, as you said, long ago, and no matter how bad it makes you feel, she is suffering more. Nothing worse than losing a child. So you are going to go see her, ease her pain."

Glen jerked as if to sit up, but he might as well have run smack into the whole navy line at once, and fell back on the pillow.

"No sir. She chose that son-of-a-bitch Barney over her own sons! I don't care if I ever see her again, and there's nothing you can do to make me."

"Really, now? But there is. You see, Glen, if you don't go see your mother, let her know you're alive, you'll never play football for me again. We'll just muster you and your bum knee out of this man's army."

Glen shut his eyes.

"I'll send your brother up. You work it out, let me know when you're going, and I'll get you a pass."

He stopped at the curtain and looked back at Glen, the thin stern line over his brow dissolving.

"Glen, if you don't go, this will be a noose around your neck the rest of your life. And then you won't be worth nothin'. Not to the army, not to anyone, not even yourself."

Ray and Glen spent the first half hour piecing together their missing decade. Ray had married Marjory, a Fort Benton, Montana, girl, and they'd come west, to the ship yards of Oakland, just before the stock market crash.

"All that farm work, fixin' Uncle Fred's combines, guess it

done me some good. Moore Dry Dock . . . they're hanging on. Don't make much, but got me and Marjory an apartment and a little whiskey money. She's a great gal. Plays piano in the bars," Ray bragged, taking the first of many nips off a flask from his back pocket.

Glen told of running away from the orphanage and the ruse with the fish blood, his years at Maxville, joining the army, his stint on the field at Fort Lewis. Ray was a stranger to him, as if the drink had taken up residence and evicted the Ray of his boyhood. His eyes were gray disks, his cheeks red and sagging, like the last tomatoes on the vine. He wasn't sure if he wanted to put his trust in this brother-not-brother character sitting on the foot of his bed. So he held back the things that really mattered: Wilbur Taft and the magical hayloft door, Huck Finn and Karl Marx, Jimmy Bird and the highline, even the two twats—as Walter alternately called the littermates.

But then they got down to it.

"How did you find them?"

"Barney and Ma? Not that hard, really. She's been writing to Uncle Fred right along, and he never answered her. Just mad she never sent for us, I guess. But just before me and Marjory come down here, I was waiting in Fred's fancy front hall and saw a note in her handwriting on the table, and by God, it had a return address in California, so I pinched it. She was begging him for news of us. Said it had been years. So I wrote her a letter, told her you were dead. And what a damn fool thing that was, because here you are. And an army football hero, to boot. Your coach says I'm to take you out there, even gave me twenty dollars for gas. Can you believe that?"

"So she doesn't know I'm alive?"

"Well, no, Glen, they ain't got electricity, much less a telephone. And I just found out myself reading about that game a few days ago! You get better, we'll go down, surprise her."

"That'll be a surprise alright. What makes you think she'll want to see us, anyways?"

"The letter she wrote me back? She'd cried all over it. So many milky tears, I could barely read it. She ain't never forgiven herself, blames herself for your death. She and Barney had two more babies in Mississippi, and left there in a damn hurry, something about Barney beating the hell outta some fella. He's started a dairy, built them an adobe house. But Ma? All she does is pine for you."

"So we just gonna go down there, knock on the door? If Barney answers, I may have to kill him."

Ray snorted and took another pull on the flask. "You always were the righteous one. That'd be some homecoming. You wanna end up in prison? Can't let you, brother. I got some big money riding on you now that you took down those navy boys. And besides, I got a better idea . . . A way to get Ma outta the house and save you from murder."

Two weeks later Glen was walking—with a cane and a limp, but walking. On the appointed day for the trip to Riverbank, he wore his uniform, as Ray instructed. And that's how he found himself standing by the side of the road, about a mile from Barney's adobe house, watching a withering cloud rack blow across the December sky. Ray's idea was that he would go see Lula, and after a short visit, he'd take her for a drive. They would come across the army private hitchhiking and offer him a ride. And of course, there'd be a reunion. Tears. Glen could tell the coach he'd seen his mother, go back to playing football, and Ray could start hauling in the winning bets on Number 16.

Ray played his part as he saw fit, throwing back the big heavy door at the adobe without even knocking, and swooping in to spin Lula in a circle. He chortled and whooped as if she was a long-lost pal discovered in a bar over a pint of beer. The boisterous act gave Ray cover for his annoyance about seeing his mother again, a woman he had stopped counting as kin that day in Uncle Fred's yard. All he wanted at that moment was to get Lula in the car, engineer the reunion with Glen, and get back to Marjory and the smokey bar in Oakland where she'd be playing that night. The thought of Marjory and whiskey were mixed like a cocktail in his mind, and his face flushed with yearning. Lula took his rheumy eyes and rosy cheeks as signs, not of alcoholic excess, but of ecstasy. She'd lost Glen but here was her firstborn son, her Ray, and she, the prodigal mother, forgiven.

Ray made quick work of reintroducing himself to his younger brothers and sister and making his acquaintance of Albert and Nora Mae, who he slapped on the fanny like she was a bar fly.

"Well, look at ya all, my goodness, aren't you something!" he exclaimed, keeping up his hail-fellow-well-met patter.

"And where's Barney, Ma? Really should see the old man."

"He's gone to town, Ray. Thinking maybe I'd rather have you all to myself," Lula beamed.

Like hell, Ray thought.

"Well, listen, let's take a drive, shall we? Just you and me? Catch up?"

"Looky there, a soldier hitchhiking," Ray pointed out to his mother. "'Spect we oughta give him a lift. Roll your window down, Ma," he said as they coasted up to Glen on the shoulder, his thumb out, his army cap tilted far back on his head.

"Well, hey there, private!" Ray sang out, watching his mother.

But instead of the crowning moment of recognition he expected, his mother glanced at Glen, showing little interest in him and then stared out the front windshield as he climbed into the back seat.

"Uh, where you headed, fella?" Ray asked nervously, eyeing Glen in the rearview mirror. Glen peered at Ray's reflection, unsure what to say. Lula, oblivious, touched Ray's arm, as if to remind herself that he was real, the soldier in the back merely a distraction.

"Town," Glen said.

"What's your name, soldier?"

"They call me Wilkie."

"Ma, say hello."

Lula turned slightly in her seat and nodded. "Nice to meet you."

The three rode in silence for a half mile, each wanting something from the other they could not get. Lula wanting the soldier gone; Ray wanting his drink; Glen wanting— and not wanting— his mother to recognize him.

Glen growled from the back seat. "Stop the car, Ray."

Lula's eyes flickered from Ray to Glen. Glen got out. His mother's window was still open, and he rested his hands on the sill, hooking his cane over the window frame.

"Mama, don't you know me?"

Lula blinked hard and put her hands on the window frame over Glen's, but Glen pulled them out from under her fingers, took his cane, and turned away toward the shoulder.

"Oh! Oh! Oh my!" Lula found her voice, flinging open the car door, throwing herself from the car like a woman escaping a burning building. She fell to her knees and threw her arms around Glen's legs, nearly making him lose his footing in the loose gravel and weeds.

"Glen! Glen!" She buried her forehead into the back of his thighs.

Glen didn't turn to his mother's embrace, or say a word. He wanted to punish her, leave her on her knees, where he was certain the goatheads and rocks must be burrowing into her skin through her thin dress, like a flagellant's whip. He wanted her to hurt, to drown in the tidal wave of abandonment he carried with him everywhere. This was the moment he hoped for. Not some saccharin reunion as Ray had imagined, but a bloody, awful reckoning in which she would be debased and, ultimately, destroyed.

Lula's wailing grew faint, until it was nothing but muted sobs, but she didn't let go of his legs. A farm truck rolled by, slowed down at the spectacle, until Ray waived him on. Then, silence.

"I'm so sorry," she whispered. "I'm sorry. Oh my son, I am so deeply sorry. Oh dear God, won't you please forgive me? It was wrong, I know that now, but I didn't know what else to do! I thought Uncle Fred would take good care of you. I thought you might even be better off without us, since we were starving. I thought I could send for you. I never wanted to leave you. Never!"

Glen leaned his weight on the cane. Where was the sweet taste of vanquishment? He felt her tears where they had soaked into his uniform britches. He looked down at her hands near his knees, worn and white in the cool breeze, veins sunken like dry creek beds. There was no triumph, no victory. Only loss all the way around, a football game with a final score of zero to zero.

They had both lost. Who could know which of them had lost the most? He pried her hands from his legs, turned around, pulled her up from her penitence, and put his arms around her.

"Mama, let's take you home."

Chapter 18

NORA MAE

Riverbank, California, 1930–1931

It had already been a day of portent: The door banging open, the florid-faced man swinging her mother around like a dish rag.

"That's our brother!" Maudie Marie told her excitedly, like she actually needed another one. He was a nuisance like Vernon, Leonard, Ernie, and Albert, she decided, when he swatted her backside, his fingernails digging into her in the most unfriendly way.

From the front window, she watched his car returning with her mother and another man, this one in uniform. The soldier got out of the back, opened the passenger door, and tenderly helped her mother out, wrapping his arm around her thin, sagging shoulders.

Her mother was crying; she'd never seen that before. She looked like a cracked egg, her soft insides exposed, revealed. Her father had just returned from town, and she wondered what he must be making of this from the milking barn, where he could surely see the car and the men and his wife. She expected to see him come running, but he never appeared. And now this big, winsome fellow with the square head and faraway stare was walking her mother to the house. All the kids gathered in a half circle inside the front door.

"Why, that's Glen!" Maudie said.

"Looks good for a dead guy," Vernon cracked.

Nora Mae stomped her foot. Shoot! Not another dang brother. In the parsing of her mother's affections, she knew that adding another two people to the family—this Ray, this Glen—would only diminish what little of her mother there was to go around, particularly when her share was less than a thimbleful as it was. She pouted as the boys and Maudie pressed around their mother and the *two* long-lost brothers.

Ray was not nearly as garrulous as he'd been just a half-hour before, she noticed. Her mother only had eyes for Glen, as she clung to his arm, her face strangely lit from within. Glen delicately slipped her arm free from his and went around the circle saying hello, giving a squeeze to Leonard's shoulder, a gentle hug for Maudie Marie, a head tousle for Albert. And then he spied Nora Mae, her arms crossed, her white blond hair in a snarl, a scowl as broad as the Mississippi. He knelt down and smiled.

"You better be careful about sticking your lip out like that. Never know when a bird might fly over and crap on it." He chuckled and stuck out his hand. "My name's Glen, but everyone calls me Wilkie. What's your name?" She took his hand reluctantly.

"It's Nora Mae. But I hate it," she said, her pout unrelenting, even under Glen's generous smile.

"Well, what shall we call you then? I've got a nickname. Let's give you one. How about . . . Jody? I like Jody."

Nora Mae considered the offer. Outside of Maudie, and once and a while her Pa, no one took her into account. Her brothers knew she hated her name, so they took to calling her Pissant, and got a pass doing it from their mother.

"Don't complain about your name if you don't like what they call you. It's your own fault," Lula told her.

Now this new brother was offering her a name without ruffles or bows. It was sturdy, short, not likely to succumb to a southern twang, the way her mother turned Nora Mae into four syllables. Jody. If she took it, she could dispense with Nora Mae, and all it represented, once and for all.

"I . . . like it," she said shyly to Glen.

"Pissant, that's what we call her," Leonard said, snickering.

Glen peered over his shoulder. "I wouldn't call her that again, if I was you."

If Nora Mae had been a mongrel cur thrown a pork chop, she could not have been more startled. No one but Maudie had taken her side before, not through her temper tantrums, her crying jags, her disputes with her tormenting brothers or her mother. No one. Lula look startled too.

Indeed, Glen had addled the entire room. A fissure had crept into the boys' universal disdain for their troublesome sister. Ray looked on jealously at the brother who always evidenced more courage than he did. Maudie, who had resigned herself as the baby's only protector, now had an ally. And Lula? Who would Lula censure for her miseries now?

It was in that moment of familial reassessment that Barney pushed through the door.

"Hello, fellas," he said. Glen stood, pressing the creases from his uniform with his big hands. Ray saw his moment to regain the room's consideration.

"Well, if it ain't Mr. Barney Stovall," Ray boomed. "Nice house you got here. Good looking kids," he said, sweeping his hand across his assembled siblings. "Course, their half brothers are handsome devils, so no surprise at all," as if Barney's genetic contribution had been of no account.

"Long time, no see."

Glen said nothing. Nora Mae edged closer to him and took his hand.

"Uh, looks like you boys have grown up just fine," Barney

offered, his eyes roaming briefly over Glen's uniform and Ray's liquor-soaked features.

"Boys, I've got two chickens in the ice box," Lula stammered, hoping to return equilibrium to a room that had tipped on its axis.

"We're going," Glen said, heading for the door, Ray trailing. Barney stepped aside. Nora Mae clung to Glen's hand. The whole family swept into the yard. A light, misting rain had started, bringing thin veils of clouds down along the road and surrounding fields.

Still holding Nora Mae's hand, Glen gave his mother a quick hug, then stooped down. "Jody, I'll see you someday soon."

And with that, they were gone.

In the night, in her small room with Maudie Marie, Nora Mae listened to the rain coming steadily down, a stiff wind blowing it against the window. She whispered it again and again.

"Jody. Jody. Jody."

Glen's impression on the Stovall family was enduring, but it was less than a week before the boys began to taunt Nora Mae again, especially when she insisted they call her Jody, even if they never did call her Pissant again. The memory of the larger-than-life Wilkie cast shadows on the adobe walls; they had no idea when he might make good on his promise to return.

Nora Mae sensed a small thawing of Lula's icy demeanor toward her. When her mother called her in to supper one night, Lula touched her daughter's head, lighter than the brush of a butterfly wing, as she came in the mudroom door. She shied away like a skittish colt. Her mother's hand had only punished her, and it seemed improbable she would use it for anything else.

Nora Mae, the most observant of lonely children, noticed other things. The extra biscuit wound up in her school lunch bag on occasion, instead of always going to one of the boys.

Her mother's voice was softer and creamier, like fresh milk. She resisted these tiny entreaties. What if Lula withdrew them, and returned to the cold, remote presence she had always been? The precarity of this new, kinder mother unsettled her.

And yet, when she came home from kindergarten in the early afternoon, she wondered what new delicacy might unfurl in her mother's heart. She often ran the last bit of country road, just to find out. Sometimes she got a smile, a handful of walnuts, a comforting pat on the shoulder for the creation of a flower picture.

She could make her mother's sky darken, though, and never more than when she questioned her about Glen.

"When's he coming back, Mama?"

"I don't know, child."

"Maybe Christmas?"

"I don't know."

"He might could bring me a present if he does."

"Maybe. I don't know."

"Do you 'spose Pa could go up to Frisco and get him?"

"Hush! I don't know. Stop pestering me. We'll see him when we see him, and not before, so just go on now."

Barney said he read in the newspaper that the army had lost their big game to the navy in November. Christmas passed without Glen, nor any word from him. Nora Mae and each of the kids got an orange and two pieces of hard candy, which Barney presented on Christmas morning as if he were delivering the Holy Grail. She made each piece of her candy last an entire afternoon, plucking it from her mouth every few minutes to gaze at its glossy, sugary perfection.

In February, she came home from school to find a broken-down wagon hauled by two emaciated donkeys straddling the road in front of their house. A woman and four children, two girls and two boys, sat huddled in the wagon. They wore the dubious distinction of appearing poorer than the Stovalls. She saw her pa coming back from the milking barn with a fellow who had been visited by every plague in the Book of Exodus. His hair was sawed ragged above red, scabby ears, his pants gnawed off about three inches above his ankles, and he wore two mismatched boots held together by baling wire. Her pa's nose twitched, telling her he didn't smell too good either. What were they doing here?

"Nora Mae, go get your ma, will ya?"

By the time she came back with her mother, the children had left the wagon and were standing on the leeward side out of the cold wind. Barney was gesturing out across the field.

"Lula, this here is the Coates family. They just come over the pass, and they haven't got a place to live, 'cept a couple of tents. The co-op sent them over here, thinking I might need a hand, and I'm gonna let them pitch their tents in the alfalfa field, least 'til the first cutting comes up. Mr. Coates is gonna help with the farming until they get on their feet."

Lula nodded at the disheveled Mr. Coates and the worn Mrs. Coates, who still sat in the wagon as if her heft, barely more than an empty cotton sack, might keep her from blowing away.

"Well, sir, we don't have much, but our neighbors helped us when we arrived, so we will share what we can."

The Coates children became a source of fascination for the Stovall boys who enjoyed the prospect of beating up on kids who could not beat back. They poked fun at their ragged clothing, awkward ways, and downcast eyes. Maudie chided her brothers for their meanness, but as in all things Stovall, Barney and Lula rarely noticed the boys' behavior. Nora Mae screeched at her brothers, "Leave them kids alone!" Her entreaties only seemed to egg them on, the Coates standing in as proxies for the sister who was suddenly off limits due to Glen. Nora Mae tried talking to them on the way to school, but they had determined that all Stovall children were to be avoided. Once again, she found herself on the lonely fringe, with no one but Maudie as consolation.

Mr. Coates, however, was a friendly sort. He followed Barney around like a puppy, offering to open a gate here, or shovel out a stall there. Nora Mae could see it irritated her pa, a man not used to such obsequiousness. She also noticed that when Barney was elsewhere, Mr. Coates seemed to be the lounging sort, taking a snooze out behind the barn or chatting her up.

"Whatcha doing, little girl?" he asked her one day as she lined small rocks up in neat windrows out near the irrigation ditch.

"Making a house for my doll," she answered warily, not at all comfortable with the scroungy Mr. Coates leaning over her shoulder. She looked toward the house, hoping for a reason to leave when she saw her Ma step out on the back porch and call her name.

"Stay away from that character, Nora Mae. I don't like him at all," her ma told her later as she stood by the sink, peeling potatoes.

A week later on a blustery March Saturday, the boys, done with their chores, went off with their pals to play baseball at the school. Barney took the wagon into the feed store; Maudie and Lula were mending clothes. Nora Mae, ever the wanderer, went from stall to stall in the milking barn, talking to each cow in Barney's growing dairy. Mostly, she bragged about her big brother.

"He's so big, why, he's taller than you, Nelly girl! And he has a nice uniform, and he plays football and the newspapers take his picture." The cows chewed along, doleful eyes watching the tiny thing as her pink fingers scratched their noses. In the midafternoon, she headed toward the outhouse, closed the door behind her, and crawled up on the seat, turning the pages of the Sears catalog, marveling at its luxuries, especially the boys clothing—the deep blue dungarees, the button-down shirts, sixty-five cents each. And then the door swung open. Mr.

Coates grinned at her, her white bloomers around her ankles, the catalog in her lap.

"Go away!" she commanded.

But instead, he pushed in, closing the door behind him.

"Now, aren't you just the cutest little thing," he said, the gaps between his yellowed teeth looking inky and bottomless in the dim light. Nora Mae shrank back as far as she could, reaching for her panties.

"You don't need those now," he said, pulling them down over her shoes and tossing them on the floorboards, his smile replaced with a grim determination. He pushed her off the hole into the corner and reached his hand up under her dress.

"No! Let me go!"

"Not just yet, little girl."

No one had ever touched her most private place, his fingers clawing into her. She screamed, and he put his other dirty hand over her mouth.

"You shut up, or I'ma shove you down that hole into the shit, and you'll drown down there." When she quieted, he fumbled with the rope that held up his pants. She looked away, not wanting to see what was behind the worn canvas. A minute passed, then two, one hand still gripping her between her legs, tearing at her. Then he moaned and stood back.

"You ever tell anyone I come in here, and I'll kill that cow, the one they named after you. And then maybe, I'll slit your throat too. Then there'll be no more Nora Maes," he chuckled. "No one gonna believe you anyhow, so you best just keep your mouth shut."

The evening slid across the valley, dragging a thick fog with it. Barney returned, as did the boys, and it was a while before Maudie noticed her sister wasn't around. She walked out into the twilight, calling to her. Nothing.

"Daddy, I can't find Jody."

"Aw, she'll turn up. Probably hiding from your brothers."

Barney headed in to start the evening milking, wondering what had become of Mr. Coates, who was supposed to show up about this time.

On down the line he milked, and when he reached the cow they'd named Nora Mae ("She bawls all the time like you, so I gave her your name") he saw Nora Mae's blond head peering out from the barn floor straw.

"What in tarnation are you doing here? Everyone is looking for you!"

Jedediah Coates had made a slight miscalculation about Nora Mae's interest in remaining alive. After all, it had been sufficient to threaten his own children with various punishments, from beatings to abandonment and death, when he'd done the same, or worse, to them. If he had left it there perhaps Nora Mae would have kept quiet too. But he had threatened a cow, and not just any cow: Nora Mae's namesake and favorite. And that had riled her up.

"I gotta stay here with Nora Mae," she said, clutching the cow's neck.

"What is the matter with you? Get on in the house. That cow is fine, look at those udders. She just needs a good milking!"

"No! He said he was gonna kill her."

"What? Who said that?"

"Mr. Coates," she said, tears stinging her eyes. "He said if I told . . ." Then she clamped her hand over her mouth and wailed behind her thin fingers.

Barney set the milking bucket down and stood over her.

"Told what?"

"He . . . he come in the outhouse when I was in there, and pestered me—"

Barney picked up the bucket, half full of milk, and slammed it onto a barn pole, milk flying in a wild spray over the cows.

"You stay right there. Don't move."

He grabbed a pitchfork and ran out of the barn.

She flung herself between the cow's front legs and curled into the smallest, most inconspicuous space she could contrive. Blood had trickled down her leg and soaked her cotton dress, and she tried rubbing it away in the straw. Soon, she heard hollering, her pa's deep voice and then Mr. Coates's high twang, then a scream, then silence. The cow huffed and stamped her feet, anxious to be milked. The barn filled with low moos as more cows grew anxious, pulling against their leads. The barn was almost entirely dark when Barney returned with a lantern.

"Get up, girl," Barney strained to look her over, head to foot, sliding the lantern closer near the bloody hem of her dress. "Now, you tell me. What did you do?"

"I come in here to protect Nora Mae."

"No before that. What were you doing with Mr. Coates?"

Instead of answering, she put both hands, flecked with straw and her own blood, over her face and cried.

"You answer me!"

She dropped her hands. "I just went into the outhouse and—"

Barney's right hand walloped the side of her face, and she fell back into the straw.

"You don't say a word about this to nobody, you hear me? Nobody. I'm sending your sister out here."

Maudie came with a bucket of warm water and clean clothes, and when Nora Mae, strangely silent, was clean and dressed, she carried her into the house like a baby and put her to bed. Neither of them said a word.

In the morning, Nora Mae saw a swath of muddy ground, empty and black, where the Coates family had pitched their tents. It was almost as if they had never been there.

Barney's big hand left a purple bruise on Nora Mae's fair skin, a scarlet letter that only she and Barney understood. The pain between her legs made her cry when she had to go to the bathroom, which she did far away from the house, unwilling to go into the outhouse again. She hid from her mother when it was time to go to school, because walking hurt too.

"Barney, what happened to her?" Lula pleaded, but Barney would not answer, and Lula was afraid to discover the truth on her own. Nora Mae wandered the fence line alone.

Four days later, a car dropped a hitchhiker out on the road, and from her perch in the rafters of the milking barn, Nora Mae saw Glen striding across the yard. She hugged the beam, wishing to disappear, to fly away with the swallows that swooped through the barn in the early evening, to become a vaporous thing no one would notice. And yet, how she longed to run to Glen! Her own arms and legs— ugly, detestable things—would not move. She pulled at her hair, extracting a handful, and dropped it into the air below where it floated away.

Her siblings came down the road from school. An hour passed. She grew weary on the narrow beams, but could not bear to come down. Maudie and Glen came out of the house, talked a while, and she pointed to the barn.

Glen saw her sitting above him. St. Jody, the patron saint of cows and barn swallows.

"Jody, come on down and see me."

"No."

"OK, what if I come up?"

"You can if you want to."

Glen scrambled up the ladder and sat down beside her.

"I brought you something," he said, turning a bright red yo-yo into her hand. For the first time in days, a smile drifted briefly across her lips.

"Here, I'll show you how it works."

The yo-yo rolled up and down the string, up and down, up and down. The soft whir as the orb ascended, the small smack as it returned to Glen's wide palm. A hypnotic calm settled on the rafters.

"You wanna try?"

Glen slipped the string over her middle finger and gently cupped her hand around the toy. Soon, it was making a wobbly return into her palm.

"Jody, where'd you get that big bruise on your face? You fighting with your brothers again?"

"Pa hit me." *Whir, wobble, smack, whir, wobble, smack.*

Glen steadied himself on the cross beam. "Why?"

"He said not to tell nobody."

"Well, I'm not just anybody. I'm your big brother, come to bring you a yo-yo."

Nora Mae considered this. *Whir, wobble, smack, whir, wobble, smack.*

"There was this man, Mr. Coates, and he come into the outhouse and . . . He hurt me, 'cause I am a bad girl . . . and Pa made him and his family move on. Now Pa is mad at me and said I shouldn't tell no one." Nora Mae lost the yo-yo's rhythm, and the toy hung motionless at the bottom of the string.

A rage flared in Glen's chest. Everything that threatened to undo him—the cold prairie wind of Montana, the hayloft door swinging open at Twin Bridges, a tree on the highline flying straight at Jimmy Bird—flooded him, and he grew dizzy on his narrow perch.

In a clanking of milk buckets, Barney strode into the barn.

Glen dropped from the beam and landed right in front of him, grabbed him by the shoulders and rushed him into the barn wall. Nora Mae watched, clutching the yo-yo.

"You rotten son of a bitch. I should have killed you the first time I saw you."

"Now, hold on Glen. Let's let bygones be bygones. I never meant—"

"I'm not talking about me. I'm not talking about bygones. I'm talking about Jody. You hit that little girl after Coates . . . What kind of a monster are you?"

Barney dropped the bucket he held in each hand as Glen shoved him harder against the barn wall and shook him, banging his head against the rough framing.

"Say you're sorry. Look up at Jody and say you're sorry."

Barney tried to get away.

"Say it!" Glen slammed him again.

"I'm sorry! I was just . . . I beat the bejesus out of that fella! Then I stabbed him in the backside with the pitch fork. You think I ain't sorry? Why didn't she scream, run like hell?"

"She's a goddamn baby, you old fool. You listen to me. If you ever touch her again, you are a dead man. I promise you. You hear that, Jody? I will come back here and kill you Barney, with my bare hands, and I will enjoy it."

Both men were breathing hard, their exhales sending a mist up to Nora Mae.

"Since you want to keep secrets, this is gonna be ours. We're going in the house, cause Ma made supper, and I'm staying this time. And you are gonna sit down and shut up and say 'Pass the potatoes' just as sweet as can be. And if you can find it in your black heart to just be nice to these kids—just a little—then I will let you live. You hear me?"

Barney nodded almost imperceptibly. Glen let him go. The

shadow of Nora Mae's short legs, illuminated by the lantern, fell over their shoulders. Both men looked up. Nora Mae was sending the yo-yo up and down in long, slow, steady arcs. *Whir, smack, whir, smack.*

BARNEY and LULA

Riverbank, California, 1931–1933

Barney behaved himself at dinner, but his polite guise was thin, and Lula saw right through it. Whatever happened in the barn had trailed Glen and Barney as they came in the mudroom door, Glen carrying Nora Mae, both men fluffed up like cold polecats.

Lula tried to extract the truth from him in bed that night, a difficult task when you are merely bedding down with a man but not intending in any way to seduce him. Lula considered trying to charm him into opening up, but realized she had forgotten how. If Barney had been a dishpan or a holey sock, she would have known her way around him, but she couldn't remember how a man tasted, or what his breath would feel like in her ear, or how to rest her hand with intention on the twitchy member between his legs. So she took the direct route.

"What happened in the barn?"

"Not talking about it, Lula. Go to sleep," he said, and rolled onto his side away from her.

Lula reconsidered her approach. She touched his bare shoulder. He flinched. She kept her hand there.

"Barney, whatever happened in the barn, and in Montana . . . Mississippi . . . I'm still your wife. And these are still our children, even Glen and Ray, though I believe we done them wrong, both of us."

He didn't move. His shoulder grew warm under her fingers.

"I can't change any of that," Barney said.

"No, but I think there's a reason those boys have come back into our lives. When I thought Glen was dead . . . Well, I thought on a lot of things I've done. Maybe this'll give us a chance to make things right."

They both lay quiet. Barney could feel Lula's breath at the base of his neck.

"And not just for them," Lula continued, "but for the other children too. Maybe even for each other."

Barney rolled slowly onto his back, not wanting to disturb the flighty little bird of her hand on his shoulder.

"You asked me to forgive you, the first night here in this bed," she continued, "and I wanted a list of how you done wrong. But seeing the boys, 'specially Glen, I know I've got lots to be sorry for too, some things you don't even know about. So I ask you again, Barney, what happened in that barn? And what happened to Nora Mae and the Coateses?"

What *did* happen to Nora Mae? Barney wasn't sure. How do you talk to a little girl about something like that? The griping started way down in his gut again, like it had every day since it happened, and he clenched his fists. Nora Mae, bloody, in the barn. Running across the road with the pitchfork, Coates standing out in the mud drinking a cup of coffee from a tin cup.

"What did you do to her?"

"Why, Mr. Stovall, I don't know what you're talking about."

Mrs. Coates and her four sorry children raised the tent flap and moved into the field, clinging awkwardly to each other. Barney lowered his voice.

"She's got blood on her dress. Said you followed her into the outhouse."

Jedediah grinned at him and whispered back, *"Why, I didn't do anything you haven't wanted to do to that sweet little thing . . . or maybe you already have. She seemed pretty eager to me."*

Barney brought the wood handle of the pitch fork down on his shoulder. Coates screamed.

"You get your brood, and get the hell off my property! Now!" Barney yelled, sweeping the pitch fork into the tent poles and reducing the moldy canvas to a heap. Mrs. Coates and the children uttered not a sound. Barney glanced at them and saw a hunger in their faces, a desire for blood and damnation. He dropped the pitchfork and began to work Coates over with his fists until Coates fell to the ground screeching. Barney kicked him, aiming for his crotch.

"Get up!" Barney commanded. Coates wailing, snot and blood running from his nose, pulled himself to standing.

"Turn around!" Coates obeyed. Barney scooped up the pitchfork, and with as much power as he could conjure in his fifty-eight-year-old shoulders, shoved the tines into Coates' backside and heaved him five feet onto his knees, unconscious, blood seeping through his clothes in a dozen places like a buckshot deer.

Barney turned to face Mrs. Coates and the children, expecting tears. What he saw instead was parted lips, flushed cheeks, a look of vindication.

"I mean you no harm, Mrs. Coates, but you can't stay here another night. I'll send my boys over to help, but you load up your wagon, including that sorry excuse of a man, and move on. Mr. Coates, there? I'd drop him off at the sheriff's office. Tell 'em some neighbors caught him stealing a cow, and you don't know what to do with him. And then, why, I would just forget you ever met him, all of you. You can't possibly be any worse off without him."

Barney sighed, parsing the memory.

"Lula, I should have taken Nora Mae with me to the feed store. She wanted to go, and I didn't want the bother. I shoulda!

And then, why, I wouldn't have nearly killed Coates, or done the worse thing I have ever done in my life."

"What did you do?"

"I hit her," he sobbed. "I hit our little girl, for no reason other than that I couldn't do anything about what had happened. I hit *her* when I wanted to beat myself up!"

Lula's grip on his shoulder grew tighter as he told her everything: Coates's visit to the outhouse, Nora Mae hiding with the cows, his blind rage with the pitch fork.

"And then Glen said he would kill me if I ever touched her again, and by God, I wouldn't blame him if he did." His belly heaved, then grew still, his truth telling scouring him out.

"But what did he do to her? Did he—"

"Lula, I don't know," Barney moaned. "I 'spect she couldn't even tell us, and I'm hoping she just forgets about it."

Barney and Lula were facing each other. She cupped his rough face in her hands. "I can't say as I ever loved you much, Barney, just the truth of it. But at this very moment, I—" She kissed him.

"I thought you shut that door behind you, Lula. No more babies, you said."

She laughed in the dusky light. "My womanhood is gone, Barney. After Nora Mae was born, maybe 'cause of that fever. Just . . . gone."

It would be impossible to call them innocent, not of their sins against each other or their children. But their lovemaking that night was pure, vestal, a dispensation of sacraments long lost to them both.

The next year offered the Stovalls a reprieve, even in the depths of the Depression. The demons that seemed to afflict them—their animosity toward each other, their yearning for advantage rather than harmony—diminished. Glen came to visit every month, and tendrils of reconciliation, persistent as English ivy, grew between him and his mother. He even spent a few weekend leaves helping Barney expand the milking barn, though they reserved their communications to talk of saw cuts, pilings, and roofing materials.

A shroud of unhappiness slipped from Lula, and she set about planting a vegetable garden and tending to the souls and bodies of her children for the first time since the early years in Montana. Barney could hear her laughing as she corralled the kids into weekly baths in the stock tank he would haul into the kitchen for them.

Nora Mae was the lone foreigner in this newer, kinder Stovall nation. She inhabited her own nightmare kingdom. Its borders: the walls of an outhouse; its continual enterprise: rape; its absolution: none. She withdrew further and further from her parents' overtures, only leaving the nightmare kingdom's confines for Glen's visits.

Lula's patience was wearing thin. Regret was one thing, but acceptance, even love, was something else again, and Lula could only offer her youngest daughter contrition. That wasn't enough to stitch her wounds.

"I have tried with that child, Glen, truly I have!" It was a Saturday afternoon in July suffuse in a kind of wet, relentless heat that made even thinking a weary affair. Glen sat with his mother on the shady eastern side of the house, snapping beans in a pan.

"Mama, she's got some pain. Could be Coates, could be . . . I don't know."

"Well, what am I supposed to do about all that?"

Glen ran through the years of his own childhood, a tattered catalog of pain and loneliness, and could not conjure up an answer. What had he wanted? Love was like a fifth cousin, many times removed from his keen. He yearned for something he could not name.

Lula sighed. “I come into the kitchen the other day, and she is standing on the table, and she’s pushed in the panel in the ceiling—I store the walnuts up there—and she’s stuffing walnuts in her pockets! She knows I’m saving those. And so I whipped her. Just when I think I’m gonna do better by her . . .Well, I can’t trust her for a minute! The rest of you kids were not like that!”

Glen shook his head. “Why did she want the walnuts?”

“I surely don’t know! I suspect . . . well, you know, Barney has to kill a cow now and again, when they stop producing enough milk. Sells some of the meat, but finally we have something other than beans and now and again, a chicken. But she won’t eat a bite of it. Says she won’t eat her friends.”

“So, she was hungry?”

“Children got to eat what’s put on their plates, not steal walnuts. It wasn’t that long ago we were practically starving. I won’t have it, Glen, I just won’t!”

They snapped the rest of the beans in silence.

After nearly twenty years of one failure after another, each year a twelve-month hurricane season of disastrous proportions, Barney had somehow hit it right, even in the middle of a depression. The simple fact was people still drank milk and ate butter, and even though the price had dropped nearly in half, running a herd of dairy cows just one hundred miles east of San Francisco turned out to be a stroke of luck. Not genius. Even Barney wouldn’t chalk it up to smarts. Plain old American luck. And hard work. If it was one thing Barney could do, it was put one foot in front of the other, day after day, when younger men would have given up and gone on the dole. Not Barney. He worked from dark to dark, planting and cutting alfalfa, feeding and milking cows, hauling tins of milk every morning and night to the co-op.

Lula’s epiphany on the night they gave in to each other that maybe, just maybe, a little tenderness was in order all the way around, changed Barney's approach too. The boys mucked out the milking barn and joined Barney on the milking line with something like bonhomie.

Why hadn't he thought of this before? These boys, his own sons, were his *men,* succumbing to an ounce of praise like the fellas in Mississippi. A word of praise here, an extra dime for the Saturday matinee there. His labor force, each with an identical dishwater-blond cowlick: Vernon, age fifteen; Leonard, fourteen; Ernie, twelve; and even Albert, at age eight. They were healthy boys, their less-than-robust diet notwithstanding.

The boys rose with Barney, propelled the dairy forward into the day, went to school, and—along with Barney—put the dairy to bed at night. His labor problem solved, Barney focused on expansion, adding a bull out in the pasture, and growing his herd to twenty milk cows.

"Why, that's ten thousand gallons a year, at four dollars per twelve-and-a-half gallons"—Barney was scratching his income on a slip of paper—"And that's . . . $3,500 for the year."

Lula kept a dirty pair of overalls riding up and down on the washboard out in the yard while Barney figured. "Is that enough?"

"Enough for a car? No, Mrs. Stovall. Enough for electricity, maybe."

"And a phone?"

"Could be." He touched the back of her neck. "Could be." That he still owed George a considerable sum didn't enter in to his calculations.

The new electric and phone lines hung like strands of pearls and precious stones between the adobe and gangly new power poles out on the farm road. Barney and Lula stood arm in arm, staring at them, the first time since Arizona that they'd had electricity.

"That telephone, Lula, it's just for emergencies, you understand?"

The sun was dropping fast on the fall afternoon. Standing in the yard, Barney and Lula watched a light show commence inside the house. Nora Mae was standing on a chair, her thin frame glowing in the window, turning the one light switch in the living room on and off, on and off.

Barney owned one suit. It was the thing he'd saved from the shack in Mississippi the night of the frantic escape in the cotton wagon three years ago. One suit—rough brown wool, a tiny moth incursion here and there—and his gold stickpin. Now and again, he wore them, feeling an old man's childish pride in donning the pin, cinching up the britches, and shooting the cuffed shirt sleeves through the jacket's arms. Funerals, bank loans, cajoling visits to George—that's when a suit was called for. And, these days, for visiting Tilly's Cafe in Riverbank, where the San Francisco Chronicle was for sale, three cents.

Barney would stand on the covered boardwalk in front of the cafe in his suit, paper folded out to the sports page, regaling the other dairymen lined up on the porch out of the October wind.

"Well, looky that, our boy Wilkie. Wins another one for the Jarheads!"

The newest headline was just above a story Barney did *not* read out loud that afternoon: Army Team Bad Boys Punished in Guard House. "Coach Johnny Baker has a surefire way of keeping the West Coast Army eleven in training. Whenever any of his players shows an inclination to break training, they spend their time—except for football practice and games— in the guard house of the Presidio here."

The story made Barney uneasy, especially after Glen's last visit in September. Glen's champion, McCormick, had been replaced, as Glen told it, by a more ruthless coach who lined them all up on his first day and said there would be no more palling around between coach and players. The army's loss to navy in the 1931 game, the first army loss in the five-year-long contest, had riled command and McCormick was replaced shortly after the game.

Glen had recounted how the new coach looked straight at him and Walter Kingsley as he said, "I'm not here to be your buddy. I'm here to win games, and right now, today, I'm laying down the law. You play ball, you play it hard, and we beat navy next November 11, or you pack it up. Plenty of miles of perimeter to walk if you fail."

That September visit was the second time Glen had brought a beautiful women, Iris, with him. It was the last time they'd seen him. They all felt the lack, even Barney and the boys who viewed him as a family status symbol. His absence left Nora Mae locked in her own private redoubt. Lula longed for his big laugh. Maudie craved the crumpled paper sack he always brought filled with cookies or donuts, and once, a silk handkerchief for her. A zoo needed a lion, and the Stovalls needed Glen.

Barney returned from Tilly's each week with the newspaper, and they laid it out on the kitchen table like a sacred text, reading of Glen's exploits. And then came the news they awaited most eagerly: The story of the annual 1932 Armistice Day encounter with the navy at Memorial Stadium. The headline streaked across the page in a deathly black ribbon: NAVY ELEVEN OVERWHELMS ARMY, 30–0.

The loss was sobering enough, but it was a paragraph near the end of the story that sent the Stovall kitchen table into stunned silence. "Army star tackle, Glen 'Wilkie' Wilkerson, suffered a broken leg in a melee on the sidelines after the final gun."

Barney read the words out loud, his tongue thick in the back of his throat. Lula gasped, and Nora Mae slid under the table.

"Barney, is this an emergency?"

"Yes, Mother, I believe it is."

"Hello, Billie?" Lula hollered into the telephone. "I'd like to make a person-to-person call to Glen Wilkerson. I don't know the number, but he's at the army base at the Presidio in San Francisco."

"Yes, Lula, we all heard about your son. I'll do what I can. I'll ring you back when I get him."

Lula walked around and around the kitchen table, waiting for the operator to call back. Fifteen minutes later, the phone rang. It was the first time anyone had heard it ring, and they all rushed to the kitchen where the phone hung by the back door.

"Mrs. Stovall? It's Billie here. I don't know how to tell you this, but no one knows where he is. They asked all around. The corporal says he don't know what's become of him, says the army mustered him out. I'm sorry. There'll be no charge, Lula, because I couldn't get him to the phone."

Weeks passed. Lula wrote letters to the new coach, the commanding officer, even to Glen himself, hoping he might return to base. Christmas came and went. They had no notion of where to find Iris, either.

In January, Barney put on his suit again, and Lula wore the dress paid for with the five dollars George tossed in the mud three years before. They drove the wagon eight miles to the sheriff's office in Modesto.

Three days later, the *Modesto News-Register* reported, "Last Friday, the sheriff's office here was asked to assist in a search for Glen Wilkerson, twenty-three, an army man, last seen after the army- navy football game in Berkeley last November. His parents live in Riverbank. Wilkerson, a football player, received a broken leg after the game and was honorably discharged and since then has not been seen or heard from according to reports to the sheriff."

Glen "Wilkie" Wilkerson had vanished.

Chapter 20

GLEN

San Francisco and Oakland, California, 1931–1932

McCormick was only half right. Seeing his mother again loosened the noose around Glen's neck, but it was still there, and it still chaffed. Something about his years as an orphan, thinking that way—alone on the prow of his life, rudderless, unanswerable to anyone—it would simply not slip away, even after his mother's ardent apology. It was like running a punt return, and running and running down an endless field, no goal post, no victory.

And yet, he was drawn back there, to the farm and milking barn, the adobe, his mother, Jody, Maudie. Barney's correction of Jedediah Coates not withstanding—he would have relished seeing Coates teeter on the end of the pitchfork—he was not inclined to forgive the old ass. Barney had never said he was sorry anyway, unless you counted his one-sided assertion about bygones being bygones. Glen could not warm up to his brothers, either. Too much of Barney in them, he suspected. Something about Jody made him want to protect her, and for that, he needed to keep an eye on Barney and his boys.

So he would spend most of his leaves out there, hitchhiking the hundred miles to Riverbank. Often took him an entire day. Sometimes, he would borrow Ray's car, but Ray himself showed no interest in accompanying him. Probably just as well. Ray calculated everything to his advantage, and the maneuvering was loud and erratic. Glen's way was subtle. A word to his younger brothers here; a sideline glance to his stepfather there. He knew some things now—what children deserved, what parents owed them. It was too late for him, a perpetual orphan of the living, but it might not be too late for Maudie and Jody.

If Glen had a home, it was inside the walls of the Presidio. McCormick, Kingsley, and most of the boys: family. With the exception of Privates Jasper Thorne and Sidney Nash, who had turned a failed hazing on Glen's first day on the field into an all-out war. Glen couldn't quite figure it. He'd heard their scorn toward Negro folks who worked at the ship yards, but he was as white as they were. He'd seen them pick on smaller, younger soldiers, but Glen was bigger than each of them. Yes, he was a Yankee, but so were most of the boys. What, then? Walter and Glen chewed it over one night on the barracks steps, blowing smoke into the perpetual San Francisco fog.

"Why me, Walter? Why us?"

"Favor, perhaps. McCormick, you know."

"Maybe. But there's something else. Something in some men that just makes them want to beat other folks down, like they ain't got enough credence on their own, got to rub out anyone who does. That's where Karl Marx had it wrong."

Walter had heard the whole story of Jimmy Bird; and of Glen's fascination with Marx; and his sidekick, Huck Finn.

"What did he have wrong?"

"I think it's what finally wore Jimmy Bird down. He could see the truth, straight in front of him: If we would only take what we need . . . But we're a selfish lot, Walter."

"So you think Thorne and Nash get a pass then? Just men doing what men do?"

"Hell no!"

And so Walter and Glen began a slow and calculated take-down of their two tormentors.

It was subtle, left no fingerprints. Being a hungry boy who remembered lean times, Glen made friends on the Kitchen Police crew, including a couple of Black civilians who worked for the base. They were happy to give a football star an extra pork chop, or hand a whole apple pie out the back kitchen door. Didn't take much convincing for them to slip an old slab of meat or a tainted potato into the littermates' rations. Food poisoning sidelined them both through a great deal of spring practice. Walter was in charge of distributing the mail each day, and hard to understand why, but the littermates rarely ever got any. They failed to pass inspection frequently too. Little infractions scuttled their weekend passes in favor of guard duty, or scrubbing the barracks.

They complained to no end, blaming Glen and Walter to anyone who would listen. But no one but Glen and Walter knew who bashed Glen's knee, and of course, the littermates couldn't reveal their one true antagonizing act.

"Should we quit? We got them pretty good," Glen suggested.

"You still having fun, though?" Walter asked.

"Hell yes."

So on it went, right on through losing the 1931 Armistice Day game to navy, 6–0, Thorne and Nash sitting it out, casting most of the blame on McCormick, Wilkerson, and Kingsley.

McCormick's departure in the spring of 1932 put Glen right back on the prow of his ship, alone. The new coach, Johnny Baker, made it clear he didn't give a horse's patootie for anything McCormick sanctioned. The 1931 season was over, and Glen had no idea what might happen when practice commenced in the spring. To make matters worse, Kingsley and several other players, now considered tainted goods, were transferred to the Presidio in Monterey. Glen was left with the littermates, like the scrapings at the bottom of the bean pot. Why he was kept, he couldn't say.

Ray, who was finding it less advantageous to bet on the army team and Glen, showed up in January on the eve of Glen's first weekend leave in months and hauled Glen off to Oakland and his cramped apartment with Marjory near the shipyards.

"Come on, Glen. Let loose! You just need some pussy and a few shots of whiskey," Ray admonished on the trip across the bay.

Feeling lower than the rocks off Alcatraz, he followed his brother into a string of smokey dance halls billowing with swing, big bands, girls, and—since Prohibition hung on like a bad cold—backroom whiskey and beer.

"It ain't illegal to drink, Glen, just to buy and sell the stuff. So me and my buddy Fritz, we just store a few cases in back rooms here and there," Ray explained at the First and Last Chance Saloon, where Marjory played the piano most nights.

"Who you getting it from?"

Ray just winked and disappeared into the back room for another belt. Glen followed him. One time, two. The boy had scarcely had a drop to drink, just a glass of sherry courtesy of Walter, a cold beer in the backseat of McCormick's car.

With two tumblers of straight whiskey in his belly, Glen returned to his bar stool, which now weaved and pitched of its own accord. The taste— charcoal, scorched sugar, and Unguentine—lingered in his throat like swamp gas. He ordered a Coke and attempted to wash it down.

At the piano, Marjory was striking the first soaring chords of *Stardust.* A woman with marcelled hair and a short, spangled red dress, floated her voice out over the melody.

"And now the purple dusk of twilight time . . ."

Glen tried to focus on the music, which beat at a more leisurely pace than the blood at his temples. His eyes settled on a woman across the room sitting with a sailor. The sailor was talking loudly and waving a cigarette. She stared vacantly over his shoulder as if he was a gnat likely to blow out on the next breeze.

"Steals across the meadows of my heart . . ."

Against the sailor's dress whites, the woman glowed like a cast sculpture under a beam of light. Her skin, oiled bronze; her lips, a deeper bronze; her copper hair, caught up in a chignon, a wide sweep of bangs curled behind her left ear. She sat motionless, a thin plume of smoke rising in a curl from a cigarette held between two of her manicured bronze fingers. Even her dress, plunging deep into a V, was swirls of copper and bronze.

"High up in the sky, the little stars climb . . ."

Glen slid carefully from his bar stool and crossed the sawdust-covered floor. "She is totally out of my league," he whispered, but the whiskey said otherwise. "She'll know you're drunk," he said to himself, but the whiskey just said, *Nah.*

At her table, he steadied himself with a hand on the back of an empty chair. The sailor glanced up and kept talking. The woman looked up at him.

"My name's Glen. Everyone calls me Wilkie, but you can choose."

She smiled. "Well, Wilkie it is, then."

"What's your name?"

"Buzz off," the sailor said.

"Iris," she said.

"Of course it is. You are the color of a beautiful flower," But it came out boo-te-full. Glen tapped his chest with a fist as if to dislodge a demon.

"I think some air might be good, Wilkie. Would you take a walk with me?"

"Hey!" the sailor said.

"Yes, ma'am."

They meandered along the waterfront, dodging donkey-driven drays and Chinese men pulling carts. Glen took off his uniform jacket, draped it around her shoulders, and lifted her at the waist to navigate a mud puddle. She weighed nothing in his arms, like air or bliss.

"What brings you to Oakland? I thought all you army boys were over in 'Frisco."

"My brother Ray. His wife, she's the piano player."

"Ah. You like the army?"

"Well, yes, ma'am, it's pretty good. But it's football for me, really. I play—"

"Oh my, you're *that* Wilkie. My mother was at the Armistice Day game! Believe it or not, she's a big fan."

"But not you?"

"Gimme some time."

Glen gave her every minute. She worked in her mother's dress shop in Oakland, and when the shop closed in the evening, if Glen had leave, he would be standing under a streetlight outside the shop door. Iris's mother was delighted to see him, but Iris was as reserved as the bronze sculpture she resembled.

She always wanted to walk. A walk, a talk. Vertical things. In which she extracted the story of his life, from his Oklahoma birth, to his misbegotten Montana years, to Oregon, Jimmy Bird, Karl Marx, and Mark Twain. She joined the army with him; sat quietly in the Kezar Stadium bleachers contemplating a field of honor, or loss, with him; lay under the branches of the redwood tree with him, gripping his shattered knee. She stood alongside the road in Riverbank with him, auguring deep into his pain and anger, feeling his mother's arms around *her* knees as Glen had felt them around his.

And with every story he told, Glen felt her bronze reserve dissolve. The day he told her about Jody, Jedediah Coates and the outhouse, Iris stopped them on their walk and gripped his arm.

"I'd like to meet your sister someday."

"Would you now, Iris! She would love you. I know she would."

Spring warmth melted the morning fog over the practice field. It was the first day with Baker calling the plays. He introduced the new quarterback, Kingsley's replacement, a brawny Italian corporal named Gallo. Baker made it clear he'd have no favorites, but that merely meant he wouldn't have *McCormick's* favorites. Gallo was one of Baker's favorites, certainly, and as if to burn a hole in Glen's heart, so were Thorne and Nash. Now it was Glen who rode the pine through most of the spring games. It dawned on him why Baker had kept him: He was an object lesson. If you were McCormick's pal, or harbored any secret allegiance to him, expect to end up like Glen, withering away, whether you were a star or not.

But Glen's irritation stayed on the field. Iris occupied his thoughts, even if the extent of their romance was long walks, her arm folded into his as if it had taken root. He took her out to the old adobe with him once that spring, and again at midsummer, her bronze skin in a yellow polka-dot sundress nearly blinded him on the drive out in Ray's car.

Jody pouted at first, seeing no reason she should share Glen with anyone, let alone this tall, willowy woman Glen followed around as if attached to her with an invisible string. Iris anticipated just such a reaction and arrived with a small doll she'd made from scraps in her mother's shop. She offered the doll and a showering of conspiratorial looks that said, "Glen is yours, but I'm hoping you'll share." It only took an afternoon. Iris snared Jody and the whole household. Her laugh rang off the warm adobe kitchen walls as she helped Lula do the washing up. Then she sat on the front stoop, smoking with Glen and Barney. Even Lula, who took a dim view of women and cigarettes, could not resist her charm.

On the long drive back to the city, the windows down, their cigarettes glowing bright as comets in the twilight, Glen looked at her as often as he did the road in front of him. He hummed a few lines from *Stardust*—*"Sometimes I wonder how I spent the lonely nights"*—into the companionable quiet.

Baker's sanctions were not so easy to shut out, though, as the season went along. Glen missed the camaraderie on the field, just playing the game, connecting with Kingsley, even the thud of his big body against the grass, the ball tucked tightly in his arms. Baker took him off offense completely, playing him at defensive tackle, when he played him at all, stripping him of everything about the army he loved.

He arrived one evening at Iris's after the team had lost another game. Glen played, but only one quarter, and at that, after they were twenty points behind. He stood under Iris's streetlamp, bruised, angry, lonely. Iris took one look at him, grasped his hand, and pulled him toward the stairs that led up to the apartment above the shop.

"What?" Glen asked.

"Mother's out. Bridge night."

Glen followed her up the stairs, a grin breaking through the wounds of the day.

"A boy can't live on walks alone," Iris said, smiling back at him.

Glen wondered if his virginity hung on him like a neon sign. Her virginity was not in question, and he could have cared less. Better that *one* of them knew what to do. He held her close, stroking her hair, her back, melting his body to glide over hers like butter. He discovered he didn't need a line coach to tell him how to play this position. He fell asleep afterward and slept like a closed book, a sleep so bewitching he would forever judge any night's slumber against it. He woke to her hand on his chest.

"You best wake up. Mother's going to wonder why I'm not at breakfast."

Glen sat straight up. He'd sneaked off base, a buddy covering for him, just hoping for a breath of Iris's bronze skin. He intended to sneak back in well before reveille. He jumped up and grabbed his uniform pants, suddenly shy. Iris let the sheet fall from her breasts so he wouldn't be naked alone, and laughed at his panic, hopping on one leg, then the other, trying to pull his pants on.

"Are you in trouble?"

"Yes, ma'am. I'm in trouble," he said, shoving his shirt tails into his pants. "But I have to ask you one thing before I go."

"Shoot, soldier."

"Will you marry me?"

Iris laughed. "Why'd you think I pulled you up those stairs, lover boy?"

Glen rushed onto the practice field, and everyone stopped to watch him.

"Nice of you to join us, Private Wilkerson," Baker called out.

"Sorry, sir. I—"

"You run laps today, rest of practice."

Glen ran for two hours, and when he slowed to a walk, Baker's whistle and wave goosed him back to speed. He'd not had any breakfast and was so thirsty, he wiped the sweat off his neck and licked his hand. He swore to himself that he wasn't going to pass out, give Baker the satisfaction. By the time Baker whistled an end to practice, he figured he'd run fifteen miles. And then he saw the MPs walking toward him, followed by Baker.

"Wilkerson, you know there's a brig here at the Presidio? It's where you'll be spending the next month, when you're not at practice. You ever leave this base again without my express permission, and you can expect a dishonorable discharge."

"Yes sir. If I could explain, sir—"

"Don't want to hear it, don't care. Gentlemen, take him away."

Glen ached, his stomach heaved and gnawed, but he couldn't stop smiling. Iris was going to marry him!

"Listen fellas, could we stop by the barracks? If I'm bound for the brig, I'd like to get a few things. Couple of books, a clean uniform."

The guards looked at each other.

"Who you s'posed won us more games, Wilkie or Baker?" the shorter one asked his partner.

They shrugged.

"Sure, Wilkie, that'd be fine," said the tall one.

Glen found himself in a small, rectangular brick cell with a bunk, a sink, a latrine bucket, his copies of *The Adventures of Huckleberry Finn* and *The Communist Manifesto*, a stack of army stationary, a pencil, and twelve postage stamps thanks to his fans, the short and tall MPs whom he nicknamed—much to their delight—Buster and Bruiser. When word reached the KP crew that Wilkie was in the brig, brimming trays of Grade-A army chow arrived. Buster and Bruiser were all too happy to deliver them. In fact, the MPs took it on themselves to be Glen's personal valets, which included mailing his letters and delivering his mail.

Dear Iris,

Well, going AWOL landed me in the brig. Baker has sentenced me to one month, except for football practice. It ain't too bad. I've got everything I need, except you. I keep thinking of our night together, and your answer to my proposal of marriage, which I intend to hold you to no matter what. How will your mother feel about you marrying a convict? Ha!

I've got nothing to do but read, and write to you, and I am enjoying both, and hope you will write me back as soon as you get this. Don't even think of coming to see me. They say I have no visitor privileges, so it'll be a sad month without your smile and the touch of your arm through mine. Please promise me a month apart will do nothing to change things between us, other than make us both pine for each other even more.

Your favorite football player and future husband,
Wilkie

Glen read his way through his two-book library once again, after the volumes had endured years of neglect at the bottom of his footlocker. When he read Jim's dialogue, his lips moved silently, attempting to get the accent just right, the despair just right, the injustice just right. He heard Jim's voice, but the face he imagined was Jimmy Bird's. Alternately reading chapters from Marx and Twain revived the despair he felt lying next to Jimmy Bird under a Wallowa night sky, brought it right into the cell, as if the stars hung in their mysterious patterns from the brick and mortar. Castaway on his iron bunk in the brig, he sank below the waves, wondering how it was that men of one color could sanction the very life out of men of another color.

But then the notions that had bloomed before Jimmy Bird's suicide—his nascent ardor for revolution, his ever-present love for the little guys—poured out of the brick walls around him, raising him up, beyond football, beyond Baker, beyond his animosity for an old, ignoble, farmer one hundred miles away in the San Joaquin Valley. There was truth in Marx and Twain he could not ignore, and somehow it had shaped him like wind on sandstone. He had pushed away such definition in his anger over Jimmy Bird, but alone in this brick box, he welcomed it now, craved its carving presence.

Then Buster and Bruiser brought him Iris's reply.

Dear Wilkie,

If you think a month apart will change a thing, you've got some things to learn about me. I'll be here, waiting, no matter what.

But I suppose I better fess up to something that might change your mind about me. I'm sure you've noticed that I am not pearly white skinned like my mother. And I've just avoided any questions you've asked about my father. So I think it's best to tell you the truth. My mother married an Indian named Owen Littlecrow, from the Red Rock tribe in Oklahoma. And that's where I got the brown skin and thick hair you love so much. But he took off when I was ten, and we changed our last name to Martin, as American as anything my mother could imagine. That's why you met me at the First and Last Chance saloon. I heard he comes there sometimes, delivering liquor to the backroom for folks like your brother Ray. I'm not sure what I would have done had I seen him: kicked him in the shins, or thrown my arms around him. He's a drunk, they say, and it breaks my heart.

I am hoping you will still want to marry a half-breed, and bring little baby Wilkersons into the world with me. I love you, Wilkie. I haven't told you that yet, but I do. You can say you don't want me now, but I ain't giving up that easy. I know what we have together.

Love,

Iris

What was this? *"I love you, Wilkie."* He jumped up on his cot and pumped his fist in the air. That her father was an Indian? He thought on it a moment, maybe two, and tested his resolve. It counted for nothing! He had grown to love Jimmy Bird in the dark of a rail car a long time ago. He loved Iris before he knew that her bronze skin and wild copper hair were emblems of the

American Indian. Then he sat on the bunk and asked himself another question. Would he have fallen for her if he knew she was Indian *first?* If someone in the bar that night had said, "See that Indian gal over there?" Would he have crossed the room, half lit-up, and walked her all over Oakland, swooning, addicted? Hell yes.

GLEN

San Francisco, Berkeley, and Oakland; California; 1932–1933

Glen licked all twelve stamps during his month in the brig, affixing each one to a letter addressed to Iris, dutifully mailed by Buster and Bruiser. Iris replied to each one. The twenty-four letters erected a scaffolding: where they might live, how many children they might have, how they might brace each other like cornerstones. Glen allowed himself to imagine life beyond the army, beyond football, but the image, like a foggy San Francisco day, was hazy. He realized that keeping Iris would require some accommodation for the Man—namely, a job. What that might be, he could not guess. Iris didn't seem to care, as long as they were together.

Her last letter arrived on November 10, on the eve of the Armistice Day army-navy game at Memorial Stadium.

"I will be in the stands, lover boy. Think of me there."

The trick, Glen thought, will be to think of anything else.

Baker called Glen into his office the week before the game, his first hour out of the brig that didn't involve practice. The coach looked unhappy, hissing like a puff adder.

"Wilkerson, they're printing the game program today. I don't like you, right down to your shoelaces. You think you're more righteous than the rest of us, you and your sad orphan story, you and your Warner Attack. You and your Indian girlfriend. You didn't think I knew about that, did ya? I've got eyes on you."

Glen stared stoically over Baker's shoulder, unsure what he was doing there.

"Truth is, Wilkerson, as much as I'd rather keep you in the brig and throw away the key, I, uh, I need to win this game. And when I look at this roster"—he tossed the pages down on his desk—"I can't see any way to do that without playing you. Starting you."

Glen cleared his throat and thought it in his best interest not to smile.

"I'll do my best, sir."

"Will you? Because I need everyone, including Privates Thorne and Nash. You understand me, Wilkerson? You play like you mean it, you play like you're on a team—*my* team—or I swear, I'll rack your ass in front of seventy thousand people, including that Indian girlfriend. Dismissed."

Glen's valets, Buster and Bruiser, walked him back to the barracks. They all three swung their heads low, like scythes against the hay.

"We heard, Wilkie. You're gonna start, seems like, though."

"Yes, boys, starting. Finishing? I ain't sure."

The army team's bus stopped near the high arched entrance to Memorial Stadium, California and US flags billowing in the westerly coming off San Francisco Bay. They stepped off the bus into a melee. There were about a hundred protesters: Black and white; men in suits and ties and brogues; women in flowered dresses, their hair styled, hats pinned in place, looking less like football fans or agitators and more like folk bound for church. They carried banners and signs, and ringed the entrance chanting, "No more war! End military football!" The signs and banners danced in the cool November breeze. FREE THE SCOTTSBORO BOYS! and WE DEMAND A FORTY-HOUR WORK WEEK.

"Come on, men! Let's enter at the next gate," Baker yelled. Most of the team followed him. A few, Glen and the littermates, lingered.

Glen watched sailors and soldiers surround the demonstrators as if they were enemy combatants. A young Black man was handing out pamphlets. Glen slid close to him.

"Who are you guys?"

"Hello, soldier. We're Communists. Here, read about us."

Glen grasped the pamphlet like a lifeline. Outside the pages of the *Communist Manifesto*, outside of Jimmy Bird and Parnell, he'd never met a Communist.

"What are you doing here?"

"See the signs?"

"I do, but . . . I'm a Communist, and I'll be playing in the game."

"Why?" Before Glen could answer, in a blur over his shoulder, the littermates rushed past and pushed the young Communist to the ground. The violent thumping opened a release valve on the crowd.

Cries of "Get 'em! Dirty commies!" flew up all around Glen. He tried to help the young man up, but in the crush, ended up on the ground next to him, as police whistles filled the air.

On the ground, Glen and the protester lay face to face.

"You better get out of here. They're going to arrest us."

Glen heeded the warning.

Glen pulled on Number 6, the uniform he'd been wearing all season since Baker moved him to defense. Starting tackle, six feet tall, 186 pounds. His photo and these scant details in the program, in addition to countless sports page stories over the years, told the crowd of seventy thousand all they would ever know about him.

Glen stared at the photo and hoped that somewhere in the stands, Iris thought he looked good. In his other hand, he held the Communist pamphlet. Each, a way forward. In one hand, the secure life of the army, the gridiron, the fluttering American flag, and banner-sized WILKIE headlines in the sports pages. And in the other hand? Uncertainty, turmoil, renown of another kind.

The team gathered in the tunnel under the bleachers. At the sound of the army's anthem, "The Caissons Go Rolling Along," they charged up the stairs onto the field. The roar from the army stands temporarily settled Glen's confusion. Football. There would be time for Iris later.

Fifteen bands strutted along playing music from World War I: "Land of Hope and Glory," "Over There," "Stars and Stripes Forever." A one-thousand-member flag corps filled the field, goal post to goal post, waving flags and banners in unison, none of them demanding a forty-hour work week, he noticed. Glen scanned the fans behind him, row upon row of khaki, men in suits, women in hats, hoping for a glimpse of Iris, but it was no good. He was off-balance, a foot in two worlds.

For the first quarter, army was in free-fall. The offense might as well have been playing in diapers against the grown-up navy defense, making only twelve yards in eight plays. When they turned the ball over to navy each time, and army's defensive line took the field, it wasn't much better. Glen had never spent so much time running in the wrong direction. He couldn't figure out what was happening. The second quarter was just as dismal. By halftime, it was navy, 14–0.

"You jackasses!" Baker yelled at them in the locker room. "We're already worse off than the 6–0 score you bozos lost by last year!" Glen looked at old patterns of crack and wear in the concrete floor, and tried to tune Baker out. Some of the guys played better after a reaming, but he didn't. There was no way up from it. He needed an encouraging word, and Baker didn't have the vocabulary, or the sense, to deliver one.

Back out on the field, he thought of Iris above him somewhere, and determined to sack as many navy receivers as he could lay his hands on. And so for the next twelve navy plays, he crushed ten pass receivers, and nailed the quarterback twice. But coming out of the huddle, Glen found himself leveled during the next three plays, and not the easy way down either. He pulled himself up off the grass the third time, and saw Thorne grinning at him.

"Like that, you fuckin' commie?"

Glen ignored him, but on the next play, when he and Thorne should have gone left toward the navy quarterback's fade, Thorne dropped back, and Glen was gored by two heavy navy linebackers. This time, he didn't get up. Navy took it all the way to the end zone for another six points. Still, Glen didn't move. The medic was cramming smelling salts under his nose. The crowd grew quiet.

"Got your bell rung, huh, Wilkie?" the medic asked when he opened his eyes to not one, but three weaving medics, all wearing the same grim expression.

"You're done, soldier. You wanna walk, or should we get the stretcher?"

"Walk me off, will ya, Carter?"

"Sure thing."

Glen sat on the bench, struggling to regain his senses, and all the while, his army team withered away. Baker paced back and forth, yelling insults at his players, at the refs, at the fans in the stands who now booed at army for every failed tackle, every poorly thrown pass, every missed opportunity. Glen couldn't blame them. At the final whistle, it was navy 30, army 0. Glen's teammates struggled to gather their gear and head to the locker room, as navy fans rushed onto the field, raising players and the game ball, signed by President Hoover, high overhead.

Glen tried standing, but the dizziness was overwhelming. Where was that medic? He almost collapsed again when he heard a voice behind him.

"Commie lover, ain't you, Wilkerson?" Thorne hollered above the roar of the fans and the navy midshipmen marching their goat with the army mascot blanket thrown over it.

"Oh, he ain't just that," Nash jumped in. "Loves them reds. Russians. Indians too."

Glen tried to back away. Nash and Thorne descended on him, pushing him onto the bench.

"Guess we didn't work that leg over enough the first time," Thorne laughed, yanking Glen's left ankle up in the air, sending Glen over the bench backward. As he fell, Thorne, twisted, wrenching Glen's extended leg, and brought it down on the bench. He landed upside down in a heap. Nash jumped on the bench, then jumped with both feet on Glen's extended leg. No one paid any attention, or heard his scream over the celebration on the field. Thorne and Nash grabbed their gear and headed, without much speed or regard, to the locker room. Glen was unconscious, alone, a dirty pile in army's Number 6, in the last light of the afternoon.

When Carter couldn't find Wilkie in the locker room, he ran back out to the field. He saw his injured tackle crumpled on the grass, one leg canted out like a used drinking straw, and a woman and a man kneeling on either side of him. The woman held Wilkie's hand and cried.

"Hey! Get away from him!" Carter yelled.

"Why? Got some more army medicine in that bag? Are you a friend of the two who did this to him?"

"What? Who the hell are you?"

"I'm his girl. My brother and I were coming down from our seats when we saw two other players beating up on him. Now he's hardly breathing—and his leg, something's wrong with it!"

Carter knelt next to Iris and checked Glen's airway, then turned his attention to the leg and the blood seeping through his uniform pants.

"You stay with him, will ya? Don't touch that leg! I've got to get an ambulance."

Deeming the leg's compound fracture too dangerous and the army hospital at the Presidio too far, Carter had the ambulance take them to Berkeley General Hospital. Two surgeons rolled Glen to the second-floor surgery wing. Carter, Iris, and her brother, Bobby, sat in stiff metal chairs outside the surgery ward for four hours.

The surgeons, when they appeared, looked whipped.

"Well, we saved his leg, in all likelihood, if infection doesn't set in, but his hip will ever be the same. That must have been some tackle."

Carter glanced at Iris.

"Thank you, doctors. When can we transfer him to the Presidio?"

Iris stamped her foot. "Why? So those hoodlums can finish what they started?"

"Miss, it's just the army way."

"We'll see about that," she said.

When Carter returned three days later with an army ambulance, the Berkeley Memorial Hospital did not include one Private Glen Wilkerson. He had checked himself out, into the care of a woman with flaming red hair.

For the next three months, Glen convalesced in Iris's bedroom. Iris or Bobby or Mildred often sat reading to him, the Martin family doctor checking in every couple of days. When he was strong enough to walk, slowly, a short distance, Bobby and Iris took him on the ferry back to the Presidio, where he was arrested almost immediately and placed once again in the charge of his valets, Buster and Bruiser.

"Fellas, while my future wife and brother-in-law are still here, I'd like to visit with Coach Baker, if you don't mind."

So there they stood in Baker's office, arm in arm, Glen between Bobby and Iris.

"You're finished, Wilkerson. Spend the next few months in the brig waiting for your court martial or take a dishonorable now and get out of my sight."

Iris and Bobby laughed. Glen thought about Wilbur Taft and the hayloft, how doors can swing open when you least expect it.

"I think I'll take the brig time, sir. And the hearing. Because that's when Sgt. Carter will testify that he left me on the bench with a concussion at the end of the game, and came back ten minutes later to find me unconscious, my leg broken in three places, and my pelvis fractured. And then I'll ask these two folk to describe what they saw from the stands, namely Thorne and Nash stomping me to pieces. And then if they ask, I'll tell them how Thorne and Nash let navy sack me, and I'm guessing, if they put those idiots on the stand, they'll give you up in the blink of an eye. 'Cause I figure they are too dumb to have conjured that move on their own. And then, I suspect, it won't take too much cogitating before the Court Martial realizes you just . . . threw the game. And then they might start wondering how much you got for that. Do you suppose, sir?"

Baker shoved his chair back and left the office like a man escaping a burning building. The three of them stood, linked, unmoving. Fifteen minutes later, Baker returned and shoved a set of papers into Glen's hand.

"Honorable discharge. Sign it, or take your chances at trial. Lots of memories fade, Wilkerson."

Iris took the pages and looked them over, and nodded at Glen. He signed.

On the way out, Buster and Bruiser met them at the gate.

"Wilkie, we saved your things, everything from your footlocker and the brig."

Glen took the canvas bag and slung it over his shoulder, the solid familiarity of Marx and Twain pressed onto his back.

"So long, boys. Thanks for everything."

A week later, on the windy first Monday of March, 1933, Glen lounged on Iris's bed and assessed their clothes, hanging haphazardly from hooks and the chair at the foot of the bed.

"Iris, wear that dress, would you for me? The one you had on the night we met?" Glen asked. He slipped his twisted leg into his army uniform, the only decent clothing he had ever owned.

Glen and Iris walked up the steps of Oakland City Hall, accompanied by Bobby, Mildred, Ray, and Marjory, and vowed to a justice of the peace to love each other till death did them part.

It only seemed right to celebrate their wedding at the First and Last Chance Saloon, while Marjory played piano.

Glen felt untethered without the army, a wayward balloon held on Earth by Iris alone. Even so, they couldn't live in Iris's bedroom forever. Life had always presented itself to Glen as an either-or proposition. Live or die; throw the ball over the fence, or rot in the orphanage; jump the freight, or starve. Now it spread out vaguely before him, no discernible options. So when Bobby's friend showed up at their wedding table with news of work, he paid attention.

"Hey, Bobby. You and your big friend here need a job? Union's hiring workers to build a bridge over the Golden Gate. I just signed on today. Promised us a forty-hour week, decent wages. All you got to have is a year's residency. That, and a little muscle."

Glen and Bobby got in line the next morning and joined the union. A week later, they were handed newfangled hard hats and took their places with 415 construction workers. In a month, Glen had learned to conceal his limp and to weld, and by two months, he and Iris had their own apartment. At night, Iris would massage away the spasms in Glen's leg. In his pain fog, he thought about his mother, his stepfather, and especially Jody, for the first time in months.

Some nights, the leg begged for opium, and he let his leg have its way.

NORA MAE

Riverbank and Oakland, California, 1933–1937

If every star in the night sky refused to shine, if the moon wrapped itself in a shroud, if the crickets silenced their wings, if the scent of alfalfa was too obstinate to rise from the field on the midnight air, Nora Mae could not have felt more alone. Each night after the others slept, she would chart a path through the milking barn, touching each cow—a string of beads on a rosary—then slink out along the fence and irrigation ditch. She paced back and forth, worrying a path in the leathery dirt. If Glen had vanished, she would too! He was somewhere, and through magic— for surely there was magic, the random good and bad that bandied her life about like a shuttlecock—she would find him. Her thin frame, her wreath of yellow hair, her bare feet, her cotton dress, the little doll from Iris under her arm, she marched and schemed. She could become smaller and smaller until she disappeared and then she would reappear wherever he was. Wearing pants! That last part was a little fantastical, she knew, maybe pressing the magic too hard. But she wished for it. She wished to wear pants forever.

"Pants!" she yelled at the indifferent night.

If there could be a Mr. Coates and his torment, why couldn't there be, on the other side of things, this magical transportment from the farm to a life in the city, a life in pants? She came out each night, alone, waiting for the lightening to strike, the magic to alight.

For their parts, Barney and Lula had no better luck finding Glen even with the sheriff's help and their newspaper entreaty. They couldn't find Ray, either, or remember Iris's last name.

The spring slipped into summer, and Lula's grief overflowed onto Nora Mae, always the child who seemed the most deserving of her ire. At eight years old, Nora Mae had become more canny and less willing to be threshed, however. If Lula was never going to love her, why not torment her?

So she bungled her chores, refused her dinner, stole her teacher's fountain pen, and recently, found great joy in destroying her brothers' shoes, throwing them down the hole in the outhouse. She patented an innocent raised eyebrow when Lula confronted her, manufacturing elaborate explanations as thin as tissue, as if she wanted to be found out for her misdeeds.

Lula tried whipping her, and when that didn't work, she ignored her even more extravagantly than she had in years past. Barney pleaded with her, late at night, while Nora Mae, unbeknownst to them, prowled the perimeter of the farm.

"Lay off her, Lula. I thought you were gonna try harder!"

"What would you have me do, Barney? She won't obey. They've sent her home from school three times now. She bit a child the other day! She's a . . . a hoodlum!"

He was flooded with images of Luzelba and Violet as they must have been in their youth. Had they been full of such spite? Maybe. It gave him a jolt. He secretly rooted for his daughter's pugnacity.

"Lula, she's just a spirited girl."

"Well, I never!" She rolled over, her heart fluttering with a powerful conviction that her youngest child was the root of all evil.

Glen finally arrived at the Stovalls' a week later in a brand new 1932 Ford Model 18, purchased for $480, on time, twenty dollars a month, a special deal offered by the brother of the cousin of the fella Glen welded next to every day. Union men with hard green cash in their pockets were rare creatures in the Depression. To Glen, the spirited little maroon Deuce Coupe gave him a sense of freedom as powerful as he felt the afternoon he threw his canvas bag over the fence at Twin Bridges. It whetted his appetite for more, for bigger, for flashier. Across the street from the Ford lot, the Cadillac dealer had placed a shiny, new straight eight out in the sun; had a little kid just shining it all day long. Glen picked up his new car and drove it directly across the street to the Cadillac dealer. Iris sat next to him, clutching her purse and beaming.

Glen got out and walked around the Cadillac, twice, then got back in the car.

"Iris, I'm buying us one of those."

"Are you crazy? See what's on the window? They cost $3,000!"

"Not this year. Not next year. But someday, I'm taking you to dinner in a Cadillac, you, and all the babies in the back seat. You just wait."

With the Deuce Coupe, his new job, his three-room apartment, his wife, he had tilted straight into the American middle class, an anomaly when men still stood in soup lines all over San Francisco. For once, things seemed to be going his way. And that gave him the courage to come back to the farm, even after the defeat at Memorial Stadium and the months that he had simply been a ghost.

He drove fast into the yard, a slice of valley dust spinning out from under the tires. Iris gathered her scarf and started to open the door.

"Wait," Glen said, touching her arm. The household was still, maybe pouting, he thought, unsure what to make of their sudden appearance. A minute passed. And then around the corner of the house, a small blond child ran toward them, her wispy hair flying.

"Wilkie! Wilkie! Wilkie! I knew you'd come," Nora Mae cried, flinging open the driver's door and jumping into his arms. Glen nodded to Iris, and they got out, Glen balancing Nora Mae on his shoulder. Lula stood on the porch, both hands over her mouth, a thin wail escaping around her worn fingers.

It took the better part of the afternoon for Glen to tell the story of the last game, his busted leg, Iris's heroics, the wedding, the Golden Gate, all of it. The boys cared little about the details and instead swarmed over the car like it was the Ark of the Covenant.

But Glen saved the best news for last, and let Iris tell it.

"We're having a baby!"

Lula, who had spent the hours grasping her cheeks and bubbling with happiness, let out a little squeak. Even Barney beamed. Nora Mae had not left Glen's side, and he squeezed her tighter. She looked from Glen to Iris, unsure where babies came from. Would she lose her spot by his side? Glen squeezed her again and brushed the blond tendrils from her face.

"You like babies, doncha, Jody?"

She nodded, not sure she liked them at all.

Nora Mae and Maudie gave up their little room for the newlyweds and slept on the living room floor. Nora Mae slipped out and sat on the bumper of the Deuce Coupe, as if it might go off on an adventure without her.

In the morning, Glen and his mother took a walk up the road.

"I'm sorry, Mama, that I didn't write."

"Or call! We've a telephone now, you know. I was just so worried."

Glen could see no upside in explaining himself, his utter

absorption with his injuries, his wife, and now, his job. The army and football, and that whole miserable day at Memorial Stadium, were things in another life. He wondered whatever became of his buddy Kingsley. Maybe he and Iris should drive over to Monterey and look for him, if he could stomach stepping onto an army base again. The thought alone caused his limp to bark, and he pressed on his thigh.

"Mama, Iris and I want to ask a favor. Will you let us take Nora Mae home with us, just for a week?"

Lula gasped.

"Whatever for? That child is nothing but trouble!"

"I think it might do her some good, and give you a break. I know it's—"

"Take her! Some days, I would say keep her too."

The next morning, Nora Mae found herself perched between Iris and Glen on the Deuce Coupe's bench seat, clutching a flour sack with a change of clothes. It gave her a particular thrill to look up in the rearview mirror and see her brothers standing in the coupe's dust as they pulled onto the road and turned west, toward the city and the sea and a world that would not include—for at least a week—her tormenting brothers and her unattainable mother.

The week with Glen and Iris was a dream, and she an apparition, floating from one astonishing thing to another. After Glen left for work in the morning, she went with Iris to her mother's dress shop and sat in the corner, watching Iris fit women for new gowns. Iris would take the afternoons off, and they'd take the street car to Alameda Beach, or the ferry across the bay to meet Glen after work. The three of them would wander through Chinatown, eating noodles and sipping tea. There were delights beyond her ken: cotton candy, soda pop, store windows full of fashions and bicycles and furniture. In the evening, around the apartment's tiny kitchen table, Glen taught her to play poker and gin rummy.

"Glen, your mother will have a fit."

"What, a girl can't play poker?"

"Not an eight-year-old, no." And they all laughed.

The laughing, Nora Mae thought, was the best part.

The only part she didn't like was when Iris and her mother measured her for a new dress.

"But I don't like dresses!"

"Really, Nora Mae? Don't you want to be pretty like Iris here?"

"But I'll never be pretty! Doncha see? I will just look silly, and the other girls will tease me. They always do. I'll have to sock 'em, and I'll be in trouble again!"

"Well, what would you like then?" Iris asked gently.

Nora Mae pawed through the bin of bolt ends until she came to a blue worsted wool.

"I'd like a suit with pants and a coat with three buttons and a big wide collar, and a pair of brown and white saddle shoes, like we seen in that window downtown."

Mildred laughed, but Iris pulled her into her lap and held her close.

"Jody, you have good taste, honey, but little girls, they don't dress like that."

"Then I don't want to *be* a little girl."

Nora Mae's return to the bosom of her family was not a happy one. Glen's intention was to distract her from her everyday troubles, but just the opposite occurred. Alone again, with only Maudie for solace, her mother as distant as ever, her father oblivious, she sank into the deep chasm separating her everyday farm life from the magical week on the bay.

School would start soon, and her mother would insist she put on a ridiculous dress instead of her faded overalls. Once again, she'd be the object of derision. Her brothers would steer clear of her, offering not a word of care or protection. The prospect made her flush with anger. She made fists and beat on her temples until the pain rinsed away for just a moment, the ugly, shameful image of herself in a pink flowered dress, and a deeper more murky memory of an outhouse, her panties thrown into a dirty corner.

One afternoon in August, a thunderstorm brewing over the eastern edge of the valley, her mother sent her out to retrieve the laundry from the clothesline. She stared at her brothers' clothes, rippling in the afternoon thermals, taunting her. Hidden by flapping sheets, she unclasped her overalls and let them fall around her ankles. She took one of her brother's shirts off the line and carefully buttoned it up, feeling the placket lay flat on her thin chest. She unpinned a pair of jeans and pulled them on, tucking in the shirt as she went, fastening the button at her waist. Then she stood perfectly still. Her eyes scanned the horizon. The undulating wind sent small dust devils out onto the road. The sheets danced around her, their whipping like whispers. She reached her hand through the open zipper, pulled out the shirttail, and grasped it as if it was a penis. She closed her eyes and tears welled at the edges.

"Nora Mae! Hurry up, the rain is coming!" she heard her mother yell from the back porch. She quickly dumped her brother's clothes in the basket, flinging the sheets on top of them as if to cover her sins, shivering in her underwear in the wind and first flush of raindrops.

She lay in the dark that night, listening to Maudie's reassuring, even breathing, and wondered what would happen if she put those clothes back on and simply ran away.

Then she lost Maudie Marie. Glen was worried that his sister, who had just graduated from high school, might be swallowed up by some lonely dairy farmer and be stuck for life in the San

Joaquin valley. He found her a job as a cook's assistant in the lavish San Francisco home of John F. Branforte, a fan of Glen's from his army football days, a member of the Golden Gate Bridge Board of Directors, and a former president and secretary of the Teamsters Union. Maudie spent her weekends with Glen and Iris, showing Iris how to laminate pastry and roast capons.

Glen and Iris kept a promise to each other that they wouldn't let Nora Mae languish away on the farm either. For the next few years, they visited just long enough to avoid Barney, mollify Lula, gather up their little charge, and take her back to the city for a week at Christmas, Easter, and a couple of times in the summer. Glen called Nora Mae's visits "furloughs," and his two new baby daughters, "Jody's little soldiers."

She saw Maudie, too, whose transition from farm girl to city woman was complete. She dropped Maudie and called herself simply Marie: marcelled hair, fingers already tinged yellow from Lucky Strikes, arms tattooed with burns from the kitchen. But she lacked the feral beauty of her younger sister. An overbite gave her a rabbity appearance, and her hair, the color of dust motes, was dull and flat. She compensated with an easy, husky laugh and a sexy two-step. Iris made her dresses that concealed her thick back and farm-heavy muscled arms. The depression could drag on, but a girl like Marie, overbite and all, could swing and drink and laugh her way into someone's heart. Nora Mae saw no upside to the dresses or the hair waves, but she envied Marie's freedom to light up a smoke whenever she damn well pleased.

In saving one sister, Glen threw the other one to the sharks. Back at the dairy, Nora Mae had no countervailing force for her mother's animus.

There would be no quick fight to the death between them, but rather, a slow, torturous war of attrition. When she grew weary of tormenting her mother, she dreamed. Could she, at ten years old, survive on her own? Dress as a boy, maybe disappear as one, go down to the coast, get a job somewhere near Glen, carrying hod or sweeping up? Too timid. So she lived for the weeks with Glen and Iris and the babies and Marie. The rest of the time? She hid her longing for a gentle touch, a hand to hold on the way to school, a smile, a nod. Better to be hard at the edges, never in need. A scowl: If she couldn't wear pants to school, she would wear that.

Albert and Nora Mae were nearly cradle mates, born eighteen months apart in the Mississippi shack. In terms of motherly love, though, there was no competition. Lula made it plain as day she preferred Albert, dressing him in new clothes from the Montgomery Wards catalog, while Nora Mae's came mostly from the charity bin at the grange.

Albert didn't excel at school, but he took home good grades anyway. He had a way of buttering up his teachers with compliments and a pint of clabbered milk or a half-dozen eggs, a bribe Lula was only too happy to send with him when he asked. He knew how to butter her up, too. He measured his sister and found her frightening, a deft, sharp-witted girl who saw right through his middling talents and guessed at his prospects. The tortured have a sixth sense that sniffs out artifice and pomposity. Nora Mae wore that discernment in her scowl, a look she often turned on Albert and his older brothers.

At school, Albert encouraged animus toward his sister. She was crazy, he whispered. Went into the outhouse with old men. Why, his own mother wanted nothing to do with her! She hung out with the cows. Lied all the time!

Nora Mae's answer to Albert's daily shun was to clamber out of reach up a sycamore tree on the playground, at recess and lunch. She ate in a crook of the tree most days, away from Albert and everyone else.

It was May, nearing the end of her seventh-grade year. Flowers punched up through the clay soil around the school, warm sun was everywhere, and Nora Mae was thinking about just one thing: In two weeks, on May 27, 1937, the completed Golden Gate Bridge would be dedicated, and Glen was coming to fetch her for the citywide party. It was just a week before her twelfth birthday, and he made it sound like the party was as much for her as for the elegant engineering marvel spanning the bay.

On that sunny May afternoon, she had retreated to her tree when she felt a slight tremble in her pelvis, and a dampness between her legs. She climbed down and went to the girls' room. The red patch blossoming across her underwear shocked her. Had she hurt herself in the tree somehow? She stuffed toilet paper into her panties and walked gingerly to her classroom, worried that if she sat down, the blood might soak through onto the back of her yellow cotton dress. She would just stand in the back of the room, she thought, and wait for the last bell of the day.

"Take your seat, Miss Stovall," her teacher instructed. Nora Mae was torn. She'd been especially compliant of late, afraid her mother might withhold the San Francisco trip as punishment if she misbehaved. She saw Albert eyeing her from his seat, and knew he'd tattle to their mother if she didn't obey. She inched to her desk and sat carefully, first on one cheek, then the other.

School dragged on. At one thirty, she asked to be excused to the bathroom. When she pulled her underwear down, the tissues were nearly soaked with blood. She threw them in the toilet and flushed, watching the blood spin in a lazy circle as the waded paper disappeared. She felt lightheaded as she stuffed more paper in her panties, wishing more than ever to be wearing pants and wondering what had turned her own blood against her.

Back in her seat, pain ran in circles around her pelvis and lower back. She squirmed, leaning first to one side, then the other. Finally, the bell rang, and she slowly stood up. A voice behind her gasped, and she heard two girls whispering. Then she heard Albert's barnyard guffaw.

"You get a stick up your butt, Nora Mae, or somethin' else?" he said just loud enough that their teacher, her back to the class, erasing the blackboard, did not hear.

She froze. She grabbed her books and ran from the classroom, sure that everyone was staring at the spreading red stain on the back of her dress.

She ran all the way home, but not alone. Albert and two of his buddies followed close behind, braying like donkeys and yelling, "Give me a ride, Lousyliz." Nora Mae had no idea what they meant, but unbidden images of Mr. Coates flooded her, and she knew, she just knew, that she'd done something terrible. She ran past her mother in the kitchen to her tiny room, threw back her covers and closed them over her head.

She heard Albert bang in the front door, breathless.

"Ma! Nora Mae, she bled all over herself in school in front of everybody! You shoulda heard them!"

And then there was silence. A while later, her mother opened the door.

"Nora Mae, get your head out of those blankets."

"Ma, I didn't do anything! I swear!"

Lula dumped a pile of rags on the bed and laid two big safety pins on the dresser. "You get up now. You pin a couple of these rags to your underwear. When they're bloody, you rinse them in soapy water and hang them on the line. You'll stop bleeding in a few days. Until next month."

How had she missed this trail of blood? How had Maudie hid it from her? Had her mother hid it too?

"Mama? You get this too?"

"Not anymore," Lula said, swinging the door shut behind her.

For the next two weeks, Nora Mae refused to return to school, claiming each morning some ailment or another, as Albert snickered and whispered to his brothers.

"Leave her alone, Albert," Barney said absently, listening to the farm report on the radio.

By the time Glen appeared to take her to the city, the mysterious bloodletting had dried up. Later that night, on the couch with Iris, Nora Mae learned what had happened in her body.

"You're not a little girl anymore, Jody. You'll be a woman before you know it."

After Iris went to bed, she thought on it and made up her mind. She wouldn't become a woman at all, and that was that.

GLEN

Moss Landing and Pacific Grove, California, 1937–1940

Glen dropped the Twain and Marx books onto John Branforte's desk like Moses delivering the Ten Commandments. "This, sir, is what I believe, and all that I know."

Branforte picked up the tattered books, one at a time, and smiled. "Hmmmn. So you're a Communist, are you?"

"Yes sir."

"Ever join the party?"

"What party?"

"The Communist Party."

Glen hesitated. "Well, sir, I didn't know there was one. Communism is my way of thinking, you see. From each according to his ability, to each according to his needs. The only party I'm a member of is the Democratic Party, and proud of it, proud of Roosevelt. But I suppose I'd join the Communist Party too, if I could."

Branforte's smile faded. "I wouldn't do that if I were you. Tends to follow a man around, and make other folks suspicious. Makes them wonder if you want to take things away from them, like money and power. Land."

"I don't want to take things away from folks so much as get them to give them up voluntarily."

Branforte laughed.

"You 'spose that'll happen?"

"No sir, I don't think it will. A friend of mine came to a bad end when he realized men just aren't inclined to revolution, or to sharing their wealth."

This wasn't the first time Glen had been to Branforte's office. Back when he first joined the union and went to work on the bridge, Branforte saw his name on the hire list and sent for him. Just wanted to meet the lauded Wilkie. Glen wasn't averse to using his fame—somewhat diminished, of course, after his last game—to get a job for Marie with the Branforte family. But on this day, Glen wasn't sure where this conversation was going, or even why he was in Branforte's wood-paneled office with a big picture window that looked over the bridge they had both spent the last four years building, Glen from the bottom up, and Branforte from the top down. But he'd been summoned. He was told Branforte wanted to talk about his future, so he brought the books. They were the only education he'd ever had; a resume, of sorts.

"Glen, your supervisors on the bridge say you're a hard worker and a natural-born leader. You started knowing nothing about steel, and ended up in charge of your own welding crew. That's quite an accomplishment. And I hear you're a union man of the first order too. I'm wondering what you're thinking you'll do next with your life."

"Well, sir, I don't really know." He pointed to his books. "But I think, somehow, I have to live as honestly as Huck did, once he came to himself, and I've got to live as much for my fellow man as my own self, like Marx said we ought to. I know that ain't the army, I know it ain't football, but I don't know what it is. I've got a wife and two babies, and a bum hip, and that's a lot to think on. The bridge was a great start in life for me, but—"

"Well, I've got an idea, if you'll hear me out?"

Glen nodded.

"There's a growing port city near Monterey—Moss Landing. Several large fish canneries there. Seems like they're always looking to find boilermen. Takes some training, but we can set that up for you. Pay is good."

Glen nodded again, but the prospect of another industrial job sent a heavy lead weight rolling down his spine, into his shoes. The bridge work had taken a toll, and his hip and leg hurt all the time. When he opened his eyes in the morning, he didn't think of Iris, didn't think of the kids. He thought of morphine. He'd watched Ray sink deeper and deeper into alcohol—the rummy eyes, the red nose, the constant restless search for the next drink. He felt the opium sneaking up on him.

"But there's another reason I'd like you to have that job. The teamsters have tried for a long time to unionize those cannery workers, to no avail. We'd like you to be our inside man, see if you could get them organized. We can't pay you anything—you can't be in our employ—but if you're successful, we can offer you a good job with the union." Branforte patted Glen's books. "And that seems like maybe a pathway to your ideals, don't you think, young man?"

Four weeks later, Glen, a fully trained boilerman with a fireman's certificate, applied for a job at the biggest cannery in Moss Landing and had himself a new job within a week. A year—two, maybe—and he'd have that job with the union . . . if his hip held out. He and Iris and the two little girls spent an afternoon looking for a house in the boom town, with no luck, and ended up twenty miles away in Pacific Grove, in a tiny cottage just a block from the ocean. The cottage suited Glen and Iris fine. Just him and his girls. Jody would be there, sure, now and again. Marie had just married a dapper English butler named Clarence, and that was one responsibility off his plate.

Just hearing Clarence's accent made him long for Kingsley. In the afternoon of their first day in the little cottage, he headed toward the Monterey Presidio in hopes that Kingsley might still be there, even if it had been five years since they'd seen each other. More likely that Kingsley and the army had parted company. He was a smart fella, smartest guy Glen had ever known, not one to re-up just to shovel stalls for the cavalry outfit stationed in Monterey.

Even in August, a cold wind blew east off the ocean across the sand dunes that swept right up to the base gate. Glen rolled down the window on the Deuce Coupe at the guard shack. Sand and a salty tang clung to the breeze. He and the guard sized each other up, one jarhead to another. Glen may have parted company from the army, but it was baked into him, the way he cut his hair, the level gaze he gave the MP.

"Afternoon. Say, I'm looking for an old friend of mine. He was stationed here about five years ago. Private Walter Kingsley. Wonder if you could check your roster for him?"

"Don't need to. No Private Walter Kingsley here. But we do have a Major Walter Kingsley."

"Major?! Well, I'll be. Do you suppose you could ring the major and say that his old friend Wilkie is here?"

The MP looked doubtful, but made the call and came back smiling.

They sat in the officer's club two hours, slowly drinking their beers.

"How the hell did you make major, Kingsley. Or should I say, sir?"

"Wilkie, you start sir-ing me, and I'll have you locked up," Kingsley joked. "I guess I never told you about that college degree."

"No sir, you did not! I thought you were just a regular guy with one hell of a right arm."

"That's what I was hoping for. After Johnny Baker drop-kicked me over here, the army offered me a chance to go to officers training school. Guess they were short on Brits. And here I am."

"Say, you wouldn't know what happened to the littermates, would you? Or Baker? I think he threw that game, but I couldn't prove it."

"You are correct, soldier. He did throw it. And it was the littermates who ratted him out. Seems he didn't want to share his payola. They're all in Leavenworth."

"No kidding?"

"Wilkie, the army owes you an apology. And a disability check. Why don't you let me talk to some people—"

"No, Walter, stop right there. I took my lumps. I learned my lesson. I might still be in the army if it weren't for that whole sorry situation, and that ain't my future anyhow. That day outside Memorial Stadium? The communists were protesting military football, and part of me wanted to pick up a sign and join them. I want to do something that lasts longer than four quarters."

Glen's hip grew stiff sitting in the wooden chair, and he grimaced, got up, paced around the table.

"Wilkie, that's some limp."

Kingsley's eyes followed Glen's tortured trek. "Walter . . ."

"Oh boy, this must be serious, using the Walter."

"Yeah." He slowly dropped back into his chair. "Serious." He sipped his beer, warm now. "Yeah, serious."

"Out with it."

"This hip, and the leg. Hurts pretty damn bad, lot of the time." He took a gulp of the warm beer and eyed Kingsley over the glass, sat it down, didn't say more.

"What are you using?"

Glen sighed. "Morphine. When I can get it. Not every day, but I think about it a lot, you know?"

"What can I do?"

"I don't rightly know. I want off it, but I can't work with the pain. This boilerman gig is some rough stuff."

"Will you see the base doctor, Wilkie? He's a good fella, you can trust him. Loves us old football heroes," he grinned.

"Maybe."

"Not maybe. You're going."

Dr. Craig whistled at the X-ray, stared hard, whistled again, and looked quizzically at Glen and Walter.

"Long story," Walter said.

"Well, here's a short story: You've got to have that hip replaced. If you don't, you're going to be a cripple for life, and by that I mean in a wheelchair. And not that far in the future."

"Replaced? With what?"

"Steel."

Glen snorted, thinking of his hours hauling steel, welding steel, riveting steel.

"Be in the hospital a few weeks and then—"

"Whoa. I just got a new job. Don't think they're gonna say, 'Sure, Wilkie, take a month off.' And it'll probably mean I'll never be able to do that job, with a hunk of steel in me."

"Well, that's where you're wrong. You'll be better than you are now. You just have to take it slow for a couple of months."

"What about pain?" Walter asked.

"Well, right after surgery, yes, but this will eliminate your pain long-term."

Glen stood up carefully.

"No. Not now. Gimme a year."

"Son, you haven't got a year. You want a job, or do you want to keep walking?"

"I'll take my chances. Thanks, Doctor. Thanks, Major. I'll be on my way."

Glen sat in his backyard with his orange tree and his patch of grass and his swing set and his pretty little girls. He held four aspirins in his palm and wondered what would get him first: the pain in his belly every time he took the tiny white pills, or the pain in his hip when he didn't. It had been nine months since he'd walked out of Dr. Craig's office at the base. He felt a pendulum swinging back and forth in his hip. Kingsley had helped him get off the morphine, the two of them pacing from one knotty pine wall to the other in a cabin down the coast at Big Sur, until Glen got past the shakes. Now he just hit the aspirin bottle, with a whiskey and milk for his stomach.

"God almighty, Wilkie, just have the surgery!" Kingsley begged him.

"I will, I promise, but I've got to get the union vote first."

It had taken him three months just to learn everyone's name, learn who came from Mexico or Portugal, whose Mama made the best spaghetti sauce on a Sunday afternoon, who could recite Robert Burns and who loved Irish whiskey. Like the men on his crew at Maxville, the football field, or the Golden Gate, Glen found soon enough that love followed familiarity. On his first day, his endgame had been winning union representation, getting the heck out, and getting that nice desk job. But by four months, he'd forgotten that goal. Now he just wanted Declan, Jose, Santiago, Finlay, and the rest of them, mostly immigrants, to unionize because dammit, they deserved it.

At five months in, he'd said the word "union" to them for the first time. They stood around a driftwood fire on the beach, a pot of cioppino nestled in the coals, their wives and kids playing in the waves. They drank cold Lucky Lagers, a bucket of them on ice, buried in the sand.

Silence at the word. Eyes peeling left and right, hands tightening on the damp beer bottles, thumbs working the labels.

"Now, Wilkie, we've been down this road before," said Declan, the Irishman. "You never met Ricardo, but they broke his arm when he started talking about such things."

"They?" Glen asked.

"They. We aren't really sure. Some *jackeens* who showed up late one night. At his house, Wilkie, with his wife and kids right there! Word came down. We all got it."

"Damn, Declan. You gonna let them do that?"

"Yes, we are. We did, and we are," said Santiago, the Portuguese. "It would make my grandfather turn over in his grave, *Deus* rest his soul, but we are."

"But that's not *right*," Glen pressed on. "We need—we deserve!—better pay, at least a couple of breaks during the day, and overtime when they want to work us all weekend. And when Tomas fell off the scaffolding? They never did *nothing* for him, or his family! A union, men, they would have to pay attention to us then."

"Oh, they'd pay attention alright, amigo. I don't want any midnight knocks on my door," Jose said.

And that was that. They ladled cioppino into their bowls and chased their kids—towheads and chocolate-brown tresses mingling like chess pieces up and down the beach.

Glen didn't let up, but nothing seemed to melt their resolve. The Depression ground on and on. This job—this grimy, dangerous, demeaning job—was better than no job. Finally, Glen just set up a meeting with a union rep.

"Fellas, Saturday night, the union's sending us a guy. My backyard, seven o'clock. I'm buying the beer. Just come and listen."

On Saturday, a thick fog rolled in at five o'clock, like the heavens dropping a cloak over Glen's tiny cottage. One by one, they came in the back gate. They stood uneasily around the fire pit, reluctant as dental patients.

The union rep wore a cheap brown suit and shiny brown brogues. His chipped front tooth and cowlick made him seem like a regular guy, a face on a billboard selling cigarettes or hot dogs.

"Fellas, my name is Mark Grearson, and I've got one important thing to tell you tonight. President Roosevelt wants you to join the union."

He let that hang in the air like smoke in a crowded bar, watching their eyes shift around the circle.

"The law is on your side," he said, turning to look at each one. "The law says it's your right to organize, and it's against the law to stop you."

"Really?" said Finlay. "Tell that to Ricardo. They broke—"

"We know all about Ricardo," Grearson said quietly. "The FBI is looking into it right now. They're mobbed up, the owners of all these operations here in Moss Landing. Working for them is dangerous, with or without the union. If you vote for a union, I think your chances are better that you'll be coming home at the end of the day, in one piece. And we'll get you better pay. You're mostly boilermen, right? How does a dollar an hour raise sound?"

Murmurs, half smiles.

"But you're asking us to risk a lot for something that might never come our way," Finlay said.

"Yeah, there's risk. But let me ask you something. You can walk out Glen's gate tonight and go back to the plant tomorrow and nothing will change. Some of you will grow old in that plant, with no retirement, nothing to show for it. Is that what you want? Or do you want a chance at something better?"

Glen could feel the mood shifting around the circle.

"I'm in," Glen said, "Who's with me?" He held his beer bottle up like a beacon in the fog. One by one, the men closed in: Declan, Santiago, Jose, eight of them. They clinked their bottles against Glen's. It was quiet. Sparks hissed in the fire; the fog hovered, motionless. Only Alphonso hung back.

"Alright," Grearson's voice, barely above a whisper, so as not to scare anyone. "Alright," a little louder. "We're on our way."

Glen lay in bed, a cold sweat soaking the sheets. It was as bad as the night in his bunk at Twin Bridges imagining Wilbur falling silently through the hay loft door, over and over again. What had he got himself into? What if someone got killed? The day they formed the committee, told management, started carrying around the loyalty cards, every one of them was terrified. They watched management call each employee down to the office, and after that . . . nada. When Glen tried to hand out loyalty cards from his overalls, he might as well have pulled a rattlesnake out of his pocket.

"Stay away from me, Wilkerson," Glen heard over and over again. "I got a new baby." "My wife ain't well." "This job . . . it took me five years to get one!" One day, Santiago was two minutes late to work, and they fired him.

"They can't do that!" Glen told him.

"Yeah, tell that to my wife, would ya?"

Two days later, the union sent Grearson, accompanied by two characters who looked more like gangsters than union reps, to see the plant manager.

The employee committee stood out in the lot, looking up at the confrontation through big windows in the manager's office.

"Looks like its thugs verses thugs, Wilkie. What the hell?" Declan said.

"Not sure."

Two days later, Santiago was back.

"I don't know. They sent a guy, told me to come back. So here I am."

"And suddenly, I ain't getting the stink eye anymore," Jose said. "This morning, someone walked up to me and asked for a loyalty card."

They can't be giving up this easy, Glen thought. But by week's end, they had enough loyalty cards to hand over to Grearson.

"We'll ask the labor department to set up the vote, Wilkerson. Nice work. And uh, we'll pass the word along to Mr. Branforte."

"That's just between us, right? I don't want the others to know."

"Neither do we," Grearson said with a wink.

Glen inched along the catwalk between two of the big boilers. He was thinking of Iris, her bronze hair falling across the pillow that morning. She lit him a cigarette and curled into his shoulder.

"Proud of you, soldier."

"Yeah? Well don't celebrate yet. The vote . . . it could go sideways. I'm thinking they got something else up their sleeve, just don't know what yet."

From behind, just a mere scrape over the roar of the boilers, Glen heard boots. It was Alphonso.

"They made me, Glen. You shoulda known better." Before he could brace himself on the open grating, Alphonso shoved him hard enough to send him over the edge, nothing between him and the ground but twenty feet of hot, noisy air.

Glen opened his eyes to Kingsley sitting in a chair next to his bed.

"Wilkie, I'm getting a bit tired of sitting by you in hospitals."

"I'm alive then, I guess," he tried to say, his rigid jaw flattening his words. He heard someone stifle a cry on his other side, and turned his eyes, his only movable feature, and saw Iris with a handkerchief to her lips.

"Or maybe this is heaven," he slurred.

"Yes, you're alive, you damn fool," Iris said. "But just barely."

"Don't worry, though. You got a new hip out of the deal," Kingsley said.

"You gonna tell me what happened?"

"Seems the goons figured out how to fuck the vote. Just kill you. Alphonso pushed you off the catwalk. Two things in your favor. Couple of your guys saw him do it. And you landed on a trash heap, otherwise, you'd be a goner."

"New hip?"

"You fractured the bad one again. So, bingo. They had to fix it anyways. Unfortunately, you also broke your jaw and your right arm. Like I said, close to goner."

"The vote . . . goddammit, Kingsley. So close."

Glen heard someone clear a throat in the corner, and swiveled his eyes to see Declan and Finlay.

"We're not giving up, Wilkie. Fact is, it backfired on the bastards. Alphonso is in jail. He ain't talkin', but everyone knows who's behind it. FBI is swarming the place. Vote is scheduled for next week."

Glen sighed, pain drifting through his body.

"Wilkie, our Scottish and Irish mothers named us with greatness in mind," Declan said smiling. "Declan: full of goodness. And Finlay here? Fair-haired hero. You think we'd back down from a fight?"

One week later, with Declan and Finlay cajoling and herding and saying, "Do it for Wilkie!" the workers at the cannery voted to unionize. The guys stood around Glen's bed that night, Lucky Lagers raised high. Glen and his broken jaw flashed a crooked smile. The fellas put a straw in his beer.

A week after that, Glen woke from a fitful nap to find Grearson at the foot of his bed.

"Branforte sends his congratulations. We expect the rest of the canneries will follow suit, easy as pie, thanks to you. But there's a problem, Glen. He says we just can't move you onto the union's payroll right now, not with the FBI still poking around. Just would look . . . suspicious."

"So?"

"You're going to have to stay on at the plant for a while, just another year or so."

"Grearson, do I look like a man who can climb ladders and scrub boilers?"

"Well, maybe not next week, but the cannery knows they'd be in deep shit if they didn't take you back."

"Except I'm not going back. I've had enough. You tell Branforte thanks for wiping the floor with me. I looked for honor in the wrong place, I guess."

A month later, when Glen could no longer make rent on the cottage, Kingsley, and Glen on crutches, put up a big tent in a field just outside the Presidio grounds, on the edge of the sand beach. Glen, Iris, and the girls moved in the next day. Kingsley sent Glen every odd job he could find on the base. At least the jobs a man with a broken arm, a shattered jaw, and one functioning leg could possibly manage.

Iris said it was grand to be on the edge of the sea, and the girls loved their giant sand box. Glen got an envelope from the cannery with a check for $2,000, his if he would sign a letter saying he wouldn't sue. The check felt like a foxtail in his back pocket. He and Iris sat on the beach. She curled into his arms, a sunny sand dune at their backs. The girls squealed at seagulls and threw them bites of their sandwiches.

"Glen, forget 'em. We've got everything we need: You."

Back at the tent, he signed the agreement with a flourish, cashed the check, and promptly bought a used Cadillac, a 1939 Series 61 model, two-door coupe, 126-inch-wheelbase, for $1,610.

"My god, Glen, that's . . . half the price of a house!" Kingsley chastised him.

"What would I do with a house? I'm not giving in to the Man for awhile, least ways not until I can walk again without these crutches, talk without mumbling, open my own can of beer. And figure out what the hell I'm going to do next."

"Well, that's ironic, Glen. I'm as authentic a representative of the Man as you will find, and your only source of income at the moment."

"Yeah, but the Man don't know that. I'm off the books, in the wind, and for a while, that's how it's going to be."

NORA MAE, BARNEY, and LULA

Riverbank, California, 1939

Nora Mae choked the guitar neck in her left hand and waved the instrument in circles over her head, warding off flies like a cow swishing her tail. She settled onto a stack of fence posts behind the barn, positioning the guitar across her lap.

She knew life's boundaries: east, the dairy; west, school; north, her untouchable parents; south, her wretched brothers—the perimeter breached by occasional visits to Glen and Iris. She had used her voice to howl, cry, dispute. But never to sing.

Then one night in the summer of her twelfth year, she and Ray, Glen, Iris, and Marie stood around Marjory at the piano and sang cowboy songs and hymns, a trashy doggerel or two. Nora Mae leaned on Iris, listening to her husky cigarette-warmed voice float up and down, singing harmony, stealing the melody from Marjory now and again. Nora Mae let her mouth open shyly, barely embracing a note. But with everyone's encouragement, she discovered she had a sweet-sounding alto that could ride on the coattails of Iris's harmony. When Iris swung into the melody, Nora Mae was surprised she could sustain the harmony, as if her voice knew the way on its own.

From then on, she begged Glen for nights with Marjory and

Ray, even if Ray unsettled her with his drinking and meaty grip on her shoulder. When an older Black man from the shipyards, Mr. Roscoe, joined them one night with a guitar, she forgot for a while the colorless world she would return to in a few days. Mr. Roscoe showed her a few chords, let her hold the guitar against her fluttering chest. She clutched it like a life preserver.

On payday, Glen took twenty-five dollars to a music store on Telegraph Avenue and on her next visit, handed her the little Regal parlor guitar.

Two years later, Nora Mae and the guitar were seldom parted.

Late at night, walking the fence line, the guitar strapped around her shoulder, she sang, a troubadour in the alfalfa and chickweed, working out the chords to songs she heard on the radio.

"Tempted and tried, we're oft made to wonder," she strummed and sang, *"Why it should be thus all the day long, while there are others living about us, never molested, though in the wrong."*

The words brought her some comfort in the starlight, her slender fingers, white ribbons against the strings, even if the promise seemed too far away to grasp.

"Farther along we'll know all about it. Farther along we'll understand why. Cheer up, my brother, live in the sunshine. We'll understand it, all by and by."

Lula thought the guitar a silly contraption, and Nora Mae a ridiculous sight with the guitar slung over her shoulder, banging against her calves as she walked. But she had little time to consider how to separate her from it now that her mother, Janette, had come from Arizona to live with them. Janette shared Nora Mae's room, sleeping in the bed Maudie had left behind.

To Nora Mae, her grandmother—lost in dementia, unable to set herself on the bedroom commode or feed or dress herself—was like a sweet old milk cow, the sort her father would send off to the slaughterhouse. She brushed Janette's hair in the morning, fished her dentures from the glass by the bed, positioning them in her grandmother's wide open, speechless mouth, where not a word could be formed any longer. Janette became her pet, led around and fed and dressed, a creature with a barely sentient animal spirit, totally dependent on her little blond shepherd.

Lula resented Nora Mae's ministrations. The child she barely tolerated caring for the mother she adored. But when Nora Mae sat next to Janette, her fretting and moaning abated. And when she strummed the guitar, Janette mewed like a kitten.

Lula's hard-hearted bias toward her daughter had become an obsession, a deep desire to undo her. Not to kill her exactly, but to erase her. She refused to revisit the root cause of her discontent—the dirt floor, the wire, the burden of the unwanted child—and now just pressed on, oblivious to any goodness or lightness in the girl at all. Even watching her mother's pain ease in Nora Mae's presence did not vibrate the slenderest strand of compassion. To do so, to feel something for this child, would take her back to that shack, her forlorn act, and she could not bear it.

Eight months after Janette's arrival, Nora Mae woke one morning to find her grandmother lying at a peculiar angle half off the bed, her mouth and eyes wide open. She ran from the room to where her parents sat at the kitchen table drinking coffee.

"Grandma . . . she's—"

"What have you done to her?" Lula cried.

Barney jumped up and grabbed his wife by the shoulders.

"Lula, enough. You knew this day was coming."

Nora Mae fled out the mudroom door with no guitar, no shoes, no solace. Her grandmother's uninhabited eyes crossed her field of vision, no matter where she looked. Two empty pale blue eyes, everywhere.

Nora Mae slept in the barn even though the cold January nights made her burrow deep into the clean straw, unwilling to go back to the room where her grandmother died. She didn't want to go to the lying in, but her mother came out to the barn in a wind-driven rain storm and shooed her into the living room where her grandmother's body lay on a plywood sheet resting on two saw horses. Someone had polished her face so that she looked like stone and applied rouge to her high cheekbones in a carnival shade of red she had never achieved in her life, even on the sun-burned Oklahoma grasslands. Nora Mae's brothers and parents stood in a line welcoming the neighbors who came to pay their respects, glance at Janette, and depart, leaving a trail of water to and from the body and the motley receiving line.

"Mama, who fixed her up like that?"

"Why do you care?"

"I . . . miss her."

"Miss her? If you missed her, I wouldn't of had to drag you in here from the barn," Lula huffed.

Nora Mae swung her eyes around the room—her dead grandmother, her equally rigid mother, the boys squirming, her father twitching against the worn wool of his one suit—a tableau into which she had not been cast or painted or carved. She would have to go, sometime soon.

Heavy winter rains continuing on into April made Barney's spring alfalfa planting a muddy, sodden business. A stream of water ran down the middle of the milking barn, and Barney found himself lifting his milkers' feet each day to search for rot.

"Barney, there's a fella here, says he knows you from Mississippi," Lula called from the barn door, the rain falling so hard on the tin roof he could barely hear her.

"What? Someone from Mississippi? What's he want?"

"Well, he's a Negro, hungry, just passing through. So I'm fixing him a sandwich, but he saw our name on the mailbox, asked if it was you."

"Send him on out, Lu. I gotta keep on these cows."

Barney heard feet shuffling through the water and muck.

"It *is* you, Mr. Stovall!"

The voice was deeper, weary, but Barney knew even before he turned to look that it was Ira Williams, the young man who had gone to prison and returned. The young man Batson had beat with his whip, ten years before. The young man whose peril, and Barney's blind anger at Batson, had sent them on a terrifying midnight journey to Gulfport hidden in a wagon with Violet at the reins. Just seeing Ira standing there, slightly stooped, graying, tattered, conjured it all up: The men bent over their cotton fields together, the scent of Violet in the dark.

"Ira Williams. My, my," he sloshed through water and mud to wrap his arms around him. Ira stiffened, and Barney stepped back, wondering if maybe Ira remembered things differently.

"Uh, well, what brings you to California?"

Ira leaned in and pulled Barney to him, into the embrace he had just resisted.

"I'm sorry, I … I am just so surprised to see you. I thought maybe I was seeing a ghost, and it shook me up a bit, but now I see you are just as much flesh and blood as me."

The men held each other at elbows' distance, their eyes roaming each other's faces in search of the ten years between them.

"Let's climb up here in the loft. It's dryer, and you can tell me what has become of everyone."

The men settled onto the rafters. Barney noticed Ira shivering, perhaps from cold, or hunger, or what, he couldn't say.

"It's been a hard ten years, Mr. Stovall."

"Barney, please."

Ira wrapped his arms around himself, searching for comfort in the cold loft.

"Ah, Barney, not sure where to begin. Ma and Pa, they've passed on, God bless them. But not before Jenkins told us, and most everyone else, to hit the grit. We moved on to the Langston plantation, but the bottom done fell clean out of the cotton market, thanks to that boll weevil and this depression. I took to felling pine, and kept at it until Pa died, then Ma, and I just didn't have no heart for it anymore. Mostly been tramping since then, looking for a place that might not spit on a Black man."

"I thought that might happen, Ira, all because of me, and I am truly sorry."

"Weren't your fault, no sir. It was that damn Batson. You left some pretty mean scars on him, though, and that makes me glad after what he done."

"Driving you all out?"

Ira looked at him quizzically and then nodded his head, resigned to it.

"I 'spect there's no way you could know, you being out here and all. Batson and his pals, they rode all over the county looking for you, sure they was gonna find you somewheres and string you up. Nobody said a word about the train, or about smuggling you out.

"But when they didn't find you, Batson got mad as hell, and started picking one 'cropper after another, hauling him out at night and just beating him good, sometimes in front of his wife and kids. Swore he was gonna start lynching us, one by one, unless someone told him where you were. Somebody, maybe one of them women, got scared and told him, and then . . ."

Barney felt as if someone had laid open a vein, and his blood was draining onto the barn floor below.

"And then what, Ira?"

"Him and his men . . . they took Violet . . . and hung her . . . from the big oak tree."

Barney gagged, clutching his throat.

"She was gonna have a baby."

Barney fell down the ladder and ran from the barn. From the kitchen window, Lula saw him running through the muddy yard, his head bare. From the living room window, Nora Mae saw him run blindly across the road, into the alfalfa field, through the muddy furrows awaiting spring planting. She watched his feet pitching left and right, until he reached the center of the field, where he threw himself down on his hands and knees.

"Nora Mae, you go see—" but she had already run out the front door and into the field, toward her father. She found him arching his back and retching in the mud.

"Pa?"

"Go on!" Barney gasped. "Leave me alone."

She ignored him. If there was anything she understood, it was grief. From wherever it came, or by whom, it didn't matter. She knelt down beside him and put her arm lightly on his shoulder, the rain cascading off their naked heads. He shuddered and retched again. She slid her arm around his neck and pulled him close.

"Pa, I'm sorry."

"For what?" Barney said, spitting vomit.

"For whatever is your secret."

It had been ten years since she pressed the Indian Head nickel into his palm at the bottom of the cotton wagon, and the years telescoped into mere seconds. In his broken state, his eyes barely focusing, all the longing— for love, land, stature—looked back at him in Nora Mae's eyes. Maybe he could do right by this child, this time, now, the very child that Violet herself had saved fourteen years ago! Make amends for Violet and her unborn baby, who was surely his child, too.

He wailed. Nora Mae had never seen anyone cry like that before, as if he might turn inside out in the furrow where they knelt.

"Pa, what is it?"

"Nothing, Nor'ma," he said, crushing her name in his mouth. "Nothing you can fix. Can you help me up?"

"Sure, I can. But what are we gonna tell Ma?"

Barney was surprised to see how much she had grasped in their minutes in the dirt. She knew he couldn't tell Lula the truth, whatever it was. She held her pain, and she knew he would have to hold his too.

"You're gonna tell her I got a belly ache, and you're gonna put me to bed. Then you say I asked you to give some food to that fella in the barn. You take him whatever we can spare, and point him into town, you hear?"

"Mister? I'm Jody," she said to the worn, graying man who still sat in the loft. She looked up at his shoes, and both had holes in the bottom. She held up a flour sack. "I brought you some biscuits, some of last summer's apples, some salt pork, an onion, a little ground coffee."

The man nodded at her.

"What's your name?" she asked.

"Your pa didn't tell you?"

"No sir, he didn't, just asked me to get you some food, point you toward town."

"Name's Ira Williams. I was hoping to talk to him some more."

"He's feeling pretty poorly. What'd you say to him?"

"I was sorry to tell him, someone he . . . loved . . . is dead."

Her father loved someone? She looked out behind her at the fading light, what little there was with the rain clouds hanging low and spewing water like broken pipes. She didn't know much about such things, but she had a feeling it wasn't smart to send a Black man out on the road after dark, and he looked kind to her, as if he really was sorry to bring such tidings.

"Mr. Williams, Pa didn't say so, but it's OK if you stay here tonight and light out in the morning. I like to sleep up there myself. If you crawl back in the corner, there's a couple of blankets. And I'll bring you some hot coffee in the morning."

"There ain't a thing wrong with his belly, and he's lying to me," Lula said to a pile of potatoes and onions on the sideboard. Who was that man in the barn? What could he have said or done to Barney to send him running across the road?

"Nora Mae, you come here, and don't you lie to me. What is wrong with your Pa?"

She looked at the floor and considered the question. "Ma, I don't know. He said it was his belly, just what I told you."

"Well, fine, then, you just keep a-lying to me, both of you. But I know. I know you are just tormenting me, like you always do." Lula stabbed a knife into a potato, cutting it in half in a fury, as if she was severing the bond between Barney and Nora Mae.

In the morning, the rain had withdrawn, and steam rose up from the puddles and wet earth. Nora Mae walked across the yard carrying a cup of hot coffee, her guitar slung across her back.

"Mr. Williams?" she called into the loft. His head appeared. "I got some hot coffee here, another biscuit."

Ira set on the bottom rung of ladder and drank the coffee in deep draughts.

"Mr. Williams, were you at the plantation with us?"

"Yes, some of the time."

"I was just little when we left, 'bout four years old. But there was an old man there, I called him Uncle Joshua."

Ira smiled. "My daddy."

Tears pooled in her eyes.

"He used to sing to me . . . like this." She pulled the guitar across her chest and sang.

"I got-a wings, you got-a wings,
All o' God's chillun got-a wings!"

Ira joined in, singing harmony.

"When I get to heaven I'm goin' to put on my wings,
I'm goin' to fly all over God's Heaven,
Heaven, heaven."

"You know it!"

"Of course I do. My daddy sang that song all the time."

"He said when he got up to heaven, he'd look down on me and watch over me."

"Then I 'spect he is."

"He's . . . dead?"

"Gone to his reward."

Nora Mae said, "I'll be right back." She ran toward the house, the guitar bouncing against her legs. She came back breathless.

"Uncle Joshua gave me a nickel once. It . . . was my treasure, but I gave it to Pa 'cause he was so sad the night we had to leave. I've been saving some money. Pa pays me for helping sometimes. I thought maybe I'd run away with it, but that ain't gonna happen. What would a girl like me do on my own?"

"'Spect you wouldn't be any safer than a Black man out there, little sister."

"Probably. So I want you to take this."

She pulled a handful of coins and some crumpled bills from her pocket. "Nah, Jody, that's very kindly of you. But it's yours, hard-earned."

"No sir, Mr. Williams. I feel my Uncle Joshua, feel those wings beating right nearby. He wants you to have this, and it don't do any good to say no to an angel."

BARNEY, LULA, NORA MAE, and GLEN

Riverbank and Monterey, California, 1940

The news of Violet's lynching tore Barney into so many tiny pieces that he lost the weave of his own existence. He could cling to only one thought: Nora Mae would become a propitiation for his sins.

But his youngest child had spent her entire life on the outer edges of the Stovall solar system. Barney's faltering advances were too late in coming and could do little to true up her orbit. She was spinning freely, a long way in her head from the dairy and the adobe, even if her body, still clad in those wretched dresses, came and went by the front door.

She was suspicious of Barney's sudden affection and interest. As if to test his kinder resolve, or perhaps because she finally had his attention, the gloves came off. She sassed him, took money off his dresser, refused her chores. Lula's fury knew no bounds. Barney simply fell on the ropes like a prize fighter who has gone too many rounds with a superior opponent.

Sensing that she may have both her parents right where she wanted them—Lula wound up like a top, Barney on his knees—she started hanging out with the other misbegotten kids at Oakdale School where she was a sophomore. With Vernon, Ernie, and Leonard newly sworn members of the merchant marines, navy, and army, only Albert and Nora Mae were left at the adobe. Her nemesis trotted home faithfully each day to report to their parents every jot and tittle of her activities, seasoned with salacious, invented details. Lula took it all as gospel; Barney brooded.

"I saw her go out behind the gym with that Walt Pinkerton, the one that got sent off to reform school last year. Everyone knows what they were doing," Albert reported.

Lula confronted her at the kitchen sink that night, Barney sitting silently at the table, a look of misery and confusion on his drawn face.

"What were you doing after school with that Pinkerton boy?"

"Huh? I wasn't doing anything!"

"Your brother says you went behind the gym with him."

"That's a lie! Him and me, we stayed after math class 'cause neither of us understood the homework. You look, I'll show you right here," she said, getting her math papers from the flour sack she carried to school. She didn't add that after that, they went behind the gym to smoke two cigarettes Walt stole from his dad.

"You listen to me, you hussy! I will not have someone like you living under my roof!"

Barney slid his chair back with a scrape. The barn cat, already skittish at the loud voices, ran toward the mudroom.

"Lula, you hush that right now."

"I'm not a hussy! I'm a good girl. I ain't never done nothing wrong with no boy. But if that's what you think . . ."

Nora Mae let her suggestive reply hang on the warm kitchen air, grabbed her guitar, and ran out through the barn, her nightly passageway to the quiet of the alfalfa field. Shame rose like bile in her mouth, even if she knew she'd done nothing wrong with Walt. She had no way to parse its insidious power over her, no one to explain to her how she carried a carbon residue of Jedediah Coates in every ounce of viscera. The word "hussy" reverberated in her head.

"I'll show her. If it's hussy she wants—"

She heard a rustle behind her and turned to see Barney coming through the ankle-high alfalfa.

"Jody."

"Yes, Pa."

"On Friday, after school, how about I drive you over to Monterey, see Glen and Iris for a few days? I'll come back and get you on Sunday night."

She took his measure. Last winter, they finally bought a car—a truck, actually. Something Barney could justify for the dairy. It was a 1937 International, which he bought used for $500. The way he told it around the dinner table the night the previous owner drove it over and left it in the yard, he'd actually been saving the money to make his final payment on the debt he owed his brother George, twelve years on from George's reluctant "partnership."

"But what the hell. We need that truck more than George needs his $500. He'll just have to wait a year."

Trouble was, Barney didn't know how to drive.

"Can't be any harder than a team and a wagon," he'd said at the dinner table that night. He drove it around the barren alfalfa field most of the winter. Nora Mae could hear him grinding the gears and wondered what might be left of it at the end of his circles in the icy mud.

She figured he was more interested in a jaunt than taking her to Glen and Iris's, but she wasn't going to let that notion scotch the trip. She hadn't seen them since Christmas, and here it was May.

"Sure, Pa. Can I call to tell them I'm coming?"

"Yep. But, girl, wait till your mother goes to bed."

Friday afternoon when they set off, leaving Lula frowning in the dooryard, the air was white, thick, and humid; but as they neared the coast, the fog burned off, flighty wisps disappearing off the highway. Both Barney and Nora Mae rolled down their windows, the temperate air granting each of them freedom: Barney, from the memory of Ira's visit, just six weeks before, and Nora Mae, from Lula's aversion. But the space between them on the worn green leather bench seat was wide. Barney searched around for a way to bridge it, probing like a water witch.

"Say, there. I been hearing you play your guitar. You're pretty good!"

"Mm-hmm."

"Sure different 'round the old farm with your brothers gone. Been thinking maybe it's time to sell. This old fella is sixty-seven!"

"Yep."

"Seems like just yesterday the depression ended and already there's war in Europe. Don't suspect we'll be in that, though. Roosevelt, he's doing a fine job."

Jody pulled the little guitar into her lap and strummed tunelessly.

"Don't know where we'll go, though, if I sell. What you think, Jody? What about the coast?"

Nora Mae stopped strumming for a minute.

"No matter to me. I'll be gone."

Barney was quiet a while.

"Jody, I don't want you to go. I know your Ma has been hard on you, but she just doesn't know how to love you."

"Maybe not. But she sure knows how to hate me."

They rode the last hour in silence.

It took awhile for them to find Glen's tent, as he moved it season to season to keep out of prevailing winds. He and Iris and the two girls had lived in the tent a year now, with no plans to move. Glen's jobs on the base, courtesy of Kingsley, kept them in food, gas for the Cadillac, smokes for Iris, and plenty of pretty dresses all around.

Nora Mae had called the number Glen had given her for Major Kingsley, since the tent had no telephone, let alone electricity.

"Sir, can you tell my uncle I'm coming out to see him on Friday? And tell him my pa's bringing me. He'll want to know that."

So when they pulled up to the tent—certainly the only tent in California with a Cadillac parked next to it—Glen was sitting out front in a rocking chair, his back to the ocean and the setting sun. The sunlight cast a golden halo around his big square head. He struggled to stand, clutching a cane, his bad leg still an exclamation point to his football and boilerman careers.

She ran to him and was surprised to hear his wide-open laugh and feel his firm embrace, potent signs that at least his jaw and his broken arm were mended.

"Jody, Lordy, you'll knock me down! Iris! The kid is here!" he yelled down the beach.

Iris and the girls, sandy and pink from the breeze, came up the dune and gathered around Nora Mae and Glen. Barney watched, leaning on the International, more chauffeur than family.

Glen acknowledged him with a nod.

"Well, I'll be going, then. Be back Sunday afternoon," he called out, casting a wave, and headed toward the driver's door.

"Now wait, Barney, I'm just about to start supper. You really should stay, have a bite with us," Iris said.

Barney raised an eyebrow at Glen, who nodded.

"Fact is, Barney, I need a walk, limber up this leg. Jody, you help the girls with supper, will you? Your pa's gonna take a walk with me."

Barney and Glen walked slowly down the beach. Behind them, Barney's worn farm boots left short, uneven footprints. Glen's old army football shoes left long, heavy indentations punctuated by a cane strike. Neither spoke.

"Sometimes when there's so much to say, it's hard to know where to start," Barney offered.

"Who says we're gonna talk about anything? This ain't a confessional, Barney. You got something to say, say it. But I'm not offering absolution."

"Abso . . .?"

"You know, that Catholic thing? Never mind. I ain't forgiving you. Not now, not ever. That's between you and God. I don't give a damn," Glen said.

"Well then, why are we out here walking, if you didn't want to talk? I see you with that leg. I heard what you did at the cannery. Iris told us when you were still in the hospital. You may think I'm lying through my teeth, but I am proud of you, boy. Those men in that plant, you gave them a better life! That's what I was trying to do in Mexico and Mississippi, but I shot it all to hell!" He stumbled. Glen saw his eyes were half shut against the setting sun and glassy with tears.

"I said I don't give a good goddamn, Stovall. Truth is, if I could get away with it, I'd kill you, bury you right here in the deep sand, but I can't see wasting my life on doing you in. Do you know what pure hate is, old man? 'Cause that's what I feel for you. Hate, right down to my innards," Glen said, almost cheerfully.

"Then you're the man I can talk to."

"What?"

"Because what I gotta tell *someone* is so goddamned awful, they'll hate me after they hear it. I can't tell Lula. Nora Mae, she's already close to giving up on me, and I don't want to lose her. But you . . . Why, you already hate me, so I don't have anything to lose. And if I don't tell someone, I might just dig that sandy grave myself and ask you to beat me with a club, throw me in, and bury me, dead or alive, won't matter."

Glen felt the sand shift under his feet. Barney wasn't talking about the Wilkerson kids or anything that happened in Montana.

"You mean to tell me you did something worse than abandon me and every last one of your children, right on down to Nora Mae?"

"Will you hear me out? Then you can tell me which is worse. Either way, I'm going to hell."

The men sat down on a driftwood log.

"I went down to Mexico, 1912, thinking I might grow bananas," Barney began.

It took him nearly an hour. The sky relinquished most of its light as he told Glen about Acayucan, Ezra, and Luzelba, about United Fruit and the banana farmers, the one year Barney held them back from United Fruit's conquest, but left them unlikely to succeed at it a second year. Glen listened silently, gathering up sand and letting it fall through his cupped hand.

Barney skipped Montana entirely as if it had been blotted out by the rising moon and picked up his life in Mississippi, standing around the big oak, trying to convince "his men" that they could work together, a union of sorts. Glen shifted on the log and turned his attention to the side of Barney's face. The sand was forgotten.

He moved through the tumblers of those years. Ira's manslaughter conviction, Barney's attempt to win him his freedom, Barney and the folk looking after Ira's parents, how they all worked together in the fields. And Violet. He gave Violet her rightful due, how she saved the lives of both Lula and Nora Mae, and he owned up to being her lover those tortured nights in that last summer on the plantation. Glen's mouth dropped open, unhinged, silent.

Barney continued, telling of that fateful afternoon when he almost killed Batson. The escape, Violet at the reins. Glen didn't move. Barney shuddered. Ira Williams showing up at the dairy, telling him about Violet and the big oak. And the baby, his baby.

Glen gasped. "They lynched a woman who was gonna have a baby?"

"*No,* Glen, I did. I lynched her, sure as I'm sitting here. I had that rope in my hand, and wrapped it around her beautiful neck, and dropped her from a high branch, the very branch we sat under, drinking water together from the same tin cup! I did it!" He turned to look at Glen, who had gone quite pale in the moonlight.

"I was messing around in things I had no business to. I was gonna save them. I told them we were gonna make money together. Buy land! What foolishness! And all I did was force Jenkins to throw them all out, forced out of their shacks with what little they had. If I had stayed and not turned tail and run, Batson would have come for me, strung *me* up . . . not Violet. Or better yet, if I had just minded my own business, chopped my own cotton, left well enough alone, no one woulda died. She took my punishment. And so did my baby—God rest their souls—if there is a god out there who gives a damn for our souls!

"Is there a god, Glen? If there is, it's me who shoulda paid. Hell, I'm paying *now,* not that it'll bring them back. I can't sleep, can't forget. You aren't the only man who hates me. *I* hate me," he said, jabbing himself in the chest as if his index finger were a drill bit. "And you didn't think we had anything in common."

Glen stood up, pacing back and forth in front of the log.

"The Man," he said, more to himself than Barney.

"What?"

"Nothing. Let's go. Iris will be worried."

They started back, the moon's arc cresting over their shoulders and gliding across the waves. Neither of them spoke. Barney sniffed, running the back of his hand over his face and red eyes. He thought that telling it to someone, unvarnished, might relieve him. But having done so, he realized there was no way out of the pit he'd dug himself.

"It's not worse," Glen said.

"Not worse?"

"Not worse than what you did to us kids."

"How you figure?"

"You were *trying* to do right by them. You weren't counting on the Man. The Man, he always wins."

"Well, I ain't sure who the man is, but I figure all that I done—to you boys, to the folks in Mexico and Mississippi—it all amounts to a hanging offense. You can't kill me, Glen. I'm already a dead man."

They sat stiffly around Iris's dinner table, the kids already fed and gone to bed in the tent. Nora Mae looked from her pa to Glen, back and forth, as if they played an invisible chess game in the lantern light. She could not figure what had happened on their long walk. Pa looked wrung out, like he'd swallowed poison. Glen, who usually ate with gusto, barely put a fork in his food before shoving his plate away.

"You best get going, Barney. It's late."

Barney nodded and picked up his hat.

"No need for you to come back over here. I'll take her home on Sunday night."

The men stared at each other, two silent adversaries whose intentions Nora Mae could not comprehend.

The next morning, Glen was expansive, witty, trying to iron over the strange exchange Nora Mae had witnessed the night before between him and Barney.

"Jody, let's go visit the army!"

She and the little girls piled into the back seat of the Cadillac. Iris sat up front, close to Glen on the bench seat. They bounced over the sand road until they hit the highway and drove two miles to the Monterey Presidio main gate. Glen barely slowed at the guard shack, lifting his porkpie hat to the soldier inside, who saluted back.

"Why are they saluting you, Wilkie?" she asked. "I thought you weren't in the army anymore."

"Not. It's just an . . . honor . . . thing. Some folks still remember ole Number 16."

Iris laid her head on his shoulder. Nora Mae could see her smile from the corner in the back seat.

"'Sides, I . . . do little things for them, now and again," Glen explained.

"Things?"

"Now, Glen, don't you go—" Iris warned him.

"Iris, I'm not gonna spoil her! She's all grown up now, aren't you, Jody? I get . . . deals . . . sometimes, on some good hooch, ya know? Just my small way of stickin' it to the Man."

Nora Mae nodded uncertainly. Her brothers would sneak beer and whiskey into the adobe right under Barney and Lula's nose. She huffed and folded her arms in the back seat just at the thought of it. All three boys had hidden girls away in the barn loft too. She could hear them up there grunting and moaning when she passed through on her nightly rounds. *Guess I shoulda stayed and serenaded them with my guitar,* she thought. *And yet I'm the hussy! Those boys coulda stomped through the house with cow shit on their shoes, and Ma woulda said, "Well don't that smell nice?"*

But Glen wasn't like them, was he?

"Is that OK—the hooch—with your friend, the Major?" she asked.

"See that, Iris? She's smart enough to stick her finger straight in my eye!"

Nora Mae shrank back on the seat. Glen saw her frightened expression in the rearview mirror.

"Listen, sister, I'm just joking," he said gently. "No, he doesn't know, but what he don't know won't hurt him. I'm helping these dog faces have a little more fun in life for a little less cash, and in return, why, they show their appreciation."

He swung the Cadillac down the neatly swept streets, lined with green lawns and acacia trees, and pulled around the back of the mess hall.

"Be right back," he said, grinning at the girls as he opened the back seat door, leaving it open to send a swirl of ocean-scented breeze through the car. He disappeared into the kitchen. Five minutes later, he trotted back down the steps, a big ham lodged under each arm like two giant footballs. A Black cook in a billowing white apron stood in the doorway, waving to Iris and the girls.

"Watch out, girls," Glen called out, tossing the hams one at a time on the floor at the girls' feet.

"Ever have ham?" Glen asked Nora Mae as they pulled away. "No? Well, you just wait. Iris is gonna roast one of these, with some butter beans, for supper."

"What will you do with the second one?"

"You've heard of miracles? Well, that second ham there, that's gonna miraculously turn into a barrel of whiskey!" Glen chuckled at his own joke, and Nora Mae smiled at his reflection in the mirror. If Glen thought it was OK, it had to be OK. Didn't it?

Like a tired boy who pulls his finger from the dike, Glen finally let the melancholy wash over him on Sunday afternoon. He'd kept up a patter, joking about the ham, flying kites on the beach with the girls, singing along with Iris as Nora Mae played guitar. But by the time the two of them climbed into the Cadillac and rolled out on the highway headed north, he sagged like an old balloon. They were quiet all the way to Salinas.

Finally, she said, "I'm leaving home."

"Oh yeah? Where you going?"

"Not sure. I was wondering about—"

"Nah, Jody, I can guess what you're thinking, but with four of us in the tent, there's not really much room for another body, much as we'd welcome you otherwise."

"Yeah, that's what I thought, probably."

Glen rolled down his window and surfed his arm on the warm air.

"Things bad there, kid?

"Well, it is with Ma. She hates me! And I don't have any idea why. The boys could get away with murder, but me? She says I'm a hussy. And school . . . Albert just makes stuff up about me all the time, and now, the other kids, they whisper about me."

"I'll talk to her. Him, too, the little shit."

"No, don't waste your breath. They don't want me. Just best if I get out of there. I can get a job in town, see about getting a room someplace."

"What about Barney? He treating you OK?"

"For a long time, he didn't seem to notice whether I was dead or alive. But since Ira Williams came through—you know about that?—he's been, I don't know, nicer somehow. Like him carrying me over here. What did Ira tell him?"

Glen didn't answer. She waited a mile or two.

"You still hate him for what he did to you and Ray?"

Glen drummed his fingers on the steering wheel.

"Jody, if you asked me that a week ago, I woulda said, 'Hell, yes.' But today, I'm not so sure. And it's making me sore!"

"Sore? Why?"

"A man's gotta know who's his friend and who's his enemy . . . Those'r the goal posts. But if I take one of those away, then where does that leave me? I wanna keep hating him, sure as God made little green apples. But now I'm not sure I can."

"Why not?"

"Well, damn it, Jody, I discovered I ain't that much different than him!"

"Why, I don't think you're alike at all! You're kind and funny and everybody loves you. But Pa, well, his own brothers think he's a no-account tramp, going from one scheme to the next. I've seen how they look at him. Even Ma, she ain't too fond of him, either."

"You're only seeing part of the picture, Jody. I'll tell ya a story now, something I've never told anyone but Iris, about two fellas, both of them dead now, because of me."

Glen went reluctantly back to Twin Bridges, Wilbur Taft and little Edward, not seeing the road in front of him so much as the milking barn, sunlight laying thin silver tracks on the floor, the kitchen knife in his hand, the dust rising in the air as he followed Wilbur up the steps to the loft, the shuddering wind, the door swinging open, Wilbur's silent fall. For the first time, he wondered what Wilbur thought in that short fall before the earth put an end to his torment. Did he repent? Was he afraid? Did he know he would die?

"Jedediah Coates," Nora Mae whispered softly.

"Yes."

"And the second fella?"

So Glen told her of Maxville and Jimmy Bird, their pitch-black freight train ride, which was, Glen realized suddenly, the most illuminating night of his life. Funny. He chuckled in the middle of his story. And then, Jimmy Bird's despair, stepping in front of the log on the highline, Glen's failure to save him.

"I'm sorry about your friend, not so sorry about that Wilbur. But how does all that make you like Pa?"

"I was trying to do right, Jody. Do right by Edward and all the little guys at the orphanage. I was trying to do right at Maxville, make a way for men like Jimmy Bird to live a life free from the Man, that bastard who controls everything.

"Your Pa, he done the same. And surely, people died because of it, someone in particular that he loved. He's gonna pay for that forever, just like me. I'll never be able to forgive myself for Wilbur or Jimmy Bird. But that ain't all, because, trouble is, there's me and Ray. He trampled over us for no good reason on his way to something else. And he *should* be sorrier than hell for that. I think he is now. And a man who's sorry, well, it's hard to hate him anymore, not when I can see all the way through him."

GLEN and BARNEY

Riverbank, Monterey, and San Francisco, California, 1940–1941

Glen parked the Cadillac in the adobe's door yard. Nora Mae reluctantly collected her things from the back seat and watched the house.

"You coming in, Wilkie?"

"Yep, I better say hello to Ma."

Glen sat at the kitchen table listening to Lula recount a housewife's day: eggs and butter money, the vegetable garden coming in.

"Why, we had our first peas last night, Glen, and my, with fresh cream and some new potatoes—I wish you coulda tasted them. I'll send some peas home for you and Iris."

"Thanks, Mama, I'm sure she'll appreciate that. Say, where's Barney?"

"Milking, I suppose."

He kissed the top of her head. "I better be going, or Iris will worry. I'm just gonna go out and have a word with Barney 'fore I head back."

Lula watched his square, burly back disappear through the mudroom door, her mouth pursed with worry. Barney and Glen together. It could be a dangerous brew.

Barney sat with his head and shoulders against a cow, a milk bucket between his feet. He guessed he'd come into the dairy world the old-fashioned way, and that's how he'd go out, hand-milking his cows twice a day. If he sold the dairy in the next year or so, sure as shooting, some young dairyman would come in, pour a concrete floor, and set up a milking machine. Progress, they called it. And if he was a younger man, he would be all over that, visiting George again for a loan to expand his dairy empire. He chuckled against the warm honey gold of the Guernsey, just thinking about how George would make a blustery refusal, and then, a reluctant agreement, like always.

But like the last whisper of sand in an hour glass, he could feel his time running out. He would just sell and be done with it, not scheme a better, more profitable dairy. The news Ira brought wiped out the last vestigial traces of his own bullheaded optimism, that everything would be rosy, eventually, someday.

The searing confessional conversation with Glen two days before came back to him, and he wondered what Glen made of it, if anything at all. The ramblings of an old man—a man he hated. Maybe he relished it, happy to see Barney get his comeuppance. He hadn't realized until he sat next to Glen on the beached log that his transgressions were threefold: Mexico, Mississippi . . . and Montana. How had he missed that? He'd simply papered it over, excused himself in his rush to go south, without any more frustrations, and grow those goddamned strawberries. Abandoning Glen and Ray seemed a small price to pay at the time for a fresh start. But boys become men, and then they come home.

Did he have any chance, as his sand trickled away, to make any of it right? And what of Nora Mae? With the three older boys gone now, and Albert nearly worthless, he depended mostly on Nora Mae to help him. She and the cows took to each other, something he couldn't say about the boys and the dairy. He'd come into the barn one day to find Vernon viciously kicking a cow in the udder. With a jolt he realized those boys—their mean, selfish ways—that was on him too.

He turned at the sound of the barn door opening, and there was Glen, taking a milking stool and a bucket to the next cow down the line.

"Where'd you learn to milk cows?"

Barney knew the answer before Glen said it, and was sorry he asked the question.

"Orphanage."

It was a long, protracted game of chess the two had embarked on, years ago now, each measuring the other's skill, trying to anticipate their opponent's next move. The first pawn had been moved right there in the barn, nine years ago, with Glen threatening Barney's life. They each moved a piece, now and again over the years, each protecting their kings. They milked quietly for a while, moving on down the line, dumping their buckets into the tins that Barney would load into the back of the International and drive over to the co-op sometime in the next hour.

And then, in their years-old chess game, Barney's king safe, still intact, protected, he gave him up.

"I'm sorry," he said to Glen.

"What'd you say?"

"I'm sorry. Sorry I left you there. I was a jackass. I nearly ruined you boys, and broke your mother's heart. She's like she is now, to Nora Mae, all because of me. I made her choose between her children, made her hate that last baby, born into that shack I buried us in."

Glen stopped milking.

"I ain't got an excuse. I can't take it back. The only thing is . . . I don't want to lose Nora Mae too."

"She's gonna leave."

"She tell you?"

"Yes, and we can't take her, not living in the tent."

"Why *are* you still living in that tent? You're well now, ain't ya? I know the union said they had a job for you. Iris told us that too."

"Just because you said you're sorry, old man, don't make my life your business. I came out here to tell you about Jody, not discuss my prospects."

"And now you have. And I'll . . . I don't know what I'll do!"

"Best if you just let her go."

"You mean like I did you and Ray, and Luzelba, and Violet? I ain't making that mistake again. Glen, why don't you let me help you? You're a smart fella. You don't want to live in that tent forever. Why, I know some folks, I can ask around, see if anyone needs a foreman or—"

"I don't need your help! You wanna know why we're in that tent? Because I ain't crawling on my hands and knees back to John Branforte. He promised me a job if I got them the union vote at the cannery. I did my part, and all I got to show for it is a busted-up body. And where's the union now? I thought they might be the anti-Man, but they are the Man too! I can't get away from the bastard!"

"For God's sake, Glen, who is the Man? You talked about him on the beach the other night, and I just don't know who the hell he is."

"The Man? The Man is United Fruit. The Man is Uncle Fred. The Man is Twin Bridges. The Man is Jim Crow. The Man is Sheldon Jenkins. Now you know who the Man is?"

Both men stood on opposite sides of the milk tins, each breathing hard, the chess pieces in disarray on the board.

"You listen to me, son—"

"Don't call me that."

"All right, fair. You listen to me, Glen Wilkerson. You said the other night that I was trying to do right by all those people, in Mexico, on the plantation. And I was, Man or no Man. It didn't turn out how I wanted, but at least I didn't live my whole life like the Man is everything, already a done deal, and we are gonna lose. If you do that, well then, the Man, he really will win. So if you try and you fail, ain't that better than not trying at all? You want to live in that tent with your Iris and your girls forever?"

Glen stared at his boots, set in a thin scrim of milk and mud on the barn floor, and said nothing.

"And you said 'absolution.' You said you weren't giving me any. I go to the library, you know that? I went and looked that word up yesterday. I 'spect you're right. There ain't no absolution for me. For you, though, you don't want to look back and need it . . . absolution, that is. Do the right thing now, Glen. Swallow your damn pride. Go see Branforte."

Glen's drive home took nearly five hours. He stopped every few miles and wandered into lush, tidy fields of lettuce, the tang of fertilizer thick on the air. We walked up arroyos through the oaks and eucalyptus. His hip, after hours behind the wheel, stiffened and keened at him. As his outright hatred for Barney waned, he found he had to take his words seriously. What if his own girls grew up despising him? What if Iris grew a hardened shell, like his own mother's? What the hell *was* he doing in that tent, filching hams and beef steaks from the base, in exchange for cheap booze and pocket money? What *if* Kingsley found out?

The answer to that question arrived sooner than he expected. Kingsley's Jeep was parked next to the tent when he got home that night at nine o'clock. Iris met him at the driver's door.

"Kingsley's down on the beach, waiting for you. He didn't look at all happy."

Glen propelled his stubborn hip over the sandy edge of the

dune and found Kingsley facing the waves and the last flamenco whispers of sunset.

"Have you been selling Army rations to bootleggers?"

Glen considered the question. He could deny it; he could justify it. But every option apart from the truth made his toes curl up inside his old football shoes. Shoes he had worn with Kingsley years ago on fields of sport and honor.

"Yes." It was an Occam's razor answer, and the only right one.

Kingsley had been hoping his snitch was wrong. His face fell.

"Well, so much for my stiff upper lip, Wilkie. What do you suppose I ought to do with you now?"

"I suppose you ought to kick me out, take away my base privileges, maybe even turn me in to the police."

Kingsley considered him, walked around him like a man contemplating a bull at auction. "You know what I want to do? I want to beat the shite out of you! But when I look at you, and I think of everything the army did, and didn't do, for you, I'm weighing you on the scales, and I still think the army got the better end of the bargain."

"No. Listen, Kingsley, it was wrong and I'm sorry, especially about hoodwinking you, and I'll take whatever punishment—"

"Shut up, Wilkie, before I change my mind. Alright, here's your punishment. You've got two weeks to get you and your family out of this tent. Two weeks. And I can't say I'm sorry I found out what you've been doing, because God knows I needed some wedge to pry you out of here. You are better than this, my friend. Better."

At nine o'clock the next morning, Glen stood outside the tent, shirtless, shaving in a tin basin. The girls ran around his feet, pelting him with questions.

"Where you going, Daddy? How come your neck is pink and your belly is white? Can we have a puppy? Mommy says we might be moving soon, but we like the tent. Will we have a beach at our new house?"

Glen grinned, tipping up his chin, shaving carefully down his Adam's apple, his reflection cut at odd angles in the small, cracked mirror hanging from the tent frame.

"Ain't sure about anything, girls, except yes, you can have a dog!"

Squeals echoed on the morning fog, and Glen could hear Iris say "Oh, geeze" on the other side of the tent wall.

By ten thirty, he was pacing in front of the receptionist's desk at John Branforte's San Francisco office, his cane strikes barely audible on the thick carpets.

"Mr. Wilkerson, Mr. Branforte says he just can't see you this morning. But he'd like to take you to lunch. Can you stay?"

Two hours later he found himself facing Branforte across a white-draped table at Aliota's. A toothy, smiling Italian waiter unfurled a napkin and placed it in his lap, another filled his water glass, and still another, as wrinkled as a Sicilian raisin, stood poised to take his order.

Branforte smiled at Glen's discomfort and offered, "Shall I order for us?"

"Sure."

"We'll have crab cocktails, followed by the sand dabs, and two glasses of the Orvieto."

This was Branforte showing Glen a measure of the distance between them. This was Branforte reminding him that he had a ways to go to be a civilized man. This was Branforte poking a hole in Glen's pique. He let the spectacle spool out for a while before he asked the question, the one he already knew the answer to because he'd been waiting, watching, his minions keeping their eyes on the great, but greatly reduced, Wilkie Wilkerson.

"How have you been?"

"I've been better, and you know it."

"How so?"

"It's taken a long time for my jaw to heal, my arm, my hip. So it's been a constant worry, for me and Iris, that the kids have something to eat, clothes to wear. No one seems interested in hiring a cripple. Least ways, you don't."

"And yet you're driving a Cadillac."

"How do you know that?"

"Now, Glen, you know the union is a tight-knit family. We've been worried about you! Things are going well at the cannery. Elections have been successful at several others too, and we have you to thank."

Glen felt like he was hanging upside down. The opulence of the restaurant, Branforte's reassuring words. Nothing was what he expected when he'd pulled out onto the highway just a few hours before and turned toward the city. He thought Branforte would be defensive, argumentative. That he might not even see him at all! Other than his little maneuver to put Glen in his place—yeah, he picked right up on that—he couldn't quite figure out what was happening.

Branforte put down his tiny seafood fork, looked Glen square in the eyes, and smiled.

"I've been waiting for you."

"*You've* been waiting for *me*? Of all the horseshit!" Glen wadded up the perfectly starched napkin, a poor substitute for crushing Branforte in his meaty hands. Heads swirled toward them at nearby tables. Branforte's smile held as steady as a quarter moon.

"Did you think I would run smack into J. Edgar Hoover and the FBI just to make good on a promise, on your timetable? A promise delayed is not a promise broken, Glen. Not at all. And I don't break promises. We asked you to wait a year, stay with the cannery if you liked, but you told us to shove it. So I've been waiting, yes, hoping you might change your mind."

And now, having proven his superiority and control, he pitched a small bone of contrition in Glen's direction.

"Now, son"—Glen's rigid leg twisted under the table—"I am sorry we had to make you wait. I truly am. But I have been in touch with Major Kingsley all along—"

"What?"

"I made sure he had plenty of work for you. Don't worry . . . he contacted me first, you know. Fine man. He's in your court, as much as I am."

Glen loosened his death grip on the napkin.

"So I am glad you finally came to see me. Because I do have a job for you. We'd like you to head up a new local for us, not too far away, in Salinas. Farm workers and truckers, Glen. They need a union too."

Glen let a brief grin twist his wide, full lips. He fingered the small fork resting in his cut-glass bowl of crab and reached instead for the soup spoon on his right. He scooped an enormous bite of Dungeness crab toward his mouth, the alabaster claw glistening in lemon and butter. Branforte might know how to order, but Wilkie knew how to eat.

NORA MAE

Modesto, California, 1941

Nora Mae and Lula stood uneasily side-by-side in the Modesto Piggly Wiggly, staring at the canned foods.

She agreed to help her mother with the shopping only after Barney's eyes pleaded with her across the breakfast table. He dropped them off and drove the International down to the tree-shaded square in the center of town, wearing his one suit and his gold stickpin.

"Got to talk to some fellas," was all he said.

Now the two of them alternately pushed and pulled the grocery cart, a token in their slow gridlocked war with each other.

"Your father likes those canned tamales. I don't know why anyone would want that Mexican food, but get two cans."

Nora Mae tossed them into the cart like live hand grenades. Lula scowled at her. A baby yowled somewhere an aisle or two away.

"Nora Mae, would you please stop!"

She smiled pleasantly, picked up one of the cans from the cart, and dropped it in again, right onto a loaf of bread. The sound of the baby drew closer. A cart came around the corner, and both Lula and Nora Mae stopped their bickering long enough to stare.

It was Velma Petersen and her new baby. Everyone knew she

wasn't married and that her parents, long-suffering Danish farmers just down the road from the Stovalls, had felt compelled to turn her out. She had taken a small apartment in the McHenry Mansion, an imposing structure on the corner of Fifteenth and I streets, abandoned in death by all the McHenrys, now divided into the Langdon Apartments, some quite grand.

But not Velma's. The whisperers around town speculated on how she managed even the tiny one bedroom, being that her sole income—at least in the daylight hours, the wags suggested and winked—came from taking in ironing and alterations.

Velma pushed her cart toward the Stovalls, the wheels wobbling on the warped wood floor, the baby wailing away, wrapped in a blanket next to a quart of milk and a box of saltines. It was hard for Nora Mae to think of Velma as anything but a farm girl, not one to be entertaining local boys after a day of ironing and mending. She was wide as a wringer washer around the middle. She looked more like a corn-fed Guernsey than an ingenue. But she had soft blond hair; a sugary, round face; and wide blue eyes like clear window glass on a sunny day.

Lula let a little snort escape her lips as the wailing and the cart drew closer. Obviously, no one had put this young woman in her place, or she wouldn't be prancing around in public with her baby like the Queen of England.

"Hi, Velma. Can I see your baby?" Nora Mae said. Lula pinched her on the shoulder blade. Nora Mae ignored her.

Velma picked the baby up, shushed him sweetly, and pulled back the blanket.

"Oh now, he's so cute! Ain't he cute, Ma?"

Lula forced a smile.

"He's got a good set of lungs," Velma said. "Just like his daddy." She put the baby on her shoulder and pushed the noisy cart to the next aisle.

"Baby look familiar?" Nora Mae asked her mother.

"What do you mean, familiar? I hardly know the Petersens."

"That baby looks just like his father," she said, catching her mother's arm above the elbow. "Yes indeedy. Just like Vernon. Vernon and Velma. Wonder if they named him Virgil? He and Velma probably made him right up in our hayloft."

Lula wrenched her arm free and swung an open hand at Nora Mae's face. The slap rang out loud enough that Velma surely heard it in the next aisle.

"Don't you ever say anything like that about your brother again," she hissed.

"Why, Mama?" Nora Mae shouted back at her, clutching the side of her face. "It's the truth!" Then she lowered her voice, her eyelids, her chin, in a crouch like a prize fighter. "You called me a hussy, and I ain't never done nothing with a boy. But my brothers? Every last one of them, they took girls up to the hayloft."

Lula looked down, her face reddening.

"Why, you knew, didn't you? You knew it and you didn't say a damn word to them!"

"Don't you swear at me!"

Women pushing carts started down the aisle and then backed up. It was more dangerous in canned goods than a bull fighting ring.

"Nora Mae, boys have different . . . urges. No one expects them to be pure!"

"Really? So it was OK for Vernon, Leonard, and Ernie to screw every farm girl from Riverbank to Visalia, but it wasn't OK for Velma and all the girls they done it to? And that baby, Virgil, or whatever his name is . . . he's your grandson!"

"You can't know that!"

"Oh yes, I can. And I'll tell you something else I'm sure about. Nobody ever wants to be born a girl. I'm sick of the whole thing.

Sick of bleeding. Sick of being good . . . For what? Sick of these stupid skirts. Sick of—"

She turned and ran from the store.

Nora Mae hitchhiked back to the adobe. She grabbed her guitar and started putting clothes in a bag and stopped. She was going, but her two dresses and an ugly plaid skirt were staying. She went down the hall to the boys' room and rummaged through a dresser until she found jeans and shirts abandoned by her brothers when they left for the service. She took those and a twenty dollar bill from Barney's dresser. The last time I'll take anything from him, she promised herself. That part was wrong, she knew, but she had her reasons. Just months before, she'd given all her money to Ira Williams, so her pa owed her. She trotted back toward the highway, stuck out her thumb, and hitched back to Modesto. She sank low in the seat of the salesman's Buick as the International, her father hunched over the steering wheel, passed by. What was that tearing at her gut as she saw her mother in the passenger seat, about as far away from Barney as she could get, her head cocked at an odd angle against the window frame? Surely she wasn't sorry to be leaving them.

She stood below the broad steps leading up to the front of the Langdon Apartments. She wasn't sure what she expected—a place to stay the night, some sisterly advice?

At the top of the stairs, a list of residents by the door showed that a Petersen lived in 305. She pushed in, walked up the center staircase, and passed door after door, a radio playing, the smell of beefsteak, two people arguing, until she reached the third floor. She walked toward the sound of a crying baby and knocked. Velma opened the door, the child in her arms.

"May I come in?"

"Might as well."

Velma paced the shoe-box-sized sitting room and kitchen,

jiggling the baby, until the crying abated. She pulled aside her dress and nursed him while she walked the tiny loop until he fell asleep.

"He's a fussy baby. The doctor says its colic. Night is the worst." Velma looked at the bag of clothes and the guitar. "You leaving home?"

"Yeah, I suppose so. But I don't have nowhere to go."

"Whatcha gonna do?"

"Get a job, I guess. Maybe find a place, something like this," she said, looking around. Two doors opened at the end of the sitting room, a bedroom and a bathroom. She'd never lived anywhere with an indoor toilet.

"Well, you're welcome to sleep here on this old couch for a while, least till you get a job. Can you help with food? Only had enough for crackers and milk today. Hard to keep nursing a baby on that."

"Isn't Vernon sending you any money?"

"You know about that, then?"

"I guessed when I saw him today. Same eyes. And I saw you together . . . in our barn."

"He was my one and only, Nora Mae, I swear!"

"I really don't care, Velma. My brother's an ass, if you ask me. If he sends you some money, and you don't have to look at his sorry face, you're better off."

Velma kept jiggling the baby and then she started to laugh. That made Nora Mae laugh too. They woke the baby, and he started to cry again.

"What's his name, anyway?"

"Virgil."

Nora Mae laughed all the harder, and that set Velma off into another round of hiccupping laughter. Someone on the floor below banged on his ceiling with a broom handle.

They giggled.

"Call me Jody, OK?"

Turns out Vernon hadn't sent a penny toward his son's survival. The two girls—Nora Mae, sixteen, and Velma, eighteen—took up housekeeping together. Nora Mae got a job cleaning rooms at the Modesto Hotel; she could wear her brothers' jeans and no one cared. She slept on the couch, paid half the rent, bought groceries, brought home things forgotten by guests at the hotel—an umbrella, a box of chocolates—and sometimes helped Velma iron sheets.

She woke in the morning to the patter of Velma's sewing machine in the bedroom and fell asleep at night to the rhythm of someone jitterbugging to the radio on the floor above them. She bought fashion magazines at the A&P for a nickel and looked hungrily at Katherine Hepburn in her slacks and loafers. She tore out the pictures and pinned them to the bare sitting room wall. When *The Philadelphia Story* came to town, she and Velma saved two quarters. Velma took one and went to the matinee. Nora Mae took care of Virgil. Then Nora Mae took the other quarter and went to the six o'clock show.

One day, three weeks into their cohabitation, Velma said, "If you want some trousers like that," pointing to the Hepburn pictures, "I can make them."

By October, Nora Mae saved enough money for one-and-a-half yards of caramel-colored worsted wool. Velma kept her word. When Nora Mae pulled on the pants with a wide waist, a back zipper and front pleats, she felt a rush of identity. This was Jody as Jody ought to be. In a bin at the thrift store, she found a pair of men's white and brown saddle shoes like the ones she'd seen in the window of the San Francisco shop so many years before. The shoes were a size too big, but she stuffed newspaper in the toes and asked the shoeshine boy at the hotel to polish them, which he did, for nothing but a smile.

Velma took her sewing scissors to Nora Mae's little girl hair and showed her how to set the new bob in pin curls, sharing her pile of rusty hair pins. Velma tweezed Nora Mae's wild eyebrows. Inch by inch, Nora Mae disappeared, and Jody emerged.

Late at night, after Velma and Virgil slept, Nora Mae would play her guitar quietly, nursing a homesickness for the cows and the nighttime alfalfa fields bathed in starlight. She missed Glen and Iris and felt a twinge of guilt that they didn't know what had become of her. She even missed Barney's steady way with her milk-cow friends. Thinking on Lula was like entering a burning building, so she stayed away from that spectacle. She did think on this, though: If Barney and Lula knew where she was, they didn't seem in any hurry to bring her home.

The shoeshine boy wanted more than a smile.

"Say, Jody, there's a dance at the Grange tonight. Good band. Wanna come with me?"

She took in the shoeshine boy as he stood up from his perch. Henry Bradshaw just kept unfolding like a letter emerging from an envelope. He was elastic, fluid, thin enough that the belt holding up his white cotton ducks circumnavigated his waist nearly twice. The only substantial thing about him was his hair, as thick and bristly as a coir mat.

"Henry, I don't know how to dance," she said.

"Aw, now, we can fix that."

He took her by the hand and led her out into the alley behind the hotel.

"We'll start slow and easy," he said, and began whistling *Pennsylvania 6-5000*, pulling her in, pushing her out, spinning her around.

"Watch my feet!" he said, stutter stepping. "Come on, Jody, swing the wing, whip the hip!"

The hotel kitchen opened on the alley and someone watching

them from the dish pit turned a radio on in the open window. Swing music poured out, echoing off the stucco wall across the way.

Henry's bony, nimble fingers were light on her rib cage, shoulder and hand. No one had ever touched her like this. Not her brothers with their rough, tormenting swats. Not Ray and his greedy clutches. Not Glen's loving, but heavy, mitt. And not—oh, the fleeting ugly memory—Jedediah Coates.

"You're a hepcat, Jody!" Henry crowed, swinging her in a wide circle and then whirling her to a stop.

"So just wear a full skirt that'll swing out—"

"I don't wear dresses, Henry," she wheezed, out of breath.

"Never?"

"Never. But . . . Katherine Hepburn? I wear trousers, like that."

"Well then, we'll just be a pair, won't we? I'll be the scarecrow. You'll be the movie star! But please, tell me at least, you like whiskey, don't you?"

"Never been to a dance, never had whiskey."

Henry bent over, clutched his ball-bearing knees, and laughed heartily.

"You, girl, are about to have quite a night."

Oh yes, what a night. Henry became her steady every Saturday night that fall. After old Mrs. Fennimen in 307 offered to take care of Virgil, he became Velma's steady too. One on each arm. But he wasn't a jealous suitor, no, not with all the sailors and soldiers home on leave, not to mention local farm boys, clamoring to dance with both of them.

The Jitterbug became Nora Mae's sacrament, grace dispensed in rock steps and Valentino dips. When she danced, she left her petulant, argumentative self sitting alone on the worn wallflower chairs. On the dance floor, her companions could do no wrong, as long as they kept the swing going.

By mid-November, guys were on the lookout for the skinny girl with the wavy blond bob in trousers and saddle shoes. Boy, could she dance!

And drink too. That first dance with Henry, sipping from the flask he carried in his back pocket, she discovered whiskey made her a better dancer. She could swing—no, fly!—around Henry and any other boy who tapped on her shoulder. Then she discovered whiskey's amnesic qualities. A few pulls on Henry's flask, refiled regularly from the boot in Henry's car, and she couldn't even remember wandering alone in the Mississippi pecan trees, her brothers' taunts, her mother's hissy fits, or even, after an extra pull toward the end of the night, Jedediah Coates.

A Saturday night, mid-November: Nora Mae had been floating like a moth from one sailor to the next, occasionally stepping outside to neck with one behind the grain silo, but only until the band fired up an especially rousing version of *Chattanooga Choo Choo.* She would break off a kiss and run back to the dance floor, the jilted boy in uniform wondering what happened. Back inside, she felt a tap on her shoulder. She turned around to find her brother Albert, a look of shock and anger on his face.

"What are you doing here?!"

"Dancing. What are you doing here?"

"You're drunk!" he yelled as strains of trumpets and saxophones swirled around them.

"Pro'ly! Wait, give me a second!" She pulled out the flask, which now resided mostly in *her* back pocket, and took a swig, then looked closely at Albert. "Not drunk enough, 'cause you still look like an ignoramus!"

"Wait until Ma and Pa hear about this," he threatened.

"You tell 'em 'hi' for me now, will ya?" And she plunged into the crowd of dancers, looking for a stray soldier.

Along toward the morning hours, Nora Mae woke up, planing across the empty parking lot, held up by Velma on one side and Henry on the other, her precious saddle shoes toe-down, dragging in the dirt behind her.

In the last week of November, Nora Mae stepped out the double glass front doors of the Langdon, right into Barney.

"Jody!"

Nora Mae shrank away. "What you want, Pa?"

"Well, first I want to know if you're OK. You look . . . good . . . Jody. Real pretty. Different. I like your hair."

If Barney had showed up with a brass band and a dozen roses, she could not have been more surprised.

"You . . . like it?"

"Why, yes. Why don't we go down to the truck, show your ma. I know she'd like to see you too."

Barney swept his arm wide toward the International, parked catawampus at the curb. Still hasn't learned how to drive that thing, she thought. She saw her mother sitting in the passenger seat, a hat pulled low on her forehead so that only her nose and some wispy gray hairs were evident.

"Why should I go down to talk to her? If she wanted to see me, she could come up here, just like you."

"Now, Nor'ma, this ain't easy for her, just coming here."

"I bet you had to drag her down here."

"No, now, girl, she wanted to come. She sent this." Barney thrust a grocery bag into her hand. She opened it and saw the familiar dresses she'd left behind. She dropped the bag as if it held a hornet's nest.

"She don't love me, Pa. Don't love me, don't know me. Cause if she did, she wouldn't have sent *that*."

"Please, child. Come home. We miss you! Albert has gone off and joined the navy. Things'll be different, I promise."

"How?"

"Well, for starters, I got a fella interested in buying the farm. With the war heating up overseas, they're talking about building a huge aluminum plant right in Riverbank! Lots of jobs, good market for milk, so I'm getting a good price for the old place. Enough to retire on, for your ma and me."

"Where will you go?"

"*We,* Jody. We. Where will *we* go. I been thinking on that a lot, and I'm thinking over toward the ocean, maybe Watsonville. Lots cooler. I can have a garden."

"Pa, that's just changing the scenery. Ma? She'll be just the same."

"Won't you give her a chance? She's real sorry, she really is. And oh, I forgot, she sent this. It's for that Petersen baby."

Barney handed her another bag, this one with a wrapped package inside. Nora Ma stared hard at her father. He showed no inkling that he knew Virgil was his grandson. So Lula was sending her a signal: "You were right. I know he's our baby, but that's just between you and me." She glanced down at her mother in the truck, who had tipped back her head and was watching the two of them on the porch. When she saw her daughter look her way, she tucked her chin down again, disappearing under the hat.

"Pa, I ain't going with you. Got a good job, making lots of friends. I don't need you! And I don't want to go back where I'm not wanted."

"But sweetheart!"

She hesitated a second, then pushed open the glass door and stood inside looking out at Barney, as if he was a prisoner in another world. He picked up the bag of dresses and walked slowly back down the steps. She wanted to see what would happen when he got back to the truck, but then she was too afraid she might see her mother smile at the news that her daughter was not coming home. So she turned, walked the long hall and out the back door. By the time she circled around on the lawn, the truck was gone. She leaned against the Langdon's cold stone wall and cried.

On December 7, everything changed. She and Velma sat glued to Mrs. Fennimen's radio the next night as President Roosevelt addressed Congress and the nation, declaring war and eventual victory. Virgil chortled away, gnawing on a roast beef bone, as if he knew something they didn't. It all seemed so far away to her, Roosevelt's round vowels intoning the names of places she's never heard before: Guam, the Philippines, Wake Island, Midway, Oahu. Even Japan. Where was it, out there across the Big Blue? How close was it to their shores, where her pa wanted to move? Mrs. Fennimen raked a handkerchief over her eyes. To Nora Mae, the edge of the known world had just disappeared, leaving her alone on its jagged maw. She wondered if the Japanese army would be marching up to the door of the Langdon any minute.

Just five nights later, Modesto held its first blackout drill. She and Velma huddled in the dark on the old sofa, shushing Virgil as if the Japanese might hear them. The next morning, there was Barney on the front porch again.

"Jody, wait. Just . . . read this." He thrust a letter in a sealed envelope into her hands. She tore it open.

Dear Jody,

Your Pa and Ma asked me to write you this letter, but it comes truly from me and Iris. I don't blame you for wanting to be on your own, but the world, it ain't the same. I don't know what's going to happen, but I can't stand the thought of you being alone in Modesto while all of us are over here on the coast. Me and Iris have a nice little house in Salinas now, and your ma and pa are moving to Watsonville. That's only twenty-five miles away! We can see you all the time, and I know you'll be safe. As for Ma, she needs you more than she lets on. And I think she loves you too, she's just ashamed of how she's treated you. You can do whatever you want, but I think you should forgive her and see what happens. I forgave her long ago. With the war coming, maybe even right here to our shores, it's better to just let it go. Please go with them.

Love,
Your Brother, Wilkie

She read the letter twice, looking for the escape clause, the place where Glen would tell her, between the lines, that she didn't have to leave Modesto. But it wasn't to be found.

"I'll think on it, Pa."

"You don't have much time, Jody. We're leaving for Watsonville a week from today, December 21. I'm coming to fetch you at nine o'clock, if you'll just say yes. We'll all have Christmas in the new house."

She searched the truck at the curb for signs of life, but her mother wasn't there.

"If I'm going, I'll be on the porch. If I'm not, don't come looking for me."

BARNEY, LULA, and NORA MAE

Watsonville, California, 1941

Watsonville was born in the usual California way. Judge John Watson obtained, under questionable circumstances, a portion of the Rancho Bolsa del Pajaro from Sebastian Rodriquez in 1852, who had, no doubt, with the might and chicanery of the Mexico Army at his disposal, taken the land from the Spaniards, who had taken the land in their time from the Ohlone Indians. Watson laid out his town and then departed, never to be heard from again.

If the Stovalls were aware of the town's provenance, it would have just seemed the way of things. Everywhere the family lived—from Oklahoma to Arizona, Montana, Mississippi, and finally California, and even before that, in the history of Barney's ancestors' westward migration from Kentucky to Indiana and Illinois, and perhaps before that, from France and England and as far back as man could touch man—humans inched forward on stolen legacies. Dirt only belonged to a man for a finite time, for as long as he could, by sweat and blood and heartbeat, hold onto it, a caretaker for those who would come to wipe him away, for his weakness, his color, his religion, or for nothing at all save the inconvenience of his occupancy.

But none of that intruded on their thoughts as the three of them, Nora Mae in the middle, sat on the bench seat of the International, rolling down the valley toward Watsonville about as far apart from each other as bowling pins in an impossible split.

Barney, still unsure behind the wheel, weaved down the highway, his thoughts and the truck swaying back and forth from the fog line to the center line. Yesterday, proceeds from the farm sale safely in the bank, he'd taken his final payment to George, which was their agreement: ten percent of the profits on last year's sales of $20,000, exactly $221.35. He brought cash—tangible, soft green bills; a quarter, and a dime—eliminating any opportunity for George to look suspiciously at a check. Barney didn't need the aggravation.

George's office, a room with no windows and dark paneled walls devoid of books or other distractions, was in the center of his massive Modesto manse. George, as usual, was behind his desk. Doing what? Barney could not say, since the desk was empty of papers or folders. George had people who handled those things, he suspected.

They were firmly beyond middle age, the two of them: Barney, sixty-nine and George, sixty-five, though a betting man would have said they bore their ages the other way around. George looked like a day-old custard-filled pastry left on the counter overnight: sagging, slightly greasy around the edges. His thin hair was mostly a suggestion of white at the temples, his eyes ringed in red. Barney found this puzzling. George had every indulgence a man could want, and yet he looked ready for the dust bin. Barney, on the other hand, still wore his vigor like a suit of armor: ramrod straight, glittering sapphire eyes, tenacious black hair just beginning to gray in the straight hank that fell across his unlined forehead. It was just as he suspected. A hard life was a good life, a worthy life, and nothing he would trade, even in exchange for George's wealth. In his brother's presence, though, he concealed everything else, all the tender, painful memories of a wounded life. There were the simple, sweet, irrigated acres in Arizona, bought, paid for, and discarded; the trail of debts never repaid in Montana; the lives torn apart and lost in Mississippi. And Luzelba . . . what of her? Had her husband died in the revolution? Did she manage to fend off United Fruit? While George fiddled with an accounts book, Barney thought of her. The memory of her scent in the warm grass threatened to flood the carpet in George's antiseptic study.

"Well, I think that settles things, Barney. Barney?"

"Sure thing, George. We are fair and square."

"So, you're moving to the coast."

"Watsonville. Bought a house, a little acreage." Land, always land.

"Well, I wish you well." George, dismissing his underling. It seemed unlikely to Barney that they would ever see each other again, their only connection being financial, and that now done with. It almost made him want to ask George for more money, just to keep the old boy animated a while longer. George was entertaining when his face turned red and he sputtered and refused, then relented.

Barney looked George over, at least as much of him as he could see above the desk.

"Let me ask you something, George. Are you a happy man?"

"What? That's a ridiculous question! I'm a successful man, Barney, and that is all that matters."

"Is it?" Barney flicked a bit of lint off the sleeve of his new tweed suit coat, bought just that morning with thirty-five dollars from his farm proceeds. He figured it was his last suit, the one he'd be buried in some day. He was back on the deck of the SS *San Juan* with Luis, watching the suicide, the sharks, the last shreds of brown wool on the bloody sea. At least he wouldn't go like that. What about it: Was *he* a happy man? He couldn't say for sure, but at least he knew the difference between success and happiness, though it had taken him nearly a lifetime to parse it out.

"Maybe I'm a Hiram after all," he said, turning to go.

"What the hell does that mean?" George barked from his desk chair.

"Exalted brother, George. Remember? That's what Hiram means."

Back in the International, he glanced one last time at George's brick mausoleum of a house and drove quickly down the circular driveway.

Nora Mae sat between her parents in a state of bereavement. She'd spent last night, her last Saturday night in Modesto, with Henry and Velma, slow dancing to *This is No Laughing Matter* on the shoulder of some soldier she'd never see again.

"*No Laughing Matter,* no kidding," Henry said, squiring her away from the soldier at the end of the mournful tune. "Do you have to go, Jody? Golly, we're gonna miss you."

She shrugged. "They'll be calling you up any day, Henry, so I'm just leaving first." She looked for Velma and saw her sitting alone in the corner, drinking punch. She could see what would become of her. She'd marry some bachelor dairyman too old to go to war who was willing to raise another man's baby, and then she'd have *his* babies, gaining heft each time, her sturdy ankles beginning to complain sometime after the fifth one. Their four months together might be the best memory Velma would ever have. The idea crushed Nora Mae, imagining a life with such a short horizon. Did she want any of that—marriage, children—in a world where men made all the choices, went where they wanted, wore what they wanted? For a moment she felt mean toward Velma, toward all women who scrambled below the table for whatever crumbs the men brushed from their plates.

"Doncha worry about me, Jody," Velma said. "Ma and Pa, the

war made them change their minds. They say I can come home now, so I'm giving up the apartment anyway. But, oh boy, didn't we have fun?" Before Nora Mae left, Velma sewed her two more pairs of trousers. "Just so you won't forget me."

The whole night, Nora Mae craved whiskey, but turned it down all the same. No use giving Lula the satisfaction of thinking her a drunk in addition to being a hussy.

She had one hundred and ten miles to imagine life in Watsonville, but the town and the future hung like an empty bingo card from the rearview mirror. Ah, well, if it didn't work out, she'd run away again, whether Wilkie approved or not. If he really cared, he'd have asked her to move to Salinas. She huddled into her space on the seat, her knees clenched, shoulders rolled in. She wanted to neither touch nor feel the animal heat of Barney or Lula.

Lula knew the feeling, had felt it so many times it was as familiar as a hairbrush or a tea kettle: the whiplash of upheaval. Once again, she was leaving behind the familiar. She knew exactly how many coffee cups would rest comfortably on the shelf above the sink. How many pots of water it took to fill the old horse trough on bath day. How long it took the wash to blow dry on a March afternoon, hot desert winds blowing in from the east.

But now? All their things were coming behind them in a moving truck! A darn site better than escaping with nothing, the threat of the hangman at their heals, like they'd left Mississippi. Or in a state of near starvation, as they'd fled Montana. Why this disquiet then? Barney said they had enough money for the new house and plenty to live on. Though she'd never seen it, he made it sound like a palace: three bedrooms, a dining room with a hutch, a living room with a fireplace, an electric ice box, inside plumbing, hot water. A lawn! Roses up the walk! A garden plot and fruit trees of apple, apricot, and plum. A stone walkway leading to a snug little garage, which Barney promised would soon hold a sedan instead of the bone-jarring truck.

What instilled such a sense of dread, then? She had resigned herself to Barney the way a gate settles into its latch. Nothing to be done about it. The thought of leaving him had never occurred to her, and she wasn't worried he'd turn her out. That was something, wasn't it? Some peace of mind?

Was it Nora Mae? She stole a glance at the girl, pressed into her eight inches of bench seat as if her parents were contagious. She's our prettiest child, she realized. If she passed her on the street she'd think, *Well ain't she sweet.* But there was something wrong with her, like a hidden crack inside a milk jug, something you couldn't see from the outside. Oh, the pity parties that girl could throw! Why did she think they were all against her? She just was so irritating; the boys couldn't abide her. And who in their right mind would rather spend the day with cows than with girls her own age? Why couldn't she be more like Maudie Marie, or better yet, Nettie. Dear sweet Nettie, always by her side. Never complained about a thing. And those pants! What a ridiculous notion. The thought of living again with Nora Mae loomed so dark it clouded the happy thought of indoor plumbing and hot water at the turn of a tap.

"Barney, I assume there's a high school? Nora Mae's got two more years to finish," she said across the mute figure of her youngest child.

"Ain't going," Nora Mae said.

"Well, you most certainly are. My Ma and Pa sent me off to high school, and I did exactly what they said."

"No. I'm getting a job. Lots of jobs for women now that the war's on."

"Why, you're not a woman! You're just a girl, and I'm still your mother, and I say you're going back to school."

"Then I'll just leave again."

"No you won't, Jody!" Barney interjected. "Lula, if the girl doesn't want to go to school, leave her be."

Ah, thought Lula. *So it is Nora Mae.*

BARNEY, LULA, and NORA MAE

Watsonville and El Centro, California, 1942–1943

Lula treated Nora Mae like a past-due bill. The debt nagged at her, but she willingly let other worries eclipse it. Four blue stars hung on a flag in the front window of the snug house on Walnut Lane, one for each of her boys in the service. They were not prolific letter writers, so she sat by the radio most days for hours listening to war reports and poured over the Watsonville *Pajaronian* every evening when Barney finished with it.

Nora Mae was right. She had no trouble finding a job and chose one that kept her in contact with soldiers and sailors, where she could wear pants: taxi driver. Her fares were a source of dates for Saturday night dances, not to mention tips—loose change they might otherwise never get a chance to spend—for the lovely girl with the soft blond curls. Barney had taken her out in a field and taught her how to drive the International. In one afternoon, she was a better driver than he was, a realization Barney absorbed with a sour countenance.

Barney puttered in the new yard. He and Lula planted a vegetable garden that first spring, and each spring after. Victory gardens.

"Do you remember, Barney, in Montana, during the war how

they urged us to plant gardens, go without meat, save gas, as if we weren't already on empty?" Lula asked as they picked beans one day.

"Yes, I do. You laughed so hard you woke Leonard up. If they'd of pinched us any harder, we'd a starved."

"We almost did, or don't you remember? Well, I suppose by then, you were already down in Mississippi, growing those strawberries."

He moved to the other end of the garden and thinned carrots. Would she ever let him forget what he'd done?

By their second summer, Barney could barely tolerate the long, yawning, open-ended hours in which he no longer had a purpose. He itched to pull on cowhide gloves and repair a fence line, or milk a cow, or jaw with the dairymen at the co-op. Just across the road, Mexican laborers tended tomatoes on ten acres of farmland. When the picking commenced in June, he lined up with the men. Lula watched him from the kitchen window as he stooped, filling his flat as quickly as the younger men. They would follow him home at the end of the day and sit drinking beer from Barney's electric ice box in the shade of the Gravenstein. Barney thought of Mississippi and the old oak and the camaraderie of the water pail, but the image soon morphed into the oak being a lynching tree, a pregnant Violet dangling from its branches.

On Saturday afternoons, he would don his suit, stickpin in place, drive the new Buick down to the plaza in the center of Watsonville, sit on a bench, feed the seagulls, and talk with a collection of fellas. "My posse." He carefully crafted the story of his life, scrubbed clean of defeat, betrayal, and murder.

Nora Mae came and went at all hours and dove deeper into her flask of whiskey, Henry's legacy. Dear Henry. She heard his mother had covered his blue star with a gold one. Her grief sobered her, temporarily, and inducted her into the adult world where friends and lovers die young. She gave up on Jody, that whimsical, childish alter ego that had never taken root except with Wilkie, Barney, Velma, and Henry. That left her with Nora Mae. In one final attempt to make the name her own, she sliced off the Mae as Velma had once shorn her baby girl locks. In hopes of winning even a shard of Nora's affection, her parents quickly adapted, and Mae was forgotten.

Otherwise, she and her parents lived in silos, silent and apart from each other, intent on their own enterprises. The war was like the roar of the nearby sea, loud enough to drown out any thoughts of reconciliation or contrition.

In early 1943, she visited Glen in Salinas, and he told her about a new company in Watsonville that was looking for workers and had already embraced his union. Bud Antle was packing lettuce, even shipping it overseas, lots of it, for the war effort. The pay was good. No more variable taxi hours, if she was interested.

A week later, wearing jeans, she stood in an ice-cold packing house, sliding wax paper, ice, and lettuce into corrugated boxes as they rolled down the production line. The work was hard, a constant stoop, and at the end of the day, she went home and crushed two aspirins in a glass of beer and drank it down, sometimes sitting under the apple tree with Barney and the Mexicans.

Lula could see them from the garden and felt a pang of jealousy at Nora's easy laughter, trying out new Spanish words, sitting on an old upturned apple crate with the men. When had *she* ever known such ease? As she watched, her daughter winced in pain from the long day in the packing shed and for just a moment, her jealousy ebbed, and something else took its place.

One Sunday afternoon in August, 1943, Nora put on a swimsuit, her first—yellow with white polka dots and black ribbing—and spent the afternoon on the beach. She'd never before exposed so much of her corn-silk skin to the sun. By the time she returned home at five o'clock, she was already a bright scarlet.

"Ma! Can you come help me take this suit off?" she called from her bedroom.

Lula's cool fingers carefully removed the suit.

"Oh my, you're as red as a sweet potato."

"Hurts like hell," she said, her teeth chattering.

Lula drew back the sheets and blankets on her bed.

"Just lay on the sheets. I'll get some witch hazel."

"Ma, you gotta call the packing house. Tell 'em I can't work."

For the next few days, Lula soaked a cloth in cold water and witch hazel and laid it across Nora's burned skin, moving it as it warmed.

Blisters bloomed on her shoulders and nose. Lula's hands grew red and papery from so much time in water.

"Ma, you don't have to do this."

"Yes, I do."

For once, Lula withheld her disdain, and Nora did not shrink from her mother's touch. Barney wasn't allowed in Nora's room, but he watched his wife come and go, filling the basin with cold water and ice cubes. He didn't know what to make of it.

Sam Rossi had been on the job only one day when Nora returned, pink and peeling. He watched her from the far end of the production line. When Glen heard Sam was leaving a packing operation in Salinas to sign on as Bud Antle's production manager, he told him about Nora.

"My sis is something. Tough. Might make a good shift supervisor, but be careful. She'll cut your dick off and hand it to you on a platter if she thinks you're a weasel."

"Sounds like trouble."

"Well, she's not easy, I'll say that, but she's as loyal as they come."

"She married?"

"Nah. Not sure she ever will be. She's a looker though. Breaks hearts like they were jelly jars. And by the way, I'd just as soon kill a fella as look at him who doesn't treat her right. At work, or love, don't matter."

Sam laughed. "I'll remember that, Wilkie."

Sam worked his way down the production line, through an inch of water and ice on the floor.

"Miss Stovall? Your brother asked me to say hello."

She lined the box, not breaking her pace. "He OK?"

"He's fine. Quite a man."

"Yes sir, he is."

"You don't need to call me 'sir.' Sam will do. All of you," Sam said, calling out to the sixteen women on the shift. "No 'sir,' no 'Mr. Rossi.' OK?" Nods all around, as the noisy conveyor belt flung boxes and lettuce toward them.

"Miss Stovall—"

"Name's Nora."

Sam chuckled. "All right, Nora. Can you come up to the office when your shift is over?"

When he left the floor, giggles broke out all around.

"Ain't he something? If he keeps coming down here, I'm gonna swoon!" Sylvia said.

"What'dya expect he wants with you, Nora?"

"No idea."

"Hey, Dolores! Didn't you say your cousin knows his family?" Sylvia called out.

"Yep. Lots of Rossis over in Salinas. Italian. Catholic. Lots of babies. I heard he tried to join up, even though he's nearly forty, but they said he was needed here for the war effort. Our boys need their lettuce!"

"He's married, right?"

"Well, if you can call it that. She's—funny name . . . Fiorella?

Something like that. She's in the loony bin, somewhere up in San Francisco. Keeps trying to kill herself. They say he won't leave her. What kind of marriage is that?"

"Maybe he loves her," Nora said above the din of the machinery.

"Doubt it! Who'd love a nut case?"

Nora sat across the desk from Sam Rossi and felt a peculiar thrumming in her chest. Her experience with men was limited to her idiotic brothers or pimple-faced teenage soldiers who offered little more than an athletic spin on the dance floor. But this man! Maybe it was his good looks, the Cary Grant kind, with just a bit more heft and muscle. Even, high cheekbones; wide brown eyes; a slight gray stubble at his jaw line; straight, white teeth. Damn. She'd bought bulls before with her pa, and if he'd been one, he'd stand out in a stock yard, for sure. She realized her skin was peeling and that her face must look like a withered pink petunia. She squirmed on the cane chair.

"Nora, sorry about your sunburn. Looks like you're healing."

"Yeah, it's better, but I'll never do that again."

"I asked you up because I've just been given a very big job. The operation will have to triple in the next month to keep up with the War Department's demands. We're going from one small shift a day to three big ones, a twenty-four-hour schedule. I need to hire a lot of people quickly, and I need leaders on each shift. Your brother seems to think you'd be a good one."

She drew in a breath and exhaled slowly.

"Well, I can run a string of milk cows. I suppose I could try."

Sam laughed. "Well alright, then. You'll need to stay a few extra hours after your shift for the next week, learn the employment laws, the union rules. I know you already know how to pack lettuce."

Nora rose to go, but stopped at the door. "You might talk to the Chinamen."

"The Chinamen?"

"Yeah, the ones downtown wearing the signboards that say, I AM NOT. My pa says no one will hire them because they think they're Japs."

"That's an interesting idea, Nora. Would you be willing to work with them?"

"Sure. Why not? I feel bad for them. Who wants to be called a Jap?"

Lula answered a knock at the front door to find a man in a black suit with a huge halo of white hair, a giant Bible tucked under his arm.

"Afternoon, ma'am. I'm Pastor Pershing from the Full Gospel Church just down the road, that little white one on the highway."

"Why, yes, I've seen it."

"I hope I'm not disturbing you, but I know you haven't been here long, and I'm wondering if you and yours have a church yet?"

"Well, no, but then, we don't go to church."

"Would you mind if I come in and visit for a while? There's some scripture I'd like to read you."

An hour later, Pastor Pershing was holding Lula's hands in prayer.

"Dear Lord, I ask your blessing on our Sister Stovall, and I pray that you will touch her heart, and Brother Stovall's too, and bring them into the flock with all your children."

On Sunday, Pastor and Sister Pershing drove up to the Stovalls' at ten thirty, and Lula walked down the steps in a new dress, pink hat, and gloves. Barney watched from the front window as Mr. Pershing ushered her into the back seat.

"Well, I'll be damned," he whispered into the lace curtains.

In the months that followed, Barney watched Lula soften like an August peach. She started saying a prayer at the dinner table.

Barney rolled his eyes. She hummed hymns during the day while she washed dishes or ironed. She patted Barney on the back when she passed him drinking his morning coffee at the kitchen table.

"Lula, have you got religion?" he asked one fall Sunday morning as she dressed for church.

"Barney, I don't know if I'd call it that. I'm talking to God, and sometimes, he talks back. I'm praying for our boys, and . . . " She grew silent.

"And what?"

"And I'm trying to forgive myself."

"Well now what in tarnation is that gonna do? That's all water under the bridge. You can't go back and do anything different."

"Barney, it's got ahold of me! All the things I did."

"Like what?"

She stopped dressing, her stockings clinging to the dimples around her knees. She started to cry. Barney sat down next to her on the bed.

"I tried to kill her!"

"What? Who are you talking about?"

"Nora Mae! In Mississippi. Remember when I told you I lost a baby, and then, well, I hadn't, really? I tried . . . with a piece of wire . . . to . . ." She covered her face with her hands and fell back on the bed. She lay there on the white chenille bedspread in her white slip, tears pouring out from between her white fingers onto her pale skin and her white hair, like a marble statue thrown off her pedestal.

Barney stood up, took off his overalls, and put on a shirt and his suit. He picked up the stickpin, held it a minute, then put it back on the dresser. He sat back down on the bed. Lula stopped crying, her hands still covering her face as if she could make herself disappear.

"Lula, get your dress on. I'm taking you to church this morning."

Within a month, Barney was saying grace with Lula at the dinner table. They took evening walks down Walnut Lane, arm in arm, into the thermals and fog rolling up off the ocean a mile away. They talked about it all. Almost all. Barney couldn't tell her about Luzelba or Violet. Some things were best left for ears, like Glen's and God's, who didn't sleep in his bed at night.

At five minutes after five o'clock on a warm September night, Nora stood in her jeans and rubber boots in front of the new Bud Antle swing shift: forty Chinese men and women, many as old as her pa. Kai, the youngest of the bunch at thirty-five and the only one who spoke fluent English, agreed to be her translator.

"Folks, today we're going to learn to pack lettuce!" she hollered nervously above the machinery, waiting for Kai to translate.

By eight o'clock the line was humming, and Nora's butterflies had flown. They were already faster than the girls she'd been packing with. She didn't miss them, those prissy girls who made fun of anyone who was just a bit different, even Sam. She was sure she'd been on the point of their spears plenty of times when she was out of earshot. *Sick of them,* she thought, *their stupid painted nails.* Who paints their nails to pack lettuce? All the gossip, their little clique that never included her, just like the girls back home at Oakdale School.

At the end of her first swing shift, she lined up to say goodbye to her new crew. Kai instructed her how to bow slightly, hands together, eyes aimed at the scrim of ice and water on the floor. Sam, who wandered in and out throughout the shift, watched from the far end of the shed.

He was waiting for her at the gate.

"Where's your ride, Nora?"

"I'm gonna walk. It's just two miles."

"No, Miss Stovall, that's not how we do it. Not at midnight. I'll take you home."

The packing house was now on a seven-day-a-week schedule. "War Hours," they called them. Nora slept in until noon most days, slowly rolling out of bed against the pain in her back. To keep up with her crew, she worked even harder than when the prissy girls set the pace. Lula, who seemed oddly kind these days, bought her a heating pad. By two or three in the morning, it brought enough relief that she could turn off her mind's constant replay of her shift and, increasingly, her conversations with Sam, and fall asleep.

She paid little attention to the home front, but the ground seemed to be shifting subtly. What *was* happening with her parents? She heard them bustling around on Sunday mornings, the smell of bacon and biscuits, the Buick backing out of the garage.

One late morning in September, just weeks before the last of Watsonville's lettuce played out for the season, Nora stood at the kitchen sink sipping a cup of coffee, watching her pa pick tomatoes across the road. She heard her mother come in from the garden. God, she wished she had a back like his, straight and true as a plumb line.

She heard a cry, like a small animal in pain, and suddenly, from behind, her mother's arms were around her waist. Nora froze. Lula laid her head on her daughter's shoulder blade and cried.

A minute passed, two.

"You've never hugged me before."

Lula's crying eased, but she didn't let go. If she held fast, could the past be transformed, a lump of coal pressed into a diamond?

"I'm so awfully sorry. Won't you let me try to make it up to you?"

"Yes," Nora whispered. "Yes."

"Can you take your lunch break with me today, Nora?" Sam asked one evening two weeks before the end of the season.

They sat across the desk from each other, Nora eating a baloney sandwich, Sam smoking a cigar.

"Bud Antle just bought a big packing operation in El Centro. I'm going down next week to set up production for the winter harvest."

Nora bit down hard on the sandwich to hide her disappointment. It wasn't like she didn't know it was coming. She hadn't even thought what she might do in the winter. Maybe she'd go back to driving taxi.

"I want you to come with me, you and the other shift supervisors. They'll have company housing for us, good pay, and in March we'll be back here. You interested?"

"Interested?" she grinned, a big bite of baloney lodged in her cheek. "Where do I sign? Can I bring my Chinamen?"

"No, you can't bring your Chinamen, Nora," Sam laughed. "We'll have plenty of Mexican workers down on the border. But you tell them we'll hire them back in the spring. You've got the fastest crew in the whole operation."

The next night, Nora brought a radio and plugged it in, turning it up as loud as it would go. She rang the shift bell.

"Hey everyone! It's the swing shift. We're gonna swing!"

On toward midnight they went, swaying to Benny Goodman. At break time, she passed out her mother's oatmeal cookies. It was the happiest she'd ever been.

Three weeks later, Sam, Nora, and the other supervisors met up at the plant for the ten-hour drive, down the coast through Los Angeles, then east to San Bernardino, and one last leg straight south to El Centro on the Mexico border. Most of the crew packed into company trucks. Sam drove his black Mercury. As the crew's sole woman, it was only logical that Nora ride with him.

By the time they arrived in El Centro at one o'clock in the morning, Nora had lost all sense of time and direction. The present moment, next to Sam on the bench seat, was the sum of her existence.

The casitas planted in the sand at the far edges of the packing house complex shimmered in moonglow. Along the manicured stone-and-sand walkways meandering between them, the cactuses cast shadows like cartoon characters. Sam and each of his supervisors had their own casita, a one-room adobe with a red tile roof, a bed draped in mosquito netting, an armoire, a carved wood chair, a wash basin, and in the corner, a kiva fireplace. Nora stood at the doorway. The moonlight behind her flowed across the threshold like a vernal stream.

She was overflowing with desire that threatened to spill out her lips and fingertips. She clutched her carpet bag close to her chest, her guitar strung around her back, and turned to see Sam in the doorway of his casita across the stone path, watching her. She closed her door, filled the basin with water from the pitcher and laved her face, hoping to cool the desperate need she felt to run in circles and sing. It was nearly two o'clock in the morning and she should be exhausted, but sleep seemed as far away as Watsonville.

She pulled a modest white cotton nightgown over her head. Lula had bought it for her just last week.

"Nora, you've got to take something besides pants! You don't know where you'll be staying, and a young lady needs something to sleep in. What if you're sharing a room?"

Nora walked in circles around the four-poster bed, the nightgown whispering between her calves, remembering the hours-long conversation with Sam, the Mercury a confessional booth. She told him everything, even about Jedediah Coates. He told her everything—leastways, she thought it must be everything, since she had bared her own soul—about his Italian family, his Catholic upbringing, his Fiorella.

"Nora, I loved her for so long, so very long. She was so beautiful when we married. We were just kids! I thought love might cure her. But I've lost faith now, even in God. I say my rosary a dozen times a day. I might as well be shouting at the moon. The girl I loved is gone, and she'll never come back to me. But I can't leave her. What if I did, and she killed herself? I'd be damned!"

Damned. There was more than one way to reach that minacious state. By the stroke of three o'clock, she no longer cared what might become of her. She threw open the casita door, ran barefoot across the sand in her nightgown, pulled open Sam's door, and fell straight into his arms.

"I wondered if you'd ever come," he said, kissing her, crushing the white cotton in his hands, the scent of starch and soap rising between them.

By the time the dawn brushed against the casita's deep-framed windows, Sam possessed all of her.

NORA

Watsonville, Santa Cruz, and El Centro; California; 1945–1961

The war ended, and Nora's four brothers came home.

"It just ain't fair that those four idiots came back without a scratch, and Henry died," she said to Sam, her head on his shoulder.

"Maybe they'll be different now."

Two of them were. Ernie and Leonard: They had seen things. Ernie's boat sank, and with it, most of his friends. Leonard swept through Germany in Patton's army, liberating concentration camps. They came home less cocky, but kinder, grateful. They took Nora out for beers, helped Barney till the garden before winter, brought their mother flowers, washed up after supper. After a few weeks sleeping on the couch and floor, they took their tender memories and moved on into lives, buoyed by the GI Bill, girlfriends, and big plans. Vernon didn't come home. He moved to Grass Valley and kept drinking. He couldn't square away the things he'd seen. Albert stopped by one afternoon, then went on to Montana with Ray and Marjory, and into insurance. Nora could still barely stand the sight of him.

Glen and Iris bought a house on a tidy street in Salinas. Despite home ownership, dental appointments, life insurance, vacation trips, and a new Cadillac each year—all the hallmarks of a middle-class life—he still resisted the Man in ways large and small. The union was his lodestar, and underdogs, his people.

Of a summer evening, he and Iris and the girls would drive over to Barney and Lula's in the Cadillac, Glen with a bag of donuts for Barney, and some sweet little thing from the five and dime for his ma: a dishtowel, or a box of canning jars.

His good hip went the way of the bad hip, so they replaced it too, and now he walked with a cane in each hand. Some evenings, he and Barney would walk west along Walnut Lane toward the ocean. Nora heard them talking about farm laborers and New Democrats, but she suspected that out of earshot, they spoke of other things.

Sam rented a small furnished house in Santa Cruz. He and Nora spent weekends there, walking the beach, dancing at the grange up in Felton where no one knew them. On Mondays, they returned to their jobs at Bud Antle and acted their parts, their love dormant inside the cold packinghouse walls.

On a certain day each December, they drove to El Centro, and on a certain day in March they returned to Watsonville, an endless circle of perfect lettuce weather.

And still, Nora stayed with Barney and Lula. She returned at the end of her swing shifts to find her bed turned down, the heating pad on and in place. Clean clothes folded neatly at the foot of her bed, a note sometimes on the pillow: "I hope your back isn't hurting too much tonight. Mom." Lula kept trying to mend all the shattered spaces between them. Nora soaked it up like the parched earth of El Centro, harboring a thirst so deep that not Barney, Lula, or even Sam, could quench it entirely.

No matter how much Barney and Lula spoiled her, how much Sam doted on her, she could not blot out the past, the years of rejection, the ever-present stain of that seven minutes with Coates in the outhouse, her discomfort with the confines of a woman's body, and of late, more than ever, a growing realization that Sam was not hers. What she had of him wasn't enough. Even by 1949, after nearly seven years together (yet not together) Sam was still a distant star. She could see his light, feel his heat, but never live entirely in his gravity.

In her turbulent state, aware that she and Sam would never be truly together, in January 1950, the worn path between their casitas in El Centro grew cold. She turned him away night after night. In February, she realized she hadn't had a period in three months. That night, she let him in to her casita.

"I'm gonna have a baby."

"But Nora, sweetheart, you can't!"

"Really?" she said, clutching her still-flat stomach.

"I can't—you know, I can't!—marry you."

Two days later, he told her about a doctor in Mexicali, just across the border, who would take care of things. He'd drive her. Coming back across the border, her anguish flashed like heat lightning.

"It was a boy, Sam. They told me it was a boy! You could have had a son!"

Lying alone in the casita, feverish, she bled for days, ignoring Sam's knocks on the locked door.

Their drive back to Watsonville a few weeks later was silent. No banter, no hand holding, no Nora, legs folded up on the Mercury's bench seat, strumming her guitar and singing. Ten hours of silence. They returned to the packing house as strangers.

When the weekend arrived, Sam said, "Come with me to Santa Cruz. Please."

They walked the beach silently. They drank coffee on their small back porch in silence. They made love silently. And then on Sunday night, Sam said the thing she always feared.

"They're releasing her. She's coming home."

Nora quit the packing house the next day and went to work driving a school bus, a split shift, early morning, then late afternoon. In the middle of the day, she sat next to her mother in the garden playing the guitar, shelling peas or playing solitaire, sinking deeper and deeper into despair.

Her mother had taken to calling her Sis, a name apart from Nora or Mae or Jody.

"Sis, why don't you come to church with us this Sunday?"

Nora strummed louder on *Farther Along*. But on Sunday, she dressed in trousers and saddle shoes, ate a biscuit and a fried egg with her parents, and rode in the backseat of the Buick for the short drive to the white church. Pastor Pershing beamed at them from the front steps like a politician on election day.

Nora had never considered God. Magic, yes. Yearning, certainly, for something precious and invisible beyond her reach. She'd been astonished by a starry sky crying silver teardrops on the purple alfalfa fields at midnight. But this man preached about a God who knew her darkest soul and was still interested in her. If she would just give up everything—her selfishness, her mendacity—and call on Jesus, why then, he would welcome her in. She'd be one of His! She'd belong! She left the pew and sat in the backseat of the Buick waiting for her parents. She didn't need an invisible all-knowing guy rooting around in the dungeon of her unhappiness.

But the next Sunday she was back, drawn by the possibility of redemption, of starting anew. Of erasing those seven years with Sam, those seven minutes with Coates, and all of her barbarous existence in between.

She came home one afternoon that spring, driving her old Ford, having a conversation with God.

"If you exist . . . go away."

Try as she might, though, the notion of God grew on her. What if there *was* Someone out there? Someone who could wipe away her desperation and, in its place, insert a new and improved Nora, immune to the vagaries of humans in general, Sam in particular.

She drove into the bus yard late one September night after driving the high school football team to a game in Seaside. Sam's familiar Mercury was parked under a street light. He met her in the middle of the lot.

"Nora, it didn't work. I've had to commit her again. I don't think she'll ever be free of it."

"Are you leaving her then?"

"You know I can't do that! But we can go back to the way things were."

Nora stood three feet from him—a gulf as wide as the craters of the moon. She wanted to leap that chasm, to return to his bed, to wake up next to him in Santa Cruz, and float down the highway with him, across the valley to El Centro, each winter. Forever. What did it matter, really, that she'd never have his name or carry his children? Then she thought of God, or he thought of her, she wasn't sure how that all worked. In that instant, her feet fighting gravity in the dusty gravel of the bus yard, she knew she would have to choose.

"I don't know, Sam. I don't know. I'll think on it."

In her small bed, the heating pad made its entreaties, cricket song seeped under the window sash. The moon rolled over the yard on Walnut Lane. But sleep did not come.

Her morning coffee and toast were a last meal, her morning bus run, a last rite. She got in her Ford and drove down to the ocean and parked. She couldn't bear it anymore. She wanted Sam to shut up; she wanted God to shut up.

"Leave me alone," she whispered at the sky.

She walked into the sea. She could not swim. *It would take so little,* she thought. The water tugged at her blousy trousers. She could just walk in and let the ocean take her. She sloshed out to her waist and then turned to look back at the earth, pearly bluffs adorned in yellow-flowered ice plant, and imagined beyond that, just a mile away, her parents, puttering, alone. Her ma spreading sandwich bread with tuna salad for her lunch. Her pa polishing his shoes on the back porch.

She looked back at the sea and slipped deeper into its gyre. If only it would take her, take away her choice, take away her breath, her memory. The water swirled at her chest, and still she stood. The sand slid away under her feet, and she thought, *Surely the moment is coming, it will snatch me and I'll be gone.* She was finally swept off her feet, and for a moment, knew the delicious sensation of floating, abandoning the anguish, the seven years, the seven minutes.

Then she heard her name. *Nora. Nora. Nora!* It came from all around her, a siren cry, a pleading, a promise. She sputtered, she choked, her saddle shoes searched for solid ground, and in a moment, a wave spit her into the shallows. She dragged herself onto the sand and struggled up the beach, her clothes and hair heavy, and threw herself behind the wheel of the Ford, where she had left the key in the ignition, and drove fast, so as not to change her mind, to the little white church, and flung open its door, and ran down the aisle, and fell like a sacrifice on the altar.

"OK!" she yelled. "I'm yours. What the hell do you want from me, anyway? Because I'm here now. I'm here." She lay on the altar, shedding salt water like a trawled salmon, cried until she had no more tears, and went home.

She drove her afternoon shift, twenty-three little kids who chattered and whistled and sang and wadded up their middling art projects, and then she drove her bus back to the barn. Sam was in his car just outside the gate. She parked the bus and sat in the driver's seat. For fifteen minutes, Sam waited. Then he drove away. When she got home and looked in the mirror, the bus steering wheel had left a red welt on her forehead in the shape of an inconsolable frown.

Glen would say the Man was everywhere. Nora's surrender on the altar came with chains and its own Man, this one in the form of Pastor and Sister Pershing.

"Nora, now that you've come into the Kingdom, we think it's important that you know: A woman of God doesn't wear pants and lipstick," Sister Pershing confided. Pastor Pershing nodded in agreement.

"She doesn't?"

"No, dear. A woman of God doesn't call attention to herself, or flaunt her God-given beauty. A Godly man, well, he just wouldn't have you, not the way you look now. And I'm sure you'd like a Godly man."

In Nora's tender state, devoid of every intention she harbored the last seven years, she was willing to believe anything the Pershings said. They were, after all, agents of the God who plucked her from a watery grave.

She entered the women's wear aisle at Ford's Department Store, and with her mother's help, emerged with two Sunday dresses and a pair of simple pumps. On Sunday, her face scrubbed bare, she went to church and was presented to the congregation as the newest member of the Full Gospel Church of Watsonville.

That Sunday, a quartet—brothers Bill and Joe and their sisters Sarah and Naomi—sang *The Old Rugged Cross.* The alto, Sarah—tall, smooth olive skin, and the sort of round bosom that suggested babies and nappies and potluck suppers—introduced herself to Nora.

"Why don't you come home with us for Sunday dinner? There's always room for one more at our house."

Sarah's parents and her brothers and sisters lived in Aptos on a small rented farm with a weathered house that was stretched to its limits. The dining room table, the biggest Nora had ever seen, held Rose and Max and their children Ruth, Jackie, Nathan, Bill, Joe, Miriam, Naomi, Danny, and Sarah, plus their friends, and their friends' children, splayed across card tables in the living room. Rose and the girls carried platter after platter to the table.

Max said a prayer, a long and involved one which Nora could not follow, so she glanced around the table. Her eyes strayed again and again to Bill—the pretty boy, the carpenter, the dreamer. The oldest at twenty-two, Sarah had whispered after they'd sat down. Everyone's favorite. Five years Nora's junior. With her new virginal bearing, she compared him to Sam: long and lean where Sam was compact and muscular; innocent where Sam was carnal; transparent where Sam was calculating. No, it wasn't possible. He wasn't for her. Too young, too inexperienced. The prayer went on, and she looked into her hands. The prayer went on, and she looked up again. Bill was looking at her. He smiled.

Their courtship lasted three years. Three years of long conversations and chaste kissing in Bill's pickup truck, *Ebb Tide* on the radio. Three years pretending the seven years and seven minutes had never happened. Because, like Mrs. Pershing suggested, she did want a good boy, and no good boy would want a girl as thoroughly tarnished as she, even if she had fallen on the altar and offered herself up. God would forgive and forget, but Nora knew that humans had less tolerance and better memories.

She stayed with Barney and Lula. She came home at the end of her bus shift one afternoon to find them sitting out under the apple tree holding hands.

"Nora," her pa said, his voice as thin as skimmed milk. "Your mother has cancer."

Nora dropped into the sod in front of them. "No, Mama."

"They say it's breast cancer," Barney said, "but it's . . . every where."

Lula put her hands on Nora's shoulders.

"It'll be soon, Sis."

Nora nursed her mother through the next five months, days splintered by bus shifts, late night pain medicine, soup sipped from a spoon, until the soup wouldn't stay down any longer. Bill and Barney carried Lula to the Buick and drove her to the county hospital. Nora lay on the bed next to her for three days.

In those three days, Lula and Nora entrusted their secrets to each other. Lula's confession to the wire and the bloody floor of the Mississippi shack released Nora from a kind of prison. Now she understood that her Ma had no power, no agency, no way out. Had she herself not done the same and succeeded? She told Lula of the baby left in Mexicali, and accepted her mother's absolution. Nora would pick up her guilt again in the years ahead, and never really escape it, but for one day on her mother's deathbed in the county hospital, she was without censure. This was Lula's final dispensation of grace, a holy act that could almost expunge a lifetime of mean-spirited neglect.

"Nora," Lula whispered on the last day. "Will you please marry that boy?"

"I will, Mama."

On June 12, 1954, in a pink knit suit, a corsage on her shoulder, Nora Mae Stovall made all the necessary pledges, accepted a gold ring, and married William David Fruh. She fervently believed life would begin anew, a clock rewound all the way back to the first movement of its second hand. But time is not that considerate.

Kathy Watson

THE HANFORD SENTINEL, NOVEMBER 30, 1955

"Fannie Forcade, 78, of the Island district and Barney Stovall, 81, of Watsonville, were married last Tuesday afternoon by Kern County Superior Judge W.L. Bradshaw in Bakersfield. When they met in 1908, Stovall was farming on the Island at Fremont and Twentieth Avenues. She was Mrs. Hall, living on an adjacent farm. For the past several years she has been living near a daughter, Mrs. W. R. Abbot on the Island and Stovall, a widower, has been at Watson-ville. He is retired. After their wedding the two came to the Abbot home and accompanied the Abbots to the coast, stopping for dinner in Fresno at the home of her son, Fred Hall. They announced their marriage there. They now are living at Watsonville and plan to move soon to Santa Cruz. Attendants for the wedding were a niece of the bride, Mrs. Inez Southstone of Long Beach, and Miss Dorothy Morris."

Nora was furious. She swept through the house on Walnut Lane, taking her mother's Fostoria fruit bowl, a flour scoop, a ring with a glass gemstone, and a picture of her parents in an oval frame.

"Don't you want your dad to be happy, honey?" Bill asked

"Yes! But not with *her*, not like *that*. You've never lost anyone so you don't know what it's like."

"I loved your mother too."

But she wasn't thinking just of her mother. She was thinking of Clemmie Mae and Uncle Joshua and Henry, and the bloody heap in the basin that was her baby boy.

When Barney told her he was marrying Fanny, his very first and long-forgotten crush, Nora refused to go to the wedding.

"How in God's name can you marry that woman?" she hissed at Barney.

"I'm lonely!" Barney said. How could he explain it to her without destroying Nora's fragile final acceptance of Lula? Barney could count on one hand the nights he had felt loved: one with Luzelba, three with Violet. All those years with Lula? They had been an American bargain, one struck to further the acquisition of land and children. Yes, he had grown to care for her, a state far less electrifying than love. He hoped that even as an old man, lightning could still beguile him.

But to Nora, it felt like her mother's second death, as if Barney were washing her away, dimming the memory of those few years on Walnut Lane when they had loved Nora, together, as parents ought to do. Now this fancy woman with her high heels and stockings and makeup, her Hypnotique perfume, her cigarette-yellowed fingers, would be living in her mother's house, the one place Nora had been loved enough.

Bill was thrilled a year later when Kathryn Marie was born. Nora wasn't. She wanted that boy, the one she'd left in the Sonoran desert, but here was a girl, a child with bangs to cut. A girl she'd be obligated to dress in frills and bows, things beyond her ken. A girl who would now be subject to all the Coateses of the world. Of that, she knew something. Bill's joy cast enough shadow that no one glimpsed her disappointment.

That December she stood under the awning of the Ford Department Store in a driving rain storm, waiting for Bill to get her. She shivered in her brown cloth coat, Kathy wrapped in a blanket in her arms. A man ran out of the rain to share the awning with her. Sam. They stood facing each other for a long minute, saying nothing. She tried to read his face. Envy? Longing? Relief? Bill's old work truck slid to the curb, and she darted away.

Aaron David Fruh, born in March, 1958, finally broke her losing streak: a healthy baby boy. She held onto him like a winning lottery ticket.

But that boy didn't fill the void. When Kathy was four, she watched her mother back her father into a corner of the kitchen. Nora leveled her index finger at him, yelling, spattering him with spit. He eased out of the corner, begging her to stop. She flew to the ironing board, picked up the hot iron, and threw it at him.

She poured her nameless, senseless wrath into Kathy and Aaron, who absorbed it the way children will do. She had just finished painting ten-foot-tall sliding doors in their first home, an old Victorian. Now Kevin, a six-year-old visiting from down the street, was throwing the children's blue and red blocks against the doors, leaving streaks and deep gouges in the fresh paint. At the sound, Nora came running, and Kevin fled. The kids shrank against the wall in the front parlor.

"Oh my god, what have you done?" Nora yelled when she came into the room.

"It wasn't us!" Kathy's voice shook. "It was Kevin."

"Liar!"

"I am not!"

Nora fell to her knees and clasped her hands. "Jesus will tell me the truth!" she said, bowing her head. Aaron clutched his sister.

A minute passed, and Nora's eyes flew open.

"Well," Kathy asked, "Who did it?"

They watched their mother through the tall bay windows as she marched down the street to Kevin's house.

The Victorian, when sold, became the ballast for Bill's new venture: building homes on eighty acres in Watsonville. He built theirs first. On December 21, 1961, Bill sat in a wingback chair in front of the fireplace, a sleeping child in each arm. His contractor's license had just arrived in the mail, and Bill had propped it on the mantel. Nora came in from the kitchen. He lifted a finger to his lips for quiet and smiled at her.

"I have everything I want," he whispered.

Two nights later, five minutes from the house, Bill, on an errand, stopped and looked both ways. He never saw the car, a drunk behind the wheel, before he pulled out.

"Sister Fruh?" the young voice said over the phone. "There's a car like yours on fire outside our house."

Nora ran down the hall and threw herself onto the braided rug in front of their bed.

"Oh God, please don't let it be Bill!"

They put what was left of him in a plastic bag, and she buried him.

Chapter 31

GLEN and KATHY

Soquel, California, 1966

Kathy contemplated the package of hamburger on the counter. Meatloaf, spaghetti . . . enchiladas? It was four o'clock. She'd better have dinner ready to go on the table the minute her mother walked in the door at six o'clock, just to keep things peaceable. If she made spaghetti—that was the quickest—she could read another hour.

Just three days ago, the librarian had handed her *East of Eden*, the third Steinbeck she'd taken home.

"I wouldn't give this to most ten-year-olds, but I think you're ready," Miss Ferguson told her. Two hundred pages in, and she had cracked open the door to a secret world. People living lives, just forty miles from her in Salinas, that she had never imagined. Wealth, murder, jealousy, sex. And Cathy, a prostitute, with her name even, who tried to abort her twin sons, and failing that, had simply abandoned them.

A rolling flash of light on the kitchen wall. A car was pulling into the driveway. *Oh no,* she thought, *she's come home early.* She felt her cheeks flush and heard her mother's voice echoing from the night before: "Stupid idiots!"

But when she looked out the living room window, it wasn't Nora's Dodge Dart, but a Cadillac. And here was Glen, coming up the front walk, a cane in each hand, rolling side to side like a buoy in a storm. She threw open the front door.

"Uncle Glen!"

"Hiya, kid," he said, handing over a white bag of doughnuts. "Where's your mother?"

"She's cashiering down at the car wash."

"And Aaron?"

"Little League."

"Well, then, it's you and me. You gonna invite me in?"

She held the door while he worked his way over the threshold. Since her dad's death, he'd made himself a regular fixture at the Watsonville house, and when her mom couldn't bear to live there any more, at a rented duplex, and then, for a disastrous year, a mobile home, and finally, at this new Soquel rancher: three bedrooms, two baths, two car garage, all electric kitchen.

Glen sent the three of them to Mississippi by train for a visit with Aunt Nettie. Sent checks in the mail, bought her and Aaron bikes, made regular unannounced visits, always with doughnuts.

"Whatcha got to eat, kid, I'm starving. How about some of your mom's fruitcake?"

"Sure, Uncle Glen. Would you like some tea?"

"God no. Got any Pepsi?"

"Mom says you're supposed to eat the fruitcake with tea," she said, pulling the giant parcel from the fridge and peeling back the brandy-soaked cheesecloth.

"There's more than one way to eat fruitcake, kiddo," Glen said.

Kathy carved a paper-thin slice from the cake.

Glen put his meaty hand around hers, lifted the knife, and hacked off a four-inch-wide slice.

"Uncle Glen! Mom says it's supposed to be eaten only in thin slices!"

"You always do what your Mom says?"

"Well, it keeps things . . . She gets so mad . . ."

She watched Glen take a hearty bite of the fruitcake and wash it down with a big swig of Pepsi. "You been in trouble lately?"

"Yeah."

"What'd you do?"

"There's this cave down by the creek. All the kids go there. She told us never to go in it, and well . . ."

"You did anyhow. How'd she find out?"

"We came back all muddy, and she beat on us for awhile, said we better fess up where we'd been and then Aaron—"

"He told her."

"Yeah. Then I got another whipping for not telling the truth."

"And your brother?"

"He took off on his bike."

"Smart kid. What about you?"

"I don't leave, really, because . . . she doesn't do too well on her own."

"How so?"

"After the cave and all, she said she couldn't take it anymore, was gonna kill herself. Said she was gonna drive the car off a cliff into the ocean. And then she drove away, real fast."

"Don't worry kid. She won't."

"What?"

"Never mind. What happened then?"

"We thought, 'Well, we're orphans now.' Aaron said he wanted to go live with Uncle Nathan, and I thought, maybe Aunt Noni, or . . . you." She looked at him, testing the waters. He took another big bite of fruitcake.

"But an hour later, she came back, driving slow, went to her room, slammed the door. I took her some soup, and when I knocked, she yelled, 'Go to hell!' I was hoping she might be in a better mood when she gets home tonight. She hasn't talked to us since yesterday."

Glen put his dishes in the sink.

"Uncle Glen, why is she so . . ." Kathy searched for the

unknowable adjectives. "I know there are reasons. Losing Daddy, and her bad back and everything, but . . ."

Glen cupped her chin in his big hand and searched her face, looking for something familiar, a telltale sign of Lula, of Nora, or perhaps Barney. But Kathy's pleading eyes showed him nothing of the Stovalls at all.

"Come on, kid, let's take a ride."

"Oh, I can't! I've got to make dinner! She'll be home soon, and there's still the breakfast dishes to wash."

"You let me worry about your mom. Come on. I'll tell you a story."

The white leather in Glen's Cadillac smelled of cigarettes and Vitalis, and hinted, like *East of Eden*, of another world far apart from the rigid, religious world inside her mother's house. The Cadillac floated over the two-lane road, winding up and up to the top of Loma Prieta, 1,800 feet above the Monterey Bay. Glen rolled down the windows. The oak, bay, and eucalyptus trees along the road filled the Cadillac with a menthol mist. Glen lit a cigarette and dangled it out the window.

"Your mom ever tell you she was born on a kitchen table in a shack in Mississippi?"

Kathy shook her head.

"Your grandmother didn't want her, tried to get rid of her."

Kathy's mind sifted over the pages in *East of Eden,* Cathy trying to rid herself of her twin sons.

"Were you there, when she was born?"

"No, I was two thousand miles away, in Montana. In an orphanage."

"But, Uncle Glen! You're not an orphan!"

Glen pulled into a turnout on the other side of the road and turned off the engine. An orange and pink sun was setting over the bay off in the distance. He put a big hand on Kathy's sandy curls.

"Yes, yes I was, baby girl. For a short time, I was. The worst kind of orphan a child can be."

References

"Thirty Thousand Dollars in Chandler Improvements," *Arizona Republican*, October 16, 1913.

Legal notice: petition for pardon, *Stone County Enterprise*, March 3, 1927.

"Elderly Pair Married by Kern Jurist," *Hanford Sentinel*, Nov. 30, 1955.

Acknowledgments

Many thanks to Stu for his unending love and friendship, and for lending a critical ear to months of "dailies" as I wrote this novel. To my grandparents Barney and Lula; my mother, Nora; and my Uncle Glen, whose mysterious lives kindled in me a deep desire to simply understand. To She Writes Press, Brooke Warner, and all the amazing writers in my SWP cohort—you are the best, and the future of publishing.

For a list of characters in *Orphans of the Living*, and for book group discussion questions, visit the author's web site: hungerchronicles.com.

About the Author

Photo credit: Blaine Franger

Kathy Watson spent twenty years as a public relations executive and journalist, including six as editor-in-chief of *Oregon Business* magazine, before embarking on a new career as a chef and restaurant owner of the acclaimed Nora's Table restaurant. This is her debut novel. She lives in Hood River, Oregon, where she writes, leads a chefs collective, and runs and hikes the Columbia River Gorge with her husband Stu and Satchel, the world's best dog.

Looking for your next great read?

We can help!

Visit www.shewritespress.com/next-read
or scan the QR code below for a list
of our recommended titles.

She Writes Press is an award-winning
independent publishing company founded to
serve women writers everywhere.